THIS
DARK
DESCENT

ALSO BY KALYN JOSEPHSON

The Storm Crow

The Crow Rider

Ravenfall

Hollowthorn

THIS DARK DESCENT

KALYN JOSEPHSON

ROARING BROOK PRESS

NEW YORK

Published by Roaring Brook Press
Roaring Brook Press is a division of
Holtzbrinck Publishing Holdings Limited Partnership
120 Broadway, New York, NY 10271 • fiercereads.com

Our books may be purchased in bulk for promotional, educational, or business use. Please
contact your local bookseller or the Macmillan Corporate and Premium Sales Department
at (800) 221-7945 ext. 5442 or by email at MacmillanSpecialMarkets@macmillan.com.

Library of Congress Cataloging-in-Publication Data is available.

First edition, 2023
Book design by Samira Iravani
Printed in the United States of America

ISBN 978-1-250-81236-0 (hardcover)
1 3 5 7 9 10 8 6 4 2

ISBN 978-1-250-32517-4 (international edition)
1 3 5 7 9 10 8 6 4 2

To anyone who has ever felt as though they are not enough

VERADELL'S HIERARCHY

THE ROYAL FAMILY

THE VAULT

ANTHIR

The city guard. Arrests and prosecutes criminals.

THE FOUR GREATER HOUSES

The bureaucratic branch of the government responsible for documentation, records, and application of the law to individual cases by berators.

The most powerful houses. Responsible for overseeing kingdom-level duties enacted by the Council of Lords.

THE EIGHT LESSER HOUSES

Oversees implementation of laws, handles city and district-level responsibilities.

THE COUNCIL OF LORDS

Consists of the heads of the four greater houses and either the ruling king or queen at the time. Creates and passes new laws, oversees military, handles kingdom-level responsibilities.

Kelbra

ZALAIRE
THIELAN

Dramara

ADAIR
BELDA

Ruthar

JACOBIS
ELRIHAN

Vanadahl

WAKELIN
FALQUERRA

THE ROYAL FAMILY

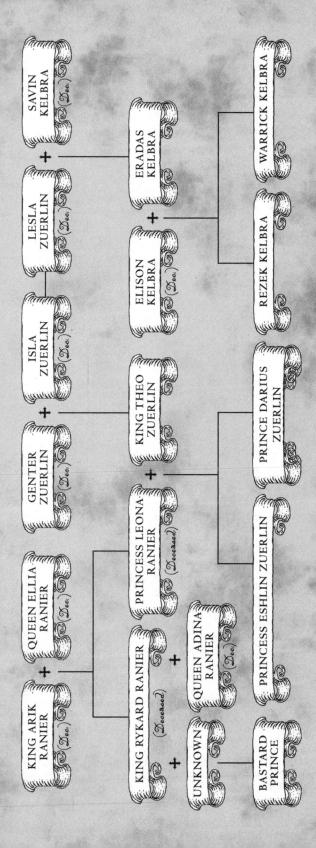

RANIER LINE

ZUERLIN LINE

SAVIN KELBRA (Dec.)

LESLA ZUERLIN (Dec.)

ISLA ZUERLIN (Dec.)

GENTER ZUERLIN (Dec.)

ERADAS KELBRA

ELISON KELBRA (Dec.)

KING THEO ZUERLIN

WARRICK KELBRA

REZEK KELBRA

PRINCE DARIUS ZUERLIN

QUEEN ELLIA RANIER (Dec.)

KING ARIK RANIER (Dec.)

PRINCESS LEONA RANIER (Deceased)

KING RYKARD RANIER (Deceased)

QUEEN ADINA RANIER (Dec.)

PRINCESS ESHLIN ZUERLIN

UNKNOWN

BASTARD PRINCE

✦ PART 1 ✦

In the beginning, the four Harbingers gifted magic to humanity.
Rach, the Armored Bull, gave physical enchantments for strength and speed.

Skylis, the Burning Light, granted behavior enchantments,
to stoke fury and invoke docility.

Lyzairin, the Great Serpent, offered energy enchantments, creating light and heat,

and Aslir, the Bright Star, bestowed ethereal enchantments,
so that humanity might always find its way home.

CHAPTER 1

MIKIRA

HORSES WILL SPEAK to you, if only you listen.

That was what Mikira's father always told her. It was in the way they pricked their ears, in the swish of their tails through still air. It was even truer of enchanted horses, whose blood thrummed with magic, bestowing untold abilities. Whether it be speed or surefootedness, good luck or the uncanny ability to always find their way home, such horses were deeply in tune with the world around them.

It was those enchantments that Mikira relied on now. Dressed in all black, from her worn riding boots to the plain mask obscuring her face, she sat tall on Iri's back as the stallion tossed his head, nickering impatiently. Enchanted for speed, the desire to run was as much a part of him as bone or blood, just as it was a part of Mikira.

The twisting maze of Veradell's tunnels—tonight's racecourse— stretched into dimly lit shadows ahead. The city's underground passages would be narrow, the turns tight and easy to miss. Breathing deep, Mikira shut out the excited murmur of the crowd, the sharp scrape of hooves against stone as horses jostled for space at the starting line, and the ever-present reminder that she could not go home empty-handed tonight.

"Are you all ready to see some action?" called Jenest, the race's owner and announcer. A slender, muscular woman with brown skin, she barely approached the riders' shoulders, even standing on an empty gun crate in the middle of the tunnel. Still, you couldn't miss her, dressed as she was in an ornate jacket covered in glass jewels and sequins—a mockery of the extravagant garments favored by the nobility—and a blue-and-white scaled mask emulating the Great Serpent, Lyzairin, one of the four Harbingers said to have brought magic to humanity.

People whooped and clapped as she dipped into a bow. "You know the rules!" Her deep voice resonated from her charmed loudspeaker. "All four types of enchantments are allowed, but no weapons! This isn't the Illinir, and I won't have blood spilled on my nice clean floors."

A chuckle emanated through the crowd. The tunnel's floor was nothing more than a swampy mixture of dirt and runoff from the canning factory above, a far cry from the flashing cameras and manicured tracks of the official races Mikira longed for. She hated being down here, but it was the only safe place to run such makeshift contests. With how tightly controlled magic was, enchanted races required a permit and a hefty tax to the city of Veradell. Jenest was risking prison by operating without one.

And by competing in them, so was Mikira.

"Twenty silver marks to the winner. First rider around the loop and back here wins the purse." Jenest jingled a small pouch above her head, the real reason Mikira was here. "Take your marks, get ready, race!"

The horses bolted. Iri easily beat half into the first turn, their enchantments either not for speed or too weak to bestow any real advantage. Mikira forgot everything but the feel of the race as they barreled along the tunnel. Her body moved with Iri's like a reflection, adrenaline rushing through her in a heady thrum, sharpening everything into stark focus.

As they leaned into the second turn, a rider wearing a green and brown half mask imitating the Harbinger Rach approached them. Something glinted, and Mikira barely dodged their blade. Freeing one of her own knives from her hip, she blocked the second swipe, then disarmed the rider with a twist of her wrist.

They rode well, their horse's physical enchantments clearly stronger than the others. But it wasn't enough—not against an enchant bred from the Rusel lines. Not against Mikira, whose father had once led Veradell's racing elite.

Taking the final turn, they entered the straightaway where the race had begun, and Mikira let Iri go. The horse's speed all but doubled as he careened down the last stretch and across the finish line.

A knot released in her chest at the crowd's cheer as Iri trotted back toward Jenest. The woman seized Mikira's pale hand, holding it up in triumph. "Nightflyer wins again!" she called to the whistles and shouts of the crowd. "I know, I know, you're all shocked. Don't you worry; I promise I'll find our little flyer a worthy competitor soon."

Mikira grinned at the applause. These people loved her, and she couldn't deny that even without the need for money, she would compete just for the way they looked at her—like she could do anything.

Feeling a different kind of stare on the back of her neck, Mikira turned, catching the gaze of the Rach rider. She was tall, with curious hazel eyes and tawny skin. Mikira could turn her in for the knife, but that wasn't the first time someone had pulled a weapon on her, and it wouldn't be the last. The rider crooked the smallest of smiles before guiding her horse into the dispersing crowd.

Everyone would leave through the myriad of tunnel entrances, careful not to raise suspicion. The Anthir didn't bat an eye when a noble house squeezed every last copper mark from one of their tenants or conscripted them into the Eternal War in neighboring Celair, but if the city guard came across an enchant racing ring without the requisite paperwork and taxes? Everyone involved would spend the rest of their lives in prison.

Her brother used to say that you could murder someone in broad daylight in Veradell, so long as you had the proper paperwork. Unless you came from a noble house—then you didn't even need that.

Jenest held out the winning purse. "You know one of these days I'd like to meet the person behind the mask," she said. "Grab a drink or two."

Guilt panged through Mikira. She liked Jenest. Her upbeat, teasing attitude reminded her of her childhood friend, Talyana, who she hadn't seen in years. But she was here for coin, not friendship, and no one could know who she was.

"Thanks for the race." She took the purse and tucked it into her pocket, pointing Iri toward one of the exits. Small engraved arrows marked the way out for those who knew where to look for them, remnants from when the tunnels were used to transport gemstones. After most of the city's mines dried up, the tunnels were forgotten.

Now the walls had become a mural of one-way messages, from peeling recruitment posters for the Eternal War to notes chalked onto the stone. Most were from Celairen refugees flooding in from the war being fought over their land, hoping lost friends and family would pass the same way, but others were last words left by Enderlish fleeing the kingdom's military draft, both driven by the war to exchange places in the tunnels' darkness.

Her brother had never gotten the chance to run—because of her.

Mikira leaned forward to scratch behind Iri's dark ears. "Someday we'll ride in a real race. For Lochlyn."

The horse's ears flicked at the sound of her brother's name. Iri had been his, once. But Lochlyn had died in the war, and all Mikira and Iri had left of him was each other.

They emerged from the tunnel into the early morning light of Ashfield Street, where preparations for the upcoming Illinir were already underway. Hosted once every ten years by House Kelbra, the Illinir was a brutal series of four magical races that would take place throughout the month alongside the Illinir festival, all in celebration of the day the Goddess Sendia sent the four Harbingers to bring magic to humanity.

People would visit from all over the continent, from southeastern Kenzeni merchants selling new technologies to Vynan politicians desperate to keep the Eternal War from spreading northward. She'd heard there was even an entrant from as far south as Yaroya, where enchants were fast growing in popularity.

Soon, vendors and performers would swarm the street, children and adults alike donning sinuous tails reflecting the Harbinger Lyzairin, or masks made to look like hammered metal in honor of Rach, the Armored Bull. Already she spotted a young girl bearing Skylis's crimson wings, her arms outstretched as if to carry her into the air like the great bird she mimicked.

A memory tumbled loose, taking her back ten years ago, when Lochlyn had gone as Aslir, the Bright Star. Mikira, displeased with her Skylis wings, had cried until he placed his mane of white feathers about her neck and said, "There. Now you shine too."

An enchanted coach blared its horn, startling her and Iri, but she kept him steady as the horseless vehicle jerked around them. The tumult was enough to spook any country horse without a docility charm, and Iri was enchanted to sense danger: to him, that meant everything in this cursed stone jungle.

Eager to escape the noise, she took a shortcut to the Traveler's Road encircling the city, where they passed only the occasional messenger or cart full of coveted grain heading for the military outposts near the border. A short ride later, she diverted Iri up the gravel path to her family's ranch—and nearly pulled him to a halt.

Something wasn't right.

She knew the ranch like her own heartbeat. The rich, earthy scent of it. The sounds of horses and gentle feel of the place that always calmed her like nothing else.

Instead, as Iri trotted up the winding drive, her family's white two-story farmhouse was quiet—too quiet, like the deafening moment after a gunshot. Her father ought to be in the pastures already, her sisters chasing each other through the long grass beside him, clinging to their last moments of freedom before they went to school for the day.

But the yard was empty.

She leapt off Iri's back and sprinted up the front steps. Throwing open the door, she staggered into the foyer, stumbling over Ailene's carelessly discarded shoes.

She'd barely regained her balance when a voice called, "Kira? Is that you?"

"Father?" Relief swept through her as he appeared in his study doorway, clutching a pale gold verillion stalk. Dark shadows rimmed green eyes heavy with sleep, his simple vest and shirt rumpled from another late night spent poring over old books. He blinked at her, then at the open door letting in the daylight.

"Is it morning already?" he asked. "I must have lost track of time."

Mikira choked out a strangled sound. He'd lost himself in his research again. That was why he hadn't been out in the fields.

"You can't keep doing this," she said tightly.

"I'm getting close, Kira, I can feel it." He held up the verillion plant. "I think the answer is in how the verillion's magic binds to things. Actually, can I borrow your knives? The stone—"

"Stop it!" Mikira snapped.

The silence that pooled between them was deep enough to drown in. Mikira adverted her gaze to the plant in her father's hand, its glow of magic gone. Like this the verillion was harmless, but when plucked fresh from a field, the stalks burning with a golden light, they were full of magic people craved. She'd seen the way it consumed people, poisoning them from the inside out like it had her mother years ago.

Her father was convinced the ranch's salvation lay in innovative enchantments, using the verillion to harness new wonders, rather than just breeding what enchants remained in their stables. But with every night of research, he put his life at risk. As an unlicensed enchanter, all it would take was one hint of magic to the wrong person, and the Anthir would come for him. The Council of Lords claimed the enchanter registry was meant to prevent a repeat of the Cataclysm, when the four Heretics destroyed the kingdom of Kinahara in their pursuit of magic, but Mikira knew the truth: it was all just for profit and power.

"I left you dinner in the oven," he said as if she hadn't just all but spat in his face. He didn't ask where she'd been. Where his seventeen-year-old daughter went every night and why she returned with bags of coin. He simply smiled, his eyes crinkling at the corners in a way that never failed to warm her. She let it, because being angry at him was more than she could bear.

If only her father could use his magic openly, they could diversify and strengthen their breeding lines, save their failing ranch. But every horse's origin was closely tracked, and people would question it if they suddenly possessed a powerful new enchant. All they could do was rely on the careful game of legal breeding and hope they made enough sales to purchase new stock.

That, and Mikira's races. Without her winnings, they would never make their monthly tax payments to House Kelbra.

"Kira!" A high voice barely preceded the girl bounding down the stairs, her alabaster skin flush with excitement. At thirteen, Ailene was already taller than Mikira, with a lean, athletic build that she put to use besting the boys in backyard races. Part of Mikira always longed to warn her that soon they'd get tired of her competitive nature, her excitability. That a time would come when instead of loving her for these things, they would judge her, like they had Mikira. But she couldn't bring herself to break her sister's spirit.

"Kira, can I stay home from classes today?" She clasped her hands together. "I'll help you with your chores."

"Don't listen to her!" Nelda appeared on the stairs, her lips pushed to the side in what Ailene called her "mothering scowl." Despite being four years younger than Ailene, she'd always had the disposition of an old lady, something their brother had often teased her about. "She just wants to go to the races with Era Keene."

"That's not true!" Ailene shot back.

Mikira smiled at their bickering, until she heard it: that sound that haunted her waking moments—the crunch of gravel beneath wheels, unaccompanied by hooves.

There was only one person who ever visited them in an enchanted coach. *Goddess help me.*

Mikira reached the door at the same moment Lord Rezek Kelbra, heir to House Kelbra, stepped out of his coach.

Iri had fled to the barn, leaving Rezek to occupy their drive like a king holding court. His light copper hair was pulled back in a bun at the nape of his pale neck, his eyes the searing, ruthless blue of a too-hot flame as he inspected Mikira.

A familiar, slow grin spread across his lips. He was several years older than her, but the almost childlike glee that filled his expression at the sight of her always chilled her to the bone. "Miss Rusel," he greeted in a voice like poisoned silk.

Her father emerged onto the porch beside her, bowing. "My lord. To what do we owe the honor?"

Mikira nearly scoffed. A visit from Rezek Kelbra wasn't an honor; it was a threat. Her father knew that as well as she, and it scraped at her to see him like this. She wanted him to lift his head and spit at Rezek's feet.

But he wouldn't, just as she wouldn't.

The Kelbras were one of the four greater houses and the king's cousins, the prince well known to favor Rezek in particular. His power was threaded into the fabric of his being, and it was those tiny moments of defiance that he lived to crush. He never touched you; he simply tore apart your world.

Then an Anthir constable stepped from the coach, and cold understanding set into her veins—someone must have spotted her leaving the underground race. Ailene and Nelda crowded at her back. She should have told them to go upstairs, should have yelled at them to get far, far away, but her throat had gone dry as sand.

Rezek inclined his head to the constable, but it was her father he addressed. "The Anthir has received a troubling report, Mr. Rusel. It appears Lord Thielan witnessed you performing magic."

Her father drew a sharp breath, and Nelda smothered a cry. Lord Thielan had been at the ranch only the other night to look at a horse. At the time, Mikira had thought his arrival suspicious. It was rare for a noble of a lesser house to challenge Rezek, who for some time had an unofficial embargo on their family's business. But they were desperate for sales, and she'd had no choice but to entertain him. He must have been looking for something Rezek could use against them, and he'd found it.

"It's not true," she blurted. "He didn't."

Rezek's frosted gaze cut to her. "Surely you aren't calling Lord Thielan a liar?"

"No, I—"

"Then are you aiding in the concealment of an unregistered enchanter?"

Mikira took an involuntary step back. She was only making it worse. But this couldn't be happening. Rezek couldn't have found out. Her father moved forward, shielding her from Rezek's view. He would know what to say, how to fix this.

"They didn't know," he said.

Mikira faltered. "Father—"

"Hush, Mikira!" The force in his voice—a voice he had *never* raised to her—froze her in place. For the first time in years, she saw her father as he'd been before Lochlyn died: straight-backed, clear-eyed, and prepared to do whatever it took to keep his family safe.

"They didn't know," he repeated.

"Kira." Ailene's voice was barely more than a breaking whisper. A plea Mikira couldn't answer, no matter how badly she wanted to. She felt her sister's hand curling into the back of her shirt, felt something inside her teeter precariously toward falling.

"Then you admit it?" Rezek practically preened with delight.

Her father lifted his head. "Yes."

Everything inside Mikira screamed at the word. Ailene tried to push past her, her hands in tight fists, but Mikira grabbed her.

"Then you have two choices, Mr. Rusel. Either I turn you over to the constable here, at which point you will be tried and hanged for evading registration. Or . . ." Rezek paused, drawing out the moment as he nonchalantly studied the diamond inlaid signet ring on his right hand. "You come work for House Kelbra."

"No." Mikira looked desperately to the constable, but if he pitied them at all, his face betrayed nothing. Everyone knew the Anthir were in the nobility's pocket, but only those from the four greater houses could get away with indenturing an unlicensed enchanter right before their eyes. As members of the Council of Lords alongside the king, the greater houses made the law—and they could break it.

"Father, please." Ailene's voice cracked.

The Kelbras were renowned for their cruelty as much as their wealth; their people worked to the bone. Most were too desperate to leave, the rest beholden to the family through debt and secrets and land, the same way her father would be. At least so far they had lived outside of Rezek's physical reach. If her father went with him now, he would not come back whole, if he came back at all.

But the alternative was death.

"Very well," her father said, and something broke in Mikira. That grim persistence, the one that drove her out of bed each morning and forced her to keep working the ranch, to keep trying, began to crumple like a post rotted through.

He descended the stairs.

"No!" Mikira lurched, barely aware of her sisters grasping her from behind and pulling with all their might. "Father, please, don't go!" They had lost too much to the Kelbras already. Given too much of their lives to them. They could not have him too.

But he didn't stop.

She broke free of her sisters' hold as their father climbed into the coach. The constable thrust an arm into her chest as Rezek closed the door.

"Open it!" She pounded her fists against the wood. The constable jerked her back; her fingers wrapped around a knife hilt.

"Kira!" It was Nelda's voice that snapped her back to herself, to the sight of the barely concealed fury on the constable's face. He could arrest her for drawing a knife on him. All it took was a word.

Slowly, she sheathed the blade. Forced her rigid fingers from the hilt and her eyes to Rezek, who made a low tsking noise. "Temper, temper."

"Please." She nearly choked on the word. "Please let him go. I'm begging you."

Rezek's head tilted. "You don't look like you're begging."

Everything inside her seized against the insinuation, but she forced down every ounce of refusal and dropped to her knees with her head bowed.

"Please."

She felt his gaze like a sword at her throat. Felt Ailene and Nelda watching from the doorway, as powerless as she was, as her family had always been before the Kelbras. There had been a time when her family's prestige might have made Rezek hesitate before doing this, a time when her father had friends in high places. But those days were long gone.

"Despite your family's constant attempts to paint me as a villain, I'm nothing if not fair," Rezek drawled. "I'll make you a deal."

She rose tentatively to her feet. "A deal?"

"If you can win the Illinir, I'll free your father and enter an official pardon for his crimes. I'll even forgive your family's debts."

He might as well have challenged her to a duel; she was far likelier to win that. Every year, one hundred racers entered the Illinir, and far fewer emerged. She probably wouldn't even survive, and yet . . .

"If I lose?" She hated how much fear bled through everything she said.

He smiled. "I get the ranch—and everything in it."

The Rusel enchants had once been mounts for everyone from the old Ranier kings to the city's best racers, and Rezek had been after them for years—a gift to present his illustrious father. Which made this deal too good to be true. Rezek finally had the leverage to get what he'd always wanted. Why make this offer when he could just trade her father's life for the ranch?

He was up to something, something more than just securing their enchants, but Mikira didn't have the luxury of figuring out what.

"Oh, one more thing," he said with an offhanded air. "Your horse can't be an enchant."

"You can't—That's not—" She bit back her words as Rezek's eyes widened. That was a look she knew too well.

"Yes?" he prompted.

She hated him for this, for always twisting the rules against them. She'd never survive the Illinir on a normal horse, let alone win. Each of the four races was specifically crafted to challenge a different type of enchantment, from spike-filled pits that opened beneath horses' hooves to illusions designed to make them go mad, and that said nothing of the dangers of the other riders.

If she refused Rezek's terms, her father would become a servant directly under the Kelbras' thumb without hope of reprieve. But if she won the Illinir, the prize was invaluable: fame, fortune, and a boon from the king himself. One that would grant her anything within the king's power—a new stock of enchanted horses, an enchanter license for her father, a ranch in a district other than the Kelbras'. The money alone would enable their freedom, but the boon would give them so much more.

"Do we have a deal?" Rezek offered her his hand.

She lifted her head. "I want it in writing."

Rezek may have a constable in his pocket and all the wealth and power that came with being the prince's favorite, but even a Kelbra couldn't break an official contract. It was the precarious base upon which Veradell's house of cards was built, the cuffs with which the elite bound each other.

Rezek sighed. "I thought you might."

He pulled a folded bundle of parchment from his inner jacket pocket and handed it to her. She scanned the contents, which already denoted everything they'd discussed. At the bottom was Rezek's signature, alongside the imprint of his signet ring—a lion's head in a pool of white wax. If Rezek were anyone else but a house lord, she'd have asked for a berator to witness the contract too, but a Kelbra's seal was as binding as any berator's.

"You have a signet ring?" Rezek asked in a tone that implied he highly doubted they could afford the yearly tax for one. They nearly couldn't, but without one, the validity of their sales could come into question. A signet ring marked them as verified by the Vault, the bureaucratic arm of the government through which every piece of paperwork in Enderlain flowed. If the product wasn't up to par or the payment didn't come through, the berators would step in to mediate.

Veradell was a city built on paperwork, and the berators were its masons.

"Here." Nelda reappeared panting at her side, proffering a plain iron band with a crest of crossed blades resting on a horseshoe, and a small pad of ink. Mikira took the ring, and Nelda looked Rezek square in the eye before marching back to the patio, where Ailene enfolded her in a tight embrace.

Rezek watched her go with a chuckle that made Mikira's stomach turn. "I'll keep your father with me until the end of the Illinir," he said as she knelt to the ground to dip the ring in the ink and press it to the paper, and then again on the second copy. Her family's symbol looked sadly pedestrian next to Rezek's ornate wax seal.

She kept one copy and handed the other back to Rezek. The contract would be filed away in the Vault, ensuring they both kept to their word.

"Until then, Miss Rusel." Rezek reached a hand toward her cheek. She braced for the cold press of his fingers, but they stopped a hairsbreadth away, curling in. He gave her one final smile before he opened the coach door and sat down beside her father, the constable following close behind. She mustered all the strength she didn't feel, willing her father to see it.

"I love you." She mouthed the words silently.

Then the door snapped shut and the coach rolled forward. She watched it go, numb.

Ailene appeared at her side, half-sobbing. "Kira, what have you done?"

"What I had to." The words came out harder than she meant, but she couldn't falter, not now. She was the strong one. The sturdy one. If she broke, her family would crumble. If she broke, she wasn't sure she could put herself back together.

Nelda joined them, wringing her hands. "We can't afford a normal horse, let alone the Illinir's entrance fee."

Mikira winced. First Lochlyn had been drafted because of her foolishness, now their father had been taken. Her sisters had never blamed her for Lochlyn's death, just like they wouldn't for this, but she blamed herself. Why was everyone constantly suffering for her mistakes? Why couldn't she stop making them?

"The first showcase ball is tomorrow night," she said tightly. "I'll get a sponsor there, and they'll provide me with a horse."

It was a flimsy hope. The showcase balls were meant to match riders with sponsors, but would anyone bother with a racer on an unenchanted horse, even if she was Keirian Rusel's daughter? Her fingers sought her knives, their worn leather-wrapped handles and bloodstone-set hilts a familiar comfort.

"It'll be okay," she said, willing herself to believe her own words.

The night Lochlyn was conscripted was the last night her father ever raced. The last night the Rusel name was spoken with awe and respect.

That name had meant something once; Mikira would see that it did again.

CHAPTER 2

MIKIRA

ALL MIKIRA WANTED was to curl up in the warmth of the barn and listen to the horses for a while. Huddled beside the stalls and wrapped in the rich scent of hay, she could pretend that when she walked outside again, her father would be sitting on the porch with a book and a cup of tea, her sisters leaning over his shoulders arguing over which story he would read.

Instead, she was back in the heart of Veradell with Iri for the showcase ball.

The city air always smelled of gunpowder and metal, like a spark would set the whole thing alight. She hated the bellow of steamship horns off the Grey and the constant press of thousands of bodies all around her, hated the way everyone looked at her as if they wanted something from her or else couldn't be bothered to give her the time of day.

But most of all she hated that everywhere she turned, she was reminded of the war.

Recruiters called for people to sign up outside government-sanctioned buildings. Enchanted lorries sent people scattering from the streets, dead-faced soldiers staring wistfully out the back. It was why she kept Iri to the side alleys as much as possible when she traveled. That, and to tear down all the recruitment posters she could.

Are you able-bodied and of fighting age? read the one in her hands. *Join us in the fight for Enderlain's future.*

Below it was a sketch of the white lion Aslir, Harbinger of ethereal enchantments and the Goddess's right hand. The Council of Lords wanted the people to believe that the war with Celair was Goddess-blessed, but it was a thin veneer for the truth—Enderlain was running out of verillion, and Celair was a verillion rich kingdom. So people like Lochlyn kept dying, while the wealthy paid their way out of the draft through the exemption fee.

By the time she boarded Iri and reached Lady Zalaire's estate in the Pendron District, Mikira felt like a wildfire that needed to consume, a hunger that only grew as she followed the winding path to the hilltop manor.

Even in her mother's nicest evening dress, she couldn't measure up to the finery of the people around her. Everyone was draped in gold and white empire gowns, or tailored jackets and long skirts studded with slices of precious gems—and most of them had arrived in enchanted coaches. It took all she had to ignore the narrowed eyes and wrinkled noses of the lords and ladies she passed as she crested the hill to the estate.

As the head of one of Enderlain's eight lesser noble houses, Lady Zalaire had the honor of hosting one of the Illinir's showcase balls, and the manor had been prepared to impress. The soaring music of two dueling pianos drifted along a stone courtyard set aglow by enchanted lights, and delicate standing tables draped in strings of crystal gathered around a fountain in the shape of Aslir in recognition of House Kelbra, under whom House Zalaire served.

Mikira blended into the line of people funneling slowly past security at the wrought-iron gate, but when she reached the front, a fair-skinned guard with a thick blond beard cut in front of her. His eyes slid the length of her gown, with its tattered hem and moth-eaten fabric, lingering on her chest and hips in a way that made her want to punch him. "You can't enter dressed like that."

"Are you serious?" She stepped toward him. "The whole point of these bloody showcases is so candidates who can't afford to enter the Illinir can find sponsors. If I can't afford to enter, do you really think I can afford a nice dress?"

"Maybe I need to be clearer," he replied. "This party is not for trash. Step back. Now."

Mikira didn't move. "My family breeds the most revered line of enchanted horses in all of Enderlain, and you're telling me this party isn't for me?"

"The Rusel line? Doesn't House Kelbra own that ranch now?" He gave a small smile, and that's when she knew: he'd been instructed not to let her in. Rezek clearly wasn't going to make this easy for her.

The man waved a dismissive hand. "Run home now, little girl. You—"

Her fist connected with his jaw before she even made the decision to swing. Pain radiated through her knuckles as a wave of gasps rose from the crowd that had quickly gathered behind her.

The man stumbled back, clutching his face. "Bitch!"

His partner grabbed Mikira's wrist. She drove her boot into his stomach with a snarl, and he tumbled over someone's leg. More guards appeared, cutting off her escape. Lochlyn's lessons came rushing back to her: *You're quick, use that. Stay moving.* But their backyard training sessions had been to teach her to deal with bullies, not armed guards.

"Is there a problem here?" asked a cool voice.

The crowd parted for two young men. One was of average height, with olive skin and dark curls shorn on the sides. A house ring of black and silver glinted on his hand. The other was tall and pale with hair darker than a raven's feathers and eyes so blue that for a moment, all Mikira could see was Rezek. Then she took in the scowl etched on his wolfish features and the piercings in his ears, and she almost laughed at the idea of mistaking him for the elegant aristocrat.

"Lord Adair." The blond guard bowed to the shorter boy. "There's no problem. We have it handled."

Shit. Mikira groaned. Running into an Adair wasn't much better than a

Kelbra. The Adairs might only be one of the lesser noble families like the Zalaires, but she made a point of avoiding anyone who could see her dead with a snap of their fingers.

Lord Adair's gray gaze swept across the scene. "This lady is a friend of mine," he said to Mikira's surprise. "Apologize for how you've treated her."

The guard stiffened, and Lord Adair cocked his head. "What was your name?"

The man floundered. "Warin Eedren, my lord."

"Mr. Eedren." Lord Adair said the name as if testing it for weakness. "Do as I say, and I won't break anything important."

Warin spun toward her, bowing swiftly. "I apologize." He'd no sooner straightened than Lord Adair was beside him, one hand on his wrist, the other twisting one finger in a sharp motion. Everything about it was so casual, a simple shake of the hand. Warin bit back a cry, and Lord Adair released him. Whispers from the people at their backs followed Mikira into the courtyard, Lord Adair and his friend a step behind.

They'd barely entered the milling crowd when Mikira spun around, her skin practically crawling. She hadn't liked Warin, but she didn't approve of Lord Adair's methods either. He was risking Lady Zalaire's fury, and by extension, Rezek's, with actions like that.

"Not to sound ungrateful, but what the bloody hells was that?" she asked.

"Funny, that still sounded ungrateful," said Blue Eyes, his scowl deepening. He looked like someone had plucked him fully formed from a grumpy shadow, dressed in all black from his silk vest to the sleek jacket fit snug to his lean frame. The rings and studs of silver in his ears contrasted drastically with the elegant cut of his clothing, and his black hair was wild as a crow's nest, complemented by the edges of midnight ink trailing down his neck.

"What are you, his shadow?" she asked.

He glowered, but Lord Adair laughed softly, which only put Mikira more on edge. Whenever Rezek laughed, it was to his own private joke, which usually involved things going very badly, very quickly.

"Allow me to introduce my friend Reid," Lord Adair said. "You can call me Damien. You are Mikira Rusel, aren't you?"

"Yes," she replied hesitantly.

Damien inclined his head. "I'm familiar with your family. Those guards were under orders not to allow you in."

Mikira's sense of unease only grew. "And yet you intervened."

A half smile curled one corner of his lips. "Yes, well, where Rezek Kelbra takes an interest, so do I, if only to get in his way."

Oh hells no. The last thing she wanted was to be the plaything in some tug-of-war between two feuding lords.

She'd already begun to edge away when Damien said, "I'm glad we ran into you, actually. I've been looking forward to meeting you."

"Thank you for your help," Mikira replied hastily. "But I have business to attend to. Enjoy your night."

She ducked away through the courtyard, praying they wouldn't follow, and stilled at the entrance to the ballroom. It was like stepping into another world, one untouched by the rising grain prices and war recruiters hounding desperate refugees. The floor-to-ceiling windows gave way to gold-veined marble floors, servants weaving throughout the party with plates of meat on slices of rich dark bread people like her could no longer afford. A set of charmed pianos stood before a crowd gathered beside the evening's crown jewel, a Ruby One motorcar imported from Vyna. She'd never seen one in person before.

Every inch of this event had been designed to reflect the Zalaires' wealth, and the wastefulness of it gnawed at her. These were the people she would have to convince to sponsor her. If she was lucky, she'd find someone from outside one of the noble houses. Someone who had nothing to do with the Kelbras and was willing to take a risk on an unknown racer. Perhaps her father's name still meant something to these people, who would be all too happy to add his prestige to theirs, another drop of power in their well.

But luck had never been on Mikira's side.

AN HOUR LATER, Mikira had driven off six potential sponsors. Granted, two of them had been women asking after her "handsome, reclusive father," and she was pretty sure at least one had just been fishing for Keirian's autograph, but they'd all fled at her mention of sponsorship. They were all too happy to take what they wanted from her family—so long as they didn't have to give anything in return.

She rushed through her explanation with the most recent prospect, Lady Kiora, an Iziri woman with brown skin and ochre eyes who worked for House Ruthar. Unlike Houses Kelbra, Dramara, and Vanadahl, it was the only greater house that didn't support the war effort, and they were known to clash with the Kelbras, which made Mikira hopeful.

"And so then we had to sell the colt from that line—no, sorry, the filly." How had she even started talking about this? "And after that—"

Lady Kiora lifted her chin, and Mikira immediately stopped talking.

"Let me be sure I understand you correctly," she said in a low, accented voice. "You want me to sponsor you to run the kingdom's most difficult competition on an unenchanted horse, which I will provide, despite the fact that you've never before raced?"

Mikira winced. When she put it like that, it sounded pretty bad. Mikira was one of the best underground racers in the city, but this woman couldn't know that.

"I know horses," she pressed. "Better than anyone. I can win that race."

Lady Kiora's rose-painted lips pressed firm. "Knowing horses doesn't mean you know racing, even if you are Keirian's daughter. I can't help you. Good evening."

She vanished into the crowd, leaving Mikira staring mournfully at a sea of delicately embroidered dresses and colorful waistcoats. These people were leagues away from her. How many of them had paid the exemption fee to escape the draft? How many knew what it was like to have your life swept out from under you?

Mikira stepped into the path of a gray-haired gentleman she recognized as a long-ago patron of her father's. "Mr. Fellington. My name is Mikira Rusel, and I'm looking for a sponsor—"

"Pardon me, young lady, but I'm already sponsoring a rider for this year's race. Perhaps next time." He stepped away, but Mikira grabbed his arm.

"They've announced all the current pledges," she said. "They didn't say your name."

The color paled from Mr. Fellington's ruddy face. "Unhand me. This is entirely inappropriate!" His voice cracked, and at the shine of fear in his eyes, her restraint broke.

"It's not my racing history or my horse at all." Her grip tightened. "This is because of the Kelbras, isn't it?"

Mr. Fellington ripped his arm free. "I have no idea what you're talking about, and your hostility—"

Mikira snarled, and he flinched. Then as if suddenly remembering his station, he straightened and lifted a warning finger. "I won't be spoken to like this by a little girl." He turned abruptly on his heel, scurrying away.

Mikira watched him go, her fury molten steel in her veins. Then he emerged on the side of the crowd, heading straight for the Zalaire security guards along the perimeter.

"Shit!" She darted into a nearby alcove, falling back against one of the thick columns and pressing her face into her hands.

She wanted to scream.

Oh yeah, that'll really make someone want to sponsor you. They already think you're trash, why not be screaming trash?

But what else could she do? Rezek had turned the entire gathering against her, and now she was moments away from being thrown out.

"Perhaps, Miss Rusel, I can help." Damien Adair emerged into the alcove, Reid a step behind.

Mikira started. "What? Why?"

"Still ungrateful," Reid remarked, and Mikira scowled in return. His gaze lingered, before he forced it away from her as if jerking free of a sudden snag.

"My family has been looking to sponsor a rider," Damien replied evenly. "If you're not interested . . ." He began to turn away.

"Wait!" Mikira lurched forward without thinking, and Damien stopped. "I can't ride an enchanted horse. I made a bargain with Rezek."

"So I've heard." At her look of puzzlement, he added, "I make it my business to know Kelbra business, and I have a solution."

Mikira only stared at him. Even the best enchanters couldn't hide the gold flecks that appeared in a charmed animal's eyes. If his solution involved any form of enchantment, Rezek would know she'd cheated with one glance.

"How?" she asked.

Damien straightened his already impeccable cuffs. "That's not something you need to know. What matters is you'll be able to race, and you'll be able to win."

Something dangerously close to hope swelled to life in Mikira's chest. Tonight had been a fool's errand from the start—and deep down she'd known that even if she secured a sponsor, there was no chance in all four hells she'd win the race. Now Damien was offering her not just entrance into the Illinir, but an opportunity to actually win.

"What about the prize money and the royal boon?" she asked. Jockeys and sponsors sometimes split them, but sponsors often took one or the other. The last winner of the Illinir had gotten their cousin freed from jail with the boon and used their portion of the prize money to start a new life outside Enderlain.

"You can keep the entirety of the prize money for yourself," he said as the crowd parted for the approaching security guards. "But if you win, the royal boon is mine."

It was a fair trade. Mikira needed to win to protect her family, but she also needed the prize money. The royal boon was a worthwhile sacrifice in exchange for what Damien was offering. Still, her father wouldn't forgive her if he knew Mikira was considering allying with a noble house, even a lesser one. The four greater houses alongside the king might make up the Council of Lords responsible for instating every decree from the draft to the rising land taxes that crushed people like her, but the lesser houses were the ones who executed them.

Damien gave her an artful smile. "If it helps, what I intend to do with it won't be pleasant for Rezek. I thought that prospect might appeal to you."

She'd heard whispers of the rivalry between House Adair and House Kelbra but knew little beyond that. It didn't matter. Just like it didn't matter that she was fairly certain Damien was using her somehow; he was her only option.

"I accept," she said, and prayed she wouldn't regret it.

Reid smirked, making Mikira bristle. In contrast, Damien only inclined his head, departing with Reid as the two security guards arrived. She let them walk her out.

As she stepped into the rapidly cooling evening air, she expected to feel relieved, but the tension inside her only coiled tighter. There was no turning back now. She would enter the Illinir, and if by some miracle she didn't get killed, she still had to win.

CHAPTER 3

ARIELLE

ONSTERS RARELY LOOK like monsters.

At least, that was what Arielle's grandfather used to tell her. Her Saba had said that monsters came in every shape and size, and the trick was not to dismiss them for how they appeared, for they could look like anyone.

So, as a child, Ari had searched for monsters in every face, in every stunted smile and hasty whisper her family received.

She never imagined that one day, she would be the one creating them.

Wrapped in the glow of enchanted lamplight and the scent of rye from last night's dinner, Ari worked a piece of soft clay against her worn workbench, kneading it like dough to mix in the powdered ruby and verillion stalk necessary for the behavior enchantment. It would form the final ear of the golem dog Lady Belda had commissioned. For now, the earthen beast stood motionless beside her, its back as high as her hips, nothing but a husk waiting for life.

Sometimes Ari didn't feel much different from a husk herself. With each hour she spent twisting and molding and shaping—and with each pang of hunger in her hollow belly—life felt farther and farther away, like a dream retreating before the morning light.

She scored the underside of the ear and a spot on the golem's head, before melding the clay into place and stepping back to evaluate her work. The ear was slightly crooked, but Lady Belda would be there shortly.

"Good enough," she grumbled. As long as she was paid, she didn't care if the dog's ears were on its ass. All that mattered was that she could send her earnings back home to her family in Aversheen and keep enough to get by herself, something that was becoming increasingly difficult with the rising grain and verillion prices as more resources were diverted toward the war effort.

Ari muttered a binding spell, threading the magic of the verillion through the powdered ruby and bonding it to the clay, her intent shaping the behavior charm into one of aggression. Then she snatched up a truth-stone from her workbench, the holy rock cool in her hand. It'd been taken from Sage-blessed ground—a rarity in Enderlain—and engraved with the Kinnish word for "truth." It was also her last one.

That's tomorrow's problem. Today she had only to finish this dog.

Ari pressed the rock into the golem's forehead before smoothing the clay. Taking a deep breath, she picked up the heavy black book from her workbench. Touching it always sent a shiver through her, like cold fingers trailing down her neck. The worn leather was soft and supple in her hands, the spine ribbed in pearlescent bone, and at the center lay a small, jade-green stone flecked with red.

It was a forbidden book. A book Ari wished she'd never touched. It had plagued her life with pain and misery from the moment she had.

Liar, whispered a familiar voice in the back of her mind. *It brought you power.*

The sort of power that made the shadows whisper and breathe. The sort that kindled life inside cold clay and could draw it screaming from warm flesh. The kind that—no! Ari nearly slammed the book shut, but she needed it. So she locked away the memories it threatened to pull free and flipped to a marked page.

Walking clockwise around the golem as best she could in the confined space, she recited the spell, speaking each old Kinnish letter carefully while holding her intent in her mind. It was a mental exercise that pushed the limits of her concentration, requiring her to channel her intent into the enchantment without fumbling a single syllable.

The power filled her in a rising tide, utterly intoxicating. Magic flowed from her lips like a breath of cold fire, streaming to the stone in the golem's head. Her voice rose as she neared the end of the incantation, the force pouring out faster and faster until—a light erupted from the dog's forehead, bright and pure as fresh snow. It rippled along the beast's body, turning clay to muscle and bone and fur.

In a final breath, Ari completed the spell, the last wisps of magic escaping her in a rush, leaving her body warm and tingling pleasantly from the sensation. The light faded, revealing a heavily breathing hound with sleek black fur and oversized canines. It watched her with dark eyes, muscles bunched and ears twitching, as if unsure what to make of this sudden thrust into life.

"You and me both," Ari muttered to the dog, placing the book on her workbench. She hesitated, her fingers curling into the soft leather. A low humming rose in the recesses of her mind.

Every time she put the book down, it felt like parting with a piece of herself. If she'd had her way, she'd have left the thing behind in her Saba's workshop. She'd tried to. Yet it'd appeared in her satchel before she'd even left town. So she'd flung it into the Greystel River when she reached Veradell, only to find it dry and unharmed in her bag once more. It was an enchantment unlike anything she'd ever seen, magic from a lost time.

Someone pounded on the door. Ari started, knocking her head on a hanging basket of dead verillion stalks. The dog was between her and the entrance in an instant, a growl like grinding stones in its throat.

"Arielle?" Lady Belda's high voice called. "Arielle, open the door."

Ari scowled. This was why her windows were heavily curtained. If Lady Belda had arrived earlier and seen her crafting an animal out of clay, it would have meant her life. She may not have recognized the golem for what it was, but she would have known the magic wasn't Enderlish, and while many in Veradell might look past her unlicensed status in exchange for cheap enchantments, they would not ignore the use of Kinnish magic. It had been illegal long before the Enderlish government established the enchanter registry.

No matter that they both relied on the same powers; Enderlish enchanters used their magic to charm objects and living animals—they didn't breathe life into clay, and that simple distinction meant the difference between steady work and a funeral pyre.

"Calm," Ari said in Kinnish. The dog relaxed at once, lowering onto its haunches and panting softly.

Lady Belda pounded on the door again. Ari crossed the room to open it, revealing the first rays of sunlight filtering through a blanket of fog and smoke from the iron smelter down the road. She wrinkled her nose at the stench of burning coal and seawater—courtesy of the nearby Greystel River that cut through the city like a jagged scar before emptying into the Eban Sea—and held up a hand to block the light.

An incredibly pale woman constructed entirely of cosmetics and furs stood on Ari's doorstep, her lips pinched, and eyebrows drawn. She wore a fox fur coat over a black silk blouse tucked into a pair of elaborately stitched pants. The house signet ring on her right index finger caught the morning light—a silver band with pink diamonds in a sun shape.

The two guards at her back weren't much better. Dressed in three-piece suits with their hands on their holstered revolvers, they surveyed the area like they expected Ari's neighbors to rob them on the spot.

Lady Belda surveyed her with a downward twist of her lips, and Ari felt a familiar, burning shame creep up her neck. She knew what Lady Belda saw. Olive skin caked in clay and sweat, her long curls frizzed and wild beneath her headscarf, and beyond her, a cramped room with peeling wallpaper, the edges stuffed with bundles of dried herbs and scavenged machine parts she hoped to sell. A small counter hosted the remnants of

Ari's last loaf of challah and the empty soup cans she'd yet to turn in for extra coin.

It was all she owned.

The noble lady lifted her chin. "My animal?"

Resisting the urge to order the golem to piss on the lady's fine shoes, Ari stepped aside, allowing the woman her first glimpse of the beast.

"Charmed for aggression and obedience," Ari said, though that last part wasn't entirely true. All golems were obedient by nature, but Lady Belda thought she was getting an enchanted dog, not a clay sculpture come to life.

She dug out a paper from her apron pocket, proffering it to the woman. "Here is the list of commands."

Lady Belda took the paper with extreme care not to touch her clay-covered fingers. She scrutinized the list, her eyebrows somehow managing to pinch even closer. "What sort of gibberish is this?"

"Kinnish."

The eyebrows drew tighter. "Are you slow, girl? I don't speak Kinnish. Give me the instructions in Enderlish."

"It obeys only Kinnish." Ari had explained this to the woman before accepting her order. Twice. Of all the millions of people in Enderlain, why was it her clients were always the most frustrating?

"How do you expect me to command something in a language I can't speak?" Lady Belda's nostrils flared.

Ari took a slow, deliberate breath. "You learn."

Lady Belda's eyebrows made it clear what she thought of that. "First you couldn't do the ethereal enchantment I wanted, now you expect me to speak this ridiculous tongue? I should have known you'd tried to cheat me with cheap work."

Ari flinched. She rarely accepted requests for ethereal enchantments, as they required higher amounts of verillion, and the powdered diamond necessary was out of her price range. That, and she struggled with the complexity of their inexact nature. To enchant something to never get lost or to detect lies, concepts that bordered on obscure, required training she didn't have.

The majority of her spellbook was in old Kinnish, and most speakers of the ancient language were lost when Kinahara was overrun by the Heretics' magic in the Cataclysm over a century ago. She could only access the first few pages her Saba had translated, and they were barely enough to figure out basic enchantments.

Lady Belda gestured one guard forward, who set a small sack of coins in her palm. She removed several silver marks, each side engraved with the royal crest consisting of the four greater house symbols: a lion's head for the Kelbras, a curving set of horns for House Ruthar, the Vanadahls' dual wings, and a serpent eating its own tail for House Dramara. A large silver Z for the Zuerlin royal family cut through the middle.

"Incomplete payment for an incomplete job," Lady Belda said. Ari's eyes narrowed, and the lady's brows rose to her hairline. "Do we have a problem, girl?"

Her clients sought her for a reason: her animals lacked the telltale gold flecks that identified enchants. They wouldn't recognize them as golems, only too happy to take the advantage it gave them with no questions asked. It made her services highly coveted, but at the end of the day, she was unlicensed, and Lady Belda knew it.

Those few who were born with magic were plucked from their families upon the discovery of their powers and sent to the royal enchanter academy, but for some reason her parents had hidden her abilities. Their warnings whispered through her head, an ever-present refrain. *Be silent. Be careful. Don't give them any reason to see you.*

"No problem," she said without a hint of irritation.

"No problem, my lady," Lady Belda corrected her, and waited.

Ari clamped her jaw shut. Something stirred inside her. Something cold and hard and unfamiliar.

Lady Belda's hand began to withdraw. Ari half lurched after the coins, swallowing against the refusal rising in her throat. She forced the words out: "No problem, my lady."

The woman smiled in satisfaction. "That wasn't so difficult, was it? Remember that the next time you try to swindle your betters." She tossed the pouch to Ari's feet, coins flying from its open mouth and scattering along the dirt. Ari didn't move, even as her instincts screamed at her to snatch up the coins before she could lose even one.

Lady Belda looked down at the list. Her lips twisted as though swallowing a slice of lemon before she butchered the Kinnish word for "follow." Still, the golem rose and trailed after her into her enchanted coach. The guards climbed into the box seat, and the vehicle trundled forward of its own accord.

The moment they turned the corner, Ari dropped to her knees and gathered the coins. Hugging them to her stomach, she retreated inside and slammed the door shut with one foot, her heart pumping fire through her veins.

It could have been worse.

After the Heretics' magic made Kinahara uninhabitable in the Cataclysm, thousands of Kinnish resettled in Enderlain, but after over a century of living alongside each other, they were still reviled. She'd been spat on and derided, tossed out of shops by suspicious owners and denied entrance to others altogether. Lady Belda was nothing in comparison.

Grumbling a string of Kinnish curses, she dumped the coins onto her workbench and counted them. Ten silver and fifty copper marks. A third of the agreed-upon price. She looked wearily from the coins to the stale challah on her counter. With the price of verillion rising as the war effort faltered, less and less was sold on the underground market, and without a license, she couldn't purchase it from legal establishments. What little made it to the underground would be too expensive to afford, especially when they upped the prices on her.

How she could be treated as both inexorably cheap and wealthy enough to be taken advantage of in the same city, she didn't know.

She swept the coins into a purse containing payment from two other golems she recently made. A hunting dog charmed for speed and a falcon with enhanced eyesight.

It wasn't enough.

Every month she sent coin home to her family in Aversheen on the coast of Enderlain, and every month it was met with silence. No letter of thanks. No inquiry after her health. Nothing.

She expected nothing more. She *deserved* nothing more.

Not after what she had done.

Monsters rarely look like monsters.

The first time her Saba had said that, she'd asked him if that was why their kind-faced Kinnish neighbors always looked at them so strangely.

"They don't like us because we are monsters?" she'd asked.

"No, Ari," he'd replied in his familiar, patient tone. "They don't understand us, so they fear us, and it is fear that creates monsters."

Ari hadn't known what fear her Saba meant. How could anyone be afraid of her gentle mother and kind father? How could they look upon the wizened face of her Saba and be scared? Her parents weren't devout, and Ari and her sister might have known little of their town's customs and prayers, but they were still Kinnish. Something more than their isolation made them different. Something that led to whispered warnings in the dark.

Don't draw attention. Don't give them any reason to fear you.

It wasn't until she'd gotten older that she'd realized it wasn't her family they feared—it was her. All their lives, her younger sister had railed against their parents' rules, but Ari had embodied them. For eighteen years, she'd been the perfect daughter. Careful. Quiet. Controlled. Yet people had still looked at her as if she were a sheyd wearing a child's skin.

A demon.

Her Saba had lifted a thin chain from about his neck, a gold cast lion's fang dangling from the end, and placed it about her own. "Promise me you will never let your fear control you. Promise me you will be fearless, a'huvati."

My love, he'd called her, and she'd promised, cradling the fang in her small fingers.

Would he still call her that if he could see her now, exploiting their people's magic for those who'd once tried to destroy it? Would he still see the fearless granddaughter he'd once held on his lap by the fire, telling stories late into the night, or would he see the young woman she'd become? The one who had broken so many promises, and whose heart had grown full of fear, no matter how she tried to control it.

The monster that made monsters.

A knock came at her door. Exhaustion swept over her at the thought of dealing with another customer or, worse, Lady Belda returning to complain about an askew ear. She had clay shavings to clean, a workbench to wipe down, and she hadn't eaten all night. Her back was sore, and she could feel one of her headaches coming, but the weight of coin in her hand, so much lighter than it should be, drove her to answer.

She'd barely turned the handle when the door burst open, knocking her to the ground. Pain radiated through her back, but she scrambled quickly to her feet as two pale-skinned Enderlish men forced their way inside. One grabbed her by the front of her apron, throwing her hard against a barrel. Her head struck the wood in a resounding blow.

"Stay there," he snarled, the words coming fuzzy through her addled mind. Scraping and shifting noises preceded the sounds of ceramics shattering and hanging pots being ripped from the ceiling.

Ari rolled slowly onto her side, blinking away the darkness encroaching on her vision. Both men were searching her workshop, overturning everything in a frantic sweep. Her fingers closed around air, and her heart leapt.

The coin pouch—she'd dropped it!

She scrambled along the ground on her hands and knees until she spotted it just beside a crate. She'd nearly reached it when something closed around the collar of her dress and flung her onto her back. Screaming, she scratched and kicked as the man held her down with one hand and snatched up the pouch with the other.

"This is all she's got," the man by the workbench growled. He held up a thin chain, the end dangling with a gold lion's fang—her Saba's necklace.

Ari lurched against her attacker's hold, her composure shattering. "You can't!" she yelled. "Put it down. Put. It. DOWN!"

He slammed her back to the ground, knocking her head into the hard earth. "Where's all your coin?"

She groaned, the haze in her vision growing. His callused fingers closed warningly about her throat, his face leaning close enough for her to smell the bitter spice of verillion smoke on his breath. "Where is it, girl?"

"That's all I have!"

"An enchanter with one pouch of silver to her name? Don't lie to me." He squeezed tighter.

"I'm not lying," she gasped, clawing at his fingers. He backhanded her hard enough to make her head ring.

Something prickled in her chest. A white-hot, vicious thing that rose slowly, like the embers of a fire whispering back to life. It longed for her to strike out, to hurt, to make this man suffer as he was making her suffer. But she had no golems, no weapons, no strength left in her weary body. And there was a part of her, far larger than she wanted to admit, that wished the man's hand would close around her throat and never let go. For him to put an end to her mistakes.

Not all monsters look like monsters.

"Shut the door," he called to his partner. "We're going to have a little talk."

CHAPTER 4

ARIELLE

THE THIEF HOVERING over Ari kicked her in the ribs hard enough to bruise. "I know you're hiding coin from us," he growled. "Just like I know you work your corrupt magic in here. I wonder what the Anthir would have to say about that?"

"Penalty's death by burning for Kinnish magic, last I heard," said his partner. He leaned against Ari's workbench, cleaning under his yellowed nails with a knife. "Don't they arrest the family too? To make sure the corruption's not spread."

Ari curled tighter, her fingers laced over the back of her neck to protect her head. She couldn't give them what she didn't have, but if she didn't give them something, they'd turn her in to the city guard for practicing Kinnish magic. It didn't matter if they had no proof. The art of making golems was nearly lost among her own people; these fools wouldn't even know what to look for to identify it. But she was an unlicensed Kinnish enchanter, and that was enough.

For one brief moment, she considered praying to the Harbingers for help, but the truth was she didn't really know how. Her family had stopped attending temple not long after she was born, and what she knew of prayer came from watching her Saba. She'd always envied the way his body had formed the right posture like the flex of a muscle. She had tried to copy the movements alone in her cramped workroom, but she felt like a shallow imitation, eighteen years too late. Now prayer felt false, as though she weren't worthy of its comfort.

Now Ari had no doubt that her gods had abandoned her.

"Last chance, girl," said the thief above her, and she braced herself.

The front door burst open. The man by the workbench cursed and drew a blade on the boy who entered. He wore all black, from his silken waistcoat to the leather of his shoes. With cut-glass features framed by dark curls and a cool, piercing stare, he reminded her of the bright white flame of her Saba's kiln fire—beautiful to look at, but too dangerous to touch. Then she saw the gun in his hand.

Recognition dawned on the nearest thief's face. "My lord—"

"Let go of her," the boy ordered.

The thief tore his hand away immediately and stood, backing toward his partner. The boy flicked the revolver toward the door. "Go."

They obeyed, leaving Ari sprawled across the floor with a mysterious stranger in her doorway.

He holstered his gun as she stood. "Are you all right?"

"Who are you?" she asked warily.

"My name is Damien Adair," he replied, and she stilled. Though she'd been in Veradell less than a year, she was familiar with its noble houses, and the Adairs most of all. Her home was in the Westmire District, which fell under their jurisdiction, and people here liked to talk, most of all about Damien.

The gossip about him was consistent: at twenty, he was the youngest Adair sibling and had worked for every ounce of respect he'd earned. He had a habit of finding people in tight spots and helping them out. Some called him a gentleman, others a scholar, but they all agreed on one thing: you didn't cross Damien Adair.

Which begged the question, what was he doing here?

Everything hurt as she sat down at her workbench. Her head pounded like a drum, her back ached, and her throat felt raw from screaming. Her hand closed again around the empty space at her collarbone, where her Saba's necklace should have hung. She always removed it when she worked. Now those men had it, the last memento she had to remember him by.

Boom, boom, boom, beat her head. She hesitantly touched the wound at her temple; her fingertips came away wet with blood. The sight of it didn't bother her. She'd seen so much of it already. Everything came back to blood in the end.

Grabbing her last clean cloth, she pressed it to her wound, regarding Damien silently. He stared back with the cool, impassive gaze of someone utterly in control. Something jerked inside her. She longed for that easy confidence, that infallible calm. It was intoxicating, like the way her magic flowed through her when she granted a golem new life.

"What do you want?" she asked, more brazenly than she intended. But she'd been humiliated, overpowered, and mugged—the quicker Damien explained himself, the quicker Ari could be alone again.

He seemed unperturbed. "I'd like you to enchant me an undetectable horse."

Ari went very still, the world slamming into sharp focus: how easily he could reach his guns, his position between her and the closed shop door, and the utter lack of emotion in his beautiful face. Had she only exchanged one captor for another?

Her hand fell away from her wound, her fingers closing around the bloody cloth. "You're mistaken," she said carefully. "I'm just a potter."

Damien toed an overturned basket of dead verillion stalks. "You weren't easy to find. I'd heard rumors of a Kinnish enchanter whose creations were undetectable, but you've been very careful. It was a stroke of luck, really, that I tracked one to an enchant dealer off Rathsborne Street."

Ari's fingers crept toward a piece of shattered ceramic. She'd heard of the Kelbras buying out the debts of unlicensed enchanters rather than see them hang, forcing them into indentured servitude. Was that Damien's intention with her? She'd sooner open the boy's throat than allow it. It would be so easy with the sharp ceramic, like a fettling knife through soft clay. It would take only a moment, and—Ari recoiled against the workbench.

Where had that thought come from? She'd never even hit anyone before. She couldn't kill someone in cold blood.

Couldn't you, though? whispered her thoughts. *You've done it before.*

That wasn't me. Ari clung to the words.

Damien's gaze tracked her hand, but he didn't stop her. "What I'm offering you is simple. Enchant me a horse for my Illinir racer, and in exchange, I will give you whatever you ask."

It wasn't until he was finished that she realized he'd been speaking in Kinnish. Surprise drowned everything else out. Almost. A flicker of curiosity sprang to life, but she snuffed it out. Her curiosity was a treacherous thing.

"You're Kinnish?" she asked in the same language, considering the olive tint to his skin with new eyes.

"Dara Adair," he said with a bow.

When Kinahara's destruction forced thousands of Kinnish to flee into neighboring countries, it became common practice to take a non-Kinnish name for interacting with the local people, whose prejudices against them were strong at the time. For those like Damien, whose family bore the public eye, it was a means of fitting in. But to have a second, Kinnish name, his family must have remained close to their roots.

"My mother was Kinnish," he told her. "But my father immigrated from Celair. My siblings and I bear both names."

Ari's hand fell away from the ceramic. "I wouldn't have thought the Enderlish would allow a Kinnish lord."

"They didn't allow anything," Damien replied. "My family took it."

Ari studied him, from the meticulous press of his dark suit to the neat curl of his hair across his brow. With his resources, his power, he could offer her many things, but he could just as easily be her undoing. It was no light decision, getting involved with the noble houses. They played with the threads of power like harp strings, and with a single strum, he could bring her life crashing down around her.

The barest smile graced Damien's lips. "Tell me what it is you want, Arielle Kadar."

Hearing her name should have set her on edge, but she was starting to understand this boy, the way he doled out information like the steps to a dance only he knew. He would not waste the hard work he'd put in to discovering her. If he'd meant her harm, he'd have put a gun to her head and forced her to enchant the horse. Instead, he gave her a choice. But what did a man like Damien Adair want so badly that he would offer her the world for it?

And more importantly, what did *she* want?

It was a question she hadn't allowed herself to ask, because the answer was something she could never have. She wanted to fall asleep in her own bed to the sound of her mother's singing, to wake up in the morning to the scent of fresh baked challah and the rhythm of her Saba's prayers.

She wanted to go home, and it was the one thing she could never do.

The thought scratched at her like the prick of a stinging nettle, and a sickening helplessness pooled in the pit of her stomach. A photograph lay facedown on the floor, overturned by the thieves, and Ari slid off her stool to pick it up. The glass had cracked across her sister's grinning face, dividing her in two. Rivkah would have taken the offer without thought. She'd have plunged headfirst into a new adventure, heedless of the risk, and Ari would have followed to make sure she came back okay.

But Rivkah wasn't here. There was only her.

Those men had made her feel weak. Her body had been useless, her magic even more so. She could do nothing as they tore apart her life and took what they wanted.

She never wanted to feel that powerless again.

She was tired of living in fear of being discovered, of losing control, of her past coalescing into a beast that would devour her.

Ah, but what a beast it would be, whispered the voice.

Her Saba's voice surged back. *Promise me you will be fearless.*

It was time she took control.

Setting the photo on the workbench, Ari faced Damien. "I want you to make me a licensed enchanter."

"Only a greater noble house has the power to retroactively grant an enchant license," Damien replied. "I can make it happen, but it will require my racer to win the Illinir."

"How so?"

"That's house business," he said, and she had a feeling it wouldn't be the last time she heard that.

"Then I want access to an enchanter's education and your protection in the meantime."

"Done." Nothing changed in Damien's expression, and yet Ari still felt his satisfaction like a soft caress. His eyes hadn't left her, the enchanted candlelight framing him in shadow.

She stared back at him unflinchingly. "When do we start?"

CHAPTER 5

MIKIRA

NOT FOR THE first time that day, Mikira wondered what in the four hells she was doing.

Damien had sent her an invitation to lunch, but as she rode Iri up the cobblestone drive of Adair Manor under a light drizzle, all she could think of was her sisters. Nelda had taken one look at her that morning and asked, "You're going to do something stupid, aren't you?"

Mikira had forced a smile. "Why do you say that, little frog?"

Nelda wrinkled her nose at the nickname. Lochlyn had always called her that. "Because you've got that look on your face, and you always do something stupid when you've got that look."

Mikira had promised her she would be careful, but she couldn't help feeling that she'd already broken that promise just by being here.

Set in the countryside at the southeastern edge of the Westmire District, Adair Manor sprawled along a low, grassy knoll, the afternoon sun limning the white marble in a silvery light. An enchanted gate granted her entrance to a circular drive, the scent of lavender filling the air from the sea of purple radiating around it. A fountain in the shape of House Adair's hawk symbol sat in the center with its wings stretched above its head.

A servant in the household's black and silver livery awaited her at the base of the manor steps alongside a stable boy.

"Miss Rusel." The servant bowed as Mikira dismounted. "If you'll follow me, I'll take you to Lord Adair. Your horse will be seen to."

Mikira reluctantly handed over Iri's reins to the stable boy and followed the servant along a wraparound deck to a back entrance in the eastern wing. The manor was quiet, the only movement from the occasional guard patrolling along the open-aired marble corridors. It wasn't near the level of luxury she'd experienced at Zalaire Manor, but it was a stark reminder of where she was.

The servant deposited her outside a set of towering doors carved with two rearing lions and departed with a bow. Mikira hesitated with her fingers on the handle. She'd spent years trying to disentangle her life from nobles, only to put herself straight into another one's path. If she walked through this door, she would officially be in business with Damien Adair.

Sorry, Nelda. She pushed open the door.

A spacious common room spread before her, set against a wall of tall, frosted windows reminiscent of still waterfalls. Before the windows stood a massive oak desk cluttered with microscopes, stacks of journals, and a small tray with vials of blood. Reid sat behind it, alternating between peering into a microscope and scribbling furiously in a journal so mangled, it looked like a horse had trampled it.

He glanced up as she descended the three short steps inside, his face already set in a glower. "Yes, please do wear your dirty boots inside. What's a little mud and horse shit on my clean floors?"

"Reid," Damien called from the armchair he occupied beside an empty hearth, a book balanced in his lap. "Be kind to our guest."

Reid scowled, but that wasn't what made Mikira stop short; it was his clothes. Silver and white, with a lion's head silhouette sewn into the breast.

Kelbra colors.

"Is this some kind of joke?" Mikira asked, one hand already on her knives.

"I don't joke about clean floors," Reid replied with such seriousness, she balked.

Damien's lips quirked. "I don't think she cares for your waistcoat."

"That makes two of us," Reid grumbled.

Damien must have seen her apprehension growing because he added, "Relax, Miss Rusel. Reid doesn't work for the Kelbras any more than I do."

"Then why—"

"Let me make something very clear," he began, and Mikira felt suddenly cold. This was the voice he'd used with that guard last night, moments before he'd snapped bone. "We may be partners in this endeavor, but the rest of my house's operations don't involve you. When you visit, you'll be escorted directly to my quarters or the stables. You won't ask questions. You won't wander. We'll conduct our business each day and nothing more. Do you understand?"

Mikira's nails dug into her leg, but she nodded.

Damien shifted his attention back to Reid. "Go change."

"I'm in the middle of an experim—" Reid paused at a look from Damien, scowling, but did as he was told. He marked a page in his journal before disappearing through an open door to her right.

"You'll have to forgive Reid his manners. I'm afraid the dead didn't make for good company growing up," Damien said lightly.

She blinked at him.

"He worked in a mortuary as a child," he clarified.

Well, that certainly explained his disposition, if not the elements scattered across the desk. "And now he works for you doing, what, exactly?" she asked before realizing that might stray too close to house business.

"A little of everything." Damien gestured at one of the armchairs that formed a crescent shape with a low-backed chaise. "Please, sit."

"I'm okay," she replied, her gaze catching on a series of black-and-white photographs of Damien with a gray-eyed Celairen man. In each, they stood alongside winning horses draped in flower wreaths, holding up medals from some of the city's most famous races she longed to compete in. She'd known House Adair built their fortune on whiskey, and that they'd since diversified into verillion, but she hadn't realized how success-ful they'd been in racing too.

Reid reappeared in the doorway, clad once more in all black, with a tiny black cat perched like a bird on his shoulder. He clutched a tray with a pearlescent teapot and cups, and the incongruence of the image made her snort.

He brushed past her and set the tray on the low table between the chaise and chairs. It was covered in stacks of books, several of which had been arranged into the same height to form an even surface. He sat down on the chaise and poured tea. She counted four cups, and only three of them.

A knock preceded a Kinnish woman's entrance. She was tall and curvy, her damp, dark curls loose down to her waist, and she wore a simple blouse and flowing skirt. It was the angry purple bruises ringing the olive skin of her throat that really caught Mikira's attention, though. They looked like fingerprints.

Damien closed his book, setting it aside as he stood. "Arielle, you're just in time for tea. Are you feeling better?"

The girl's deep brown gaze settled on Damien, narrowing in a consider-ing way that Mikira couldn't fathom. What about a dangerous lord made her so bloody curious? She might as well be fascinated by death.

"Much, thank you." Arielle descended the stairs and took the seat Damien indicated to his left. She had a keen elegance to her, the kind of graceful movement that drew the eye, and not in the way Mikira did. Mikira made people uncomfortable, made them angry. Arielle made them want to look and linger.

Damien inclined his head to Mikira as he retook his seat. "This is Mikira Rusel, our sponsored Illinir jockey. Mikira, Arielle is the solution I told you about. She can create undetectable enchants."

Mikira started. "What? How?"

He gave her a shrewd smile. "*That* is house business."

Arielle's dark eyes watched Mikira, her face unreadable. There was something tight and controlled about her, like the hammer of a gun about to snap down. Only a powerful enchanter would work for someone like Damien Adair, but to be able to create undetectable enchants? That was something else entirely.

Damien continued, "What I can tell you is that I know you race in the tunnels. I know the Kelbras want your ranch, and I know your father's an enchanter."

"That's not tr—" Mikira broke off at the look on Damien's face.

"What we're about to do is both dangerous and difficult," he said mildly. "Let's not make it more so by lying to each other."

Mikira bit her lip. How had he learned all of this?

Damien interlaced his fingers. "What I'd like to know is what your exact bargain with Rezek is."

Mikira folded her arms. "If I win the Illinir on an unenchanted horse, he'll pardon my father and forgive our debts to his house."

"Well, that was a stupid bargain," Reid muttered, and Mikira considered upending his cup of tea over his head.

Arielle's hand stilled where it'd been reaching for one of the books. "That's why you want one of my enchants? To win your bargain?"

"If I lose, he gets my family's ranch and my father," Mikira told her. There was no point in hiding it. Damien was right; for what was to come, the least she could do was be honest. "My family will be put on the street."

Arielle's fingers curled slowly into a fist, but she didn't speak again.

Mikira eyed Damien. "And what about you? What do you get out of all of this?"

Damien stood and approached a drink cart behind the chaise. He poured two glasses of whiskey, returning to offer Mikira one. She took it, uncertain of his intentions.

"I want this to be a partnership, Miss Rusel, and for that, I need you to trust me." Damien swirled his drink. "I want to see this city change. The Council of Lords fuels the Eternal War for their own gain, and no amount of repudiation from House Ruthar is going to stop them. Not when they all stand to lose so much."

Mikira's breath quickened; this was dangerously close to treason. It was no secret that the greater houses benefited from the war. Verillion, gemstones, enchanted objects—they all had a stake in one of them, and those industries were thriving beneath the wartime demand. She'd thought these things a thousand times herself, but it was something else entirely to hear them from him.

"I want to put an end to the Eternal War," Damien continued. "But only the Council of Lords has the power to do that. Which is why I've made my own bargain with Rezek Kelbra: his family's rights to run the Illinir against House Adair's racetracks and horses. If we win, it's the first step in my plan to stop the war."

An end to the war—it sounded like a dream, and she felt foolish for wanting to believe in it. But what if he could do it? House Adair was the first in ages to usurp an old house, granted their position at the newly crowned King Theo's behest some twenty years ago. Perhaps Damien had ties she wasn't aware of, a means of influencing the Council of Lords.

Damien lifted his glass to her. "So what do you say? Do you want to help me tear the Kelbras down?"

Not for the first time, Mikira had the distinct feeling she'd walked into a game she wasn't prepared to play. Some part of her knew that Damien wasn't telling her everything. It whispered that he couldn't be trusted, that he'd left out how exactly taking the Illinir from Rezek would change anything, but she also couldn't ignore what he offered her: a life free from the Kelbras.

And she'd help deal a blow so vicious to them, it would take them a generation to recover.

"To conning House Kelbra." She lifted her drink, the glass cool against her hot skin, and tapped it against his, the clinking sound like a chain pulling taut.

CHAPTER 6

ARIELLE

LISTENING TO DAMIEN talk was like watching a conductor lead an orchestra.

She'd seen one once, a woman in a traveling band of Celairen musicians who'd performed in her town edah. She and Rivkah had snuck out to the town square to watch. The woman had been so calm, so controlled, each smooth motion she made reflected in the sound that swelled from her musicians with the organization of a well-oiled machine.

Damien was the same in the words he chose, the actions he took. He'd done his research on Mikira, but rather than use it against her, he showed his hand, knowing the truth was what she needed. Together they would both get what they wanted.

He'd used the same trick with her.

Conning the Kelbras was akin to sticking your hand under a falling blade and hoping it wouldn't cut you. By doing it with a bunch of strangers she'd only just met, she might as well be holding the blade herself. If Damien had told her this back at her workroom, she might have refused his offer. Instead, he'd waited until she'd seen the room he'd offered her on his gated estate, the guards patrolling the perimeter with their imported Sherakin shotguns. He'd wanted her to see that she would be safe here, and it was the only thing that kept her from walking out the door.

That, and the table full of books.

Each and every one was about Kinnish history and lore, culture and society, from a leather-bound Arkala full of prayers and teachings on the Harbingers she'd never read to books of ancient mythology. How much did he know about who they were?

More than I do.

She felt again that longing to be like him. To be in control not just of herself, but of the world around her, so no one could ever hurt her like those thieves had again.

So she could never hurt someone like she had again.

Mikira downed her whiskey in one go and wiped her mouth with the back of her sleeve. "How long will it take you to enchant the horse?"

"Three weeks," Ari replied.

"Three *weeks*?" Mikira gaped. She was short and wiry, with a freckled, hawkish nose and pale skin that was already flush from the drink. "I thought charms only took a few hours."

"And what exactly do you know about enchanting?" Reid asked, still slumped into the chaise. "Is that a common topic of education on a ranch?"

Mikira's knuckles turned white from gripping the glass. "More common than in a mortuary, or do the dead have much use for magic?"

Reid's gaze snapped to Damien, who shrugged, leaving Ari sure she'd missed something. Mikira forced a breath and turned back to her. "Okay, three weeks, though that only leaves us a few days before the first race. If you can charm it for speed, endurance, obedience, and to never get lost, that'll give me an edge in all four races."

"Anything else?" Reid asked. "Would you like it to have six legs and be enchanted to fly?"

"I think someone might notice that," Mikira replied tightly.

Ari almost smiled. "Binding two enchantments to an animal is incredibly hard. Binding three requires an expert hand. Any more than that, and the beast will go mad."

That was technically true. Golems could handle more, but this girl didn't need to know that—not before Ari knew if she could do it. The physical and behavioral enchantments shouldn't be difficult, but she'd never tried combining them with ethereal enchantments, which were arduous on their own.

Mikira grimaced. "Oh." She set her glass down on an end table. "I only really know breeding enchants, not charming them."

At that, the girl's last name clicked into place. "Your family breeds enchanted horses, is that right?"

"Yes?" Mikira tensed as if she expected the answer to bite her.

"I'd like to hear more about how that works sometime." As a breeder, Mikira would be dependent on the careful curation of bloodlines, on the complex game of inheritance and long process of distilling the purest enchantments into her animals, but that was the extent of Ari's knowledge.

Something like suspicion lingered in Mikira's gaze, but she nodded before addressing Damien. "We should attend a couple of the showcase races over the next few weeks to scope out competition."

The showcases were the last chance for unknown riders to display their skills in hopes of securing a sponsor before the opening Illinir ball. After that, the real race would begin.

"I'll arrange for someone to do that." Damien tucked one hand into a pocket, a surety about him that she longed to possess. "In the meantime, our private track is at your disposal for training. Reid can show you to the stables."

Reid spluttered mid-sip of his tea, but at a look from Damien, he muttered something under his breath and set his cup aside. Standing, he swept his cat onto his shoulder and grumbled, "Come on."

Mikira looked less than enthused as she followed him out, leaving Ari alone with Damien. She wasn't afraid of him, but he did make her nervous. It was a thrilling sort of nervous, though, like the moment before she brought a new golem to life.

"I have something I'd like to show you." Damien offered her a hand up.

She took it, his fingers rough with calluses grazing along her skin. What had a man like him done to earn hands like that?

Damien's gaze dropped to the line of bruises around her neck. She covered them with a hand. "They're not as bad as they look."

His fingers tightened briefly on her own. "Follow me."

He led her back into the open corridor, the arches reflective of the Kinnish style. From what her Saba had told her, only the city buildings in Kinahara had been large enough to warrant corridors like these. Each one was open aired to take in the warm natural light, and to promote a sense of connection and cohesion among the community, as dictated by the Harbinger Lyzairin's teachings. Which made them an unusual choice for the cold, rainy weather of Enderlain.

Perhaps a choice of Lady Adair's? Damien had told her on their way to the manor that his ailing father had not lived there since his mother passed, but nothing more than that. Some rumors said Lady Adair had died from a disease when Damien was only a child; others said a rival house had murdered her. She hadn't asked, not wanting to pry open old wounds. She knew something of the work they took to keep closed.

Damien slowed outside a guarded door, a Sherakin rifle resting in the sentry's gloved hands. Like Damien's revolvers, the rifles were as much a status symbol as the estate itself. With Enderlain's import restrictions on guns from Celair and Izir, they must have cost a small fortune.

The guard opened the door, revealing a narrow, descending staircase illuminated with enchanted lights.

"When I told you how I found you, it was the truth, but it wasn't the entire truth," Damien said as they started down the stairs into a small, cold room, where another guard unlocked a second door. This one opened into a short hallway, rows of cells running along either side. Ari paused on the threshold, curiosity warring with uncertainty.

Damien slowly removed his jacket, revealing broad shoulders and the Lonlarra revolvers holstered against his ribs. "You see, Arielle, I know the truth about you."

The words drove straight through her. She calculated if she could get back up the stairs and down the hall fast enough. Would the guard outside stop her? Shoot her? What if—she silenced her rising panic, forcing her expression to remain carefully neutral.

"I don't know what you mean."

His soft laugh prickled along her skin. "I know you practice Kinnish magic."

"You don't know what you're talking about," she bit out.

Damien's eyes came alight, as if finally seeing something he'd expected to find all along. *Calm down calm down calm down.* This was getting out of control. She needed to breathe, to get away from him, to—

"The enchant I tracked—to anyone else, it might have looked like nothing, but I've seen golems before."

The words carved a line of fire through her. A line of fear, and pain, and dark, bloody memories. Her mother telling her not to meddle with things she didn't understand. Her Saba begging her not to go looking for the book again.

She hadn't listened. Oh, how she wished she'd listened.

Blood on her hands. Blood on the walls.

Be silent. Be careful. Don't draw their attention.

But she had more than Damien's attention; she had his interest. He watched her like a hunter before a trap, waiting to see if his prey would be caught. She could see it in the lift of his brow, the question in his eyes.

Will you run? they asked.

Part of her wanted to, but that morning's attack had shaken something loose inside her. She'd been so very careful with her work, so very careful with her customers, and still her secret had slipped, still those men had found her. Still they'd stolen everything she'd worked so arduously to collect and left their handprints around her neck like vicious tattoos.

Promise me you will be fearless, a'huvati.

"If you tell a soul what you know, I'll send a golem to tear you apart." She felt a sparking thrill with each word she spoke, a lightness she hadn't known for years, like a beast stretching its legs after a lifetime of confinement.

To her surprise, he laughed. A short, booming sound that echoed in the chamber. "Not afraid of me, not afraid of the law, not afraid of magic. What are you afraid of, little lion?"

She flinched at the nickname, at the true meaning behind her Kinnish name. A lion was courage, a lion was strong. Like Aslir, the Bright Star, a lion was not consumed by fear. She could not remember a time she'd ever felt worthy of her name.

"I have no intention of telling anyone about your abilities," Damien said in Kinnish. "You have complete freedom to practice your magic however you wish here. I promised you access to information, and I'll ensure you get both Enderlish and Kinnish texts on enchanting. You can even build the golem here."

Ari stared at him. The idea that she might be able to work her magic openly and unafraid was so foreign, she struggled to accept it. But despite that, she believed him. Beneath his reticence, there was an earnestness to this boy, a sincerity that put weight behind his words.

"You know what I'll need to create it, then?" she asked. "This horse."

"Dirt from holy ground, and water that has never before been poured into a vessel," he said. "The materials are already on their way."

He hung the jacket on a hook in the stone wall, before removing the holster from his chest and setting the guns down with reverent care on a stool. Each movement was methodical, almost ritualistic. Undoing his waistcoat, he hung it atop the jacket, leaving him in just his shirtsleeves. Then he carefully unbuttoned the cuffs at his wrists and rolled his sleeves up bit by bit, baring forearms corded with lean muscle beneath olive skin.

"I brought you here for another matter, however." His eyes dropped again to the bruises at her neck, and this time she didn't cover them.

He stepped toward the cell in the back, and she followed, drawn by an invisible lure. The faded lamplight barely illuminated two ragged forms suspended from the ceiling by their wrists. A strange, wild feeling crept over Ari as Damien unlocked the cell door. Her eyes never left the bodies as she stepped into the full glow of the lamplight.

Pale and bruised, their heads lolling against their chests, were the two men who had attacked her.

They looked like animals hung for the slaughter. Both blinked dazedly at her, before one of them—the one whose handprints she wore—finally recognized her and cursed.

Something glinted in the dim light, and Ari tore her gaze from the men. Dangling from Damien's fingers like a star in the sky was her Saba's necklace. *He got it back.* She held out her hand, and he placed it gently in her open palm, the fang cool against her skin. Her fingers curled against it, and she pulled her fist to her chest.

Then he offered her a set of brass knuckles.

"I thought you might like to return the favor," he said.

A shiver dripped down Ari's spine, something dangerously close to anticipation. Some dark, quiet part of her wanted this. Wanted to make them feel the fear that had immobilized her, the pain that still plagued her.

She wanted to make them feel powerless.

"We're sorry!" one of the men stammered out. "We ne—ah!" He choked off as Damien's elbow slammed into his sternum.

"You don't speak to her," he said.

The man gasped, struggling for air. Ari expected to feel sorry for him, and to an extent, she did. But there was also a part of her that felt this was right.

He'd brought this on himself. He deserved it.

And yet she couldn't bring herself to take the weapon from Damien.

He must have seen the decision in her eyes, because he retracted his hand with a small nod. One of the men let out a choked sob of relief.

Then Damien slid the brass knuckles over his fingers and entered the cell.

CHAPTER 7

MIKIRA

THE ADAIR GROUNDS were something out of a fairy tale. The sea of lavender plants stretched around the entire estate, undulating in the gentle afternoon breeze. Even in the midst of summer, the Veradell sky was overcast, but the air was filled with the scent of lavender and pleasantly warm.

Mikira wanted to stretch out on her back on a patch of grass and just breathe for a while.

It would have been idyllic—if not for Reid. He trudged along as though the task of showing her the stables was the most absurd thing anyone had ever asked him to do. Why did her family's fate have to rely on her getting along with this gloomy cloud of emotion?

"What's your problem?" she asked.

Reid shot her a dark look. "I have better things to do than babysit you."

"Ah, yes, like stare at slides of blood under a microscope all day. You must be really popular at parties."

"At least I can get into parties."

Mikira's cheeks flushed, but Reid had already turned away. She was still considering flinging a knife at him when they rounded a final corner and the stable spread out before them.

She'd never seen anything like it before.

The Adair stable stretched the length of her family's several times over. It sat at the forefront of acres of emerald grass divided into neat pastures by white picket fences and filled with horses of every color. Her gaze leapt from a circular arena where a woman lunged a piebald horse, to a rectangular course set with jumps of varying heights, before settling at last on the racecourse.

It was easily four hundred yards in length, the dirt track a pale brown in the filtered sunlight and peppered with the imprint of hooves. Several other racers were taking their horses in easy laps, the rhythm of their steps echoing up to where they stood.

"Well, at least now I know how to shut you up."

Reid's voice broke the spell, and Mikira glared at him. "How is it no one's pushed you under a galloping horse yet?"

He sneered at her and stomped toward the stable. The fresh scent of hay and leather greeted them inside, where horses poked their heads out through the half-open doors of their stalls. Each was one of the finest she'd ever seen—sleek heads and muscular necks, coats that shone and luxurious, neatly trimmed manes.

"They're gorgeous," she breathed before she could stop herself.

She expected Reid to make a scornful comment, but he seemed as enthralled by the beasts as she was.

"Where's Iri?" she asked. "I'll ride him."

"That's a stupid idea," Reid replied, shattering whatever strange image she'd been constructing of him. This was the boy she expected. "Your stallion's not been trained at the gate. At best he'll do nothing when it opens, at worst he'll throw you. Pick another horse."

Mikira started to object on the sheer principle that agreeing with Reid felt like impaling herself on a jagged spike, but held back. He was right. Iri had never been pinned into a starting gate with a mechanical door that snapped open and a bell that rang in his sensitive ears.

Folding her arms, Mikira jerked her head at the line of stalls. "Fine. You choose."

Reid looked her over, and Mikira tensed beneath the intensity of his bright blue gaze. Then he was off down the aisle, leaving her feeling strangely cold.

Shaking the feeling away, she followed him to the stall of a beautiful black mare. She was about sixteen hands and had a single white sock on her left hind leg, as if the dark had tried to swallow up the light. A silver plaque on the stall door read EILORA'S FLIGHT.

Reid haltered her, falling into a routine that betrayed his familiarity with horses. Eilora let him work without concern, her posture relaxed in a way that suggested a docility charm. It was a line of enchants often sold to parents of young riders who wanted a safe horse to learn on.

By the time Reid had finished tacking her up, Mikira was flat-out staring.

"You have a way with horses," she said begrudgingly. "And here I thought they'd run away screaming."

Reid peered out from around Eilora's hindquarters. "I like animals. It's people I can't stand." He gave her a pointed look.

She rolled her eyes as he undid Eilora's halter and slipped it from beneath the bridle. Damien had said that Reid did a little of everything for him, and apparently that stretched from science experiments to racing to being a thorn in her side.

A short walk later, Mikira was standing on the track before the racing gate clasping Eilora's reins. The other House Adair jockeys had relocated to a second track nearby, and Mikira's attention lingered longingly on them. They were what she'd always wanted to be: normal riders running normal races on the finest enchants in the kingdom. They split their winnings with their sponsored house, but with how lucrative betting was at the official tracks, the purses were ten times what she won in the tunnels with Jenest.

"Any day now," Reid remarked. He stood on the bottom rung of the fence surrounding the track, eating an apple he'd filched from the barn. The cat had taken up residence in a patch of sun on the fence.

She eyed the narrow stall she was supposed to walk the horse into with a frown, before swinging up into the saddle. Eilora shifted beneath her, and Mikira gathered the reins, whispering gently to her.

"Direct her into the stall," Reid instructed. "I won't shut the gate behind you the first time."

"Doesn't the gate crew usually do this part?" she asked.

"Do I look like an assistant starter?"

"You look like a dissatisfied woman just threw you out of her bed." Mikira ignored his scowl and slid her boots into the high stirrups, squeezing her knees gently against Eilora's sides. The horse had a slow, loping gait that hinted at her age.

"What's the point of this anyway?" she asked. "The Illinir races don't start with a gate." The last Illinir had been ten years ago when she was seven, but she remembered the races taking place all over the city, from beside the hilly Greenwark District to along the Traveler's Road.

"The final race does," Reid replied. "And the point is I want to time you." He plucked a pocket watch from his pants, and a flutter of nerves buzzed through her. Surely Reid would report everything he observed back to Damien. Would he retract his offer if she wasn't up to par? He had something depending on this too, after all.

Wrangling her doubts into submission, she guided Eilora into the stall. The mare entered almost of her own accord, clearly comfortable with the process.

"On one," Reid called. "Three, two—"

The horn sounded and the gate fell open. Eilora burst forward before Mikira was ready. She cursed, but her instincts took over, and she clung tight with her knees, taking her weight off Eilora's back. She kept a firm grip on the reins and leaned low over the horse's neck.

The wind buffeted her braid, tearing red strands free to whip about her face. Eilora soared along the track, keeping close to the inner fence. As her heart calmed from the sudden start—something she intended to *thank* Reid for later—Mikira settled into the ride.

It'd been so long since she'd raced in open air like this, the way she'd once done alongside her brother and Talyana. She loved the feel of the wind in her hair, loved the sound of thudding hooves against the dirt, loved the knowledge of the sheer strength and power of the majestic beast beneath her.

It felt like flying.

All too soon, they reached the end of the course, and Mikira slowed Eilora to a trot as they approached the starting gate. They were both panting heavily, sweat streaking hair and skin, and Mikira had a grin plastered across her face.

That had been amazing. She had to do it again. She had to go faster. She—something struck her in the chest, and she pulled back reflexively, nearly toppling off Eilora. The horse whinnied as she jerked the reins, taking several quick steps back.

By the time Mikira regained her seat and control of the horse, Reid had stepped onto the racetrack.

"What the four hells just—" She stopped, spotting the apple core where it lay on the ground. She swung off the horse, boots driving into the dirt, and stalked up to Reid.

"What is your problem?" She jabbed her finger into his chest. "You could have gotten me hurt, or Eilora!"

Reid didn't back down, and for the first time she was struck by how much he towered over her. She was short, but he was taller than average, and had a way of looking down at her that made her want to break his nose.

"The Illinir isn't some jaunt around a track," he snapped. "It's four cross-country races through enchanted terrain with the city's most dangerous criminals dressed up as jockeys. You can't lose yourself to the ride like that, or come the race, it won't be an apple hitting you in the chest!"

"It was a practice race! Hells, it wasn't even a race. It was a *ride*."

"And you only have three weeks until the Illinir." Reid leaned toward her. "You need to make every ride count, or you don't have a chance."

Mikira shoved her hands into his chest. He recoiled a step, scowling, and she turned back to Eilora. Reid could describe the weather and it would probably infuriate her; what made this so much worse was that he was right. Despite all her dreams of becoming a jockey, she had never wanted to run in the Illinir. Not since she'd begged her father to take her to watch the race as a child, and he'd replied, "That's not a race, it's a bloodbath. No one who cares about their horse enters it."

It wasn't until she'd gotten older that she'd realized what he meant: the quickest way to take out an opponent was to take out their horse. All it would take was a moment's distraction, and her life or her horse's could be over in seconds.

She splayed her hand against the warmth of Eilora's neck. "I want to meet the horse Arielle will be enchanting."

"It won't be here for a while." Reid's voice was still tight with annoyance. "After that Arielle wants privacy to work on it. You can meet it when she's done."

"But that's—" She stopped as something over his shoulder caught her eye. He followed her gaze to where flashes of blue and white flickered through the branches of the trees from the road beyond the estate.

"Shit." Reid marched for the fence, the cat leaping onto his shoulders as he passed.

"What's going on?" She scrambled after him, waving down a nearby stable hand to take Eilora. By the time they reached the back porch, the pounding of hooves echoed from the road. Reid hurried back toward the side door they'd left from. Ahead, a line of horses surged through the open manor gate and raced along the drive.

The Anthir.

Reid broke into a run, and Mikira considered turning back for the stable, grabbing Iri, and getting the hells out of there. The last thing she needed was trouble with the Anthir.

But she couldn't afford for anything to happen to Damien either.

She caught up to Reid as he stopped to open the side entrance. They thundered down the corridor and curled around a corner just as a door down the hall clicked open. Arielle stepped out. She frowned, then moved aside as Damien emerged.

"Anthir," Reid wheezed as they arrived.

Damien's eyes flared, but that was all Mikira saw of his reaction, for her gaze had snagged on his forearm. The once pristine white of his shirtsleeve now bore pinpricks of red like splattered paint.

When she looked up, it was Arielle's gaze she met. The girl shook her head, just the slightest.

And then the hall filled with guards.

CHAPTER 8

ARIELLE

ARI FELT LIKE she'd been unmoored and set adrift in the ocean—weightless and without direction. She didn't remember waiting for Damien to roll down his sleeves and strap on his guns once more. She didn't remember walking back up the stairs, the faded sunlight too bright for eyes that had grown accustomed to the dark.

She'd watched Damien beat those men within an inch of their lives, and she had not looked away.

Not when the blood splattered his arms. Not when bone cracked. Not when her Saba's voice asked her how she had gotten here, with him.

Monsters rarely look like monsters.

Was she a monster for not stopping him? Would he have stopped if she'd asked?

She hadn't asked, and he hadn't stopped, and Ari couldn't bring herself to regret it. Not fully. Even as her stomach tilted and the sound of metal against bone reverberated in her head, she couldn't ignore that flare of relief inside her. The knowledge that those men had gotten what they deserved and they would not harm her again.

She couldn't ignore that she felt safe for the first time in a long time.

And so it was when the corridor flooded with Anthir, a stern, fair-skinned young man at their lead, she shook her head at Mikira's wide-eyed stare.

Say nothing, she willed her.

Damien put his back to the door they'd just exited, his jacket slung over one shoulder. Whatever surprise he felt at seeing the constables was buried beneath a practiced mask.

"Sergeant," he greeted. "Is there a problem?"

The sergeant bowed—barely. "My apologies, Lord Adair," he said, not sounding sorry at all. "We received a report claiming that you were seen abducting these men who work for the Kelbras."

He held out pictures of the two men who'd attacked her. One short and square-faced, the other lean with a jagged nose. "Do you know why someone might have said such a thing?"

Ari had to force herself not to look at the door behind Damien. To his credit, he didn't so much as blink.

"Not in the slightest," he replied smoothly. "As I'm sure you know, my family is old friends with Inspector Elrihan and a dedicated supporter of the Anthir."

The sergeant's lips curled in distaste. "Yes of course. I wouldn't dare to insinuate. But neither can I simply dismiss such claims, you understand."

"Of course." Damien's voice was light, but the Adair guard holding the Sherakin shotgun fell into line at his back. The constables responded by reaching for their enchanted batons.

Mikira shifted, her nervousness nearly as tangible. Ari willed her to stay still. All it took was a noise from the men downstairs, or the wrong turn of a head, and the Anthir might realize just how close they were to the truth.

The blood.

As though the thought drew him to it, the sergeant's gaze fell on Damien's red-stained sleeve. "Are you wounded, Lord Adair?" he asked with hollow concern.

Ari acted before she could think. She drove her palm into the point of her Saba's necklace hard enough to draw blood and tugged it free with her other hand, tearing the skin open with a sharp burst of pain.

"That's from me." She held out her wounded hand. "Damien was inspecting it before you showed up, and if you don't mind, I'd like to get it tended to sometime today."

Visible annoyance flicked across the sergeant's face. "I see. My apologies, my lady." He inclined his head to Damien, adding begrudgingly, "I'm sure this was all just a misunderstanding. Please accept my apologies, Lord Adair."

"Of course," Damien replied. "Though I didn't quite catch your name, Sergeant."

The sergeant paused mid-turn. "Jac Eedren, my lord."

Mikira stiffened in recognition at the name, and it brought something of a smile to Damien's lips. "My family recently made a sizeable donation to a hospital with a Mr. Eedren in residence. A relation of yours?"

"My father." Jac's face had gone pale, the threat received. The Anthir's job was to enforce the law, but they never would have dared question a member of another noble house this way without solid proof, which meant someone had sent them. Someone whose reach with the Anthir went farther than House Adair's.

Ari could practically see Damien recording the slight, a notation in his mental ledger. Jac's only saving grace was that they hadn't brought any enchanted animals with them. A bird charmed to detect lies or a hound to track scents would have been far more than a slight.

It'd be an attack, and Damien's response would not have been a simple threat.

Damien adjusted the cuff of his sleeve. "You may go, Sergeant Eedren."

The sergeant performed a hasty bow, then scrambled from the corridor, his compatriots a step behind.

"How did you know that?" Mikira blurted out once they'd gone. "That guard at the ball—they have the same family name."

"If you're going to make an enemy of someone, you best know everything about them," Damien replied, and Ari didn't miss the warning underneath.

Something clicked into place in Mikira's expression. "Rezek sent them."

"I don't imagine he likes the idea of us working together." Damien turned back for his room. "This won't be his last move."

ARI SAT STILL as a bird on the chaise as Reid meticulously bandaged her hand with a skill that bespoke training. She still wondered at herself over what she'd done. Involving herself like that—it went against everything her parents had taught her to do in such precarious situations. But Damien had been threatened because of something he'd done to protect her. The least she could do was return the favor, even if she didn't understand why he'd done it in the first place.

With the Anthir gone, they'd gathered around the book-strewn table before a crackling peat fire. Thick gray clouds had filled the sky, and several enchanted lamps burned along the perimeter of the room.

Mikira kept glancing outside. She looked anxious, like an animal backed into a corner.

"Do you have something you want to say, Miss Rusel?" Damien asked from his position by the fire.

"Mikira," she corrected him with a shudder. "Did you take those men?"

Damien regarded her with an unreadable look. "I didn't, no."

But your people did. Ari could practically see him stepping around the question. It was like watching a chess game unfold; he always thought several moves ahead.

"Would it bother you if I had?" he asked. "They're Kelbra men."

Mikira's jaw set, the nervous shaking of her leg ceasing. "That doesn't make it right. People can't just take people off the street."

"Apparently they can." Reid tied off the last of Ari's bandage and released her hand. "Good riddance to them."

Mikira cast him a narrow-eyed glance but didn't respond. Instead, she started for the door. "I have work to do at the ranch. I'll be back in the morning."

Ari debated if she should follow, but in truth, she didn't want to be alone right now. The events of the day had left her feeling swept away. Instead, she watched as Damien took apart and cleaned his revolvers, and Reid hunched over the microscope at the desk, making notations in his journal. She half expected them to ask her to leave, but they absorbed her presence without so much as a batted eye, and she wondered if this too was a move on Damien's part, a carefully calculated decision to make her feel more comfortable.

"What will you do with those men?" she asked, thinking of the Anthir sergeant.

Damien looked up from carefully wiping down the outside of a revolver. "I'll let them go in the morning."

The thought of them being on the street again where they could hurt her made Ari's chest tighten, but what had she expected? For him to keep them imprisoned forever?

Damien's sharp eyes missed none of her reaction, and he set the gun down on the cloth laid out before him. "They won't come near you again. You're under my protection now. You're safe."

Safe. She almost laughed at the thought. She hadn't been safe since the day she fled her home with nothing but the clothes on her back and a book she couldn't be rid of no matter how hard she tried.

"From them, perhaps," she said. "But you won't be the last to figure out I'm unlicensed. The Anthir will come for me eventually."

"If you're referring to the enchant dealer I spoke of, he won't be a problem." Damien picked up his whiskey. "We'll make sure he understands his discretion is appreciated."

She shivered but didn't protest. Her gaze shifted to the dismantled guns. She wanted to be able to protect herself, to not have to depend on the Adair name to shield her. She was tired of relying on other people, of bending herself to their whims. Perhaps Damien wasn't like the haughty nobles who'd sneered down at her, but he still wielded immense power, and she did not.

She was going to change that.

A servant knocked and entered. "Lord Adair, the materials you requested have arrived."

"You can put them in the study," Damien replied.

Reid's head snapped up as workers began carrying in barrels of dirt and water to the open door to his left. "You're putting her in my workshop?"

"Mikira will see if she's out here, and I'm not shutting her in some far-away room. Besides, you only ever use my desk."

"The light in here is better!"

"Then what are you complaining about?"

Reid muttered something unintelligible in response and rose to follow the workers, his annoyed instructions floating out from the other room. Damien had told her that Reid knew the truth of her powers, but it still made her uneasy to hear them discussed so openly.

By the time the last of the materials had been delivered, Reid was pale-faced and overwhelmed. He sunk onto the chaise with the world's largest teacup and his cat in his lap. "There's dirt on my floor," he grumbled at them. "Dirt."

"We'll leave you to grieve in peace." Damien invited her toward the room with a nod. She followed him inside, where the workers had organized the materials into sections: dirt and water for the golem, verillion for the magic, and powdered gemstones to bind the spells. The room itself was spacious, with a built-in desk along an entire wall hung with anatomical diagrams and landscape sketches. The bookcases on the opposite wall were a neatly organized assortment of glass tea containers, scientific equipment, and tomes thicker than her fist.

Another door led to what looked like Reid's bedroom, now nearly blocked by the barrels of dirt.

"Do you have everything you need?" Damien asked.

"I think so." She dragged forth a stack of buckets. "I'll need to make the clay first."

Damien had changed into fresh clothes after the Anthir left—a silver waistcoat over a white shirt—and he removed the waistcoat now and rolled up his sleeves. "If you tell me what to do, I can help you."

She instructed him on the ratio of water to dirt and the means of mixing, after which the buckets would be left to sit to allow the clay to separate from the sediments in the dirt. They worked alongside each other in silence for some time, Ari being careful of her injured hand as they prepared bucket after bucket.

"Will you build the horse and then bind the enchantments or bind them to the clay before crafting it?" he asked as they neared the last of the buckets. He had mud splattered on his white shirt and caked along his forearms that stood in stark incongruence with his neatly styled hair and fine clothes.

"I'll fold the verillion and gemstones into the clay, then build the horse and bind the enchantments before bringing it to life," she replied, each word stranger on her tongue than the last. She'd never talked about creating golems with anyone before. It was a task she did alone in her workshop, with the knowledge that should anyone discover her, it would mean her life.

Damien held a small jug underwater in a barrel until it filled and then carried it to his bucket of dirt. "It's a crime how little of this art remains." He poured the water into the bucket, then used the mixing stick to stir it, the muscles in his forearms flexing. "I wish I could have seen it at its peak."

Ari stilled in stirring her own bucket. To build a golem was not so different from enchanting a living animal, merely a different application of the same magic, and yet it was condemned and driven into obscurity because a kingdom with power sought to possess one without.

"I've never understood why the Enderlish hated it so," she said. "Why they hated us."

"They saw it as a threat," Damien replied. "Golems kept the Enderlish army at bay for years before they finally broke through. The day the Enderlish flag rose above the Kinnish royal palace, the first thing they did was crack down on Kinnish magic. Before long the Sendian Church was calling it an abomination, a perversion of Sendia's gift to humanity."

"The Harbingers brought magic to humanity, not Sendia." She might not know much about her own religion, but she knew that. Even the Enderlish agreed on that point, though they believed the Goddess Sendia sent them. In the Kinnish religion, there was no goddess, only the Harbingers. "Their religion stemmed from ours, didn't it? How can they turn around and call us a perversion?"

Damien scraped the mixing stick along the edge of the bucket, then set the mixture aside among the rows of others. "You can do a lot of things when you're backed by an army of that size. This continent had never seen anything like it before or since. If the Cataclysm hadn't wiped out so many Enderlish troops, the Eternal War would have been over years ago, but Enderlain still hasn't quite recovered."

Most of that army was now in Celair, half made of conscripted farmers and shopkeepers. She'd heard whispers that the Council of Lords kept the real soldiers in the castle barracks and garrison towns throughout Enderlain, sending those they saw as expendable to die on the front lines. It wasn't the level of the invasion of Kinahara, but it was enough to disrupt an entire kingdom.

Ari moved her bucket over to join the others. "How do you know all of this?" It was the sort of information she'd craved for years, but never had access to.

"My mother was a historian, and I take a particular interest in history,"

Damien replied as he secured another bucket and filled it with dirt. "I also collect old books on the subject. You're welcome to them any time, though for Reid's sake, I have to ask that you be careful not to get clay on them. He can only take so much."

A smile pulled at her lips. "Do you believe, then? In the Harbingers?"

"I put my faith in things I can see and feel." Her disappointment must have showed on her face, because he added, "But I have books on Kinnism too, including an Arkala, and people who would be happy to discuss them with you, should you want that."

She wasn't sure yet what she wanted. There was far more to her culture and religion than belief and prayer, though those were two of the central tenets. Damien clearly excelled in another: the practice of study. Kinnism placed a high value on learning and using that knowledge to better the world, as the Harbingers had for humanity.

Ari was aware of those things, but that was as deep as her knowledge went. Everything she did know was only a reminder of something else she that didn't—she could craft golems, but lacked the understanding of their past and purpose, knew the importance of community to her people, but had never experienced what it meant. Her culture was like a piecemeal tapestry cloistered away in a dark room, sewn together with stolen books and whispers overheard when her parents thought her asleep.

Her family had even lived outside their town's edah, the community square central to all Kinnish towns. Because of all that, she'd never felt properly Kinnish. So much of her history, her culture, her people's religion, had been kept from her by her parents. She had only the smallest pieces, a thin thread connecting her to another life that she wanted, more than anything, to know more about.

"I think I'd just like to start with the books," she said at last, and he nodded.

Ari dragged over the last bucket and surveyed the lot of them. "Do you think we'll ever go back?" she asked. "To Kinahara."

When the Heretics' magic erupted across the island, it did more than destroy buildings and take lives. It settled in the animals and trees, the water and the earth, a blanket of magic so thick it could suffocate. People near the epicenter of the explosion died from exposure mere hours later, rotted away from the inside as if from a verillion addiction. The stories she'd heard said that to this day, even minutes on the island were enough to sign your death warrant.

Damien came to stand beside her, and she found his nearness to be a comfort, though his words were cold. "No," he said softly. "I think it's gone forever."

CHAPTER 9

MIKIRA

MIKIRA WAS FLYING.

She forgot the worries weighing her down like saddlebags, forgot their dangerous plan and the even more dangerous man she was in league with. The world fell away as Eilora barreled down the track, the wind pulling at her hair, the heavy thud of the horse's hooves a steady rhythm that matched the racing beat of her heart.

Then they turned the last corner, and Mikira gave the mare her head, putting on a final burst of speed as they crossed the finish line. Eilora slowed and the dream fell away, nothing but a beautiful illusion. Each of her worries latched back into place like leeches thirsting for her blood, refusing to be shaken loose—her father's predicament, the worried looks Nelda and Ailene couldn't hide when she left each morning, the looming competition.

She led Eilora in loping circles, letting both of them catch their breath. It was the third run they'd done that morning, Eilora's second enchantment for endurance lending her extra energy. Not many charms paired well with endurance during breeding, but docility was one of the rare few that wasn't overridden by it.

"Not bad," Reid called from where he leaned over the fence. Widget, his cat, sat on his shoulder like a small crow.

Mikira nudged Eilora toward him. "Are you feeling okay? That almost sounded like a compliment."

Reid shrugged. "You're getting better. Though you're still giving Eilora her head too late, and your starts are sloppy. Also, do you have to grin like an idiot the whole ride?"

She rolled her eyes. "There we go."

Four days of training and enduring Reid's snide comments had left her mostly immune to them. She'd quickly figured out that he was all bark and no bite. No amount of sniping erased the fact that he made everyone tea each morning or that he got to the track at dawn when Mikira asked and stayed long after the sun had set. He reminded her of Talyana in that way, always so aware of the people around him.

Her heart wrenched at the thought of Talyana. She wasn't the first friend Mikira had lost, but she was the most painful. They'd been inseparable until one day Rezek came to collect their monthly payment, and Talyana had told him to go to all four hells. He'd shot the vase of carnations she'd been holding right out of her hand.

After that, her parents never let her come back.

Dismounting, she led Eilora back toward the stable, already calculating how long she could stay today. Her sisters had stepped up to help out around the ranch in her absence, but she didn't want the work to fall on them. The ranch was her responsibility, and she'd been away from it too much recently. Away from them, though some guilty part of her felt relieved. She'd been dodging their questions about the race—how she'd entered, who her sponsor was, the horse's name—since she'd returned home that first night.

The less involved they were in this, the better if it came crashing down around her.

Reid followed her, somehow managing to look like he was skulking through the shadows even in broad daylight. As always, he wore all black despite the warm afternoon, though without a waistcoat or jacket, and his sleeves were rolled up to reveal a twisting mess of leather bracelets and black ink against pale skin.

"What's with all the tattoos?" She nodded at his arms. Reid set his gaze on the stable ahead, clearly pretending he hadn't heard her. "What, one too many drunken nights out?"

His head whipped around. "That," he growled, "is none of your business. Or would you like me to start asking what it's been like bending to Rezek Kelbra? I'm sure the two of you get along splendidly."

Mikira stilled, a cold fury bubbling up inside her. Then she shoved Eilora's reins into his chest. "Fine. I don't even know why I asked."

She stomped back toward the manor, ignoring the heads of jockeys and stable hands turning in her direction. It wasn't that she expected to be friends with these people—Reid was an ass, she rarely saw Arielle, and she'd yet to be convinced Damien wasn't just as bad as Rezek—but was a simple conversation too much to ask?

"Stupid, temperamental—"

"You're done early." Damien's voice slid over hers. She'd reached the main courtyard outside his suite without realizing it, and he was approaching from the adjoining corridor.

"There's only so much Reid I can take," she replied.

His lips quirked in a smile. Unlike Reid, he was dressed head to toe as a proper gentleman, the silver of his waistcoat glinting like steel in the sunlight. Or maybe that was the Lonlarra revolvers. The thought of the weapons sent a shiver down Mikira's spine. She'd never liked guns. They were cold and impersonal, and far too deadly for how easy they were to use.

"I have a meeting now, but you're welcome to remain," Damien said. Mikira followed him inside, where a man with tired shadows purpling the pale skin beneath his eyes sat across from his desk, turning a bowler hat round and round by the brim.

He leapt to his feet when Damien entered, bowing. "Lord Adair, thank you for seeing me," he said in a thick Vynan accent, the vowels pinched at the back of his throat.

Damien sat down across from him, where a stack of correspondence awaited. His attention remained squarely on the man. "Mr. Vonner, what can I do for you?"

Mr. Vonner huddled back into his seat. "I, well, I've come about a loan. With my daughter—the funeral costs, they've taken everything my husband and I had, and the royal army's refusing to pay. They say she's a deserter, but I know it's a lie. My Evie would never. And now the shop—I can't keep up with orders without her, and I can't afford to hire help."

It took a moment for Mikira to understand what was happening. The lesser house lords were responsible for the day-to-day matters in Veradell, the city divided by district among them, but she'd never heard of a house member taking direct meetings with people, let alone giving out loans. Yet she watched as Damien pulled out a prewritten document from the desk and picked up a pen without even a debate.

"I'll cover the funeral costs," he said, writing something across the bottom of the document and folding it in half. "Take this to Tavi and Sons, and they'll provide the funds."

Mr. Vonner made a small choking noise, his hands tightening around the hat. "Thank you, my lord."

Damien poured a dollop of heated wax onto the paper, then pressed his signet ring into it, marking the contract as legitimate.

"Not what you expected?" Reid's voice made her jump. She was still standing at the top of the stairs, waiting for the scene unfolding below to make sense. If this had been Rezek, he'd have made the man beg. Then he would have ensnared the loan in so many conditions that he'd end up owing more than he borrowed, until he had nothing left to give him but the shop itself.

"Does he do this often?" she asked.

"If I say yes, will you stop looking at him like he might suddenly shoot you at any moment?"

Mikira clenched her jaw against the caustic response she wanted to spew. Mr. Vonner finished thanking Damien and strode past them with a nod, the document clutched to his chest and his head held high. It was difficult to slot this information alongside the rumors she'd heard about House Adair, and neither could she ignore what Damien had done to the guard the night they'd met. There was a brutality to him layered beneath that pristine exterior.

Reid trudged past her into his room. She heard running water and the clatter of a kettle. Damien was making notations in a leather-bound book, and Arielle was still shut up in the workroom. She felt suddenly out of place. Should she sit? No, she'd ruin the furniture with her dirt and sweat. Arielle had made it clear she didn't want to be disturbed while working, and there was no chance she was following Reid into his room. She was half convinced it was full of skeletons and caskets.

How in the hells was she going to make it through another few weeks of working with these people if she couldn't even make a decision as simple as where to sit?

"Lunch will be here in a moment, and then we can discuss our plan for the first race," Damien said, closing the book he'd been working in.

Mikira hated how relieved she was that he'd spoken, but she latched on to the conversation. "You keep saying that. The plan is to win."

"Bad plan!" Reid called from his room.

"No one asked you!"

Reid appeared in the doorway, a cup of tea in hand. She was starting to doubt that he consumed anything else. He dropped into his usual spot on the chaise with Widget. "Have you even ever watched the Illinir?"

Her cheeks flushed. "No, but I know what it's like. What's your point?"

"His point," Damien said, rising to join him in the sitting area, "is that the Illinir is as much a battle as it is a race. The moment you're away from the starting line, all those weapons everyone claimed not to have are going to start finding their way into people's backs."

Mikira was well aware of the race's bloody reputation. "So?"

"So winning the first race is a good way to paint a target on your back." Reid slouched into the plush chaise as if hoping it'd envelop him deeply enough that he could escape this conversation.

Damien sat down in an armchair. "The serious contenders are going to try to take out any worthwhile opponents as early as possible. If you establish yourself as competition, that will mean you."

Mikira had known she'd have to defend herself in the race, but hearing herself spoken of as a target made that possibility feel all the more real. What if, after everything, all she got for her trouble was a knife in the side? If nothing else, she had to survive, or her sisters would be alone.

She swallowed hard. "Okay. So what's your plan?"

"Make them think you're terrible," Reid said. "Shouldn't be too hard."

Oh, she was going to pour that scalding cup of tea right over his head.

"You want me to lose." She glowered at Reid.

"We want them to underestimate you," Damien clarified with a disapproving look in Reid's direction. "The race fields a hundred riders. Only fifty will make it to the second round, twenty-five to the third, and ten to the final. You should progress to each stage, but don't win outright. That way they won't think you a priority, and you'll be in the final race before anyone realizes what you've done."

Mikira didn't know why the plan sat with her so poorly. It made sense. But the thought of looking like a bad rider in front of so many people who knew her, knew her father, needled her pride. Her family's name had been trodden on enough as it was.

"Can you do it?" Damien asked, and it felt like a challenge.

She folded her arms. "Of course I can bloody do it."

"Good."

Lunch arrived then, an assortment of light cheeses, fruit, and bread, which the servants spread across the tops of the stacked books as though they were used to them being used as a table. By the time they left, Arielle had joined them, her face and hands freshly scrubbed, and her dark curls bundled atop her head in a brightly patterned kerchief. The bruises around her throat had faded to a pale yellow, the bandage gone from her injured hand.

Mikira approached at Damien's behest, ignoring Reid's muttered protests about the state of her clothes as she sat down on the chaise.

"The reports from the showcases were about what we expected," Damien began, holding up a stack of papers. "Most of the riders being picked up are little more than criminals hoping to fight their way through, but I had some people go through the registrations for the other riders, and it appears there's a heavy trend toward speed enchantments this year."

"I can include that," Arielle said, already through her third pairing of bread and cheese. Mikira picked at the food alongside her, but Reid only seemed interested in his tea, and somehow, she couldn't imagine Damien eating, as if he subsisted solely off of stoic looks and a steady diet of information.

"Are you aware of the order of enchantments for the races?" Damien asked her, setting the papers aside.

"Energy enchantments first," Mikira replied, giving up on pretending to eat. "The course will test a horse's agility with enchantments for movement, energy, and light."

It was the same every Illinir. House Dramara began with a course molded by energy enchantments, followed by House Vanadahl's course of behavior enchantments, House Ruthar's physical enchantments, and last, House Kelbra's ethereal enchantments. Each race was meant to honor a different Harbinger's given magic, but in truth they'd become a stage for the greater houses to show off the skills of their enchanters, each trying to outdo the other.

Damien nodded. "The enchantments change each Illinir, and their design is kept secret, so I think a general agility charm is a good option."

"Endurance would round out the physical category," Mikira said thoughtfully. "But I'm more tempted to go with a behavior charm to keep the horse calm or something ethereal to help with the final race."

Damien tapped one finger on the arm of his chair. "Historically, both the ethereal and behavioral races tend to target the riders more than the horses. I think we're better off planning for the energy and physical."

"So speed, agility, and endurance?" Arielle piled a plate with half the tray's provisioning of fruit. "I can do that."

"Good." Damien stood and checked the pocket watch he kept in his vest. "I have another meeting to attend. In the meantime, Mikira, we'll begin crafting your persona with the opening ball—by not attending."

Mikira blinked. "What?"

The opening ball marked the start of the Illinir, the first of three others hosted by the greater houses before each of the races, culminating with the closing ball at the castle. They were an opportunity to place bets, craft alliances, and scope out the competition. Skipping one didn't make any sense, even if she dreaded the idea of attending them.

"The more people see your face, the more they'll remember you." Reid scratched Widget behind one ear. "And considering you probably couldn't go five seconds without saying something to piss someone off, it's better if you're not around them at all."

"You're one to talk," she muttered.

Damien snapped his pocket watch shut. "Your goal for the next couple weeks is not to draw attention. The more of an unknown you are, the easier it'll be for you to slip through the first race undetected."

Mikira let out a long sigh. This wasn't going to end well.

CHAPTER 10

ARIELLE

*A*RI SETTLED INTO a rhythm in the passing days. She ate breakfast with Reid and Damien each morning, Mikira joining them on occasion, before locking herself away in the workroom. With the last of the clay prepared, she'd begun folding in the powdered verillion and emerald for the physical enchantments Mikira had requested, alongside the powdered diamond for the ethereal enchantments she planned to add.

It would be difficult to thread the numerous physical enchantments alongside the ethereal ones, and Ari still wasn't sure she could accomplish it, but with her enchant license riding on Mikira winning the race, she wanted to give the girl as much of an advantage as she could. A horse that could sense danger and never got lost would be invaluable.

She spent her evenings in the sitting area with Reid and Damien poring over *The Book of Enchantments*, a basic charming text Damien had secured for her, before attempting to apply what she'd learned alone in her room. With the boys out for the morning, however, she'd taken her latest project into the workshop with her: a bronze mark, which she'd been attempting to charm to detect danger.

To employ the verillion and diamond, she'd added them to an adhesive paint, which she'd applied to the coin and left to dry overnight. Now she held it out in her palm and muttered a binding. The coin resisted, and she struggled to force the magic through it. By the time she finished the spell, she couldn't tell if it'd worked or not, and her head was pounding with a familiar ache.

"Hello?" Mikira's voice rang out in the sitting room.

Ari rushed through the open workshop door, shutting it behind her so Mikira couldn't see inside. The coin, predictably, did nothing. So much for detecting danger. She tucked it away in her blouse pocket.

She poses no danger to you, hissed the voice, and the weight of it startled her. Ever since she'd discovered her magic, her thoughts had felt a little unwieldy, a sensation she'd chalked up to the way her headaches often fogged her brain. But lately, she'd begun to feel more than just off-kilter.

It wasn't until the morning she created the golem for Lady Belda though that it really began to feel . . . *off*, as though with each use of her magic, each golem she brought to life, it grew stronger.

Don't be absurd, she told herself, and pushed the thought away.

"Mikira," she said. "What are you doing here?"

The girl was dressed to ride, her hair done in a haphazard braid that Ari's fingers itched to rearrange. The freckled bridge of her nose was pink with sunburn. "What do you mean? I'm here to train."

"Didn't Reid tell you they'd be out on house business for the morning?"

"No, because that would require him not to be a selfish ass." Mikira dragged a hand down her face, then winced as her fingers brushed the burn. "I spent all morning getting my chores done so I could get over here. Do you know how hot it is outside?"

"Too hot," Ari agreed, thinking of the clay she had stored in the darkness of Reid's workshop. Perhaps today would be better spent on non-golem-related tasks. "I have some errands to run. Why don't you come with me?"

Mikira hesitated. "Damien said not to draw attention to myself."

"We're shopping, not robbing a bank," Ari replied. "Come on."

They took one of the enchanted coaches Damien had put at her disposal. She'd ridden in one the day he brought her to the manor, but the second time was no less disconcerting, and she held on to the seat with both hands as it rumbled along. Mikira stared out the window the whole way with her arms folded and a look of deep irritation.

"So, what is it like running an enchant business?" Ari asked to distract herself from her rising discomfort.

The question startled Mikira out of her stare. "Oh, um, it's great. Or it used to be."

Ari couldn't tell what was causing the girl more distress: the casual conversation or the topic. She wasn't much used to this type of thing either. If she hadn't spent the last few days in conversation with Reid and Damien, she'd probably have just sat in silence the whole ride.

"I really like working with the horses," Mikira continued, warming up to the topic. "The day-to-day stuff, but my dream is to have other people doing that so I can focus on the enchant lines. I've been wanting to spend some time going over my grandmother's old research. She was a biologist, and she knew a lot about crossing enchantments."

"Is it complicated?" Ari asked. "How do you decide which ones to breed?"

Mikira unfolded her arms and leaned over her knees. "It's a science, really. Certain enchantments can't mix with others, and crossing the same one often makes for a really strong enchant. Crossing within the same type of charm is the best strategy, which is why you see a lot of animals with endurance and speed as a packaged set. But certain ones will still override others, which is why it's really rare to see something enchanted for both strength and another charm."

The more they spoke, the more open the girl became. She told Ari about her sisters, how Ailene had wanted an enchanted dog since she was a child and the way Nelda inhaled books like air. When they arrived at the row of shops along Tea Street in the Pendron District, it took them both several moments to realize the coach had stopped moving.

"It's been a while since I've been able to just talk about this stuff,"

Mikira said as they descended from the coach into the sweltering afternoon. "Sometimes I feel like all I talk about now is Rezek."

"He sounds very unpleasant."

"Colds are unpleasant. Rezek is one bad day away from homicidal."

They entered a narrow shop called Fox and Quill, a Kinnish bookshop where the walls were lined with secondhand volumes Ari had longed for from afar for months. Now, two weeks into her service, Damien had handed over her first wages that morning, and she'd known exactly what she intended to buy. A short time later, she had her own personal Arkala, the front inscribed with Aslir's silhouette.

What she really wanted was a Kinnish book of enchantments, but Damien had warned her it'd be difficult to find authentic Kinnish texts, and he'd asked that she leave doing so to him, as he could do it quietly and without connection to them. Normal enchanter texts were heavily regulated enough; they couldn't afford the attention that came with Kinnish ones.

They emerged from the cool darkness of the shop into a street that had grown congested in their absence.

"Let's walk toward the square." Mikira rose on her toes to see over a gathering crowd. "I think the royal address is starting."

"The what?" Ari asked, returning her book to the coach before trailing after her.

"The royal family always addresses the city the night of the opening ball. It marks the start of the Illinir festival." Mikira pointed at a corridor of wooden booths along the street's edges. Cloth and jewel figurines of the four Harbingers hung between the lampposts. Rach's massive emerald horns glinted black in the fading sunlight, Skylis's wings stretched out in all their sunset glory. Aslir's star-white coat shone like a beacon, but it was Lyzairin, the Great Serpent, whose likeness was most frequent.

For all that Sendism railed against Kinnism, it drew so much from it, and she wondered if they even understood why. Did they know the reason

Lyzairin's visage was associated with festivals, why her long body was often pictured in a circle, symbolizing the unification and community tenet central to Kinnish culture? Or did they just like the way she looked, with scales that sparkled like lapis lazuli and teeth and claws bared in warning?

Until recently, Arl hadn't known any of that herself. Nor that it was against Kinnish practice to create idols of the Harbingers, but she'd come to realize over the course of her time in Veradell that most treated the Harbingers like myths. The Order of Sendia still drew decent crowds to their churches, and she frequently saw the clerics out preaching in the streets, but most seemed to think them nothing more than stories.

They joined the people thronging toward Canburrow Square, where a large stage had been erected. A representative from each of the four greater houses stood to one side, save for House Ruthar. Were they late, or intentionally missing? Either way, it sent a message: they didn't support whatever the king was about to relay.

It was a dangerous balancing act, seeing as house status was granted by the king, but the last thing he could afford was instability in the Council of Lords. Removing House Ruthar would just draw more attention to their opinion on the war, and with the other three houses in support of it, the king had the votes he needed for any measures.

Guards in pristine white surrounded the platform, keeping the gathering crowd at bay as three people took the stage. Ari recognized Princess Eshlin Zuerlin first. A gown of midnight green hugged her full-bodied figure, a thick layer of kohl outlining eyes of the same color. Even in an elegant dress she had the imposing bearing of the skilled swordswoman she was known to be, a talent she was said to have acquired from her departed mother.

Prince Darius surveyed the crowd with a wide smile that bared his teeth. He had their father's coloring, with hair nearly as fair as his skin. There was something cuttingly cold about his manner, as if they were all gathered here for his amusement. But where the two royal siblings stood like pillars ready to bear the weight, King Theo Zuerlin was hunched and willowy, a once powerful frame reduced to wiry muscle and a thin, wispy beard.

Ari felt something brush her arm and turned to find Mikira rigid, her hands drawn into tight fists. "Are you all right? You're shaking."

"I'm fine," she ground out as the ailing king approached a Sendian cleric behind the podium. The cleric reached out with supplicating palms in the Goddess's gesture of blessing, and the king returned it. Once, only the king would have bowed, the cleric touching his open palms to bestow the blessing, but the balance of power had shifted; the church was mainly a symbol now. A symbol the king clearly meant to capitalize on.

"Does he think parading a soldier on the stage erases the hundreds of veterans sleeping on the street?" Mikira hissed, and Ari followed her line of sight to a military officer standing straight-backed on the right, his lapel decorated with gemstone pins in honor of his service.

This whole stage had been carefully arranged like a set piece, and the show was ready to begin.

King Theo stepped up to a charmed microphone, his children on either side of him. "People of Enderlain," he called in a voice that hinted at his former strength. "I welcome you to the twelfth running of the decadal Illinir, so held in honor of the holy Goddess who watches over us."

A cheer went up among the people, but Ari and Mikira weren't alone in remaining silent. Several other grim-faced spectators stood with arms crossed, waiting to hear what the king had to say. More than one was dirty and gaunt, the rising price of grain having carved its consequences into their bodies.

"We run this race to remind ourselves of the great gifts we were given when the Goddess sent the Harbingers to humanity, and also in remembrance of the potential for great destruction that magic carries. Over a century ago, four enchanters sought power beyond their station. In their pursuit of godhood, the Heretics' magic erupted in a devasting explosion that took several thousand Enderlish lives and destroyed Kinahara."

Ari drew a sharp breath. Nearly four times as many Kinnish died from the Cataclysm, and all he cared to mention was the territory Enderlain no longer had.

"It is for this reason that magic must be carefully controlled. It is for this reason that the enchant registry was established, and the Illinir alongside it. With this race, we celebrate what magic should be. With this race, we remind ourselves of what our friends and family are fighting for in Celair."

"Liar," Mikira hissed through clenched teeth.

Liar, echoed Ari's thoughts.

"Over the course of the years after the Cataclysm, we withdrew our troops from Celair and Vyna, shrinking Enderlain's might below its station. This was a mistake. To show weakness was a mistake. Today, I am honored to report that we are making more headway in recovering the Celairen territory than ever before."

A murmur radiated around them, and Ari moved closer to Mikira as the mass of people pressed eagerly inward. Was this what it was like so many years ago, when Enderlain made the same choice to invade Kinahara? They already had Vyna and Celair under their domain, but their greed was depthless. Since the Cataclysm, their weakened military couldn't hold, and both countries reasserted their independence. Her Saba had thought their days of overreaching finished, until the last Ranier king died and his brother-in-law ascended the throne, promising to return Enderlain to its former glory.

People whispered that he stole the throne from his brother-in-law's line of succession. King Theo said his brother-in-law had died childless, but there were rumors that out there somewhere, there was an illegitimate child who could challenge his claim to the throne, and the Eternal War was nothing but a distraction, a means of keeping the eye busy while the trick was done elsewhere.

"Each day our soldiers risk their lives to ensure Enderlain's future is bright." King Theo brought a hand to his heart. "We thank them for their sacrifice, as the Goddess thanks them."

"Liar," Mikira said again.

"Mikira," Ari warned when, this time, nearby heads turned.

The girl's gaze snapped to her, green eyes bright with fire. "That stupid war has nothing to do with Enderlain's future, or the Goddess, or any of that horseshit. It's all for them and their greed."

Ari didn't doubt that for a second, but neither did she want Mikira openly preaching about it where people could hear. "We should go." She took Mikira's hand, but the girl refused to move. Her eyes were back on the king, her hand a solid fist beneath Ari's fingers.

The crowd had begun to move, people fighting their way forward alongside a growing murmur. At the front, the guards' hands went to their swords.

"Today, I am honored to announce the start of the Illinir with the opening ball," the king continued, oblivious to the rising tumult. The only one who seemed to have noticed was Princess Eshlin, who'd stepped nearer to her father and pulled a thin rod from her intricately braided hair that looked sharp enough to puncture flesh.

"Let the festivities begin!" the king called.

"Murderer!" someone shouted.

"Free Celair!" cried another.

The guards closed ranks as the front of the pack pushed forward, separating from the confused gathering behind them. A chant rose up as they pressed up against the guards. "No more war! No more war!"

"Mikira!" Ari called when the girl began leaning toward the mob. People were staring at them now, staring at *her*, their expressions locked in mirrored looks of dismay. "We need to go."

"You with those traitors?" asked a young man in a newsboy's cap, his afternoon round of papers tucked under one arm. The question drew more eyes, and Ari pulled hard on Mikira's arm. The girl blinked at her, her fury clearing as she realized what was happening.

Something rattled against Ari's chest, and then the coin she'd charmed earlier leapt from her pocket and flung itself at the newsboy. It bounced harmlessly off his chest, but his pale face flushed a heavy red.

"Kinnish witch!" He thrust a finger at her.

"I'm sorry," Ari said quickly. "That was an accident."

Two other boys had joined the newsboy. On the platform, Princess Eshlin was ushering her father down the stairs to a waiting coach, and the crowd was beginning to shove. Others fled the growing tumult, forcing a ripple of motion back through the remaining spectators that jostled them from all sides.

"Don't touch her." Mikira's hands went for her knives.

"So you are a traitor." The newsboy sneered. "I heard what you were saying. I served in the war, you know. Nearly lost an arm in it." He jerked a sleeve up, revealing a knotted scar by his shoulder. "And you think it's stupid, do you?"

"That's not—"

"Now you're defending this Kinnish leech. The only reason we're even in Celair!" The boy spat at Ari's feet.

She recoiled. "What? The Kinnish have nothing to do with it."

"Your corrupt magic is what caused the Cataclysm," said one of the newsboy's companions. "It killed our soldiers and destroyed acres of verillion."

"Verillion that belonged to my people," Ari shot back before she could stop herself. What was she doing? She needed to be deescalating this situation, not adding fuel to the fire.

You are done being afraid, answered the voice.

"It belonged to Enderlain!" said the newsboy. "You hoarded it and the wealth it gave you for years until *we* won it from you."

"We *stole* it," Mikira snapped. "Just like we're doing in Celair."

The newsboy dropped his papers and pulled out a pocketknife. At that moment, a gunshot went off, and the throng broke apart in a flurry of screams. Ari seized Mikira's hand and pulled her away from the crowd, but the boys pursued them.

Mikira was faster than her and took the lead. "This way!" They ducked into a nearby alley, taking several quick turns into the narrow maze, before cutting a hard left Ari expected to send them toward Tea Street. But Mikira wasn't the only one who knew the alleys, and as they barreled around the corner, they came face-to-face with one of the newsboy's friends. Before they could backtrack, the newsboy and his other friend boxed them in from behind.

Mikira drew her knives, pressing Ari toward the wall so she could see both sets of opponents. "I'm going to take the one on the left," she whispered. "When I attack, make a run for it."

"I'm not leaving you here—"

"I'll be fine."

"You'll be dead."

"Ari—"

A sharp thud cut her off as the boy to their left dropped like a sack of grain. A slender woman with dark curls spiraling about her oval face and a bored expression stood behind him, flexing her fingers in a set of brass knuckles.

"I'd like you to know," she began in a soft rasp, "that beating up vagrants in a back alley was not on my list of things to do today."

One of the boys lurched forward, but the newsboy caught him by the arm. "Her ring," he hissed. The other boy took one look at the black and silver wing embedded on the woman's ring before both bowed low.

"Apologies, Lady Adair," the newsboy said. They didn't even stop to check on their companion before both fled.

"Lady Adair?" Ari asked at the same time Mikira groaned, "Not another one."

"You can call me Shira." The woman toed the unconscious body before her with one boot. They were military style, made of thick black leather that went midway to her calf.

"What do you want?" Mikira asked with about as much tact as a stampeding horse. "And how did you find us?"

Shira's lips quirked. "You're my brother's jockey." Her gaze slid to Ari. "Which means you must be his latest project."

Ari recoiled. "What?"

"Damien has a way of finding the lost and broken and putting them back together, and entirely in his debt, of course." Shira waved an absent-minded hand at her. "So tell me, what skill do you have that he wishes to possess? Connections with rival verillion growers? A talent for getting into places you don't belong?"

It wasn't lost on Ari that she and Mikira were a part of some grand plan of Damien's, most notably winning his bet with Rezek, but hearing herself spoken of like a tool to be used made her hands curl. She was nobody's pawn.

"My business with your brother is between us," she replied.

Shira sighed, crossing her arms and leaning one shoulder against the alley wall. Her dark brown gaze was tired, but her posture was the lounge of a relaxing predator, an image aided by the array of knives strapped to her body in plain view.

"Are you so loyal to him already?" she asked pityingly.

Ari bristled. "You know nothing about me."

"I know you're keeping secrets for a man you hardly know from a woman who could slit your throat and leave you bleeding to death behind a pub owned by someone who will do whatever she tells them to. Like drop your body in the Grey weighted to sink."

For the first time, it struck Ari exactly who she was talking to. This woman was no less a threat than her brother. Even dressed like an assassin in the night, Shira had all the wealth and power that came with being an Adair. Damien had told her that both of his siblings no longer lived at the manor; had they left on good terms, or would she and Mikira have been better off with the newsboy?

Mikira's grip shifted subtly on her knives, and she angled herself between Ari and Shira. That was twice now she'd done that, thought to protect Ari before herself.

You could protect her instead, whispered the voice, and Ari shuddered as its solidity.

"But that would be far too much work. I'd much rather us be friends." Shira pushed off the wall with a wink at Mikira, who seemed torn between defensiveness and utter perplexity.

"Come with me," Shira said. "I'll return you to my brother."

When they didn't follow immediately, she said over her shoulder, "Or you can take your chances with the mob."

THEY RODE IN silence back to the manor, Mikira fidgeting nervously with her knives the whole way, despite the fact that Shira's attention sat squarely on Ari. She kept thinking the woman would get tired of staring at her and look elsewhere, but she remained steadfast until the moment the carriage curved around the circular drive.

Ari was the first through the door, Mikira and Shira following. A light drizzle had picked up on their way home, and Damien and Reid stood under the cover of the porch on the manor steps. Someone must have seen the coach coming.

"We heard about the riot." Damien descended the stairs to meet them. "Are you both okay?"

"They're fine," Shira answered, her attention on the boy at Damien's back. "Hello, Reid."

A flush filled Reid's face, and he took one large step sideways behind the nearest pillar. Widget, on the other hand, came trotting down to Shira, and she crouched to scratch behind his ears.

Whatever Damien felt at seeing his sister, he kept it locked behind an impenetrable mask. "Thank you for your help, Shira. You can go."

"Not going to invite me in for a drink?" she asked, straightening.

"You don't drink."

"I make exceptions in all things. Just ask Reid."

Ari looked between them. Though the exchange felt harmless enough, Damien was clearly trying to get rid of her, and Shira was just as clearly refusing to play along.

"You never told us how you found us," Mikira cut in, and both sets of Adair eyes fell on her. To her credit, she didn't falter. "Were you watching us?"

The question was like a trigger. Nothing changed in Damien's expression, but his dissatisfaction bled into the air around him, turning it sharp. He hadn't wanted them to reach that conclusion.

The smile that split across Shira's lips said that she had. "You know, I think I will go. I only came to say that Father has requested a family meeting at the pub later this week. His health is deteriorating quicker than we expected." She turned for the coach, throwing a hand into the air. "Until next time, Reid!"

"Wait!" Mikira called, but Shira was already climbing into the coach. With a snick of the closing door, it set off.

Only then did Reid peer out from behind the pillar. "Is she gone?"

CHAPTER 11

MIKIRA

MIKIRA DIDN'T NEED Iri to know that something was wrong. Damien might be an impenetrable stone vault, but even she hadn't missed the way that he'd tried to get Shira to leave as quickly as possible, nor how he stared after her departing carriage as if recalibrating for its sudden departure.

"Is she watching us?" she pressed again, ignoring Ari's look of warning. If they were being followed, she wanted to know why.

"This is a family business, Miss Rusel," Damien replied, still watching the carriage. "You shouldn't be surprised to find my family involved."

"It's Mikira," she ground out. When he called her that—it reminded her of Rezek, and she suspected he knew that. "Then you asked her to look after us?"

Damien's gaze slid to her, as cold and impersonal as the falling rain. It'd begun to soak through her clothes, coming faster now.

"All that matters is that she saved our lives," Ari cut in in that ever-calm way of hers that was beginning to grate on Mikira's nerves. She had a habit of defending Damien that made Mikira want to shake her until the girl saw what he was: a dangerous man with far too much power.

Ari gave her a look that said, *And yours relies on him, so don't push it.* Mikira was treading on delicate ground, but neither could she just ignore this. They were playing far too perilous a game to tolerate unexpected players.

"Are you all just going to keep standing there getting soaked, or can we go inside where it's not dumping buckets of water from the sky?" Reid asked miserably from the top of the stairs, Widget now bundled in his arms.

Damien took the opening, making for the stairs, but Mikira didn't move. Ari faced her as the boys retreated down the hall. "You made a deal with him. Telling you everything wasn't a part of it."

"I know." She ran a hand through the damp crown of her hair. "But I've been here before. These people—they'll take everything from you if you're not careful."

Ari's brow furrowed. "Is this about what happened at the square? What you said about the war—"

"I meant every word of it." Her foolishness had nearly gotten them killed, but she didn't regret a single thing she'd said.

"What happened?"

It was the genuine concern in Ari's voice that pulled the story out of her. She'd never told it to anyone, and they never spoke of it at home. "House Kelbra has been after my family's ranch for years. Just over a year ago, I filed a complaint against them. A few days later, Rezek showed up at the ranch with an order saying my brother had been drafted."

It had been Lochlyn's birthday. They'd strung enchanted lights in the barn, the radio playing some old song tinged with static. Her father strummed along on his guitar, his face alight with the sort of glow that only came after winning a big race. They danced. For a little while, they were happy.

Then Rezek's men arrived.

She remembered the music cutting off sharply, remembered Lochlyn yelling at her and her sisters to run, to hide, even though it was him they'd come for. He was seventeen. An adult. And under Enderlish law, he could be conscripted—one member of each household to serve the king.

The Council of Lords managed the draft, and it had been all too easy for Rezek to ensure Lochlyn's name was put into the next lottery. They'd wanted to make an example of her father. Except it had been Mikira who'd filed that complaint. Mikira who'd ignored her family's warnings, who'd been so afraid they were going to lose the ranch that she'd thought she could put her faith in the law to do what was right like her father had always said.

Oh, how wrong she'd been.

Her throat tightened, the words digging like claws in her chest. "They took him away. It was the last time I ever saw him."

Ari bowed her head. "He died in battle."

It wasn't a question, so Mikira didn't respond. She only turned her face up to the sky until the threat of tears receded.

"I understand why you're so angry," Ari said quietly. "The people of my town were terrified of being conscripted. We'd already lost our home to Enderlain and its war; we didn't want to lose our lives too."

Mikira couldn't imagine how that felt, to be asked to fight in the very army that had once killed your people. Probably a bit like being forced to work for the man who murdered your son. Her heart clenched, and not for the first time, she wished that her sisters were there, if only because before them, she was only ever strong.

"I am sorry about your brother, Mikira." Ari's gentle tone broke her from her reverie. "But Damien is not Rezek, and we need him. We don't have to trust each other, but we have to work together."

Mikira wiped the rain from her face. "You have something relying on this too?" She'd just assumed that Ari was an enchanter employed by House Adair, her only stake in the game the payment that came with enchanting the horse.

Ari's expression shuttered, and she turned away. "No, not like that."

It was a lie, Mikira was sure of it, but Ari looked one step away from bolting, so she didn't press. "We need each other too, Ari," she said instead. "We're two small fish in a bay of sharks, and if we don't protect each other, we'll get devoured."

Ari looked back at her. "What are you asking of me?"

What was she asking? She didn't know Ari any more than Reid or Damien. She'd spent every day of the last two weeks with them and yet it felt like there were oceans between them. But after today, Ari knew more about her than anyone had in a very, very long time, and there was something comforting about that.

In the end, she only shrugged and said, "It's been a long time since I've had a friend."

The word had a strange effect on Ari. Her eyes grew wide with alarm, her lips parting to silently repeat it.

Worried she'd gone too far, Mikira backtracked. "How about just partners, then? You watch my back, I'll watch yours."

"Partners," Ari said softly, then nodded. "I'd like that."

When Mikira smiled, Ari did too.

THE RANCH WAS quiet when Mikira returned late that afternoon. She ought to have spent the rest of the day training with Reid, but the rain had picked up even more, and she wasn't sure if she could face him or Damien again so soon without pressing for answers. It bothered her not knowing exactly what she was involved in, but she couldn't risk her position with Damien.

"How did we end up here?" she asked Iri, leading him into the barn to brush him down. Her father never would have made a deal like this. Their family did things right. Or at least, they used to. Before doing what was right cost them everything and the only way Mikira could see to protect her family was to make the rules bend in her favor for once.

She leaned her forehead against Iri's, her fingers pressing into his black coat. "Lochlyn would know what to do," she whispered, and Iri nickered softly at the name. She gave herself to the count of three to focus on the silence, on the warmth of Iri and the scent of hay in the air, before she returned to the house.

She was kicking her muddy boots off in the foyer when Ailene's voice echoed from the kitchen, "Ow, Nelda! That *hurts*."

"Don't be a baby."

"I am not—ow!"

Mikira crossed through the sitting room adjacent to the kitchen and stilled in the doorway. Ailene was sitting at the round kitchen table, her head tilted back and her nose plugged with two strips of bloody cloth. Nelda hovered over her, dabbing at a small cut on her cheek, her latest book tucked into her apron pocket.

They spotted Mikira's horrified look at the same time. "What happened?" she demanded.

Ailene gave her a sheepish grin. "This is nothing. You should see the other guy."

"She got in a fight with Era Keene." Nelda rinsed her cloth in a bowl of water on the table.

Mikira pressed a hand to her head. "I thought you *liked* Era Keene?"

"I did," Ailene replied. "Until he said you were going to lose the Illinir because our enchants were shit—"

"Language."

"—now and our dad was all washed up."

Mikira dropped into a chair with a groan. "Ailene, Era Keene's father is a berator. He could file charges for assault with the Anthir. We can't afford that fine."

Ailene's head snapped forward with a look of grim determination. The purple bruising around her nose and eye only made her look fiercer. "He called you a loser, Kira. Said you were going to die in the first race."

It was only then that she noticed Nelda, who'd washed and wrung the rag in her hands past the point of cleanliness and into compulsion. She was staring at a spot on the table without blinking, something she only did when she was trying not to cry. Ailene's hands were balled into fists in her lap, both of them waiting for her to say that it was a lie, that she'd be fine.

She'd been spending so much time with the others preparing for the Illinir that she hadn't realized the effect it was having on her sisters. They'd lost their mother, their brother, now their father—they couldn't lose her too, yet here she was risking her life in the kingdom's most dangerous race. There was a very large possibility that she wouldn't make it through the first leg, even with Ari's undetectable enchant, which the girls couldn't even know about.

They were terrified, and she didn't know how to fix it.

"Era Keene is an ass," she said at last. "I'm not going to die in any of the races. I'm going to win, and I'm going to be the most famous racer in all of Enderlain, and you can shove it in his face every time you see him."

A wobbly smile broke across Ailene's face, and Mikira stood to gather her and Nelda in her arms. "I promise you both. I'll be okay."

IRI WAS HALF asleep when she roused him from the barn, but he greeted her with a huff of warm breath and a low nicker. She'd been a fool today, pressing Damien the way she had. He was her only chance of running in this race, her only chance of winning, of making sure Era Keene's predictions didn't come true. She would not abandon her sisters, and if that meant abandoning her scruples instead, it was a worthwhile sacrifice.

The rain had abated, allowing them an easy ride back to Adair Manor, where the enchanted gates granted her access. She went straight down to the track, where the light of the full moon breaking through the clouds was all she and Iri had to see by. They'd just finished a warm-up lap when the enchanted lights around the track turned on. A moment later, Reid appeared at the fence with Eilora in tow. He swung up into the saddle and joined her.

"What are you doing awake?" she asked, expecting him to yell at her for disturbing him.

"I'm always awake." He maneuvered Eilora alongside Iri and pulled something from inside his jacket, flinging it into her lap.

She scrabbled to grab it before it could fall. It was the front page of a newspaper, the date printed for tomorrow.

The headline read "Adair Jockey Overheard Spouting Rebel Rhetoric at Royal Reception."

Below it was a picture of her and Ari facing off against the newsboy, Mikira's hands on her knives.

"Damien had the story killed," Reid said. "The editor of the paper owed him a favor. But for the record, that is not what lying low looks like."

Mikira crumpled the paper into a ball. "We didn't do anything wrong. Those boys—"

"It doesn't matter." He shook his head. "If you were suspected of being a rebel, you could be detained and barred from the race. You have to know that Rezek will use anything he can against you. Even something as personal as your brother's death."

Mikira inhaled sharply. It shouldn't surprise her that Reid knew about

Lochlyn; she was starting to realize just how far Damien's connections extended. It still felt like an invasion, though, having the choice to tell them taken away from her.

"My personal life is none of your concern," she ground out.

Something pressed into her ribs, and she glanced down to see Reid holding a pocketknife just above her kidney. She had one brief, harrowing moment in which she was sure that Damien had decided that she was more trouble than she was worth, before Reid pulled the knife away and snapped it shut.

"Your emotions are a distraction," he warned. "You can't let people use them against you, or come the race, the knife won't stop short."

Her hands tightened on the reins. "I can't just shut them off, either. I'm not Damien."

Reid slid the knife back into his pocket. "Then keep them close. Everything that they can use against you. You make them a shield so they can't make them a weapon."

There was something about the way he said it, something that made her wonder if he was talking about her, or himself.

"I can't." Her throat tightened. "It hurts too much." She didn't want to think about Lochlyn. About the horses they'd lost and the look on her father's face when Rezek took him away. About what might happen if she failed.

"You have to learn to live with the pain, or it will destroy you." He angled Eilora alongside Iri. "Because the moment you let them use it to make you feel small, you've lost."

He eyed her sidelong, his smirk turning wolfish in the moonlight. "And I have a feeling you don't take losing well."

She choked out a laugh, surprising herself. Never in a thousand years would she have expected Reid to be the one to make her feel better, even if he'd still insulted her to do it.

Reid leaned low over Eilora's neck. "You shut them up by winning, Mikira, and this is how you win."

With a click of his tongue, he sent Eilora flying down the track. Iri tossed his head, eager to pursue, and Mikira let him go. They shot through the chill night, the scent of rain still heavy in the air, only the rush of the wind and the beat of the horses' hooves punctuating the silence and the dark.

✦ PART 2 ✦

The Harbingers lived among humanity, learning and teaching in turn.
Rach was wary of their thirst for knowledge,

while Lyzairin sought to share all she knew.

Skylis wandered among the people in disguise,

and Aslir sat high above them, like a star unwavering in the night sky.

CHAPTER 12

ARIELLE

BY THE END of the third week, Ari had finished all but the enchantments and detail work on the golem. The first Illinir race was only two days away, which wouldn't leave Mikira much time to practice with the horse, but with the litany of enchantments Ari intended to instill in it, she hoped it wouldn't be necessary. Besides, she'd learned by now that Mikira was a more than competent rider. Reid had brought in a steady stream of jockeys over the last week to challenge Mikira on the track.

She won every time.

Ari only wished she had half as much confidence in her own skills. Since the fiasco with the coin nearly a week ago, she'd practiced the danger enchantment several times, all with the same result. The charm felt like it worked, but when she asked Reid to test it by throwing something at her, the coin only sporadically responded. Meanwhile, Damien watched them with such steadfast intensity that eventually Reid refused to do it again.

The Book of Enchantments held no answers for her. In fact, every book on enchantments Damien had was woefully light on the instruction of actual magic, a result of the government's strict control of the practice. Enchanters were educated at the royal academy; the only ones who'd need an outside text were unlicensed.

Enderlain was a kingdom built on magic, but like everything else in this cursed land, that power belonged to the nobility and the royal family alone.

None of them said a thing about hearing voices, either. Each time she used her magic, the voice was there, whispering, until she decided her spell-work was good enough and cut off using it entirely. Since then, the voice had been mercifully absent, so much so that she'd begun to doubt the strangeness of it. She'd been sacrificing food money for verillion for months, eating far less than she needed before coming to Adair Manor—her exhaustion was bound to catch up with her. Surely she only needed a break.

Ari stepped back to inspect the horse. She had only the mane and tail left and was rather pleased by the elegant result. Once the rest of her clay dried overnight, she'd complete it in the morning. Then she'd speak the binding spells and bring the beast to life. Only then would they know if it could handle the flood of magic in its veins.

Feeling the press of eyes, she looked to where Reid scrutinized her from his desk. Over the last few weeks, Damien had opened his library to her, and she'd spent countless hours poring over Kinnish texts and stories. They talked philosophy and history, from the central tenets associated with each Harbinger to the royal line decimated during Enderlain's invasion, and the longer she sat by Damien's side, the more she noticed Reid staring at her like a mother bird watching her nest.

Tonight had been particularly bad, as the two of them were alone in the workshop, and he'd given up even pretending to be subtle about it.

"Will you just say whatever it is already?" she demanded.

Reid's jaw shifted as if grinding down the words. "I've seen the way you look at him."

"The way I look at . . . ?" She raised an eyebrow.

He scowled. "I'm only going to say this once. Damien's been through enough without you adding to it, and he's got a lot depending on this. If you hurt him, I'll make you regret it."

Ari groaned, a burgeoning headache flaring. Yes, Damien was attractive, and she'd developed a fondness for him the more she'd gotten to know him, but he was not her focus. Romance never had been. In truth, she had never been sure whether it was something she even wanted. Rivkah had giggled over the boys in their village, plotting how to capture their attention, and Ari had shrunk away from it like some shelled creature cloistering to protect itself.

She felt different around Damien, though. The more she got to know him, the more comfortable she grew with his nearness, with the intensity of his searching gaze and the way she caught him staring at her. With each passing day, she found herself drawn to those things, to him, but right now, she had other things to worry about.

She waved Reid off. "I'm here to make this golem, Reid. Let me make it."

Kneeling on the blanket she'd laid out to protect the floor—at Reid's demand—she began rolling thin strands of her remaining clay to serve as the mane. She would craft the finest racehorse the world had ever seen, they would win the Illinir, and Damien would make her a licensed enchanter. The rest could wait.

The sitting room door burst open.

She and Reid exchanged looks, then leapt to their feet. Reid beat her out, and Ari drew the door shut behind them.

"Shit," Reid muttered.

A broad-shouldered man with golden skin and a neatly trimmed dark beard surveyed the room from the top of the stairs, a servant scurrying in after him. She thought at first it was one of Damien's district tenants come to seek his help—then she saw the fear in the servant's eyes. A low growl shuddered from the desk, where Widget balanced on the back of Damien's chair, his fur raised on end.

"I apologize, sir," the servant said quickly. "Lord Adair was in too much of a hurry to wait for an announcement."

Ari's eyes flashed to the man's right hand, where a hematite and diamond signet ring encircled one finger, just like Damien's. His father was much older and ailing, which made this his brother.

"Is this not my home?" Lord Adair's voice boomed. The servant bowed swiftly and backed out of the room.

"You don't live here anymore, Loic." There was an edge to Reid's tone that surprised her. She'd heard him both grumpy and annoyed more often than not, but this sounded different. "In fact, I distinctly remember your father kicking you out years ago."

Loic smiled the kind of smile that promised everything was just fine, right up until he snapped your neck. "Reid," he said as if he'd discovered a rare prize. "It's been far too long."

"That would be because I go out of my way to avoid seeing you."

"Afraid, are you, little spider?" Loic asked, and Ari had the sudden desire to wipe the smile off his face. She expected Reid to snap back, but the boy only clenched his jaw and looked away.

Loic descended the stairs into the foyer. "Not so brave without my brother here to protect you. Let's say we play a game, like old times. It's been so long since you've gotten a new design."

Reid went utterly still. Widget leapt down to brush his leg, but he only stared at a spot on the ground as though it were the only thing he could see.

Be silent. Be careful. The familiar refrain began inside her. If Loic had even noticed her, he paid her no need. She could slip out the back door and be gone. Reid was Damien's friend; surely Loic wouldn't hurt him?

If you believed that, you wouldn't be thinking about running. She gritted her teeth. Running was what she did before, abandoning everything at the first sign of trouble. It'd kept her alive, but it'd also kept her isolated and alone. It'd kept her afraid.

Be fearless, my love, said her Saba.

Ari stood, her cut-off wire still dangling from one hand, her fettling knife in the other. "Can we help you?" she asked. "Damien isn't here."

Loic halted, turning to her. Unlike his brother, his face was an open book. She could practically see the calculation in his gray eyes. Another person meant another variable. Did she matter? Would she interfere?

"And who," he asked slowly, "are you?"

She forced herself to smile despite the nervous buzz rising in her ears. "I'm Arielle, a friend of your brother's. Would you like to leave a message for him?"

Loic surveyed her clay-covered arms and the tools in her hands that suddenly felt very much like weapons. She clasped them tighter, funneling her nerves into her grip and trying to hold herself like Mikira in that alley.

"And what do you do for my brother, Arielle?" Loic asked.

"He commissioned her for a sculpture, obviously." Reid gestured at her arms. He seemed to have recovered, but the edge to his voice was weaker now. Widget was still staring Loic down as if intending to devour him.

"I'm sure Lord Adair realized that, Reid," Ari said with fake sweetness. "He'd have to be a fool not to figure that out, and you're not a fool, are you, Lord Adair?"

Loic smiled rigidly. "Yes, you do seem like the sort he'd like. Tell me, girl, where is my little brother?"

"It's beyond me to keep track of someone like him." She grasped the other wooden toggle of her cutting wire and pulled it taut. "I'm just here for the sculpture."

Loic eyed the wire. Ari simply smiled.

Then he came toward her.

She couldn't help it—she stepped back. Loic was twice her size, his hands easily capable of wrapping around her neck. But it wasn't her he reached for—it was the door.

"Loic!" Reid lurched after him, but it was too late.

He shoved past her into the workroom, where he took one look at the horse before his hands slammed into the soft clay of its neck. He tore it back out, pulling a fistful of clay with it. Then Reid was there, grabbing his arm. Loic sent him crashing into the desk. A snarl ripped through the air, and Widget launched at him, claws digging into his leg.

Loic kicked the cat off, sending him tumbling. Then he tore free the golem's ear, raked his fingers through its eyes, and slammed his forearm into the beast's neck, crumpling its head. He drove a foot into its two front legs, sending the body crashing to the floor.

Hours and hours of painstaking labor fell apart before her into a pile of limbs. And when Loic was done, his hands dark with clay, he grabbed Ari by the chin, forcing her to look at him.

"I won't forget your face," he said.

Then he was gone.

Ari stared at the decimated sculpture. At the smears of gray like blood and the dismembered body that had once been whole. She stared and saw something else entirely.

Though her parents had tried to hide it from her, she'd snuck out night after night to explore the spellbook. To run her fingers over its humming surface and feel the rough cut of its pages. That was how she'd discovered the spell, translated in her Saba's careful hand.

DIRT FROM HOLY LAND.
WATER NEVER BEFORE POURED INTO A VESSEL.
A TRUTHSTONE TO BIND THE MAGIC.
THE BINDING, CLEARLY SPOKEN.

He'd had all the ingredients, perhaps intending to try the spell for himself, the clay already made, the truthstone glinting in the moonlight upon his desk. So she'd shaped the rough approximation of a creature, pressed the stone into its head, and said the spell.

Her Saba had walked in when the last wisps of white light had left her lips.

He'd startled the golem. *Her* golem, half-mad with weak spellwork. It'd attacked, tearing into him with teeth and claws. She'd screamed at it to stop, but it hadn't listened. Then Rivkah was there, ripping the beast from their Saba's flesh.

Ari had seized a hammer, driving it into the creature's skull again and again until it fell still. Its body slowly melted from blood and bone and fur to the soft clay from which it'd been born. But it was too late to stop her Saba from bleeding out, too late to prevent her sister's fearful gaze.

Ari stared at the decimated horse, at her hopes of earning her license, at the truth of what she was exposed, and watched as the horse crumpled.

CHAPTER 13

ARIELLE

ARI KNELT IN a sea of clay.

Reid hovered beside her like a mourner standing vigil. It would take days to reconstruct the horse and finish the detail work, time that they didn't have. The race was in two days, and Mikira expected the horse in the morning.

A shadow fell across them from the doorway.

"What happened?" Damien had a gun drawn, his back pressed into the doorframe so he could see both rooms simultaneously.

Reid clutched Widget to his chest. "Loic."

A preternatural stillness overcame Damien at the sound of his brother's name. His hand tightened on the revolver. Reid's booted toe nudged his, and something passed between them in silence, until at last, Damien's finger slid away from the trigger, and he holstered the gun. He approached her, faltering for only a moment when he saw the clay fingerprints staining her face, and reached out to gently take her hand.

Ari watched him help her to her feet as if from a separate place inside herself. The images of her Saba's death were still fresh in her mind, alongside the knowledge that someone else had witnessed her creating a golem, someone who clearly wasn't on good terms with Damien.

"The horse . . ." she whispered.

Damien pulled a handkerchief from his jacket pocket and dipped it in one of the clean buckets of water Ari had been using for the clay. "My brother is a fool," he assured her, lifting the cloth to her face. As he carefully carved away the clay, his fingertips brushed her cheek, and she felt his hand tremble. It was only for an instant, but she felt it all the same—the barely contained rage.

An unfamiliar feeling stirred deep inside her, warming her from her core. She could practically feel Reid staring at them.

"He's so detached from his heritage he wouldn't know a golem from a statue." Damien cleaned away the last of the clay and let his hand drop. She resisted the urge to lift it back to her face. "He probably just thinks he destroyed a commissioned piece of work, but I'll have him followed nonetheless to make sure."

It wasn't a surety, but it was enough to release the knot in her chest. She forced herself to face the dismembered beast. "The race is two days from now. What are we going to do?"

Damien surveyed the golem's remains. "Can you rebuild it in time?"

"Perhaps, but sloppily. And I intended to do the enchantments in batches, and then bring the horse to life the following day. Now . . ."

"You'll have to do them all at once."

She nodded. Damien was familiar enough with enchanting to under-stand how dangerous an endeavor it would be. Five enchantments, two of them ethereal, and a golem spell? Even the most powerful of enchanters couldn't manage all that at once without pushing their bodies to the limits of survival.

Damien sighed reluctantly. "I have an idea, but I don't like it."

Ari looked at him questioningly, but Reid only groaned. "I'm not call-ing her."

"Calling who?" Ari asked.

"My sister," Damien replied. "She's an enchanter."

IT TOOK TIME for Damien to convince her that Shira could be trusted, a truth she only accepted when he revealed that she too practiced Kinnish magic and knew about crafting golems. It was because of her that Damien had recognized the golem he'd seen in the enchant dealer's shop on Rathsborne.

He took Widget from Reid, handing the cat to Ari to inspect. "She made him for Reid years ago, when he became a target for Loic's temper."

Reid rolled his eyes. "She made him to protect you and gave him to me because she knew you wouldn't accept him."

Ari marveled at the creature, the first golem she'd seen from another enchanter, even as she wondered why Shira had picked something so small to act as a protector. Golems were strong and loyal, but even they could only do so much wrapped in such a petite form. It was more than enough of a reason to trust Shira, but more than that, Ari couldn't pass up the opportunity to talk to someone else like her.

A few hours later, which Ari spent diligently reshaping the larger pieces of clay, Shira arrived. Her dark curls were braided down her back, her outfit still an amalgamation of black leather and knives that Reid seemed unable to look away from. She slid off her jacket and rolled up her sleeves, getting to work without a word.

Ari didn't know what to make of operating alongside another Kinnish enchanter. She'd spent so long hiding her powers that the idea of what she was doing now had never seemed possible. There was a comfort in Shira's presence that stemmed from more than the reassurance that they'd make the race deadline.

Ari peered at her over the horse's back as they finished reattaching the legs. "If you've known about golems all along, why didn't Damien just ask you to do this? Why go through all the trouble of finding me?"

Shira smiled. "Because I would have told him no."

Ari recoiled. "Why? Do you want him to lose?"

"No," she replied. "I don't want him to play at all."

Apparently, the skill for cryptic answers ran in their family because she got nothing more out of Shira. They worked late into the night and rose early the next morning. Reid brought them tea and scones, refusing to look at Shira, whose flirtation clearly got under his skin.

Mikira arrived around noon, and they overheard her arguing with Reid at the sitting room door. She'd expected the horse to be ready that morning, and the excuses he gave her were poor, but he ushered her outside and the door closed on their conversation. Ari could only imagine how nervous this news must have made the girl. At this rate, she'd meet the horse only a few hours before putting both their lives at risk.

Damien was nowhere to be seen the entire day. She assumed he was tending to house business, meeting with tenants and running numbers with bookies, but Shira dropped several remarks about it until Ari finally gave in and asked, "Do you know where he is?"

"Not a clue," she replied. "But you should ask him when he returns."

Ari had the distinct feeling of being a fly that had wandered into a spider's web. It wasn't the same feeling she had around Damien, whose every interaction felt like moves on a board, but something far more assessing, as though Shira was waiting for *her* to make a move.

They finished the last of the clay sculpting early that evening, Ari's fingers weaving the final bits of mane into place before she stood back to take the beast in. She was covered in clay from head to toe, her dark curls a wild mess, but it was done. With a sleek, muscular frame that would be the envy of any racer and keen, knowing eyes, it was a work of art even immobile.

Now there was only the magic.

"How many enchantments are you doing?" Shira asked, washing her hands in a bucket of water.

"Five," Ari replied. "Speed, endurance, and agility for physical, and then a charm never to get lost and one to sense danger."

Shira nodded. "The golem's natural strength is practically a fourth physical enchantment. Smart." She dried her hands on a clean cloth. "Which ones do you want me to do?"

Ari hesitated. Her reflex was to ask Shira to handle the ethereal ones, since she'd been unable to figure them out with the coin, but after all the work she'd put into the golem, she wanted to finish it herself. Shira was licensed. She'd been trained to do magic. Perhaps she could teach Ari to do the same.

"I've been struggling with the ethereal enchantments," she said. "I've been practicing them on objects, but I don't think they're working, and they're sporadic when they do."

"Most enchanters struggle with them. What are you associating them with?"

Ari frowned. "What do you mean?"

Shira must have realized then how little she really knew, because she leaned back against Reid's desk and explained, "Think of it this way. A large part of the spell's effectiveness comes from your intent, right? Spells cast with a weak intent are in turn weaker. One of the easiest ways to strengthen your intent is by associating each type of enchantment with something. For example, if you associate strength with physical force, then you keep a representation of that force in the forefront of your mind while working the binding."

This was the sort of information Ari couldn't find in any textbook, the kind that could take her spellwork to the next level.

"And ethereal enchantments?" she asked. "Why are they more difficult?"

"Because it's easy to come up with an association for strength. But what about for never getting lost, or sensing danger? They're far less concrete concepts. That's probably why the spell works sometimes and not others. If a charm for danger doesn't contain a clear idea of what danger is, the charmed object won't either."

Ari stepped up to the horse, already running through associations in her mind. For speed, she thought of Mikira flying down the track on Eilora's back, and for agility, she pictured Widget on Reid's shoulder. For endurance, she thought of herself, toiling endlessly on her golems.

As she spoke the binding spell for the physical enchantments, she focused on the warm thrum of dormant magic in the clay, weaving it through the powdered emerald packed inside. She kept each of the ideas at the forefront of her mind, letting her intent shape the magic first into a speed charm, then one of agility, and then endurance.

"Impressive," Shira said when she'd finished. "I can feel the spells in the clay. They're strong. Do you want me to do the ethereal ones?"

You don't need her, whispered the voice. *You can do this yourself.*

Was it her imagination, or was it louder than before? A twinge permeated the edges of her mind, threatening to grow into a full-blown headache. But the voice was right—she *could* do this herself, and more than that, she wanted to.

"I can do it," she replied.

Shira looked like she wanted to argue, but Ari had already shut her eyes to concentrate. What did she associate with never getting lost?

Home.

She thought of her family's small house on the edge of the town edah. Of the colorful walls and the too-small kitchen. She conjured up the scent of garlic and onions sizzling in oil that filled the house when her mother cooked, the sound of her Saba's voice.

The binding spell slipped through her lips and into the clay, locking the magic in place. Now only the danger charm remained. She thought of the feeling of when those men broke into her workroom, of the sense she'd had that no matter what she gave them, it would not be enough. Then she thought of the safety she'd felt the last few weeks, sitting by the fire surrounded by books, with Damien, Reid, and Mikira, and she carried both sentiments with her into the spell.

It slid seamlessly into the clay, locking into place with an ease she hadn't felt with the coin. By the time she finished, her stomach growled with hunger and her head ached as it often did after performing magic. She'd long ago learned that though the magic was not the cause of the headaches, it was one of several triggers, and she often didn't know when one would spring upon her.

Well done, praised the voice, and Ari shivered.

Shira placed a steadying hand on her shoulder. "You should rest. That was a lot of magic." But it wasn't just concern that Ari saw in her eyes. There was something else there. Something she couldn't place.

"It's remarkable."

Ari spun at Damien's voice. "You're back," she said, an undercurrent of excitement in her voice that surprised them both. Without thinking, she took his hand, pulling him around so they faced the beast head-on. When he didn't let go, she let her fingers curl about his. Shira looked between them, her face inscrutable.

Reid joined them on Ari's other side. "Now what?"

"Now stand here and don't move." Ari released Damien's hand and darted to her satchel on the desk, where she withdrew the spellbook. It hummed welcomingly in her hands, and she had the distinct feeling that it was glad to see her.

"Ari." Shira eyed the spellbook uneasily. "I don't think you should attempt this until the morning."

Ignore her, the voice growled.

"I'll be fine. The golem needs time to adjust before Mikira rides it tomorrow." Even as she said it, her nerves rose. Working enchantments in front of someone else was one thing; bringing a golem to life was another. It was at once an intensely personal experience and an entirely horrifying one, because each time she spoke the words, she thought of that night with Saba, when everything went so terribly wrong.

Blood on her hands. Blood on the walls.

Taking a deep breath, she locked away her fear and flipped open to the marked page. She began to circle the horse, reciting a string of Kinnish as she went. Light flowed from her lips, swirling and dancing in wisps, before vanishing into the horse's clay forehead. The beast began to radiate, bright as a full moon.

Ari spoke faster, louder, and the light grew brighter, wisping off of her like rising steam. The magic filled her in a rush, and she met Damien's gaze over the back of the horse. There was a look in his eye that spoke to her, as if he longed to reach out and touch her, to see if the heat that blazed in her eyes also burned beneath her skin.

"What in the four hells?" Reid whispered.

In a flash of power, the light rippled along the horse's form, turning clay to flesh and bone, hair and hooves, like a fabric turned inside out to reveal a new pattern. The horse snorted, the last wisps of light dissipating with its breath.

Black as ink, its coat lustrous and radiant, the horse held itself like the steed of a conqueror, its depthless gaze surveying them all.

Ari couldn't tell if her heart was thundering from the expenditure of magic or from the way Damien was looking at her, as though he'd discovered a rare jewel nestled among a pile of coals.

She held his gaze as she said, "Lady and gentlemen, I give you Atara."

A slow smile spread across Damien's lips at the Kinnish name she'd chosen.

It meant crown.

Beautiful, breathed the voice, and in it, Ari *felt* its satisfaction. It coursed through her, entwining with her own until she could no longer deny that whatever it was, whatever it meant—that voice was not hers.

Then she dropped to the floor.

SHE WOKE TO the sound of people arguing in Kinnish.

"Listen to me, Dara. What she did—she should be dead! No one has that kind of power." That was Shira.

"You're overreacting," Damien replied. "Clearly someone does have that kind of power, and I'm not going to tell her to stop using it the moment she's discovered it."

Her eyes fluttered open. She was on the chaise in the sitting area, a pillow beneath her head and a blanket tucked over her shoulders. Her thoughts felt as though they were swimming in honey, unable to detach from one another.

"Arielle?" Damien noticed her first.

She wanted to tell him that she was fine, but she couldn't find her voice. There was something . . . *wrong.* Just as suddenly as she was sure of it, the feeling passed, and her mind cleared. With it came an aching pain in her head so sharp she hissed.

"Arielle!" Damien dropped to a knee before her.

"I'm okay." She pushed herself up. "What happened?"

"You used too much magic." Shira held up the spellbook. Ari lurched as if to grab it from her, but movement only made her nauseous, and she stopped halfway.

Shira watched her impassively. "What is this book, Ari?"

"I don't know." She pressed a hand to her head, trying to make the room stand still.

"Where did you get it?"

"I don't know." That one was a lie, but she felt as if she had no choice. As though telling Shira the truth would result in the book being taken away.

Damien rose to face his sister. "She needs to rest. You can ask your questions later."

Shira looked reluctant, but in the end, she handed Damien the book. Her voice dropped to a whisper, and Ari strained to hear, but she could already feel herself fading again. The last thing she saw before her head hit the pillow was the color drain from Damien's face.

CHAPTER 14

MIKIRA

MIKIRA DIDN'T SLEEP the entire night.

Not only was the first race of the Illinir tomorrow, but something had gone wrong in enchanting the horse, and it wouldn't be ready until the morning. Reid had refused to tell her what exactly it was, claiming that it didn't matter.

She was gone before Ailene and Nelda woke, after making them promise the previous night that they wouldn't come watch. They'd finally stopped peppering her with questions, but the distance that had opened between them was even worse. She'd told herself that she'd kept them away from all of this for their safety, but the more time she spent in this world, the more she started to think that she was only protecting herself.

By the time she reached the manor, her nerves had coiled tight in the hollow of her throat, and her hands sought her knives for comfort as she neared Damien's suite. Her father had given them to her when Lochlyn died, suspecting they were enchanted, and she'd clung to them for security ever since, though she'd never seen a wisp of magic.

"I hope you have good news." Damien's voice drew her to a halt. A door just behind her had been left cracked open.

"That's hardly a proper greeting," responded another in saccharine tones. "What happened to 'How are you, Hyle?' or 'Can I get you a drink, Hyle?'"

"Hyle," Damien said quietly.

A beat of silence, and then, "Oh. I see. What happened?"

"Nothing that concerns you," Damien replied. "Now tell me what you found."

She should have kept moving. This was exactly the sort of thing Damien had made clear was not her business, but as she started forward again, Hyle said the one name that she could not ignore.

"Your brother visited Rezek Kelbra."

She pressed back against the wall behind the door as Damien asked, "Loic went to the Kelbras that night?"

"I was quite surprised myself," Hyle replied amusedly. "I was under the impression he wanted to take Rezek Kelbra apart into tiny little pieces, burn them, and then feed the ashes to pigs destined for slaughter." He paused. "Oh, wait. That's you. Still, I do believe your families are mortal enemies, are they not?"

Mikira smothered a sound of surprise. She'd known that Damien and Rezek weren't on good terms, but she hadn't realized it stemmed as far as a family feud. Or did it? If his brother was friends with the Kelbras, was his sister too? Had Shira been watching them for Rezek? That would explain why Damien had been so determined to get her to leave.

"Before that, I had word he'd been talking with Velrose Kelbra, the Illinir race coordinator," Hyle continued. "Your brother's making the rounds, it seems."

There was the snap of a lighter, and the spiced scent of verillion flowed out of the room. Mikira covered her nose as her bile rose. She hated that smell. It reminded her of her mother's room, the air stale with the scent of death.

There was a smack, then the telltale sound of a boot grinding something into the ground.

Hyle gave a defeated sigh. "That was my last cigarette."

Mikira could practically hear Damien's dark stare. "What of my ring?"

"No luck finding it."

She leaned closer at that. Did he mean his house ring?

"Handle it," Damien commanded. "Quietly."

Hyle laughed. "You know me, quiet as a mouse."

"I'm serious, Hyle."

"All right, serious as a mouse."

Damien drew a measured breath. "And find out why my brother is suddenly so keen on Rezek's friendship. Quickly."

The finality to his tone sent Mikira scurrying onward. She'd just turned the corner toward his suite when she heard the door bang open in the hall behind. She ducked into the sitting room, praying he hadn't seen her enter, and stopped.

The floor-to-ceiling windows on the far side of the room were gone, slid aside along a movable track to grant entrance to the courtyard beyond. Standing among the tall grass and flowers was the most beautiful horse she'd ever seen. Easily nineteen hands and pure black from nose to tail, the beast glimmered like obsidian in the sunlight.

Reid was brushing it down, while on the far side of the courtyard, stable hands prepared a trailer at the end of a wide arched corridor. The horse nipped at him, and he kept pushing its face away.

"Her name is Atara."

Mikira startled at Damien's voice, and he peered at her curiously. She stifled the urge to ask him about Rezek. There was more at play here than just their bargain, and she was starting to worry that the consequences of winning the race might be just as dire as losing. If Rezek lost the Illinir to Damien, would he seek revenge? Would he blame Mikira too?

Her eyes dropped to Damien's hand—his signet ring was gone. House members rarely took off their rings. The status symbol aside, the rings granted them access to bank accounts, records, everything. When it wasn't on their hand, it was a target any thief would salivate over. Was that what Hyle was looking for?

Swallowing the questions, she asked instead, "Where's Ari?"

"Resting," he replied. "The enchantments took a lot out of her."

Mikira sent a silent thanks to the girl as she descended the stairs. The horse watched her approach, unblinking, until she reached out a tentative hand. All horses were different, from their temperaments to their gaits. There was nothing about her knowledge of and experience with them that guaranteed this one would trust her, and yet she needed her to from the start.

"Hi, there," she said softly.

Atara's ears pricked. Mikira placed her hand reverently on the horse's nose and felt Atara press back.

"She's beautiful," Mikira whispered. "Too beautiful."

Reid tossed his brush into a bucket. "Rezek's going to suspect something's off, gold flecks or not."

"But he won't be able to prove it, and that's all that matters," Damien replied as he joined them.

Mikira looked up into Atara's dark gaze and grinned. "Either way, he's going to lose."

MIKIRA'S CONFIDENCE DISINTEGRATED into nausea on the way to the race in the Houndswood. She wasn't ready for this. What had she been thinking? Attending the showcase ball, competing in the Illinir, conning Rezek Kelbra—this wasn't her. That life belonged to someone who didn't ruin everything she touched.

It didn't help that she'd only had time for a brief trot around the front drive with Atara before they were off. She knew nothing about how the horse ran or what she responded to. Ari had barely woken from her sleep long enough to wish her luck, leaving no time for questions.

"Mikira? Mikira!"

She snapped back to herself. Damien frowned at her from across Atara's back, her hands still tangled in the stirrup she'd been adjusting. They were in a cordoned area off to the side of a grass field at the edge of the Houndswood Forest, the site of the first race. The chatter of other jockeys and sponsors filled the air with a tangible buzz, tightening her stomach into knots.

"Did you hear a word I said?" Damien's bare fingers tapped once, twice on his leg, the only sign of his annoyance.

She winced. "Sorry."

"Remember what we discussed. You want to end up in the middle of the pack, not win outright. The first race is a straight shot. You'll start on one side of the Houndswood and end on the other, where I'll meet you."

"I remember everything I'm supposed to worry about," she replied more sharply than she intended.

Damien continued unperturbed. What did it take to get under that man's skin? "I've made some arrangements to find you alliances. They—"

"No."

His eyes narrowed. "No?"

Creating race alliances was common practice. Riders would band together to watch each other's backs, but eventually, those alliances had to break, and you never knew when someone was going to turn on you preemptively.

"I have enough to think about without fretting over when they'll betray me," she said. "It's easier if everyone is my enemy from the start."

"Do you know the odds against you winning?" Her expression must have been answer enough because he continued, "You're the greatest underdog in this race. Anyone betting on you is about to make a fortune. They have as vested an interest in you crossing that finish line as their own riders."

Mikira's nails dug into her palms. It had been a long time since she'd relied on other people. In her experience, everyone walked away eventually. All of her father's friends, her family's connections, Talyana, even her father himself, though he hadn't meant to. It was hard enough for her to rely on Reid, Ari, and Damien—now he wanted her to put her faith in complete strangers?

She shook her head. "I'm not leaving my fate in the hands of your house of cards. The answer's no." She freed Atara of her halter and guided her out of the makeshift stables.

Spectators streamed along the main thoroughfare, dressed in suits with colorful waistcoats and flowing dresses that stopped above the ankle and wide-brimmed hats. Milling vendors sold meat pies and popcorn, hard candy and cups of cold ale and spiced wine. Makeshift stalls and tents had been erected along a nearby embankment, peddling everything from Skylis wings and Lyzairin tails to enchanted looking glasses to watch the race with, and she caught snippets of people discussing bets and odds.

All of it tugged on memories she'd almost forgotten. Evenings spent with her best friend and brother, eating rock candy until they were sick, Lochlyn narrating the races under his breath while she and Talyana rattled off stats. How distant those moments felt, as though someone could simply brush them away like dust off a forgotten shelf.

The starting line was a flurry of activity as horses began to gather. Cameras flashed, voices calling for the riders to pose and wave. The shouts of fans and vendors rose over them, melding into the clanging of metal gates and the wet thud of horse hooves in soft grass.

One of the gate crew guided them toward the starting line, where horses jumbled and jostled for space. The other racers all looked older than Mikira, and most were hardened, gruff-faced men that looked plucked straight from the Anthir's cells. Atara's ears flicked in all directions, and she pawed the ground restlessly. Mikira fiddled with the knives strapped to her forearms beneath her sleeves. Not for the first time, she wished she knew if they were truly enchanted. If ever she could use a little magic on her side, it was now.

"Miss Rusel?" a crewman asked. "It's time to mount up. The race is about to start."

Mikira laid a hand on Atara's neck. The mare stood taller than any other horse there, her coat the pure black of a starless night. She watched Mikira with obsidian eyes that felt too keen, as if she were staring into her soul. "I snuck you a treat," she whispered, pulling a couple apple slices from her pocket. The mare gobbled them up with delight, then snuffled her hand for more. "Please don't throw me."

Wiping her sweaty hands against her pants, she swung up into the saddle.

Atara started forward at an easy clip. Her gait was incredibly smooth, and Mikira fell into the rhythm of it with ease. But by the time they'd slipped into the tumult of horses and riders, her anxiety had swelled once again. Only fifty of them would progress to the next race, and somehow she had to survive long enough to be one of them, all without doing *too* well, lest she draw attention.

She scanned the riders, surprised how many she recognized. Alren Zalaire, who came in second place at the last Illinir, in which he'd lost his left arm. There was Arabella Wakelin, the dark skin of her forearm tattooed with the names of the famous races she'd won. She was shaking hands with Dezaena Fyas, the Yaroyan prodigy who'd traveled kingdoms to be here. Mikira wanted to ride over and talk to them, to tell them she was a racer too, but the idea felt laughable. Her father's name could only take her so far—she had no merits of her own to support her here.

"You're quaking where you sit," grumbled a jockey in silver and white— House Kelbra colors.

With a start, she realized she recognized him: Gren Talyer. He'd been a legend once, one of the youngest jockeys in history. Until her father had exposed him for sabotaging his competitors' horses. He'd been banned from the races for ten years, and from the way he was looking at her, she had a feeling his fury hadn't dulled the slightest in that time.

"What can I say?" Mikira ground out. "I'm excited."

"You don't belong here." Gren's dark eyes glinted. "Even your coward of a father knows that."

The words snapped Mikira's spine straight. "My father is not a coward."

Gren laughed. "A washed-up, useless, coward."

The announcer said something over the loudspeaker, but it was lost to the roaring in Mikira's ears, to the desire to drive her fist into that man's sneering grin. She tried desperately to claw the anger back, to do as Reid had said and forge it into a shield his blades couldn't penetrate.

The crowd echoed the announcer's countdown. "For Enderlain! For the Harbingers!"

Gren turned back to the track. "You're in over your head, little girl."

"For Sendia!"

The starting bell rang.

CHAPTER 15

MIKIRA

*A*TARA BOLTED.

Mikira threw herself forward with a yelp, holding on for dear life as the horse galloped toward the woods at breakneck speed. Dirt and grass flew up behind them, the world turning into a blur of color on either side of her. She slowly relaxed back into the saddle, unclenching her white-knuckled hands from the reins. Even Iri's speed enchantment wasn't this strong. Exactly how powerful of an enchanter was Ari?

As Atara raced forward, her stride easy and graceful, the burst of fear-laden adrenaline that'd erupted through Mikira melted into utter delight. She whooped into the roaring wind.

Then the Houndswood swallowed them.

The cheering crowd vanished, replaced by the thunder of hooves and shouts of riders. Metal clanged as weapons were drawn and the melee began. Dezaena Fyas fended off a baton from another rider, Alren Zalaire riding at their back in an alliance formation. Arabella Wakelin was already pulling ahead of the pack, Gren hot on her tail.

Mikira shifted her reins to one hand and unsheathed a blade with the other as another rider bore down on her. She deflected their knife and drew Atara away to open space.

They wove through the trees, keeping well away from the other riders.

There was no path to follow, and the thick canopy above cast the forest floor in shadow, making it difficult to spot any warning signs of enchantments.

The ground began to shake.

Atara slowed but kept her footing. Other horses spooked, darting wildly left and right as leaves rained from the trees. Ahead, the ground split like a yawning maw, revealing a bed of sharp spikes.

Dezaena's and Alren's horses sprang across the gap as it opened. Another slammed to a halt, throwing its rider over its head. Screams rent the air as he disappeared into the pit.

Mikira tried to turn Atara aside, but she was going too fast. She swallowed a yell a second before the horse leapt the pit.

She landed effortlessly on the other side and kept running.

Mikira glanced back at the gaping chasm. The rest of the racers had slowed in time, now forced to go around. She'd been the last to make it across—something that should have been impossible. Atara was only charmed for speed, endurance, and agility. How had she made that leap?

Swinging back around in the saddle, Mikira caught a glimpse of another rider. A girl with brown hair and a green Rach mask on a chestnut bay, racing along beside her. There was something familiar about her. The girl turned, revealing curious hazel eyes.

It was the rider from her last underground race, the one who'd drawn a knife on her.

She stared in wonder at the girl a second longer, before a sharp pain seared through her arm.

Crying out, she flattened herself over Atara's neck just as something whizzed overhead. Hanging from the branches all around her were spiked balls attached to long strings, swinging back and forth like pendulums. More than one rider lay groaning on the leaf-strewn ground.

A mace swung toward Atara's side, but she dodged it. It was all Mikira could do to cling to her as she darted through the swinging spikes with the fleet-footedness of a gazelle. Her control, her agility—they were unlike anything Mikira had ever experienced.

She leaned close and put her trust in the horse's instincts.

They burst from the spikes and into open woodland. Relief tore through Mikira as she sat upright, the motion pulling at her wounded arm. She hissed, but there was nothing she could do for it now. With how deftly Atara had handled the beginning of the course combined with her speed, they could be near the front of the pack. But between the pit, the maces, and whatever other obstacles the forest hid, there was no telling how many riders remained.

"Watch out!"

Mikira didn't get a chance to locate the voice before the world turned white. She shut her eyes against the flood of light and slowed Atara reflexively. The horse tossed her head, pulling at the bit, and Mikira felt her speed up again. Even through her closed eyelids she could tell the lights still blared, yet Atara surged forward confidently. Could she see somehow?

The light faded, and she blinked until her vision cleared. She marveled at Atara, whose stride only grew quicker, steadier, as if falling into a rhythm she'd been born to. The forest edge parted ahead, a handful of racers pushing their horses into an all-out gallop for the finish line.

Atara let out a high whinny and veered to the side a second before another horse nearly crashed into them. Mikira swung out wildly with her knife but cut only air. A man laughed as Atara regained herself, forced to a stop by the sudden strike.

Gren Talyer's white stallion blocked their path.

His lips parted in a jagged smile. "You're lucky to have made it this far on an unenchanted horse, but it's as far as you'll go." He lashed out with a blade and Mikira deflected it, urging Atara away with her knees.

But the horse didn't listen. She lunged forward, teeth skimming along the stallion's shoulder. The white horse reared back, screaming, and Atara reared with him, front hooves striking at the stallion's chest.

When the horses came down, Gren jerked his away with a curse, driving his heels into his stallion's sides and forcing the startled creature into a canter.

Atara huffed heavily, tossing her head. Mikira tried to soothe her, but she was frenzied, like a beast drunk on its prey's blood. She sidestepped, then reared again, neighing.

Mikira laid a hand on her neck as they came down. "It's okay!"

Atara turned sharply as if to snap for her hand. The moment stretched, Mikira frozen by the look of utter ferocity in the mare's eyes.

Then flames blazed to life at their backs.

Atara bolted and Mikira lost her stirrups. The enchanted fire raced alongside them, funneling them aside into a small clearing. Mikira clung fast with her knees, her hands fisted in Atara's mane as the fire encircled the clearing, cutting off their escape. Atara ground to a halt, and Mikira tumbled over her shoulder, barely managing to throw herself clear.

She hit the ground hard and rolled, stopping just before the line of flames. Atara stamped and tossed her head, and Mikira fought her way back to her feet, body aching. The mare cut toward her, and Mikira leapt away, holding up her hands.

"Easy girl," she called, the heat of the flames pressing at her back. Atara lowered her head, panting nearly as heavily as Mikira.

"We're okay," Mikira breathed. "We're okay."

Enchanted fires lasted only as long as their verillion source; this had to burn out soon. But that look in the mare's eye, the frenzy—the only horses she'd ever seen act like that had been enchanted for aggression or protection. Her family sold them as warhorses. Atara didn't have either of those charms, though that didn't mean she hadn't been trained for battle. Had Damien gotten her a warhorse instead of a racehorse and not told her?

With a whoosh, the flames went out around them, leaving the ground blackened and the air scorched with smoke. Mikira didn't move, holding Atara's gaze. The horse stared back at her with a look she couldn't decipher, an intensity bordering on zealousness.

They needed to go. They had to be near the end of the pack by now, and only Atara's unnatural speed would have any chance of regaining their position. But some part of Mikira didn't want to get back on her.

She couldn't remember the last time she'd been afraid of a horse.

Atara pawed at the ground, turning aside as if to let Mikira mount. Forcing her burgeoning fear aside, she approached cautiously and swung up into the saddle. When Atara didn't snap at her, she gave her an experimental nudge, and the horse trotted on. Mikira's fingers quivered on the reins, and she closed them tighter. She couldn't afford to be afraid right now. She had a race to win.

They tore through the trees, Atara's strides eating up ground. The tree line thinned, then broke, emptying them into a wide stretch of rolling hills. A stream of horses stretched out before them, the finish line a dot on the horizon.

"Go!" Mikira called, giving Atara her head.

The horse flew.

They passed the stragglers in a blur, then reached the end of the pack. They galloped past horse after horse, until the finish line was only an open stretch of green away. Mikira forgot the pain in her arm and the fear crouching in her bones and lost herself to the race as they soared across the finish line.

It was only as Atara slowed to a walk that she noticed the massive group of horses and riders at the end of the clearing. Only then did she hear the announcer call, "And Mikira Rusel in the fifty-first position."

She was too late.

They'd lost.

MIKIRA COULDN'T BREATHE.

Every once in a while, her lungs would burn so viciously that she'd choke down another sob of air, but then her throat would close, and her body would seize and the realization that she'd lost everything would threaten to crush her.

She sat huddled on a bench in the jockeys' locker room. She'd found a private corner, and incredibly, no one had disturbed her. Not even Damien, who she couldn't bear to face. She'd lost him his family's racing business. His reaction would not be kind.

The door swung open with a low groan, and a familiar voice *tsked* quietly. The sound trailed cold claws down her spine.

"My, my, Miss Rusel," Rezek practically purred. "What a mess you've made."

The room was in shambles around her. The wooden locker was broken, the shelves askew, the mirror cracked. She didn't even remember destroying them.

She fought to control her breathing, to seal away her pain so Rezek couldn't feed on it, but it was too raw. She'd lost the ranch, trapped her father in a life of service to a demon, and put her sisters on the street.

So much for wanting the Rusel name to mean something again. She'd only ground it deeper into the dirt.

She felt Rezek behind her a second before his hand came down on her shoulder, his fingers digging beneath the bone. It wasn't the pain that nearly made her sick. It was the realization that Rezek had never touched her before, as if he'd been waiting for this moment.

"You're bleeding," he said simply.

Her left arm was coated crimson. The wound had mostly crusted and dried, but still leaked rivulets of red.

Rezek brushed his fingers down her arm, lingering over the wound. They came away stained with blood, and Mikira shivered. He slid onto the bench facing the opposite direction of her.

"You came so very close," he lamented. "That horse of yours is rather remarkable."

Atara.

She'd left the mare standing in the clearing and staggered into the locker room before anyone could stop her. Had someone tended to the horse? Guilt shuddered beneath the numbness.

Rezek gripped the bench and leaned back so he could see her face. For a moment, he simply drank in the sight of her. Then he said, "I want to make you a new deal."

Her heart lurched. "What?"

"A new deal," he repeated slowly, as if warning her not to make him do it again. "Losing their racing business will be a blow to the Adairs, but it won't crush them the way I want, and Damien will find a way to recover. I need something that will destroy them—that will destroy him."

Finally, she forced herself to fully meet his gaze. He stared back, seemingly pleased that she had. "What are you asking of me?"

"I want you to spy on Damien Adair."

She stilled, memories rising of breaking bone, of red flecks on a pristine white sleeve. Then her gaze dropped to Rezek's bloodstained fingers.

"And in exchange?"

He laughed once, short and sharp. "Bold of you to assume you have the power to ask anything of me. I hold everything you care for."

His words were weapons, each one tearing a new hole. She felt herself sway. Rezek's hand closed around her arm, too close to the wound to be accidental, and she hissed against the flare of pain.

"But as I said, I am not a villain." His voice dropped low, almost caressing. "If you accept, I'll reinstate you into the race. Our bargain from before will continue. You will still have your chance to win."

"Why?" Rezek had finally gotten what he wanted, and now he was willing to risk it again?

He released her, his palm stained red. "My reasons are my own. Do you accept?"

"Damien will never believe you just let me back in. He'll be suspicious."

"Let me handle the little Adair."

Mikira hesitated, and Rezek eyed her. "Come now, Miss Rusel. Don't tell me you've grown attached. Damien is everything you hate."

"He's better than you," she snapped.

"He is me."

She thought of the man whose finger Damien had broken, of the Anthir flooding the hall the first day at the manor and his conversation with Hyle. But she'd seen him do good too, things Rezek would never do, for people he owed nothing to. Had it all been a performance?

As if summoned by their discussion, she heard Damien's voice at the door. "Move aside, Kyvin."

"My lord has asked not to be disturbed," an oily voice replied.

Rezek raised his pale brows. "Last chance."

"Fine," she growled. "I accept."

"I won't ask again." Damien's voice turned sharp.

Rezek stood. "Let him in, Kyvin."

Damien burst into the room. "What is this?"

Rezek laced his fingers behind his back. "I was just telling Miss Rusel that I'm willing to let her back into the race, for a price. What do you say to upping the stakes of our bargain, old friend?"

Mikira stilled—old *friend*?

Like a clock shifting gears, Damien's face changed bit by bit. The anger melted as he adjusted for the situation, no doubt sensing the opportunity to turn the odds in his favor.

"What do you propose?" he asked.

"Simple," Rezek replied. "In addition to our current bargain, you will wager all of House Adair's verillion fields."

Damien regarded Rezek without expression, but Mikira could guess what he was thinking. If they lost, House Kelbra would have a monopoly on two of Enderlain's main trades: racing and verillion. They would own over half the city, and House Adair would be broken.

Of course, Rezek didn't know what they did about Atara.

Damien looked to her. She recoiled. He couldn't mean to let her decide.

No. But he doesn't know what happened. Damien didn't know how the horse had lost herself to blood like a lion tearing into a kill. How Mikira hadn't been able to control her, had been afraid of her. If winning was impossible, he wanted to know.

She didn't know what to tell him.

Damien's jaw set. "Very well."

Rezek clapped his hands together in delight. "Wonderful." He brushed past Damien to where a narrow-faced man with slick black hair waited. "Best of luck, Miss Rusel." He lifted one red hand before closing the door behind him.

Mikira expected Damien to yell, to close the space between them like Rezek had and make her feel even smaller than she already did.

Instead, he let out a quiet breath and said, "Let's get you home so Reid can look at your arm."

She blinked at him. "That's it?"

"We'll discuss the race in the coach."

Because they were too exposed here. These were the sorts of things Damien Adair thought of that Mikira did not, and yet somehow, she was supposed to spy on him? Rezek wanted damning information he could use to crush Damien, but Mikira needed him. And if he found out she was involved, there was no telling what he would do.

But she didn't have a choice.

CHAPTER 16

ARIELLE

SOMETHING WAS WRONG.

Ari didn't know what it was, only that it was off, like a picture frame slightly askew. The feeling needled at her, lingering ever since she'd created Atara early that morning, but every time she tried to examine it, it slipped away.

"Ari? Ari?" Reid's voice pulled her back to herself. "What the hells are you doing?"

"What?" She started, realizing she was standing in the middle of the foyer. When had she gotten up from the armchair? She turned about, taking in the bookcases she didn't remember approaching.

Ignore him, hissed the voice that was not hers, and she steeled herself against it.

"Ari?" Reid asked again.

"Nothing," she replied tersely. This feeling—she'd had it before after working magic, but she'd put it off as the drain of energy on her body. This loss of time was new, as was the weight in the back of her mind. "I—I was just thinking."

He brushed past her toward the chaise, Widget balanced on his shoulder. "Pretend I never asked. Not like I care, anyway."

She rubbed her temples. The persistent headache she'd had all day had only worsened, and her temper was short, but Reid had only been making sure she was okay, which was a step above questioning her intentions with his best friend. Ever since Loic's attack, he'd been far warmer toward her. If *warm* was even a word that could describe Reid.

"I'm sorry." She followed him back to the sitting area. "I'm not myself."

"Does your head still hurt?"

She nodded, and he poured a cup of tea from the enchanted kettle keeping it warm.

"Thank you." She settled back into her armchair with it and breathed in the relaxing scents of vanilla and chamomile. Little helped once her headaches took root, but she'd grown used to the pain, the way it'd sweep an afternoon's plans out from beneath her and leave her head tender for days.

The suite door flew open.

Ari reflexively reached for a butter knife on the end table before Mikira entered with all the grace of a derailed train. Her eyes were red from spent tears. Mud caked her boots, and dried blood coated her left arm.

"Clean! Floors!" Reid exclaimed a second before he took in the whole picture.

"What happened?" Ari asked, half-afraid to raise the question.

Mikira stopped like she'd struck a wall. Then Damien swept inside, his orderly appearance in blunt contrast to Mikira's dishevelment. His sharp eyes took in Mikira's deerlike immobility and Ari's rising panic, and he said calmly, "We are not out of the race."

"What?" Ari placed a hand against her pounding heart.

"Mikira lost, but Rezek offered me a deal. If I added House Adair's verillion fields to our bargain, he'd allow her back in."

"That doesn't make any sense," Reid said with a frown. "Why?"

Damien strode to the drink cart. "Because he thinks she has no chance of winning. This race only confirmed it."

Ari looked to Mikira, but the girl was staring at the floor, her arms wrapped around her stomach. Standing in the midst of the pristine foyer, plastered in blood and dirt, she looked lost.

"The verillion isn't yours to give, Damien," Reid said quietly.

"I'm aware." Damien poured a glass of whiskey, took a long draw, and then refilled it. "I'll talk to Shira tonight."

"What of Atara?" Ari asked.

"She's fine," Damien replied. "Mikira said she was great until another racer attacked her, and Atara became aggressive. She couldn't pull the horse out of the fight, and it led to them getting caught in an enchantment."

Reid scowled at Mikira. "You let them distract you, didn't you?"

Mikira snapped back to herself. "Yes, I get it! It's all my fault. I don't need you to tell me that!" She stalked from the room.

Reid rose to go after her, but Ari was already moving. After all, this was her fault, not Mikira's. The girl didn't know the truth about Atara. If she had, she might have been prepared for the golem's defensive reaction. Instead, it'd nearly cost them everything.

Mikira was gone from the corridor, but Ari had a feeling where she'd be. Sure enough, she found her sitting on the stable floor with her back against Iri's stall, the horse lipping gently at her hair.

Ari hesitated. She had no idea how to do this. The closest thing she'd had to friendship in her life had been with Rivkah, and so much of that had been looking after her sister, keeping her safe. Perhaps this wasn't much different. Mikira was trying to balance the weight of her family on her shoulders; perhaps she simply needed someone to look out for her for a change.

So Ari did what she would have done had she seen Rivkah curled with her knees to her chest and her face buried behind them.

She sat down beside Mikira and hugged her.

The girl started, and for a moment, Ari thought she might pull away, but instead she leaned into Ari's arms. They sat side by side against the stall for some time. Neither of them spoke, but Ari didn't mind the silence. She'd never been good with words, never known the right thing to say. What could she say when the truth was something she couldn't give?

Mikira wound a piece of straw around one finger. "Do you ever feel like no matter what you do, it's always the wrong thing?" Her voice sounded as bruised as her body looked.

Ari's fingers brushed her Saba's necklace. "Yes. As a child, I was so afraid of doing something wrong that I rarely did anything at all."

So much of her life had been filtered through other people. Looking after Rivkah, obeying her parents, performing the chores they gave her as if afraid what she might do left to her own devices. She couldn't think of a single time she'd done something because she wanted to. Something for herself.

Except the night she'd gone looking for the spellbook.

Except the night you took back your power, said the voice, and she couldn't shake the feeling that this time, it wasn't going to leave. She could no longer deny that the more she used her magic, the more she felt her thoughts changing, slipping away from her like water through her fingers. But neither could she let go of this power, the strength it gave her.

Whatever this was, exhaustion or confusion or something else, she would figure it out.

Mikira snorted, tearing off a piece of straw and tossing it across the barn. "I can't seem to stop myself from doing things. No matter how much I muck stuff up, I just keep stumbling into the next bad decision. My family would be better off without me."

The words panged in the hollow space around Ari's heart. Her family was certainly better off without her. So far away, she couldn't hurt anybody else. It was why she'd left. That, and the fear in their eyes. The blame. But Mikira had done nothing but try to help hers. She couldn't be faulted for trying to survive in a game of kings.

"I know what you've done to protect them," she said. "No one who you care about that much would be better off without you."

Mikira's fingers closed around the straw, and she squeezed her eyes shut. "But what if I can't do this? You're all relying on me. My family is relying on me. I already ruined this once, and now Damien's risking even more. What if—"

She cut off, opening her eyes as Ari laid a hand over hers. The warmth of it surprised her. When was the last time she'd touched someone like that? In friendship, not in fear.

"You're not alone, Mikira," she said gently.

The girl stared at Ari's hand, transfixed. Then she drew a deep, shuddering breath, and placed her other hand over Ari's. "Neither are you."

Ari nearly pulled away, but Mikira's hand tightened. "I know you have something at stake here too, and I know you don't want to talk about it, but whatever it is, you're risking a lot to help me, and I'll never forget that."

Words hovered at Ari's lips. For the briefest moment, she had the absurd notion to tell Mikira everything. To prove her wrong or to prove her right, or perhaps to simply speak the darkness into existence, if only to unwrap it from her soul. But she didn't want to destroy this moment. The way Mikira was looking at her; it was like Rivkah had once looked at her, as if she would always be there.

She liked the idea of being there for someone again.

"When's the last time someone took care of you instead?" Ari asked.

Mikira's attempt at a smile faltered. "I don't remember."

Ari squeezed her hand. "Well then, maybe we can take care of each other."

This time, Mikira's smile was bright. "I'd like that."

Iri dropped his head over the stall door, huffing hot air into Mikira's face. She laughed and stroked the horse's nose. "Yes, I'm here for you too, you oaf."

Ari marveled at the way Mikira's face changed when the horse appeared, shedding a thousand worries. Was there anything in her life that transformed her so completely?

Making golems, she thought. It felt like a part of her, a part she no longer wanted to deny. She might not be able to tell Mikira everything, but she could tell her enough.

Be careful, warned the voice, but she pushed it aside.

"Atara isn't a normal enchant," she said, and braced herself for Mikira's look of puzzled suspicion. "She's what's called a golem, a Kinnish creature of clay given life. They're incredibly protective by nature. I suspect that's all she was trying to do in that fight—protect you."

She expected Mikira to pull away, to react like the boys in the square when they discovered her magic, but the only look that crossed the girl's face was clear understanding.

"That's why you didn't let me see the horse before she was finished. Practicing Kinnish magic is even more dangerous than being unlicensed . . ." She trailed off. "Ari, do you *have* a license?"

Ari looked away. "If you win the Illinir, Damien promised to get me one."

Mikira's head dropped back against the stall, her mouth parted in astonishment. "Rezek's going to find out. He'll use it against us. All of us."

"He's not. Damien will make sure of that. He'll keep us safe."

"Do you really think he can?" Mikira lifted her head, staring at the crusted wound on her arm.

"I do." It was only when she said it aloud that she realized the truth of it: she trusted Damien Adair, but more than that, she'd begun to trust herself. As soon as she was feeling better, she intended to discover just how far her power went. She would keep them safe herself.

Mikira scrubbed a hand across her face with a groan. "I hope you're right. And, Ari?" Ari met her gaze, and Mikira smiled. "I know a little of what it's like to keep secrets like that. Yours is safe with me."

The words wrapped Ari like a warm cloak, and she too smiled. "Come on." She brushed her skirts free of hay before offering Mikira a hand up. "The boys are probably lost without us."

Mikira took her hand with a derisive snort. "I'm sure Reid found something to complain about just fine. Maybe he found a speck of dust on his desk to lecture."

"Yes, but who is Damien going to stare at pensively and overanalyze? He knows Reid far too well already."

Mikira groaned. "I swear he can see straight into my soul."

Ari laughed as they stepped out into the rapidly falling night. "Oh, I don't know. He's not that bad."

"That's because you like flirting with danger." Heat flushed Ari's cheeks, earning a playful elbow from Mikira. "I knew you liked him!"

"I find him interesting," she mumbled, uncertain about the blossoming warmth in her chest. It was a foreign feeling, though not an altogether unwelcome one, and it'd been growing. Over the last few weeks, she'd learned more about Damien than she felt she had any right to: she knew he was a scholar, a man of numbers and figures. She knew how rarely he shared his smile, and how often he sought a stiff drink. She knew that as serious as he could be, he was full of passion. He cared for Reid, and his house, and he would stop at nothing to get what he wanted.

"It's a new feeling for me," she continued, not sure what she intended to say. She'd never described this out loud before. "At first, I thought relationships just weren't for me, as I've never felt attracted to anyone before. But I'm starting to realize that I just need to get to know them first."

Mikira tilted her head. "You need an emotional connection to have a physical one, you mean?"

"Yes, exactly."

"I get that," Mikira replied thoughtfully. "I just want someone to sit on the porch and watch the horses with."

Ari smiled. "That sounds nice."

Mikira clapped her on the back hard enough to make Ari start. "Good luck! That man is like a locked vault."

Well then, she would just have to find the key.

BY THE TIME Mikira finished recounting everything that had happened in the race, Ari was simply glad that she and Atara had made it out alive. She'd heard stories about the dangers of the Illinir, but she hadn't thought about what a toll it must take on a rider, not just to have their life at risk, but to watch people die so brutally around them.

She'd only seen death once in her life, and it was with her always.

"Atara still almost won it for me, though," Mikira finished in a rush. "She shot past the competition like—ow!"

"Would you hold still?" Reid snapped. He was halfway through sealing her wound with a row of tidy stiches Ari's mother would have been proud of, though Mikira's gesturing made it difficult for him to aim.

Mikira glowered back at him. "You're literally stabbing me right now."

"I will stab you if you don't sit still. How did you get so much bloody dirt in this? Did you roll around in the mud?"

"Oh, I'm sorry. I must not have been paying attention when I was *riding for my life from an enchanted fire.*"

"Whenever you two are done." Damien's cool voice cut through the argument from the desk, where he was sifting through a pile of messages that'd been delivered for him earlier. He held up a blood-red envelope between two fingers. "It appears the racer who came in the fiftieth spot in today's race is no longer able to compete. Mikira has been invited to take his place."

Mikira paled. "Is he okay?"

Damien tossed the letter onto the desk. "It's Rezek."

"Right." Mikira stared down at her bare feet—Reid had made her remove her boots at the door—no longer seeming to notice the sting of the needle.

Ari's fingers curled about the edge of her chair. She'd never met Rezek Kelbra, but she was beginning to understand why Damien was targeting him. If he truly cared about improving things the way he'd told Mikira, Rezek was a good person to start with. Still, she suspected there was more to it than that. The way he said Rezek's name . . . it was like a curse.

Reid tied off the last stitch and cut the thread free of Mikira's arm, then neatly bandaged it all. "You're welcome," he said flatly when all Mikira did was poke at it.

He dropped the needle onto a pile of bloodstained cloth and gathered it all with his supplies, disappearing into his bedroom. Mikira's gaze followed him, and Ari wondered if the girl even realized the way she watched him.

Reid returned with Widget on his shoulder. "So, what's our new strategy? Clearly trying to go unnoticed didn't work."

"Are you blaming me for that too?" Mikira snapped. She hadn't moved from her spot on the chaise, something Reid not only seemed to have noticed, but appeared unsure what to do about.

He hovered at the edge of the rug. "Who should I blame? The cat?"

Shutting out their bickering, Ari secured two cups of lavender tea from the drink cart and set one before Mikira and the other beside it. Casting Mikira a final sour look, Reid sat down beside her, snatching up the tea as though he'd only come for it.

Damien joined them. "Anyone who saw Mikira make the comeback that she did will wonder if she's a threat. I've already had reports that Arabella Wakelin's team was hunting for racing records of you at the Vault. Slipping by unnoticed is no longer an option."

"What do we do, then?" Mikira cradled her teacup.

Ari's fingers played absently with her Saba's necklace. She traced the sharp point, remembering those long minutes spent in the cell with Damien and the men who'd hurt her. "We make them fear you instead. Most of the people entering this race are like you: desperate and just trying to survive."

Mikira winced, but Ari pressed on. "Those people are going to do what we were trying to, which is hope they can slip by unnoticed long enough to make it to the finish line first. You can outrace them with Atara, so they don't matter. That leaves the real racers like Arabella and the fighters. You've got the fighters' attention, so the best we can do is reduce the number of them that think attacking you is worth it."

A slow smile curved Damien's lips. "If people think Mikira is dangerous to fight—"

"Which I am."

"—then they'll focus on competition they know they can best first and hope someone else takes her out in the meantime."

Ari nodded. "Exactly. But by the time they realize they have to deal with her after all, she'll be long gone."

"That won't take care of everyone." Reid held his teacup away from a curious Widget. "Rezek will try to make sure you don't finish, and you still have to outrace the best."

"But it at least means fewer people I'll have to contend with." Mikira sat forward. "It's a good plan. How do we do it?"

"We start by ensuring the next time you race with Atara, you're in full control, which means training from now until the next race a week from now," Damien replied. "We'll also make a statement at the next ball, which is in four days. I'll introduce you to as many people as I can. By the end of the night, everyone will know your name. You'll seem untouchable."

Reid lifted his teacup in a salute. "Then come the next race, you destroy them."

CHAPTER 17

MIKIRA

MIKIRA FIDDLED WITH her empty teacup. Reid had disappeared into his workshop, and Ari had excused herself to go lie down. Between the dark shadows under her eyes and the way she kept flinching at the light, Mikira suspected she was nursing a headache.

Only Damien remained, sorting through ledgers at his desk. Until her talk with Ari, she'd been set on following through with Rezek's demands. He had so much power, so much influence, that the idea of trying to wriggle out from beneath his thumb felt impossible. But perhaps Ari was right. Perhaps Damien could keep them safe.

She made herself a promise then. She would ask him about Rezek, and if he told her something, *anything*, true, she would let herself trust him.

Setting her teacup aside, she came to stand across from him, praying she was not about to make a terrible mistake.

"I wanted to ask you something about today," she said when he looked up. "Rezek called you his old friend. Were you . . . ?"

Damien set down his pen. "We were. Once. Now I intend to see his house burn." His hand strayed to the pocket watch at his waist. On the coach ride home, he hadn't said a word to her, but his fingers had flicked the pocket watch open and shut, open and shut, as if seeking its calming rhythm. It was the most restless she'd ever seen him.

"You don't believe me, do you?" he asked.

"It's not—I don't—" She clenched her teeth. She actually found herself wishing Reid were here, if only for someone else to take up a little of the space that Damien so easily consumed.

"What do you see, when you look at this city?"

She looked up, but Damien had angled his chair toward the courtyard, where Veradell stretched in the distance.

"People with too much power," she replied without thinking, but she didn't take it back. The royals, the noble houses—they all had too much. The power to take kingdoms and lives, the power to redraw the lines of the world. Enderlain had done it before, and it would do it again. The war wouldn't end with Celair. Eventually, Enderlain would seek to expand again, and more people would lose loved ones like she had, sacrificed to an endless war.

Damien's brows lifted. "You say that as if power is a bad thing."

Rezek's sinuous smile flashed in her mind. "It is." There were no consequences for people with power, only for those without it. "Powerful people are dangerous."

Like you.

"What I do, I do for this city, this kingdom," Damien said softly. "It has suffered at the hands of people like the Kelbras for too long, and I will see it freed."

He didn't look away from her, as if waiting to ascertain if she believed him. She was just a pawn in his plans, and yet the earnestness in his eyes—he seemed to genuinely care what she thought. But after tonight, could she be anything but his enemy?

The thought of being Damien Adair's opponent sat with her about as well as a sharp stone wedged beneath her ribs. She was no match for him. But perhaps he could be one for Rezek.

"I need to tell you something." Damien waited, and she fortified herself with a deep breath. "In exchange for letting me back in the race, Rezek wants me to spy on you."

His fingers curled slowly around his armrest. "And you're telling me because . . ."

"Because I don't want to, and I need your help to fool him, or he'll hurt my father."

He was silent long enough to make her think she'd made a terrible mistake. Long enough for her to calculate how quickly she could free a knife, whether she could make it to the exit.

Then he said simply, "Thank you."

She started. "What?"

"Thank you for telling me the truth." He picked up his pen again, the motion drawing her eye to the signet ring that was back in place on his right hand. Had Hyle found it while they were out? "I'll feed you information to give to Rezek. Enough to satiate him until your father is freed. I'll keep you safe from him, Mikira."

Those words stayed with her. By the time she returned home with Iri that night, she felt like an old, moth-eaten rag someone had wrung dry. The sickening realization that she was far, far too tangled up in Rezek's web had yet to leave her, and like a foxtail seed burrowed beneath the skin, he wouldn't be removed without tearing apart as much as possible.

So when Nelda crept into her room, long after she'd given up trying to sleep, and slipped under the covers beside her, she let her stay, thankful for the companionable silence that came with knowing someone so well, words weren't needed. She enfolded her sister in her arms, the knowledge that she had almost lost her, lost everything, burgeoning in her chest like a swelling river.

Nelda didn't ask. She just wrapped her thin arms around Mikira's neck and let her hold her for as long as she needed.

THE NEXT MORNING, Atara greeted Mikira with a toss of her head where she waited saddled outside her stall.

Mikira had forgotten how huge the horse was, how imposing with her midnight coat and knowing eyes. She'd been in such a fugue state yesterday that she hadn't fully processed the truth about her origins. Her knowledge of Kinnish magic was even weaker than enchant magic; all she knew was that Atara had been like a warhorse charmed for aggression, crazed by blood, and there'd been a moment when she'd been afraid the horse might attack her too.

Ari had explained it was because golems were protective by nature, but Mikira couldn't shake her doubt. Atara didn't behave like she expected a horse to.

Isn't that the same thing people say about me? Her nails dug into her palms. Reid could snap and grumble and Damien could break bone, but no one called them aggressive the way they did her. That race had been grueling and violent and heady. Could she really blame the horse for getting caught up in it?

But what if she does it again? It wasn't just Mikira at risk here. If Atara's behavior betrayed her, Ari would be discovered too. But she couldn't let her fear rule her. One way or another, she had to learn to work with Atara, for all their sakes.

Forcing herself to close the distance between them, she laid a tentative hand on the mare's velvet nose. "You're not going to eat me, are you?"

Atara nickered softly, leaning into Mikira's touch. There was a life behind the golem's eyes, a familiar spark that she cradled inside herself, even when all the world tried to put it out.

"Maybe you're just like me," she whispered. "A little angry. A little scared."

"Are you going to ride the horse or just stare at her all day?"

She cast Reid a sour look where he slouched against the stable door, arms folded. He looked so comfortable there, so in place. What was it like to be so unabashedly yourself, secure in the knowledge that you had people that accepted you, no matter your faults? Mikira ached for that kind of camaraderie. To not have to bend and shape herself into what other people wanted, and the last few weeks, she'd started to feel it here. Perhaps that was why she'd been honest with Damien about Rezek's deal last night.

She didn't want to lie to them.

Reid shifted uncomfortably. "Staring at me isn't any better. We haven't got all day."

"Maybe I like staring at you." She said it with the express purpose of getting under his skin, but the last thing she expected was the blush that filled his pale cheeks, or the thoughts that spurred to mind at the sight of it. At first, she hadn't thought of him as handsome, but the more she looked at him, the more the piercing blue of his eyes and the sharpness of his features grew on her.

Muttering under his breath, Reid fled from the barn with a backward call of, "I'll be on the track when you're ready to actually do something productive!"

Grinning, Mikira led Atara out into the gray morning sunlight just as Ari descended the final steps to join them. She twisted her curls atop her head with a cerulean kerchief, then offered Mikira a flask of tea from her satchel.

"You're a goddess." Mikira took the container and gulped the hot tea.

Ari laughed as they approached the track. "Damien said you were looking for me?"

Mikira held one of her sheathed knives out to Ari. "I've been meaning to ask if you can tell me if these are enchanted?"

Ari took it, turning it over in her hands. "I definitely sense magic, but I'm not experienced enough to identify one enchantment versus the other. Give me a few days to do some studying, and I'll try again."

She handed the knife back and joined Reid by the fence as Mikira led Atara onto the track, where several other jockeys were running their horses. At a look from Reid, they departed out the rear gate.

Ari scratched Widget under his chin where he lay across the top of the fence. "You should know I also enchanted her to sense danger, and to never get lost. Other than that, golems are obedient by nature, but I can't guarantee her temperament or behavior otherwise. The longer they're alive, the more they become their own creatures."

"Then I'll figure her out like any other horse." Mikira laid a hand on Atara's neck, and the horse's tail swished. She knew Iri like the back of her hand. How the horse ran, the way he took jumps, how he liked to be brushed extra hard behind his right ear. Over the next few days, she needed to learn the same about Atara. It was the only way to keep Ari's secret, and for her to win.

"She's not quite like any other horse," Ari warned. "Golems are highly intelligent. Atara can understand you more than any normal creature, but if you truly want to command her, you will need to learn the Kinnish words."

"Command, as in *force*?" Mikira's stomach squirmed when Ari nodded. The idea of taking Atara's free will away, of using magic to control her, didn't sit right. Besides, the horse's instincts were sharper than her own—she had to learn to trust Atara, not control her.

"I'll manage without the commands," she said, drawing the reins over Atara's head. "Here goes nothing."

Placing her foot in the stirrup, she hoisted herself into the saddle, her injured arm twinging in complaint. Atara pawed at the ground.

Reid lifted his pocket watch. "Let's see what she can do."

Mikira already knew. Barreling along at breakneck speeds during the race had been both enthralling and terrifying. But this was different. Here her life wasn't in danger. It was just her and Atara.

Drawing a deep breath, Mikira nudged Atara.

The horse shot forward.

Mikira lifted up with a yelp, fisting her hands in Atara's mane as the horse flew around the track in record time. By the time they slowed to a walk at the end, the horse wasn't remotely winded. In fact, as she tossed her head, flowing mane rippling in the breeze, Mikira could have sworn there was a challenge in her dark eyes. She wanted to run.

Laughing, Mikira directed her to where the others waited. Ari grinned, an expression that lit up her entire face, and Reid—he was staring at her strangely, his expression so open, so natural, that he almost looked like another person entirely.

Then he seemed to get ahold of himself, and his scowl returned. "You're going to have to learn to control her."

Mikira grinned and let Atara loose.

AFTER THREE DAYS spent on the track with Reid and Atara, Mikira finally began to feel as if she understood the horse. There was a playfulness to her that belied her austere appearance. She nipped at Mikira's hair every time she dismounted to get water and spent too long talking to Reid, and when she went to climb back into the saddle, the horse danced around just out of reach until Mikira gave her an apple. But the moment she was back in place, the mare abandoned herself to the race and they flew.

Damien brought in several of his family's jockeys to simulate real racing conditions, and it quickly became clear that Atara's aggression didn't show only when Mikira was threatened. She tossed her head at the other horses and even snapped when they pressed her into the inside fence, but nothing more so long as Mikira wasn't in any real danger. Mikira had also begun to read her tells. A flick of her right ear, and she was thinking about snapping. A shift in her gait meant she was readying to throw her body into the horse beside her. In time, Mikira would be able to anticipate and compensate for the horse's quirks.

The night before the ball, she and Reid went for a walk on the grounds. Atara strode alongside them, exploring the trail with childlike curiosity.

She sniffed at flowers and munched at grass, poked her head into trees and eyed holes in the ground in hopes they'd offer up their secrets.

Things of particular note she brought back to Mikira and dropped at her feet, like a cat delivering a hard-won mouse—long-stalked flowers with bright blue petals, a crimson ribbon that'd gotten caught in a bush, a pinecone painted with vibrant moss.

Mikira had tried to thank her and set them aside, but Atara had stared at her with such a complex look of confusion bordering on disappointment that in the end, she'd tied the ribbon to the end of her braid to give to Nelda and carried the flowers. She made Reid hold the pinecone.

The Adair estate had nearly fifty acres of land, most of it rolling hills dark with lush woods and hidden crystal lakes. Their trail traced the edge of one forest where the gathering fog threaded through the trunks. Mikira closed her eyes and breathed the scent of wet bark deep into her lungs. She listened to the sound of a gurgling creek nearby and the soft *clump* of Atara's hooves in the damp earth. Even the chill air on her skin felt right.

For once, she could forget the worries hanging over her and believe, if only for a moment, that everything was going to be okay.

"Branch," Reid called.

Mikira threw up a hand, expecting the scrape of leaves, but found only air. When her eyes opened, she found nothing but clear space.

"You're insufferable," she said, though a smile tugged at her lips.

Reid smirked. "I try."

The more time she spent with him, the more she realized just how true that was. He did try, and she couldn't for the life of her understand why. As much as Reid wanted people to think it, he wasn't quite so horrible as he seemed. Yes, he was as grumpy as a cat that'd had its tail stepped on, and yes he couldn't resist making bitter, sardonic remarks about almost everything, but he also made tea for everyone at the end of a long day, and reorganized Damien's books when he'd made a mess of them, and helped Widget onto the sofa when the little cat pretended he couldn't do it himself. Yet he poked everyone around him with a sharp stick without care for who bit him.

You make them a shield so they can't make them a weapon.

"Why are you such an ass all the time?" She asked it lightheartedly, both hoping he'd sense the real question underneath and simultaneously afraid of it. Getting to know him, to know Damien and Ari, hadn't been a part of her plan. Yet she'd come to realize that despite her attempts to keep them at arm's length, she *liked* arguing with Reid, Ari was gentle and kind, and as much as he could make her nervous, Damien also made her feel like someone was watching her back.

"Why do you have the self-control of Atara before a bushel of apples?" Reid tossed the pinecone up and caught it.

"Because I spent half my life trying to be what other people wanted me to be, and they just tossed me aside anyway."

Reid stared at her. Clearly he hadn't been expecting a real answer. She shrugged, uncomfortable. It was the closest she'd ever come to talking about her childhood. She hadn't even told her sisters what had happened. How one day she'd had friends, and the next she'd been completely, utterly alone.

"It started with a neighborhood boy I grew up with," Mikira said. "At first, he didn't mind me hanging out with him and his friends. He didn't even mind me beating him in races. Until suddenly he did. I started losing on purpose after that."

She thought of Ailene in the kitchen, skin bruised and eyes fierce. Of the way the world would try to control her like it had Mikira. As much as she'd tried, she couldn't stop the way people had looked at her and whispered behind her back. She tried to curb her tongue, to be polite and respectful like they wanted, but it was like bending her bones into a new shape: she couldn't be something she wasn't.

"One day he tried to kiss me. I shoved him into the mud." She flinched at the memory. "I laughed, thinking it a game, but he was furious." The things he'd called her sat engraved in her memory. Bitch. Whore. Worthless girl.

"'You're just like everyone says you are,' he said. 'You just can't keep your mouth shut.' So I threw him into the mud again. After that, they wanted nothing to do with me."

No matter that their mothers were royal magistrates and army sergeants. No matter that their sisters won gold in the city's top races. They could handle strong women, so long as they still acted like they thought a woman should. Mikira's frankness, her physicality—they were too aggressive, too much.

Reid studied the pinecone in his hand as though it might offer the secrets of the universe. "Their loss."

Her gaze snapped to him, but he wouldn't look at her. Surely she'd heard him wrong. That had actually sounded . . . nice. The edges of a smile pulled at her lips, but it quickly faded as she thought of Talyana. She'd stayed. At least at first. Then Rezek had come.

Reid tossed the pinecone again, his expression pinched. "I grew up in a mortuary," he said at last. "I worked there most of my childhood."

"What was that like?"

"People can be cruel when they're in pain." He ran his fingers along the sleeve of one forearm absently, tracing the lines of the tattoos beneath. "They only ever came to us when their world had been torn apart, and when we didn't look at the body of their loved one and break down like them, they hated us for that too. Toss in a pale, spindly kid who looked more like a corpse himself and liked to talk about blood vessels and arteries, and, well . . ." He shrugged.

Mikira could picture his childhood with discomforting ease. The way he must have stood apart, turning instead to study and experiments, solitary things that couldn't reject him. She could see how someone like that would grow thorns.

She'd done the same.

She cast a sidelong glance at him. The sunlight lent his unruly black hair a blue sheen, like the glisten on a raven's feathers. He was still tall and lean, but far from spindly, and he held the pinecone to his chest as though seeking comfort from it.

"That sounds . . . lonely," she said softly.

Reid smiled wistfully. "That's how I first met Damien. His mother had just died, and we handled her burial." His smile faltered, and he slowed to a halt, studying the black lines poking out beneath his sleeve.

"Ari told me what happened with Loic and Atara." Mikira faced him. "She said it sounded like you had a history with him."

"Something like that." Reid tugged his sleeves down, and she didn't press him further.

By the time they saw Atara to the stables, the clouded sky had grown dark with promised rain, and dusk had fallen. As they returned to the manor, Mikira felt oddly lighter, even with Reid griping about the mud on his boots.

"I'm taking a very long bath," he said as Mikira pushed open the sitting room door.

A tiny white shape barreled into her. She caught it, stumbling back, and Reid caught her. They both stared at the wriggling mass of fluff in her arms.

It was a dog.

It turned about so its little snout could reach her face and proceeded to lick her cheek repeatedly.

"What in the—" She caught sight of Ari in one of the armchairs by the fire. Damien sat at the desk, half-buried in house ledgers. He'd been in meetings all day, a steady stream of jockeys, bookies, and district tenants knocking on his door.

"You said your sister wanted one." Ari gestured at the dog. "Enchanted for companionship and protectiveness."

Mikira gaped at her. She had no words. What did you say to someone

who granted your little sister her heart's desire? She hadn't even realized Ari had been paying attention when she said that.

"Thank you," she croaked out at last. "I—thank you."

"Keep it away from Widget." Reid marched past her into the foyer. "Or I'll feed it to Atara."

Mikira clung to the wriggling ball and grinned.

CHAPTER 18

ARIELLE

THAT EVENING AFTER Mikira had left, Ari set the spellbook on
Damien's desk. He looked up from the letter he'd been writing to his
father. He spent hours on them, often rescheduling meetings and turning aside
messages to focus, but when his eyes landed on the spellbook, they widened
with the slightest wisp of curiosity. That she could recognize that thrilled her a
little. She enjoyed the challenge of reading him, though she'd started to suspect
that he'd been letting his mask slip more and more around her.

She'd been studying him most of the night: the sharp slope of his jaw,
tight with concentration. The flare of his slate-gray eyes. With each purposeful stroke of his pen against the page, she remembered the heat of his
gaze when she brought Atara to life. He had never flinched away from her.
Would he if he knew the truth of what she'd done?

No.

She didn't know how she knew it, but she did. And it scared her. Because
perhaps, for once, she was not as alone as she thought.

It was why she was willing to share the book with him. That, and the
fact that the voice had only grown stronger after she'd charmed the dog,
confirming her suspicion that using her magic was making it worse. Her
attempts the last few days to find answers in books had failed, which left
only one person who might be able to help her.

"Do you know what it is?" she asked.

Damien ran a reverent finger along the book's binding. "Shira suspects that it's a book of the old magic."

"The what?"

"You're familiar with the Burning?"

"Generally." Her parents had homeschooled her and Rivkah, and had never spoken much about it. "It was when the Enderlish government commanded the burning of all the texts they saw as profane after the Cataclysm. I always thought it was part of their control of magic."

Damien leaned back in his chair. "It was. After the Heretics' magic made Kinahara uninhabitable, it wasn't just Kinnish magic the Enderlish feared anymore, it was all magic. So the Council of Lords ordered the Burning, destroying centuries of research and knowledge, and instated the registry."

A move that had effectively stripped the Order of Sendia of a large portion of its power. With people's newfound hesitancy around magic, the Order struggled to preach its merits to a frightened flock. Enderlain itself hadn't fared much better. With its army weakened, the Empire broke apart.

"Most of the history of that time was lost during the Burning," Damien continued. "As were, supposedly, the books the Heretics used to gain their power. They were called the Racari, and they were said to have belonged to the four Harbingers. Some stories say the Heretics stole them, others that the Harbingers left them behind when they departed from humanity. Sendism and Kinnism differ quite dramatically on the subject."

It felt strange to know that information herself. After weeks of reading books she'd only ever dreamed of having access to, she knew that while Kinnism believed the Harbingers moved on once they'd taught humanity all they could offer, Sendism preached that humanity drove the Harbingers away with their greed and lust for power, a sin all souls had to atone for when they died.

"Do you think this is one of those books?" She felt foolish asking it, but whatever the spellbook was, it wasn't normal.

It is strength, said the voice.

"Shira thinks so." His gaze dropped to the book. "Would you let me inspect it?"

Her reflex was to refuse. Parting with the book, leaving it in someone else's hands—she shut the thoughts away. They weren't hers, just like the voice that whispered in her ear. The spellbook was doing something to her, and she needed to understand what, preferably without revealing that she was hearing voices.

"You may," she agreed. "But in exchange, I'd like your help furthering my magic."

He smiled, a soft, tentative thing that looked out of place on his cool features. She liked it. "You don't have to bargain with me, Arielle. I'll give you whatever you want."

She looked up at him, and he stared back with an intensity that she'd come to crave. It was like having a rifle trained on you. It made her feel real. Here. Alive.

Damien joined her on the other side of the desk. She tracked every inch of space disappearing between them, swallowed her anticipation when he stopped before her. "I don't know what you intend to do when this is over." His voice was soft, intimate, like a song played only for her. "But you are welcome here as long as you wish to stay."

He offers power, whispered the voice. *He offers strength.*

Ari hadn't thought about what came after the Illinir. Their goal was so grand, their plan so dangerous, that life after it felt impossibly far away. But a license would alter everything. She could open an actual shop, work legal enchantments she could sell honestly, perhaps even control her magic enough to feel comfortable returning home to face her family.

Except she didn't want to stop making golems.

She loved everything about it—the art of sculpting, the power of her magic, the challenge of getting it all just right.

All save the memories it tore free each time.

But she couldn't go on as she had been. Risking herself as an unlicensed enchanter had been worth it when she needed the money to survive, but it was only a matter of time before someone found her out. If she worked here with Damien, though, she'd be safe. More than that, she'd have everything she needed to push the boundaries of her magic, and someone who wanted to explore them with her. She'd already begun to practice identifying enchantments to help Mikira with her knives—what else was she capable of?

A tentative smile spread across her lips as she imagined it. "I'd like that."

Damien shifted, a tension she hadn't noticed before slipping away from him. Had he—did he look *relieved*? He laid a hand atop her own, and she turned her palm to meet his. Relishing the heat of his touch, she laced her fingers with his, closing tight.

"But if I'm staying," she said, "I want to understand what it is I'm getting involved with."

A shrewd smile turned one corner of his lips at the challenge, and she felt his satisfaction like a thrum deep in her belly. It had taken time for her to realize it—that Damien Adair *liked* to be challenged. That when she or Mikira pressed him, no matter how he deflected, he respected them for standing their ground. It was something Ari had once thought herself incapable of, but as she tugged Damien with her to the sitting area and he willingly came, for the first time she wondered if she was capable of more than just standing firm.

Perhaps she could push back.

Settling into one of the armchairs, she released his hand—and didn't miss the way his fingers curled inward as if to capture her touch.

"Tell me why you're so intent on destroying Rezek Kelbra," she said.

"That," he replied, "is a rather long story."

He strode past her to the drink cart, where he poured them both a glass of Adair whiskey. "Let's just say my family hasn't always been what it is today." He picked up the glasses, handing her one as he came back to the sitting area.

Damien took the armchair beside her. "My parents were both immi-
grants who struggled to find work when they arrived in Veradell. By the
time they were expecting Loic, my father had taken a job working the
Kelbras' verillion fields. He worked there for years. When my mother got
sick, my father couldn't afford the treatment, so he went to Eradas Kelbra
for help. He laughed in my father's face and took his job for his impudence."

The callousness of his story shocked her, and yet she could see it with
ease: the cold indifference of Enderlain's elite, the scorn, the disgust. She'd
seen it over and over again in the eyes of her customers.

"I'm sorry," she said softly.

Damien's fingers tightened around his glass. "When my father left, he
stole verillion seeds from the Kelbras. Did you know that verillion can
actually grow anywhere? But it's only when it's planted in certain areas that
it possesses the magic necessary for enchantments."

She frowned. "It's the dirt. The magic is in the soil." Damien crooked
a smile, and she traced the rim of her glass with one finger. "How can no
one know this?"

"Because it's common knowledge that verillion can only grow in certain
areas, and those already belong to someone. There'd be no point in plant-
ing it elsewhere."

And so no one had bothered to try. No one but a desperate man trying
to save the woman he loved.

"And," Damien continued. "Because it requires knowledge of Kinnish
magic, which uses holy dirt in its enchantments. But that's just another
term for verillion-rich land. The Sages theorize they're places where the
Harbingers walked or spent a great deal of time. It's why so many temples
were built in verillion fields in Kinahara."

"What did your father do with his magicless plants?" Ari asked.

Damien lifted his glass of whiskey in a salute. Ari took a sip of hers.
The liquor was rich and oaky, but it changed as it passed over her tongue,
sweetening into notes of vanilla and orange, before sliding down her throat

smooth as honey, leaving behind a smoky aftertaste that made her mouth tingle.

"Oh," she breathed.

"Exactly." Damien sipped his own drink. "My father built an empire on Adair whiskey. Soon he was buying the verillion fields of other lords, coalescing what became the second largest verillion holding in Veradell, and eventually ousting one of the old lesser noble houses not long after King Zuerlin took the throne from the Raniers."

He paused, eyes dropping to a spot on the table. "But he couldn't save my mother."

There was something more to the story than he was telling her. Something that made his eyes glaze over as if he'd receded into some dark, depthless place. But she didn't press him, even as the curiosity burned.

"She was a scholar of the old Kinnish magic. It's from her that I got my interest." He ran his fingers along the Arkala nestled in one of the stacks of books. "There is a tenet in Kinnism about making the world a better place. The Arkala will tell you that's why the Harbingers shared their magic with us, why Skylis walked among the people in human form and Lyzairin established the first Kinnish academies. I've never been the religious sort, but that aspect has always called to me. My mother always talked about it, and it's what I'm trying to accomplish."

He met her gaze. "My business with the Kelbras is personal, but it's not my only focus. I intend to see that this city changes. That it becomes more than the shadow that has consumed it."

"And then?" Ari asked, though she nearly didn't. There'd been something almost reverent about the way he spoke. Something that left her not only believing him but believing *in* him. That he could truly fix this place and stop what had happened to his family from happening to any others.

Damien was resolute as he said, "Then I change everything."

⋅✦ PART 3 ✦⋅

In time, humanity began to clamor for the divine.
They sought power beyond their station
and would not rest when they were denied.
Sensing darkness in their hearts, the Harbingers left,
and took their secrets with them.

CHAPTER 19

MIKIRA

MIKIRA STARED AT her reflection in the mirror and saw another person.

The dress Damien had sent her for the ball belonged to a different girl. Someone who was always looking down at the world instead of reaching up. The bodice clung to her chest in a waterfall of sapphire silk and silver gossamer, emanating from a single strap on her left shoulder, wrapping down around her waist, and rushing toward the ground in a seamless flow.

It was only Ailene's face over her shoulder that grounded the image, her thin fingers drawing the last of Mikira's red hair into the braided crown she'd been working on for the last few minutes.

"You look like a princess!" she exclaimed when she stepped back. Nelda nodded her agreement from where she was curled up on her bed with Wolf, the golem dog, and a small book she'd had in hand the last few days.

Mikira certainly didn't feel like a princess, but she smiled for her sisters' benefit. They didn't need to know that she felt like a sheep walking into a lion's den. Her job tonight was to be bold, confident, intimidating, and to do it all with a smile for Veradell's elite, bolstering their plan to make her untouchable.

But she wasn't a princess; she was a girl playing dress-up in a gown worth more than everything her family had left.

Someone knocked downstairs, likely the driver of the enchanted coach Damien had sent. He'd been doing that more often, so that she needn't ride Iri across town. She missed being around the stallion, though, her time almost entirely absorbed by Atara now.

"I'll get it!" Ailene darted from the room.

In the resulting silence, Mikira's nerves bundled into her chest. She caught Nelda watching her in the mirror, her dark eyes full of a very simple message: *Don't do anything stupid.* Sometimes Mikira wondered which one of them was actually the oldest. Her sister had taken one look at her injured arm the night of the race and become her personal medic in the days since, though Reid had removed the stitches yesterday.

Ailene burst back into the room. "He looks gorgeous, Kira!" she whispered excitedly.

Mikira frowned. She didn't know Damien's household staff very well, but she didn't know who among them Ailene would refer to as gorgeous.

Ailene ushered her to the door. "He's waiting!"

Sighing, Mikira slipped past her sister into the hallway, one hand holding up the folds of her skirt. As she descended the second flight, the wall curved away to reveal a man standing just inside the door.

She froze. "Reid?"

He turned, frost-blue eyes bright against the set of his dark lashes. Gone was his normal casual attire, replaced instead by a black silk waistcoat over a crisp black shirt, his jacket tight through the shoulders and tapering to his waist. Someone—likely Ari—had even gotten ahold of his hair, slicking back the strands that usually hung over his forehead. A few had still escaped and curled slightly against his pale skin.

He looked completely different. Not just because of the suit and the hair, but because for once, he wasn't scowling. She might even say he was staring.

A giggle reminded her that Ailene was lurking, and she quickly regained her composure, descending the steps. "Did Damien send you to keep an eye on me?"

He cleared his throat. "Something like that. Are you ready? We're going to be late."

"Aren't you supposed to bring flowers or something?" Ailene called from where she clung to the banister.

Reid blinked, and for a moment he looked so innocently perplexed, she almost smiled. "Flowers," he repeated.

"For your date. People usually bring flowers."

"This isn't—I'm not—" Reid looked to Mikira for help, but she merely grinned.

"Yes, Reid, dear. Where are my flowers?" she asked silkily.

Reid took one look at her and about-faced, marching back outside. Mikira winked at Ailene before hurrying after him. As they climbed into the coach, the door swung shut to the sound of Ailene yelling, "Bring her home before midnight!"

VANADAHL MANOR WAS even more beautiful than the Zalaires'.

Intricately carved pale rose stone encompassed stretches of enchanted glass. White painted birds fluttered across the panes, perching on the ruby framework before swooping low to touch wingtips to a rippling lake. Enchanted violins played a gentle rhythm against the backdrop of laughter and the clink of glass.

The beauty of it at once entranced and infuriated Mikira. Like the races themselves, the balls were an opportunity for the greater houses to display their wealth and enchanters' skills, never mind that people like her couldn't afford the verillion to refresh the most basic enchantments—lights, cold-boxes, heated water. But Goddess forbid the Vanadahls' windows didn't dance.

The moment she and Reid entered the ballroom, that anger fled in place of nerves. Eyes roamed over her, judging, evaluating, finding her wanting. Snippets of whispered conversation drifted past as they walked in, mentions of destitution, of desperation. She was a glass figurine in a room full of barbed words and piercing stares. Each one left behind a new crack.

She longed for a little of Ari's grace, her composure. The enchanter had a sensuality to her that Mikira could never mimic, a femininity that she'd never felt comfortable inhabiting. Where Ari was long, graceful lines, Mikira was coiled fists and scraped knuckles. She was a mouthful of glass, not a whispered sigh between soft lips.

Mikira wished she were here.

The crowd shifted, and she spotted Damien among a small group. He beckoned them over, and Mikira's heart rose into her throat. She wanted to disappear, to flee back to the coach.

"Mikira?" Reid's voice was soft, a dam in her dizzying spiral. The look he gave her was knowing, and she straightened beneath it.

Make them a shield.

She'd already ruined one plan; she couldn't jeopardize another. The fate of the race, of her family and Ari's future, relied on her holding herself together. She wouldn't let these people break her apart.

She lifted her head as they arrived.

Damien gestured at her with one black-gloved hand. "Gentlemen, may I present Miss Mikira Rusel, daughter of Keirian Rusel."

Mikira shook each of their hands.

"I was quite impressed by your last leg of the race, Miss Rusel," said a dark-skinned younger gentleman with warm brown eyes and the trace of a melodic Yaroyan accent. "You rode remarkably well."

"My father taught me everything he knew," she replied, happy to use the advantage Damien had lent her.

An older, golden-skinned man with a sapphire-blue waistcoat and flushed complexion gave her an evaluating look. "It's great to have a Rusel at the races again. I look forward to seeing what you do next."

They discussed the race a little while before Damien excused them from the group and led her away. She looked around for Reid, but he'd disappeared.

"That wasn't so terrible, was it?" Damien asked lightly.

Mikira snorted. "The night's still early. How long do we have to stay here?"

"Not long." Damien readjusted the cuff of his black jacket. Unlike the bulk of Veradell's elite, his outfit was as austere as he was: a dark embroidered jacket over a black silk waistcoat and crimson tie. "I'll introduce you to a few people, make sure you're well seen, then leave you for a bit to give Rezek a window to approach you. Then we'll go."

She shivered at the thought of being alone with Rezek again, though she had proposed the meeting to pass him information herself.

Damien offered her his arm, and she allowed him to escort her through the thrumming crowd. People swept out of their way in a sea of bobbing heads and swift curtsies. Some greeted Damien by name, others averted their eyes, but it was clear that everyone they passed knew who he was.

What must it be like to wield that kind of power? She'd be lying if she said she didn't envy it. Walking at his side, watching the crowd part before her—it felt the same as the moment after she won a race in the tunnels, when everyone chanted her name.

If she won the Illinir, this would never stop.

It was an aspect of their success she hadn't considered before. Her family would be free of the Kelbras, and she would become more legendary a rider than even her father.

History would never forget the Rusel name.

"That," Damien said in a low voice, "is not the smile of a ranch girl in leagues over her head."

Mikira touched a finger to her lips. She hadn't even realized she'd been smiling. "Isn't that what you wanted?"

"Indeed. I just didn't expect it to come so naturally."

Something about his words disquieted her, but then he was sweeping her into a small group of nobles who bowed and preened like jeweled peacocks. Mikira forced her expression into neutrality and offered her hand to each one. She kept her head high, interjected herself into the conversation, spoke of her family's renowned lines and her intentions to win the Illinir, and they loved every moment of it.

The same performance carried her through the next conversation, and the next, but as the evening waned, she began to lag. By the time Damien promised the next group would be their last, she was exhausted.

"I hear the Enderlish forces have been forced to retreat in Celair," said a pale man in a ruby-encrusted waistcoat. He had a strong Ranoen accent, likely one of the many merchants visiting in hopes of striking a trade deal with Enderlain's wealthy houses. "The Eternal War won't last much longer, mark my word."

The Enderlish woman at his side rolled her eyes. "Please, like you know anything of military tactics. Our forces have been pushed back that far before, and we've rebounded every time. More importantly, the Council of Lords won't let the endeavor fail. High Lord Vanadahl was just saying so himself."

Mikira swallowed back her agreement. The more verillion Enderlain had, the more they could continue relying on magic instead of foreign technology, and the more valuable House Vanadahl's stakes in the gem industry became. Like Houses Dramara and Kelbra, the continuation of the Eternal War meant the deepening of their pockets, no matter the impact on the people they were meant to serve.

The woman's partner laughed. "Oh, and we're to believe you an expert on such matters, then?" he teased, making her blush and look away.

"I don't really care how far back we're pressed so long as the army keeps buying canned goods by the truckload," said a third Enderlish man with a drooping mustache. "My factories can't keep up with the demand it's so high, and I'm selling everything at a premium." He released a deep-bellied laugh that curled Mikira's hands into fists.

"You won't be laughing when Enderlain loses," the Ranoen man said. "If Izir is truly backing Celair, you haven't the numbers to win."

"Of course they are," the woman cut in. "They don't want to risk that they're next, and Celair's freedom means a buffer between our countries."

The mustached man waived a dismissive hand. "So we conscript a few more soldiers."

Something snapped in Mikira. "It's that simple to you, is it?"

"Excuse me?" asked the mustache.

"Is this all a business venture to you?" she demanded, dismissing Damien's cautionary look.

The man smiled patronizingly. "My dear, everything is a business venture. If there's money to be made, this nose'll find it." He tapped a finger to his small nose.

The Ranoen man clapped him on the shoulder. "You miss her point, Mr. Barta. I think you've upset the girl."

"Ah, yes, the thought of violence can do that to some," Mr. Barta agreed. "Calm down, my dear, it's nothing to worry your pretty little head over." He laid a hand on Mikira's back, his fingers uncomfortably warm.

She seized his wrist, twisting. He released a small noise of surprised pain. "How dare you talk about the war like that? It's not your family fighting and dying. You think you can just take our loved ones and feed them to the war like cannon fodder?"

"Mikira," Damien warned.

For an instant, Mikira met the gaze of the woman across from her, and she stared back with the intensity of a flightless bird trapped in a cage. Mikira's nails dug into Mr. Barta's jacket. Then she thrust his hand back at him. "Never touch me again."

He clasped his hand to his chest, face red. "Lord Adair, get your jockey under control. She forgets her place."

Damien's gaze fell on him like a blade. "And what place is that, Mr. Barta? As one of Enderlain's foremost enchanted horse breeders? As the sponsored Illinir racer of House Adair? Or as a woman whose worth outweighs your own, no matter how much blood money you make?"

Mr. Barta gaped at him, but Mikira's satisfaction couldn't outweigh her anger. Damien excused them and led her away to the nearest refreshment table. "I'll leave you to wait for Rezek here," he said. "I have one last matter to attend to and then we can go."

Mikira nodded absently as he departed, her fingers fumbling for the note she'd tucked into her pocket. It was a list of betting patterns at the Adairs' most lucrative track. Not the sort of thing that might be immediately damning to someone like Damien, whose connections with the Anthir would keep him safe from any claims of rigged races, but hopefully enough to buy her more time from Rezek.

She spotted him cutting toward her through the crowd and restrained the reflex to go the opposite way. He snatched up the note she'd left on the refreshment table, pausing alongside her. "This had best be something useful. My patience grows thin."

"It's what I could get," she replied.

Rezek's gaze slid the length of her dress, making her uneasy in a way no one else could. There was nothing carnal about his stare, only the cool, detached evaluation of a hunter before his prey. Then he flipped the paper open, read its contents, and crumpled it into a ball.

"This is worthless." He lit the edge on fire with a nearby candle and left the remnants to smolder on the marble table.

Mikira's heart stuttered. "I have to be careful. If Damien realizes what I'm doing, you'll lose your opportunity to take him down."

"Perhaps I didn't make myself clear enough." Rezek curved toward her. "I want something I can destroy him with."

"I don't—"

"You do." Rezek's gaze flicked to the side, where she could just make out the edge of Damien's profile as he conversed with someone. "I know him. No matter how much he pretends to cut himself off, he can't help caring. Which means he's let his guard down around you, and you know more than you think."

He straightened. "Find something better, Miss Rusel, or your father will face the consequences."

"Wait!" Mikira called as Rezek started to merge back into the crowd. He turned back expectantly, and she hesitated. Damien would never give her anything damning enough to satisfy Rezek, and he'd made it clear her next chance was her last. She had to come up with something.

"His ring," she said, grasping for anything she could. "It was missing for a while."

It felt inconsequential when she said it, but the words had an odd effect on Rezek. "So it is a fake," he mused. "He wasn't lying to me after all."

"Who?"

Rezek waved a hand. "No one. Now, that wasn't so hard, was it? Consider our bargain complete." Then he was gone, swallowed up by the crowd, and leaving Mikira off-kilter as his words slowly settled.

Damien's ring was a fake.

It seemed innocuous. So Damien had lost his ring and made a replica in the meantime. It made sense. If people knew an Adair signet ring was floating about, they'd be looking to use it for themselves. But why not just get another one commissioned?

Unless he didn't want anyone to know he'd lost it.

She had no idea why that mattered, but she did know that Damien Adair did nothing without a carefully considered reason. Rezek would use this against him somehow, and it would be her fault.

She buried her face in her hands. "What have I done?"

She didn't know when she'd begun to care about Damien, but she did, the same as she did Ari and . . . and Reid. Because she did care for Reid. More than she wanted to admit. And betraying his best friend, betraying *her friend*, was wrong. But leaving her father to suffer at Rezek's hands was impossible, and she'd had to do *something*.

"Well, aren't you friends with interesting people," said a voice at her ear. She spun, coming face-to-face with the girl from the tunnel race, her Skylis half mask fitted firmly in place.

She wore an ice-blue dress suit that clung to her lean, muscular frame. A sleeveless, jacket-like bodice tapered over a cobalt pair of pants, cinched at the waist with a gold rope. Her hair fell around her deep bronze shoulders in warm waves, several intricate braids running back from the crown of her head, and a dusting of gold powder around her eyes sparkled in the enchanted light.

"You," Mikira breathed.

The girl smirked. "Me."

"Who are you?"

A strange look flickered across what she could see of the girl's face. Then the smile was back, and she dropped into a melodramatic bow.

"Quinn Falar, Illinir jockey of House Ruthar."

"I've never heard of you." Mikira followed the races closely, knew everyone there was to know. She hadn't even seen Quinn in the tunnels before that night, and Jenest was militant about who she allowed in.

Quinn straightened. "You just did. And now that we're acquainted, I believe the next dance is about to start."

"What?"

But Quinn had already seized her hand, dragging her through the crowd and onto the dance floor.

"What the hells are you doing?" she demanded as Quinn lifted her hand, placing the other on her hip. They were standing incredibly close together.

Quinn grinned. "Leading."

The music swelled, and the dance ignited. Quinn knew her steps well.

Mikira was a passable dancer, but Quinn moved as if the music carried her every step. Mikira allowed herself to be drawn along with her even as part of her mind screamed that this was absurd. She didn't know this girl, and the unease in her stomach warned that something was wrong.

The dance quickened, and Mikira became very aware of her fingers clasped in Quinn's, of the girl's hand at her waist. She looked up and nearly started to find Quinn watching her intently. There was something disquieting about her hazel eyes.

"What do you want from me?" she demanded as they turned about the room.

"I thought that was rather obvious." Quinn glanced at their clasped hands.

Mikira's frustration redoubled. "I've had enough of veiled meanings for one night. Either answer my question, or I'm done with this dance."

"There's that fire." Quinn grinned and guided Mikira through a turn. When they came back together, she added, "Very well, since you're intent on being so boringly direct, I want an alliance."

Mikira stiffened. "Did Damien send you?"

Quinn rolled her eyes. "No one sends me anywhere, least of all a spoiled noble brat."

"He's not like that."

"And a desert lizard doesn't spew magma," Quinn said sardonically. "He's dangerous, violent, and self-obsessed. Just ask Fen and Cardix Ridoux."

"Who?"

The girl watched her carefully, and Mikira couldn't shake the feeling that'd been some sort of test.

"Are you so enamored by your new sponsor that you've forgotten who he is?" she asked. "I'd have thought you wanted nothing to do with Veradell's elite."

Mikira's hand tightened on Quinn's. "You don't know anything about me."

The other girl started to respond, then stopped, her lips curving into a wry smile. "Of course not. Forgive me." She pulled back to twirl Mikira before drawing her close again as the music faded and the dance slowed to an end.

"So what do you say?" Quinn pressed. "Partners?"

Mikira nearly laughed. "You haven't given me a single reason to trust you. You won't even take off your mask. Besides, I have no interest in an alliance."

She pulled away, but Quinn grabbed her wrist. "Mikira—" she began, but then her gaze snagged on something over Mikira's shoulder, and she let out a low curse. Quinn released her hand and ducked into the crowd.

Mikira watched her go, feeling like she'd missed something.

"Were you talking to someone?" Reid asked as he joined her.

"No one important. Where have you been the entire night?"

"House business," he replied. "Usually Damien's job, but since you hogged him all night, I had to deal with it. Are you ready to leave?"

Reid looked nearly as haggard as she felt. She supposed balls full of snobbish nobility and socializing weren't his cup of tea either. Still, something about what he'd said felt off. He'd said it so quickly, hadn't met her eye.

He was keeping something from her.

CHAPTER 20

MIKIRA

THE DAY OF the second race arrived in a blur of nerves and anticipation. Mikira had barely sat still long enough for Ari to braid her
hair before they departed, and she'd already worried the edges of it free. It
wasn't just the race eating away at her, but the knowledge that she may have
handed Rezek the very thing he needed to destroy Damien.

It'd been days since the ball, and nothing had come of Rezek knowing
the truth, but a pit still sat in her stomach. He would not have let her out
of the bargain if the ring meant nothing, but it seemed benign, and all she
could think about was what would happen if Damien learned what she'd
done.

He would not forgive her.

Her thoughts hounded her as Atara jostled for position at the starting
line, which rested at the crest of the sloping Ashfield Street. Tall, sooty
buildings knocked shoulders along the wide boulevard, casting long shadows in the late afternoon sun.

A section of the Pendron District had been cordoned off to form a
square-shaped course laden with behavior enchantments. Unlike the first
race, which pitted the environment against them, this one would turn them
against themselves, something that unsettled Mikira far more than any
living fire or spiked pit.

The scents of sweet dough and frying meat only made her nervous stomach twist tighter. She tried to ignore the press of eyes, the curious whispers, the shouts of excited children so at odds with the waiting danger. She could only hope their plan worked. If her reputation had spread at the ball and the other racers focused on each other, she could fly right by them all.

A beautiful bay mare stepped up beside her, its rider clad in a deep forest green and white racing shirt, the colors of House Ruthar.

"This ought to be fun." Quinn's Rach mask glinted in the sunlight. "I always love having my own worst fears and most unruly emotions turned against me, don't you?"

Mikira groaned. "What part of 'I don't want to ally with you' didn't you understand?"

"The part where you clearly haven't thought it through. Who wouldn't want a face like this on their side?" She set her chin against the back of her hand and fluttered her eyelashes.

A flush warmed Mikira's cheeks, completely ruining several acerbic retorts. It was just as well. She could deny it all she wanted, but even with the half mask, Mikira could tell Quinn was gorgeous, from the sheen of her long braid to the warmth of her golden-brown skin. Even that little freckle just above her lip—*Nooo no no no!* Mikira reeled back to herself, her cheeks flaring hotter.

She was saved from Quinn's laughter—a sound, she couldn't help noticing, that was like a particularly sonorous bell—by the booming voice of the announcer as she welcomed the crowd. By the time she finished her speech about the rules and Princess Eshlin had accepted the Sendian cleric's blessing upon the race, Mikira's nerves had redoubled.

She'd been too nervous to notice the royal viewing platform last time, but now she watched the princess return to her brother's side, his attention captured by the beautiful woman on his arm while Princess Eshlin surveyed the riders like troops lined up for the kill. Fitting, since she'd served briefly in the Eternal War herself, a calculated show of the royal family's dedication to the cause.

Mikira ran a hand along Atara's neck, suddenly wishing it was Iri with her. Though her and Atara's relationship had grown over the last week, it was Iri she knew like her own heart, Iri who settled her nerves and made her feel grounded when the world was spinning out of her control.

Seeming to sense her doubt, Atara's head curled back, and she fixed one dark, knowing eye on Mikira, as if to ask, *Do you trust me?*

"I trust you," she said softly, and meant it.

"To the starting line!" roared the announcer, the last call for riders. The thick scent of horses and sweat turned suffocating as the competitors boxed them in from either side, pressing her and Quinn closer. Atara snapped at the too-close bodies, compelling people to shift away.

Mikira forced herself to breathe, to focus on the details: Arabella Wakelin had her silver stallion at the front of the pack. The last race was the first she'd ever lost, and she'd be looking to prove herself. Mikira would have to stay away from her. Dezaena Fyas sat beside her, tying off their dark curls in a thick braid. They were a still spot in a sea of turbulence, easily ignoring the antagonizing grins Alren Zalaire was flashing their way.

She couldn't find Gren.

"For Enderlain!" The noise of the crowd faded to a dull roar as she searched the riders. Gren wasn't at her back, and there were too many competitors to check. "For the Harbingers!"

Focus, she told herself. She couldn't let him get under her skin.

"For Sendia!" The crowd's roar drowned out the announcer's call as the starting bell rang.

The horses surged down the sloping street, and Mikira instantly pulled Atara to the side, slowing. She didn't want to be anywhere near another racer sooner than necessary, lest Atara's aggression expose them.

The bulk of the competitors reached the bottom of the slope, where arrows indicated three different paths. Most of the racers went straight to avoid the loss of speed around the turns. Some turned, probably assuming the straightaway was filled with the most difficult enchantments.

When another large group veered right just before Mikira arrived, she sent Atara left.

The road narrowed to an alley, then cut right. Mikira cursed, her reflex to slow Atara, but their hours of riding together paid off as she remembered the horse's unnatural agility. Atara took the corner expertly—just in time to see Arabella Wakelin disappear into crimson smoke ahead.

Mikira nearly jerked the reins back but forced herself to think. The entire alley was filled with smoke. There was no getting around it. She could turn around—Atara could make up the time lost to backtracking—but she had a feeling they'd find something similar down each path.

"All right," she breathed. "Let's see what they've got."

Atara raced into the smoke. Mikira held her breath and counted. She'd just passed half a minute when her lungs began to burn. With no end to the smoke in sight, she gave in, swallowing a deep lungful of it. It stung like normal smoke, making her cough. Then they broke into open air, a red tinge clinging to her clothes.

The alley bent ahead, turning them back toward the central road. As they emerged onto the main thoroughfare, a big bay horse came barreling perpendicular to them. Mikira managed to turn Atara up the road at the last second, but her leg still slammed into the other rider's as their horses paralleled.

The woman blinked dazedly at her. She looked down at the reins in her hands, then at her horse as though she had no idea where it'd come from. Both were stained with blue powder.

Atara snapped at her horse, and it shied, dropping into a loping trot. Mikira pulled Atara away before she could attack again, but thankfully, the woman didn't seem to notice. The last thing Mikira saw before the road curved was the horse slowing to a stop and the woman just . . . sitting there.

"What in the hells?" Her hands tightened about the reins. "I don't like this."

Atara tossed her head in frustrated agreement.

As they surged down the straightaway, Mikira caught sight of the bulk of the pack nearly fifty yards ahead in an open square. Then the strangest things began to happen. One man turned his horse with a yelp and galloped past her in the opposite direction, fleeing the race. Another's horse walked in drooping circles, the rider seemingly unaware. Arabella Wakelin and Alren Zalaire were screaming at each other.

Fools, she thought. *What's the matter with them?*

Atara navigated the melee, whinnying harshly at anything that stumbled too close. Mikira searched faces for Quinn's mask, then cursed herself for doing so. What did she care about the girl? She could die in the damned race for all it mattered.

Mikira frowned. Something felt wrong about that thought.

A pouch flew past her head, striking a wall and spilling blue powder.

Her frustration flared as a shout went up and the road emptied into an open square full of dangling pouches of different colors. Blue and red, yellow and white, orange and purple, they hung from wires strung across the square like festival lights. Riders were ripping them free and flinging them at other racers. They exploded in powders of the same color, their effects immediate.

The yellow powder sent the riders or their horses into a fearful frenzy. The blue glazed their eyes with confusion.

"The powders are enchanted," Mikira said with slow realization. "The smoke too."

Mikira swiped a finger through the red powder on her skin. As if it'd simply been waiting for her to recognize it, the simmering frustration bloomed into all-out fury. She wanted nothing more in that moment than to punch something and to keep on punching until her knuckles were bloody and raw even as she understood: she'd been enchanted into anger.

Movement at her side made her duck, and she narrowly avoided a yellow bag that slammed into a man behind her. She thought about seizing one of the pouches, but the square was quickly turning to mass chaos. Where the red pouches struck, anger rose like thorns, and where the fear pouches exploded, horses became unpredictable, lashing out with sharp hooves and bolting wildly. Stopping to fight would only slow her down. All that mattered was getting to the finish line.

She urged Atara toward the road directly ahead of them, and they tore into a wide corner just as something flashed beside Mikira. Atara tried to dodge, but the thing still crashed into her, knocking Mikira from her saddle. She hit the ground hard, the air bursting from her lungs in a pained gasp. Some distant thought warned her she was hurt, but it paled in comparison to the all-consuming rage that swallowed her.

She leapt to her feet with a scream, knives in her hands. Atara had already doubled back to her side, tossing her head wildly.

Two horses blocked their path, two more at their back. One of the riders held the baton that had knocked her from the saddle.

"Back off," she snarled.

One of the men grinned down at her. His pale skin was free of powder, as was the brown-skinned woman next to him. A hot wire of fury wound its way through her. This had been planned. Whoever these people were, they had skipped the first enchantment, and she had no doubt it was Rezek's doing. Just because he let her back into the race didn't mean he wouldn't interfere.

She tightened her grip on her knives. No matter. If she had to cut her way through them, she would.

The man kicked his horse toward her and brandished low with a knife. She leapt aside, slashing back with her blade to catch him in the leg. His snarl thrilled the enchanted anger in her veins. Another man made a move for Atara, but Mikira put herself between them, the flash of her blade driving the advancing horse back.

Atara moved with her, and Mikira sheathed her blades, swinging back up into her saddle as the woman struck down at her with a dagger. Atara danced away, then lashed out with a hoof that caught the woman's horse in the knee. The horse screamed and buckled to its forelegs, opening a gap in the street.

She should have ridden through it. Some part of her knew that, but it was drowned by the fury, the frustration, the endless, endless anger. These people worked for Rezek. Rezek had ruined her life. Rezek had driven her into this race, into working with Damien, into cheating and lying and keeping secrets from her sisters. Because of him, she had to sacrifice what was right for what was necessary. To make choices she never would have otherwise and carry the weight of them all on her own.

A baton slammed into Atara's shoulder.

The mare took the blow with unnatural strength and snapped at the attacker's leg. The man screamed, jerking his horse back and tearing flesh free. Blood spattered Atara's snout, dripping stark against the pale stone.

The sight pulled at something, a memory.

Not again. Panic began to writhe beneath the anger, a voice yelling at Mikira to run before it was too late. If she let Atara lose herself to the bloodlust, to the anger infecting them both, they would never win, and who knew what assumptions people would make, what would get traced back to Ari. She knew that she had to turn Atara and go, but she knew it like a childhood memory—it kept slipping away from her, leaving nothing but the desire to run her knives through the other riders.

It's over, she thought.

A whistle cut the air, and a bay horse galloped toward them, the rider on its back clutching a blue pouch. Quinn grinned at her a second before she let the pouch fly. It slammed into the face of the fourth rider, exploding with blue powder. His eyes glazed over.

Quinn reeled in her horse, releasing a yellow pouch at the man whose leg Mikira had cut. He yelped, shoving the powder away, but the contact with his skin was all it took. Already his breathing quickened, his pupils dilating. His horse skittered nervously, then bolted when Quinn let out a loud whoop.

The woman whose horse had crumpled mounted up behind the one Atara had bitten. Quinn held up another blue bag. It was all the threat they needed to flee.

Quinn watched them go with a grin, tossing the bag up and down. "I have to say, this one's turning out to be pretty fun."

"How did you escape the enchantment?" Mikira demanded, the words harsher than she meant. Or than she thought she meant. She couldn't tell anymore.

"I didn't."

Mikira peered closer, and sure enough Quinn's clothes had a bluish tint to them.

"The enchantments are just starting to wear off." She glanced over her shoulder at the square, where the fighting and chaos had ebbed. "Which means we should probably get going."

Mikira wheeled Atara around to face her, and Quinn's eyes widened. Blood flecked the horse's mouth and Mikira's face, and the fury pumping through her felt palpable. She could only imagine how they looked.

"I'm getting tired of you interfering." She angled her blade at Quinn. "If you won't leave me alone, I'm going to make you."

"This is the enchantment talking, Mikira," Quinn said uneasily.

Some part of her knew Quinn was right, but that part was lost beneath magic and years of pent-up fury.

"Stop talking like you know me!" She brandished her knife.

A pouch struck her in the face. White powder exploded, covering her skin and Atara's coat like a shock of cold water. Just like that, the anger was gone, leaving behind a strange sort of hollowness. Her shoulders slumped as her energy drained, and she blinked down at the chalky substance, rubbing it between her fingers.

"A calming enchantment to cancel out the anger," Quinn explained.

That's what the other bags' colors had been for; countercharms to undo the enchantments. And if she and Quinn had found them, then others would have too.

"We need to go." Mikira turned Atara about.

"A thank-you would have been nice," Quinn replied lightly. "But for now, I'll just be satisfied that you said 'we.'"

Mikira swallowed a bitter laugh, the undercurrents of the enchantment still buzzing beneath her skin in an unwelcome reminder of what she'd nearly done. She couldn't afford to think about it, though, not now.

So she put her head down and raced.

CHAPTER 21

MIKIRA

MIKIRA AND QUINN crossed the finish line near the front of the pack, joining a bundle of racers dusted in different colored powders. Quinn had a slice across her forearm, and Mikira could already feel the bruises blooming on her side from the fall. Thankfully, her arm wound had healed enough not to reopen. Medics rushed forward to tend to them and their horses, but oddly, the eyes of the crowd weren't focused on them.

Whispered rumors flew across the concourse. Mikira caught only pieces of it as she returned to the saddling area and dismounted.

". . . an attack on the prince."

"Thank the Goddess he escaped."

"It's the rebels, I'm sure of it."

Atara lipped at her sleeve, asking for an apple, and Mikira laid a distracted hand on her head. Had a rebel really tried to attack Prince Darius? Princess Eshlin had been on that viewing platform too—why go for one royal sibling and not the other? Granted, Eshlin didn't have the womanizing, cruel reputation that her brother did, but she was still a royal.

Atara snorted warm air into her face.

"All right, all right." She undid the girth and removed the saddle, setting them aside along with the bridle. The horse had made it quite clear that while she'd tolerate them for the duration of rides, that was where her patience ended.

Atara's midnight coat gleamed red with dust, but the enchantment had been weak and short-lived, making it harmless now. Still, they'd both nearly lost control back there.

Did lose control, she corrected herself. The charm had spoken to something in each of them, a hidden seed of fury that took only a drop of anger to sprout. Mikira had come undone in a way she'd never allowed herself before. Had let her anger fuel her first and foremost. It had been terrifying, but it had also been freeing.

Mikira leaned her head against Atara's. "No one else has ever seen me like that," she murmured. "I'm not sure I ever want them to."

The horse pressed comfortingly against her, and Mikira closed her eyes. She could never be that person in front of Ailene or Nelda, never let herself falter. She didn't have the luxury of a moment's weakness. She was the one who had to stay strong, who always had to do the right thing. She was holding herself together with nothing more than fury and sheer determination.

All she wanted was to break.

"I don't know what was more exciting, the race or the attempt on the prince's life." Quinn's voice pulled her back to the present. The girl brought her bay to a halt and dismounted.

Mikira nervously scanned the area. "Say that a little louder, will you?"

Quinn lifted an eyebrow. "What? They're not even meant to be ruling. They usurped the throne from the last Ranier king's son."

Mikira had heard rumors of the lost illegitimate prince, supposedly born to the king's mistress, but it was the sort of thing one only whispered about in close quarters. It toed the line of treason.

"Do you disagree?" Quinn asked. "Don't tell me you of all people actually care about Prince Darius?"

"What's that supposed to mean?" Mikira secured a brush from a bucket.

For once, Quinn seemed uncertain. "Nothing. I just meant the royals prop up the noble houses, most of all their cousins. The prince treats Rezek like a favored rabid dog he refuses to leash, and it's common knowledge your family has had their share of trouble with him. You're not the only ones."

"That doesn't mean I want the prince dead." Mikira started brushing Atara's coat, trying not to think about the veracity of her own words.

"But you wouldn't mind if Rezek was." Quinn said it so quietly, Mikira almost didn't hear. She hated Rezek. She could deny that with her dying breath, and no one would believe it. But did she want him dead?

Some innate part of her recoiled at that. For all she railed and resisted, for all her anger and her aggression got the best of her, Mikira hated violence. She hated blood and death and pain. She hated being the one to cause it, even when it was necessary.

Doing harm to do good is a false promise, her father had told her. *It's never all that it seems.*

She turned around and jolted to a stop. Quinn stood just behind her.

"Tell me the truth, Mikira." This close Mikira could smell horses and spiced verillion from the powder, and beneath that, something floral and familiar. "Do you want him dead?"

Mikira's lips parted. Her father would have said no. She wanted to say no. But after all Rezek had done: to Lochlyn, to her father, to her, forcing her into this bloodbath of a race, into putting her ranch at stake and spying on and betraying Damien, it felt like a lie.

"We shouldn't be talking about this here," she muttered at last. "I don't know why you even care."

Quinn's long fingers skimmed across Mikira's hip as she slid a card into her belt and said quietly, "Find me tonight, then. I'll show you why."

Mikira's eyes tracked her hand all the way back. Her sleeve had been pushed up from a medic attending to her wound, and just below the bandage, the edges of a jagged mess of scar tissue poked out. Quinn slid her sleeve down to her wrist and returned to her horse, taking all the heat and presence of her body with her.

"Miss Rusel?"

Mikira steeled herself, already on edge and uninterested in adding anything more to it. But it was only a small group of teenage girls, their blouses neatly stitched with gold thread and tucked into ankle-length brocade skirts. Each one worth more than anything Mikira owned, and yet they were staring at her as if *she* were the treasure.

The oldest, a girl with tawny skin and intricately braided hair, gave her a tentative smile and asked, "Can we, um, meet Atara?" Her gaze flicked to the horse.

It took Mikira a moment to understand what was happening. To connect the gleam in their wide eyes with the way people had looked at her in the tunnels, like she was something more than herself.

"Yes," she said automatically, and stepped back as the girls flooded Atara with a series of giggles and soft coos. The horse ate up their attention, letting them pat her and feed her slices of green apples. It was all Mikira could do just to watch, a shift in understanding slowly sinking in.

Then one of the girls gasped, and all three scurried away. She whirled to find Damien approaching, a bundle of white cloth pressed to his bleeding forearm and a roll of bandages in hand.

"Hells! What did you do?" Mikira took the bandage from Damien, which he was all but fumbling. He frowned at her but didn't stop her as she snatched up a clean towel and wiped the blood away.

"I got between a fool and the prince," he replied as she wrapped the bandage neatly about his arm. Mikira nearly said that sounded like three fools to her, but she bit back the words and finished tying off the bandage. She'd heard someone say that a house lord had stopped the attack—somehow, she wasn't surprised to find it was Damien.

Damien inspected the bandage. "Reid might actually be impressed."

She barked a laugh and picked up another brush. "Before or after it rains gold?"

His measured gaze cut to her. "That might not be so impossible, actually. I've been discussing Rusel enchants with the prince after our encounter. He was under the impression your lines were all but decimated, but I told him you still have one left descended from your father's stallion, Nightflyer."

Damien couldn't be implying what she thought he was. "Starling," she whispered. "A mare."

"Good." He slid his sleeve down over his injured arm. "I'll coordinate the remainder of the details, but you can expect Prince Darius's stable master the day after the next ball."

The brush dropped from her hand, and for a wild moment, she considered flinging her arms around Damien. He must have seen it in her face, because he recoiled, staring at her like she might burn him. She laughed.

Royalty wanted one of her horses.

All this time, fear of the Kelbras had kept buyers at bay. Nightflyer was one of the most recognized names in racing, and Starling and Iri were both descended from him. But while she'd refused to sell Iri, she'd been unable to sell Starling. Now Damien had found one of the few people in this kingdom who had more power than Rezek, someone he wouldn't dare challenge. If the prince bought a Rusel enchant, others would follow suit. This could change everything.

She grinned. "Thank you."

Something like a smile turned Damien's lips. "Let's take Atara home."

THE MUSIC OF the Illinir festival echoed from streets away, the sky bright with enchanted lights and resounding with laughter.

Mikira walked alone toward the glow, her hands shoved into the pockets of her coat. She ought to be home with her sisters, not chasing some woman she didn't understand into a festival she despised. The laughter, the lights, even the smells—they all reminded her of Lochlyn and Talyana, of the nights they'd spent here together as children during the last Illinir.

She turned the card over in her pocket, running her finger along the embossed address of the Petal Shop on the surface. There was something about Quinn she couldn't get out of her head. She barely knew the girl, and yet she felt an ease and comfort around her she couldn't explain. More than that, Quinn had opened a door with her questions about Rezek and the royals, a door Mikira couldn't bring herself to shut.

Do you want him dead?

Quinn had said it like she could make it happen. Had talked about the noble houses and royal family as if they were simply obstacles to be removed. And in that moment, more than her personal desire to see them defeated had taken root. All this time, she'd been thinking only of herself, of her family. But they weren't the only ones who'd lost people to the war, to the noble houses' cruelty and the royals' greed.

She wanted to hear what Quinn had to say.

Ducking through a narrow alley lined with recruitment posters, she emerged onto Tea Street, the entirety of which had been swallowed by the festival. Some of it was commissioned and paid for by the Kelbras, but much of it was donated by enchanters looking to get their name out, and they held nothing back.

Tree branches hung heavy with enchanted lights, some small and star bright, others large and round as pumpkins with charmed images sliding across their faces: glowing fish in a rippling pond, rain falling over an empty bench bathed in moonlight, Aslir roaring soundlessly against a backdrop of night. She skirted around a vendor selling color-changing masks emulating the Harbingers. Two children each wearing Lyzairin's sapphire tail burst past her, sparklers held aloft, leaving a trail of fleeting light.

The scent of roasting chestnuts curled around her from a nearby cart. Her father had bought some for her and Lochlyn last time, and she'd loved them so much, Lochlyn had given her his entire bag. They were enchanted to change flavor, turning from cinnamon to nutmeg to brown sugar in a bite. She slowed, watching the vendor scoop nuts into thin paper bags for two men holding hands, and wished, more than anything, that her brother was there with her now.

Lochlyn had always had such an unyielding sense of what was right. He was the peacemaker in their family, sorting out arguments between his little sisters with promises of trail rides and sweets. Sometimes she wondered if it was that softness that had cost him his life in the war. He'd never been able to make the difficult decisions.

Those had always fallen to her.

Except maybe now she didn't have to do it alone. She thought of Ari sitting next to her in the stables after the first race, of her belief that they could do this together, and a little of the tightness in her chest unwound.

"Excuse me?" A young girl stood before her, a paper and pen clasped in her sugar-dusted hand. She wore a silver fang like Ari's. "Are you—are you Mikira Rusel? Can I have your autograph?"

Mikira blinked at her in stunned silence. The girl shifted nervously, letting her pale hair fall over her face to hide her rising blush, and Mikira realized she was embarrassing her.

"Oh, um, yes?" She took the proffered pen and paper. Did she just sign her name, like she would any document? That seemed too ordinary. Her father's signature had been a flash of a *K* and an *R*, more art than name. She tried for the same, looping the *M* into the *K* with a flourish and handing it back.

The girl's eyes lit up. "Thank you!" She darted back to where her parents were waiting at the corner.

"I thought I recognized you!" The vendor was grinning at her now. "Congrats on the race, Miss Rusel. How about a bag, on the house?"

"Oh, I couldn't possibly—" But he was already filling it up, and she accepted it with a nod of thanks, scurrying onward before anyone else could take notice of her. It hadn't occurred to her that people might recognize her now. After two Illinir races and with her father's name behind her, suddenly she was someone to know, a change she suspected was also due to Damien's introductions of her at the ball.

Thanks to him, the Rusel name meant something again.

And she'd betrayed him.

Guilt turned her stomach, and she ended up giving the nuts to a woman wrapped in blankets on the street. She wasn't the only refugee bundled up for warmth and with nowhere to go, and it wouldn't be long before the Anthir forced them out of the festival. The Council of Lords didn't like reminders of the cost of their war.

Mikira gave her directions to the nearest shelter along with the few copper marks in her pocket before heading toward the corner housing the Petal Shop.

Quinn waited outside.

Her dark hair was half up, half down, the top coiled into an intricate series of braids. She wore knee-high boots over dark pants and a loose pine-green shirt that turned her hazel eyes the dark, vivid color of the forest. She held one hand behind her back, the stem of a flower poking out.

"You came," she said.

Mikira eyed the stem. "What's that?"

Quinn held a flower out to her. It was a red carnation.

It was such a small thing, a flower, yet it brought Mikira crashing to a sudden stop. That feeling of familiarity that had haunted her for weeks enclosed her, immobilizing her with the threat of understanding.

A vase of red carnations. The sound of a gunshot and shattering glass.

Quinn gently tucked the stem of the flower behind Mikira's ear, the scent of sugar and cloves clinging to her skin. Mikira seized her hand, her thumb tracing the scar tissue on the girl's wrist, etched there by shattered glass.

Quinn didn't pull away. She simply watched, her eyes dark and resolute, as Mikira slid off her mask.

"Talyana," she breathed.

Her childhood best friend gave her a small, sad smile. "Hey, Kira."

Then they were wrapped up in each other's arms, and Mikira was squeezing her tighter than she'd ever held anyone in her life, and Talyana's shoulder was pressing the satin petals of the flower against her cheek, and she was hating, hating herself for having taken this long to figure it out.

"I don't understand," she rasped into Talyana's shirt.

Talyana leaned back, brushing the tears from Mikira's cheeks. "It's a long story."

"Why didn't you just tell me? Why pretend?"

Talyana gave her a sheepish smile. "I thought if you knew it was me, you wouldn't let me help you. Not after I . . ."

"After you left." Mikira didn't say it coldly, just plainly. One moment Talyana had been her strength; the next she had been gone, the last break against the storm that had consumed her. She'd always blamed Talyana's parents. After Rezek shot the vase, scarring Talyana's arm, they'd never let her return to the ranch. When Mikira had gone looking for her at their house days later, they'd moved.

Mikira dragged the back of her sleeve across her eyes. "But that night in the tunnels. You knew it was me. How?"

She laughed. "Really, Kira? Nightflyer? Your dad's racehorse was your favorite as a kid. You never stopped talking about him."

"You remember that?"

Talyana's expression grew solemn. "I remember everything."

And Mikira had forgotten. Had she really buried Talyana so deep that she hadn't recognized her best friend, mask or not? It'd been nearly eight years, and she was a far cry from the short-haired, round-cheeked girl Mikira had known, but her eyes—they'd been the thing that unsettled her from the start.

Mikira just hadn't wanted to see it.

Talyana slipped her arm through Mikira's. "Why don't we walk for a while. We have a lot to catch up on."

Talyana told her everything as they walked. The day after Rezek, her father had packed her bags and sent her to a military academy at the edges of the kingdom. She'd trained to become an officer, a position she owed to her father's history as a royal guard.

It pained Mikira to think of Talyana trapped into the rigidity of military life. It was everything she'd never wanted. The schedule, the structure, the repetition. Talyana wanted untraversed seas and forests that had never seen a human hand. She wanted to see desert lizards and scarlings and northern Vynan rivers that froze so deeply in the winter you could go sliding across them on skates.

Yet it also healed something in her to know that Talyana had not left her willingly, and she had never forgotten her.

Talyana told her how she'd spent several months fighting, before being honorably discharged when a blast left her mostly deaf in one ear. How she'd entered the Illinir for a last burst of freedom before she intended to join the Anthir, and how she'd agonized over finding Mikira after she returned, and upon seeing her in the tunnels, had been unable to resist talking to her.

"But when you didn't recognize me, I was too much of a coward to say anything," she finished. They sat on the edge of an enchanted fountain in Canburrow Square. The water was filled with sparkling gold dust that caught the light as it leapt into new patterns, forming ribbons that spun and danced.

She squeezed Mikira's arm. "I'm sorry I didn't say something sooner."

"It's okay." Mikira squeezed back. "I'm just glad you're here."

A silence fell between them, at once as uncertain as it was familiar. Then slowly, in bits and pieces, they started telling each other the little stories they'd missed. They talked about the ranch and everything Mikira had learned about breeding enchants, about the friends that'd rejected her, about Talyana's first time firing a gun, and when she'd accidentally gotten drunk on cheap whiskey.

Eventually they left the fountain for a vendor selling festival cakes on the edge of the square, and Talyana bought her more than she could carry, and they laughed as she tried to balance them in her arms and eat at the same time. The cakes were warm and spiced and molasses sweet, and slowly the memories she'd built with Lochlyn years ago faded just a little bit more in the light of the new ones.

When they were full of sugar and sick from it, Talyana laced her sticky fingers in Mikira's and dragged her over to a crowd that had gathered before a stage, where actors dressed as the four Harbingers danced to a quick string rhythm.

"You never answered my question," Talyana said above the speeding music.

Mikira knew what she meant, but she still didn't know how to answer. She watched as Lyzairin, the Great Serpent, spun about Rach like a rope. "Rezek has done a lot of terrible things to my family, but he's only one man. What I need isn't to get rid of Rezek; it's to have the means to protect my family from more like him."

"And yet you're working with Damien Adair." Talyana didn't take her eyes off the stage. Rach had broken free, and now stalked Lyzairin across the stage while Skylis, the Burning Light, swirled around them in trails of enchanted fire.

"I don't have a choice." The wind picked up, carrying her words away on a chill breeze, and she pulled her jacket tighter against its bite. "Besides, he's not like Rezek."

Talyana laughed as Rach tackled Lyzairin, Skylis's flame encircling them both. "He's just like Rezek. I've heard rumors about an Anthir sergeant investigating him, looking into everything from his finances to business deals. He's as corrupt as any house lord."

Mikira thought of the flood of Anthir in the hall, of breaking bone.

Talyana stepped in front of her, forcing their gazes to meet. "Kira, Damien Adair is a murderer."

At that moment, a roar overtook the stage, and Aslir erupted onto the stage. Dressed in glittering white from the mane of feathers about his neck to the lion's tail at his back, he reflected the enchanted lights like the bright star whose name he held, his sheer presence bowing the other three into submission.

Mikira studied Talyana, uncertain. "What do you know?"

"Exactly what I said."

"Do you have proof?"

Talyana bit her lip, the action at once so familiar and so foreign, it twisted something in Mikira's heart. "There was a time you wouldn't have asked me that."

Mikira turned back to the stage, where the performers were bowing to the clapping crowd. "Things have changed."

CHAPTER 22

ARIELLE

ARI TURNED MIKIRA'S knives over in her hands. The girl had left them with her for the morning while she and Reid trained, something Ari recognized as a sign of trust on her end. After a week of studying the signatures of other enchantments, she'd spent the last hour comparing the magic in the knives and coming up empty.

Whatever enchantment they held, she'd never seen it before.

Frustrated with her lack of knowledge, she set them aside and picked up her Arkala. Damien had spent the morning taking meetings with House Adair's bookies, a distiller from their whiskey business, and several district tenants seeking his help, but for the last hour, he'd been deeply engrossed in the spellbook, reinforcing her relief that she'd shared it with him. Not only was he very good at research, but unlike Ari, he could read the old Kinnish, which only just resembled the modern tongue.

She was halfway through a section on the Sages' theories around Skylis's desire to walk among humanity as one of them when Damien's chair scraped against the marble floor and he strode over, a thin leather journal in hand.

"The spellbook is remarkable." He paused at the edge of the rug. "I haven't gotten very far—it's incredibly dense, and my old Kinnish is rusty—but it's equal parts magic, philosophy, and history, leading me to believe it is a Racari. It's also very focused on the golems."

She swung her feet to the ground. "Do you think it's where the Kinnish learned how to create them?"

Damien's gaze grew distant as he considered the idea. It was a particular look he got when faced with an interesting question. She liked it—it softened the lines of his face, made her want to trace a finger along his jaw.

"I'm honestly not sure," he said at last. "We're bordering on religion now. Both Kinnism and Sendism teach that the Harbingers brought magic to humanity, but where Sendism is centered on the four kinds of enchantments and their stones, Kinnism has always held a much broader definition of magic. With how much knowledge was lost with the Burning, it's possible magic is capable of far more than we know. New enchantments, additional ways of applying them, perhaps even other gemstones capable of conducting enchantments."

He flipped the journal around for her to see. "For example, I found information on how to expand and control your abilities as an enchanter."

Control. Ari nearly snorted at the word. Controlling the magic that came flowing out of her was like trying to control a river. With each new golem she crafted, she balanced on a cliff edge, seconds away from tumbling into darkness—she worried one day it would overpower her.

Do not be afraid of your own power, said the voice. *Embrace it.*

"You look uncertain," Damien said.

Her fingers brushed her Saba's necklace. "What if I can't control it? I might hurt you."

Damien set the journal on the table and crouched before her as she sat up, close enough that his forearm brushed her knee. "You have an incredible power, Arielle Kadar, and I am not afraid of it."

Listen to him, coaxed the voice.

He took her hand in his, guiding her to her feet as he rose. They stood eye to eye, a handsbreadth apart. "I am not afraid of you."

Something inside her shifted, like the click of a lock. His hand was warm and large around her own. Secure. This was what she wanted, after all. To learn to control her power, to *have* power.

Be fearless, my love.

Her fingers curled about his. "Tell me what you found."

An hour later, Damien had presented her with such a thorough, well-organized explanation of his discoveries, that it seemed impossible he'd only had the book for a few days. She marveled at the way his mind worked, like a vault of information always at his fingertips.

"Let me get this straight," she said from her perch in the armchair, a fresh cup of tea in hand. Damien stood at the edge of the rug, arms folded loosely. He'd removed his guns and his jacket, and even unbuttoned his waistcoat, rolling up his shirtsleeves to reveal the neat bandage on his left forearm. Reid had stitched the wound cleanly but warned it would probably scar. She'd felt the strange urge to chastise him for getting hurt.

"You think I can use enchantments on myself?" she asked. "Say, make myself stronger or faster or luckier?"

He nodded. "Sendism claims it tarnishes a person's soul to be enchanted, but the only real reason it's illegal is because consuming verillion is dangerous to most people. But enchanters are immune to verillion's poisonous effects."

He started pacing the length of the rug. She'd noticed he did that when he was caught up in an idea. It reminded her of a lion stalking about a cage. "If you can consume it, you can contain it and, according to the book, use it."

The idea of holding raw magic inside herself both thrilled and terrified her. She'd never smoked verillion, but she'd always felt a pleasant humming sensation around the plant.

"Enchantments require more than just magic." She drained her teacup and set it on the end table. "I would need the conducting stone."

Damien strode over to one of the towering bookcases and returned with a glittering emerald that he tossed to her. The gem was cold against her palm and easily the size of an acorn. In his other hand he held up a glowing gold verillion stalk. He drew a switchblade from his pocket, flipped it open, and cut off a small piece, throwing it to her too.

She looked down at the emerald, worth more than anything she'd ever held in her life, then to the verillion stalk.

"You certainly don't waste time," she muttered.

He smiled, and the ease of it coaxed free one of her own, even as her stomach twisted with worry. This was reckless. Dangerous. They had no idea what the magic would do. What *she* would do, and yet still he looked at her as if she held the world in her hands.

"Go to the other side of the room," she instructed. He frowned, but she gave him a pointed look and he relented, retreating to beside Reid's doorway.

Ari stood, the emerald slippery in her sweating palm. Approaching this power felt like turning to face a beast that'd been chasing her for years. She'd avoided it for so long, afraid of what she might do.

And what did that get you? asked the voice. *Nothing but pain of another kind.*

She felt the press of phantom hands against her throat. Her bruises had long faded, but she hadn't forgotten the sheer terror that enveloped her the day those men attacked. It wasn't the first time she'd been helpless. In the face of Enderlain's elite, in the face of her bloody past and bleak future, she'd felt defeated more than once.

What would her life be like if she learned to control her power instead? If rather than locking it away, she claimed it?

You could have anything, said the voice.

She ate the verillion. The plant had a celery-like texture and a spiced tang to it, like the chamin her mother made. It filled her mouth with a strange warmth. The sensation spread as she swallowed, extending through her body in a gentle hum. She knew this feeling. It was a wisp of the power that surged through her when she gave life to a new golem.

Magic.

"I can feel it," she told Damien. He stepped toward her, but she held up a hand, keeping him at bay. "I'm going to try charming myself for strength."

Strength was one of the simplest physical enchantments, requiring minimal intent. To enchant something, she had only to thread the verillion magic through the stone and bind it to her target. The magic's journey through the stone acted like a chemical reaction, producing the charm.

Except normally, all three elements—stone, magic, and target—were all one being by the time she set to work. Was it even possible to push magic from herself to the stone and back again?

Only one way to find out.

She commanded the magic into the stone and gasped aloud when it obeyed.

"What is it?" Damien asked, but she was too caught up in the magic shifting through her, passing from her hand to the emerald.

Binding the energy to the physicality of the stone was like embroidering a cloth. Normally she worked with powders, since the materials then had to be folded into clay. She found the stone more resistant to her attempts to infuse it. It was like forcing a needle through canvas instead of silk.

In the end, she succeeded at binding it, the magic combining fully with the stone. This was the point at which an enchanter would bind the charm to the object or animal while forming a specific enchantment in their mind, guiding the magic through sheer intent.

She tried to pull the magic back to her from the stone, beginning the spell, but it resisted. She pulled harder. The magic snapped, dispersing, and she gasped against the sudden loss of it.

"What happened?" Damien moved toward her.

She held up a hand. "I'm fine. I bound the magic into the stone and then tried to bring it back into my body, but it didn't work."

Damien picked up the journal he'd left on the table. Flipping to a marked page, he ran his finger along several lines. "I don't think you need to bring the magic back into yourself. With normal enchantments, the stone, magic, and target are all one. I think the same is true when you're holding the stone."

"So once I bind the enchantment with it, I have it?" she asked.

He retreated to his spot across the room. "Try it."

Focusing on the flow of magic once more, she performed the same steps. Except this time when she threaded the magic into the stone, she left it there while she spoke the spell. A soft glow emanated from her skin, just like when she raised a golem.

"Lift the table!"

Damien's sudden shout almost broke her concentration, but she managed to lean down and heft the table edge with one hand. Two legs came clean off the ground with ease, sending books toppling. Gaping in surprise, she forgot to funnel the magic, and her sudden strength began to dissipate. The table grew heavier. She pushed more magic into the stone, burning through it like kindling in a fire, and the strength returned. Then all at once the magic store inside her vanished and the table thumped to the ground, nearly taking her with it.

She fell to her knees on the soft carpet, the absence of the magic leaving her panting. That feeling—the strength, the *power*. She felt the soft purr of something satisfied deep inside her, heard the voice whisper her name, and she wondered if once, hundreds of years ago, the Heretic who'd stolen this book had felt the same.

She flexed her fingers, marveling at the remnants of strength flowing through them. If those men had attacked her just now, what could she have done to them? Damien had offered her a chance for revenge once, and she'd refused it, because revenge was not what she wanted. Control was. Control of herself, her power, her fear. She wanted to show herself that she was master of them all.

Then do it, said the voice. *Crush what remains of your fear.*

But to do that, she needed to understand this power. Then she would find those men and show them just how unafraid she'd become.

A slow grin spread across her lips. She lifted her head to find Damien staring at her like he too might fall to his knees.

"That was incredible," he breathed.

"Let's do it again."

She tried a couple more times before Mikira and Reid returned. Finding them in the midst of an experiment, Reid promptly told them everything they were doing incorrectly before setting up a proper series of tests for them to conduct. They worked only with emeralds and the strength enchantment. The amount of verillion she consumed and the size of the emerald were their variables, though they only changed one at a time. The more verillion she consumed, the larger her magic store, and the bigger the stone, the more magic she could funnel through it, and therefore the stronger the enchantment.

The other thing they discovered was how utterly, bone-achingly tired it all left her.

An hour later, she was sprawled across the chaise like a corpse, head propped on a plush pillow, where she swiftly fell asleep.

She woke around noon to Mikira's worried voice asking, "What did you do to her?"

"She's the one who didn't want to stop," came Damien's reply. "You try telling a woman who can lift an entire marble table no."

"I'll be fine," Ari murmured as she pushed herself up. Damien had laid a blanket over her, and she pulled it tight around her shoulders. "I just need something to eat."

"Food is on its way," Damien replied, already hovering over the Racari again.

"Ari? Ari!"

Ari blinked, finding Mikira beside her on the chaise, her brow furrowed with concern. A tray sat on the table stacked with empty plates, and her stomach was full, yet she didn't remember eating. Had she blacked out again?

"Are you sure you're all right?" Mikira asked softly, as if to keep Damien from hearing. Did she think he was pressuring her into this?

Ari seized hold of the conversation as an anchor. "I'm better than all right," she replied with a fervency that surprised her. "I wish you could have felt it. That kind of strength . . . I wish I could give you some of it."

A longing Ari knew well passed over Mikira's face. Everything she was doing was to protect her family, to not have to wake up every morning afraid. She smiled forlornly. "Well, you'll just have to be strong enough for the both of us."

Ari took her hand. "I will." The girl had been right when she'd said they were two small fish in a bay of sharks, but with magic like this, Ari would have teeth too, and she would bite anyone who came for either of them.

Mikira's smile faltered, her next words tentative. "What happened, Ari?"

She read the words underneath: *What made you this way?*

Blood on her hands. Blood on the walls.

Ari squeezed her eyes shut against the memories of her Saba and told Mikira instead about the men who came to her workshop. It wasn't the whole truth, but it was part of it, and the look of understanding on Mikira's face was enough to make her heart ache. Fear lived in them both, and she wanted to crush it.

Mikira squeezed her hand. "They win when they make you afraid," she said quietly. "Don't let them win, Ari."

And Ari promised she wouldn't.

CHAPTER 23

ARIELLE

FOR THE FIRST time in a very long time, Ari didn't feel afraid.

Even as she strolled through the tumult of Rathsborne Street, side-stepping dusty horses and dockworkers heading to the pub for an evening drink, she didn't worry if one of them might stare at her too long, if the horse's rider might be the Anthir, come looking for the unlicensed enchanter from the Westmire.

Her conversation with Mikira that afternoon had steeled something inside her. She walked with her head held high and the belief that if she did not bend, then people would bend around her.

It was with that mindset that she strode into the enchanted animal shop.

A bell dinged overhead, nearly swallowed by the piercing call of a charmed falcon perched nearby. She ducked under a hanging cage of colorful birds and between crates of enchanted kittens, disturbed by the cramped, dirty space they'd all been crowded into. The whole shop smelled distinctly of animal piss.

She finally reached the back counter, where the glow of a candle illuminated the shopkeeper reading the evening's broadsheet. "RISING REBEL RUCKUS" was printed atop a photo of Prince Darius surrounded by his guards at the last race. Below it was an article about Mikira's win. People were starting to bet on her for the upcoming third race, and Damien had practically been bombarded by requests from reporters to interview her.

The shopkeeper flicked the paper down to peer at her. With beady black eyes and blond hair that hung in a greasy curtain about his pale face, Welzin Carswoth looked more like a rat than one of Veradell's foremost enchanted animal dealers, let alone the man that had changed the course of her life. He'd given not only Damien the chance to find her, but likely the men who had robbed her—or so Ari intended to find out. Though from the acerbic look he leveled at her, she had a feeling he wouldn't be quite so chatty with her.

"Mr. Carswoth," she said.

"Do I know you?" His voice was gruff and wheezing and laced with the remnants of a Vynan accent.

"A friend of mine gave me your name. They said you might have an unusual enchant. A cat."

Welzin raised a verillion cigarette to his thin lips, taking a long draw as he evaluated her. He let the smoke out in a perfect ring and folded up his broadsheet. Sliding his thin body around the corner, he disappeared into the shop long enough that Ari started to wonder if something had eaten him, before finally returning with a sleek white cat in his hands.

She knew it on sight—it was a golem that she had made for Lady Vanadahl, heir to House Vanadahl. The woman had swept into her workshop flush with cash and looking to burn it, and had wanted a cat enchanted to detect lies. It was one of the few ethereal enchantments Ari had been able to manage.

Welzin huffed. "Well, don't just stare at it all day. You want it or not?"

Ari's fingers curled around the emerald stone inside her skirt pocket. The steady buzz of verillion hummed low and hot in her stomach.

Make him give you the truth, coaxed the voice.

"What did you give Lady Vanadahl in exchange for my name?" she asked. "Or did she give it for free?"

Welzin's narrow face constricted. "Your name? What in the hells are you talking about, girl?"

"My name is Arielle Kadar."

The shop owner only blinked at her in confusion. Either he was a fantastic actor or he had no idea who she was. But that didn't make any sense. Damien had gotten her name from him, and she'd assumed that meant the men had too.

"You didn't answer my question," she said.

Force him, said the voice.

"That's because it's none of your business." Welzin brandished his cigarette in her face, hot ash singeing her cheek. "Now, stop wasting my time. Either buy something or get out of my—" Ari's enchantment-enhanced punch smashed into his face. He dropped the cat and stumbled back into the wall beside the cage of a snarling wolf.

Ari advanced on the reedy man, pinning her forearm against his throat. "Let me be very clear," she said, ignoring his wheezing. "You are going to tell me what Lady Vanadahl told you, or I'm going to feed you bit by bit to the wolf." She jerked his fingers toward the snapping jaws of the beast.

"Okay!" he rasped, and Ari nearly gagged on the stench of verillion smoke and rotting gums on his breath. She let up on his throat but kept her verillion burning. "Look, the lady didn't tell me anything. She got herself into some gambling debts her father wouldn't pay and needed the coin. She only came in to sell me the cat."

"But she gave you my name?"

Welzin hesitated, and Ari shoved his hand between the bars. He yelped as she snatched it back, barely avoiding the wolf's teeth. "No! She didn't give me any names. Just the cat."

That didn't make any sense. She was missing something.

Welzin squirmed in her grip. "Come to think of it, a bloke came in asking after that cat. He had someone else with him, but I didn't see their face. They were awfully interested in the beastie, though."

"Were they big men?" she asked. "Dark hair, tall, broad shouldered? One carried a baton, the other a blade."

Welzin shook his head. "The one I saw was lean and blond. I remember him because he kept riling up my animals. Right annoying, that one. If you're looking for the rough sort, you should go to the Drowned Crow across the way. A lot of them that operate around here like to go in for a drink."

Ari barely heard him. If Welzin never knew her name, then how had Damien gotten it? Though now that she thought about it, Damien had never said he'd heard of her through the enchant dealer. Only that he'd tracked a golem of hers down there. She'd come here looking for revenge on the men who harmed her and gotten only more questions in return. What was she missing?

Ari released him. "If you're lying to me, or if you ever tell anyone about this, I'll be back." She didn't bother to stop the golem cat from escaping as she shoved open the door and strode out.

THE DROWNED CROW sat on the edge of the Greystel River, crammed between a recruitment building and an inn. They leaned over the pub like an arch missing its keystone, casting its worn wooden exterior in shadow.

A warm orange glow washed over Ari as she entered, illuminating a clean, well-kept pub. The air was thick with the scent of freshly baked bread, and she drew a deep breath, the familiar smell working away at her burgeoning headache. The gentle whisper of a brass band warming up in the corner rose over the steady hum of voices from the half-filled tables.

The place felt far homier than she'd expected for the drinking establishment of criminals.

"Can I help you, darling?" A dark-skinned person with thick eyebrows and short, curly black hair looked up from the table they'd been wiping down. They were tall and thin, all elegant lines with kind eyes, and had the fading hints of a Yaroyan accent.

"I'm looking for someone." Ari eyed the half-eaten stew the table's patron had left behind. Her stomach growled. She'd left off burning the verillion, but the small amount she'd expended had still left her hungry. The more she used it, the more tolerance she built up, but she still had a long way to go.

The barkeep smiled. "Why don't you have a seat at the bar."

Ari followed them to where a dark cherrywood counter separated the room from the kitchen behind. She settled down in one of the well-worn stools as the barkeep ladled her a fresh bowl of stew.

"Oh, thank you, but I don't have any coin," she said quickly. Though Damien had paid her several times now, she hadn't gotten used to carrying the coin around and often forgot to take it with her.

"Don't worry yourself over it," they replied. "I have quite a bit left and a coldbox with a dead enchantment."

It was a common story on Rathsborne Street, where few could afford to maintain enchantments with rising verillion prices. From the looks of it, she wasn't the only one eating for free. There was a Celairen family still with their luggage, and two gaunt-faced kids at the corner of the bar inhaling their stew.

Two more problems the Council of Lords could alleviate if they chose. They could stop the price gouging of grain and release verillion from the royal reserves, or fund refugee and veteran housing like the Adairs. Perhaps that was why Damien had accepted every invitation the prince sent his way since the day of the rebel attack—he could be a means of influencing the council.

"Name's Vix, by the way." The barkeep stuck out their hand.

Ari shook it. "Arielle."

"Ah, a Kinnish name. My mother was a Sage in our town in Yaroya, though

I myself have never been the religious sort." Vix folded their arms atop the bar, an ease in their voice Ari wondered at. They spoke so definitively about their Kinnish identity; something she'd never felt comfortable doing.

Her Saba had always said that there wasn't just one way to be Kinnish. Some people were born Kinnish, some became Kinnish through marriage, and some converted, but they were all equal in their welcome, no matter how deep their roots ran. Whether their connection came through religion, or culture, or heritage, they were one people. Yet somehow, she still felt leagues apart.

Ari scooped another bite of stew. It was warm and spicy on her tongue, reminding her of something her mother made when the weather turned cold. The memory sent a pang of nostalgia through her.

What for? It's not as if they miss you too, said the voice.

She flinched. *You don't know that.*

Then where are they?

"Now, who was it you were looking for?" Vix asked, startling her from the conversation. When had she started speaking back to the voice?

"Two men." Ari focused on the present. "They'd have been in here just over a month ago." She described them best she could, which was very well indeed. Their faces were seared into her mind.

Vix nodded slowly. "I know who you mean. They ran up a tab and refused to pay. If Lady Adair hadn't stepped in, I'd have been out quite a bit."

Ari nearly dropped her spoon. "Lady Adair?"

As if summoned by her name, there was a rustle of cloth at Ari's side like the flutter of wings, and Shira Adair folded herself into the seat beside her. Dark curls spiraled about her tired face, but her smile was warm.

"Always happy to help, Vix," Shira said. "Would you give me and Arielle a moment alone? I'll be back to fix that coldbox for you in a bit."

"Sure thing. Let me know if you need anything." Vix snatched up their rag and ambled back into the pub.

"What do you want?" Ari blurted.

"And here I thought we'd become friends." Shira leaned over the counter, snatching a roll from a basket. Tearing off a piece, she stuck it in her mouth and turned her stool to face Ari. "What interest have you in Fen and Cardix?"

Ari's hand went to her throat. "They attacked me."

"And?"

"And—" Her eyes narrowed. "And it's none of your business. Unless you want to tell me where they are?"

"They're dead, of course."

Ari's spoon clattered to the counter. A complex web of emotions spun through her. She knew she ought to care, if only for the loss of life. She ought not to feel so relieved. Damien had promised they wouldn't harm her again, but she'd still thought about them constantly. Or rather, about the fear they'd left behind in her like the seeds of some vicious flower.

"I don't understand," she said at last, aware of the way Shira watched her like a specimen beneath a microscope. "Who killed them?"

"My brother, or someone who works for him, more likely." Shira tore off another piece of bread. "Did you expect otherwise?"

"He said he'd let them go . . ." She trailed off.

"For all his faults, my brother doesn't lie, Miss Kadar. Though he may occasionally omit the truth." She tossed the bread into her mouth.

She was right. Damien had said he'd let them go; he'd never said he wouldn't do anything to them after.

Shira finished the last of the roll and wiped her hands. "Most likely, he thought to spare you the burden of knowing. But he wouldn't allow someone to live who was so obviously a threat to you and, by connection, him." She reached for another roll, though her eyes never left Ari. "Does it bother you? Those men had done terrible things, after all. I'd count you among the luckier of their victims."

Ari didn't know how to answer that. Those men had known dangerous information about her. Information she'd just threatened to let a wolf tear off a man's hand for knowing. Still, she hadn't wanted them dead.

Didn't you, though? asked the voice. *Doesn't it make you feel powerful, knowing he had them killed for you? Knowing that if you found them, you could have done it yourself?*

I wouldn't have. She clung to the thought.

"Are you all right?"

Ari looked up, realizing she had a hand pressed to her temple as if to shove the voice out. But she couldn't. She might as well tear away a piece of her own soul. That voice, that darkness, they were a part of her. They *were* her.

She lowered her hand. "I'm fine. I don't know what your motivation is for interfering, but stop following me."

She expected Shira to refute her, not to look at her with a quiet sadness in her dark eyes. "I love my brother, but he has a way of losing himself to his scheming. He doesn't know when he's in over his head. I know he's up to something. Be careful that you don't get caught in the undertow."

She placed a gold mark on the counter and stood, something shifting about her neck. A necklace with a lion's fang, just like her own. Shira's fingers closed around it.

"If you decide you want out, ask for me at my family's pub, the Dark Horse," she said. "I'll find you."

"Why?" Ari asked as the woman turned for the door. "You barely even know me."

"Let's just say I have a long history of cleaning up my brothers' messes. Good evening, Miss Kadar."

Ari watched her go. She had no need of Shira's help.

What she needed was to talk to Damien.

SHE FOUND HIM sitting by the fire in his room, whiskey in hand, his shirtsleeves rolled up to reveal his forearms. The firelight cast a warm glow across his olive skin, lending depth to his gray eyes as he watched her descend the stairs.

"Is something wrong?" he asked.

The simple question almost stopped her cold. That he could see through her so easily, as though she hadn't spent years of her life honing her emotions into silent blades, was something she still wasn't used to. Yet as much as it terrified her, it also thrilled her. She missed having someone that knew her.

She stopped at the edge of the rug. "I went looking for the men that attacked me."

There—a flicker of surprise. He might be able to read her, but she could decipher him too. He set his glass on a stack of books and stood, giving her his full attention. "Why did you do that?"

She opened her mouth to respond, then stopped, uncertain of how to explain. Her hand slid into her pocket, finding the cool edge of the emerald. The last couple days of training with her magic had changed her. They'd made her feel stronger, more confident. She'd seen an opportunity to destroy her lingering fear, to not let them win like Mikira had said, and she'd taken it.

But what had she meant to do? Show them what she was capable of and walk away?

The voice laughed. *No. Oh, no no no.*

"I was still angry," she said at last, realizing her hands had curled into fists. She drew them tighter, savoring the sting of her nails into her palms. "I was angry and scared, and I thought if I faced them down, I could erase what remained of both."

She met his gaze, unwavering. "Did you kill them?"

"Yes." He didn't hesitate.

For all his faults, my brother doesn't lie.

Her fists trembled, and she realized this was what she'd wanted: to know if he would tell her the truth, no matter how bloody.

"Good," she said and the look in his eyes nearly undid her.

She closed the distance between them. "I found the enchant dealer. You didn't get my name from him, did you?"

"No." He didn't look away from her as he spoke. "I'd been following the rumors about you for some time when I learned Lady Vanadahl had an undetectable enchant. I won a game of cards against her, in which my prize was a piece of information. Your name is what she gave me. She'd already sold the cat, so I tracked it to the enchant dealer to confirm it was what I suspected."

"Who else will she give my name to?" Ari asked.

When Damien smiled, there was an edge to it. In it, Ari read a thousand different promises that sent a thrill through her. "She won't. Shortly after, Lady Vanadahl received a visit from the pit boss of the gambling den she owed. Last I heard, she hadn't woken up."

CHAPTER 24

MIKIRA

THE NEXT FEW days before the third race settled into a routine Mikira came to crave: training with Reid and Atara in the afternoons, lunch with everyone in Damien's quarters, then evenings with Talyana at the festival. They spent the nights swapping stories and eating more sweets than they could stomach. Even her fear of accidentally sabotaging Damien had begun to fade as each day passed without incident. Perhaps Rezek had hoped the information about the ring could turn into something but it never had.

Ari caught her halfway out the door on her way to one of her meetings with Talyana, and promptly redirected her to her own bedroom, where she commanded Mikira to sit on a stool while she fixed her hair into an intricate plait.

"I'm just seeing a friend," Mikira complained. "She doesn't care what my hair looks like."

Ari snorted derisively. "You practically fly out the door every time you go to meet her, Kira, and you're always trying to smooth the wrinkles out of your clothes. Even Reid noticed."

Mikira recoiled into the stool. "He did?"

"If you're not aware of how much attention he pays to you, then you're twice the fool over."

She groaned, burying her face in her hands. Never in her life had she imagined that she'd have two people in her life that she cared for so deeply, and who were so completely different from each other. With Talyana, there were years of friendship behind them, and yet a thousand things to learn about each other again. She'd only just told her about her situation with Rezek, and why she was so reliant on Damien.

But Ari was right. She'd seen the way Reid looked at her, known that when he brewed her a pot of tea and stayed on the track with her until midnight, it was not out of loyalty to Damien—it was for her, and the sheer attention to detail he put into everything he did for her was unlike anything she'd ever experienced. Like Ari, he'd been there for her in ways no one had for a very long time.

"I honestly don't know if I can think about this right now," Mikira said as Ari tied off the braid. "There's too much else going on. I just . . . want to enjoy it."

"Then enjoy it," Ari replied. "But enjoy it after I do your hair every night."

Come the night of the third ball, Mikira sailed through conversations with Damien's acquaintances, accepting praise and congratulations from people who once wouldn't have given her the time of day. She took her own words to heart from her conversation with Ari: being scared of these people felt like letting them win, and she was done conceding to them. She might not have the enchanter's newfound physical strength, but she had another kind of power now—a name that meant something.

Word had spread of the prince's impending acquisition, and many were asking after the Rusel lines. Once the prince's stable master came for Starling tomorrow and people saw the horse in his possession, things would change for her family's ranch. She only wished her father were home to see it.

Having played her role, she feigned an upset stomach to leave the ball early, planning to meet Talyana at the festival. By the time she retrieved Iri from the stables, a storm had set in, and she cursed herself for not bringing the horses into the stable before she left. She'd have to stop by the ranch first.

Iri's ears danced to and fro the entire ride, and he jumped when thunder cracked in the distance. She brought him back under control with the press of the reins and a reassuring voice, but he wouldn't settle. His restlessness only grew as the rain fell harder, biting through her clothes to graze skin.

As they followed the drive toward the house, his ears pressed near flat to his skull.

Something was wrong.

Splintering light burst across the darkened sky. Iri reared, throwing her from his back. She hit the muddy ground hard as the horse bolted. Gasping for air, she rolled slowly onto her side, wincing at a pain in her hip.

She hoisted herself to her feet using the pasture fence. Lightning lit the sky followed by another deafening crash, and this time, Mikira saw it. The fence at the far side of the pasture had been struck by lightning. Whatever fire it'd caused had died quickly in the pouring rain, leaving behind scorched wood and a gaping hole.

A sound echoed in the distance, carried on the rising wind. Loose hairs buffeted her face as Mikira strained to hear. Had that been a voice? No. Not a voice.

Barking.

Vaulting the fence, she sprinted for the far side of the field. The squelching grass pulled at her boots like hands seizing her from below and the wind shoved her back with every step, but she pushed through the obscuring rain until she reached the gap in the fence. Wolf, Ailene's enchanted dog, was barking madly at something below.

The hill dropped away steeply before sloping into the rocky bank of the river. And there, struggling with a lead line attached to a frightened horse's halter, was Ailene. The horse was half submerged in the turbulent river, trying and failing to find purchase on the slippery, moss-covered stones. Each time she put pressure on her front left leg, she let out a high-pitched squeal and drew the leg up against her body, which only served to destabilize her more.

It was Starling.

"Ailene!" Mikira yelled.

Her sister turned, eyes wide and frantic. "Help me!"

Mikira dropped to the ground and hung her legs out over the ravine, sliding down on her side. The ground tore at her skin but she pushed to her feet, rushing to Ailene's side.

"We need to get her to a different part of the river," Mikira shouted over the tempest and Wolf's wild barks. "Somewhere she can get footing."

She reached for the lead line, but as she turned upriver, her heart stopped.

A wall of water was hurtling toward them.

"Flash flood!" Mikira seized her sister's arm, dragging her away from Starling and toward higher ground, but Ailene refused to let go.

"We can't leave her!" She ripped free of Mikira's hold, stumbling toward the horse. At the same time, Starling's hoof struck out, seeking purchase. It caught Ailene in the shin. She screamed, her leg giving out beneath her. Blood spurted from the wound, stark against the pale white bone protruding from her skin.

Mikira hauled her back to her feet even as Ailene cried out. The sound tore something apart inside her, but she didn't stop as she slipped under Ailene's arm. They staggered toward the incline. Mikira leaned Ailene against the slope and clambered up ahead of her. Sharp teeth pulled at her arm as Wolf tried to help drag her up.

The water was nearly upon them. She seized Ailene's hand, pulling with all her strength, but it wasn't enough. With Ailene's injured leg, she could barely help propel her weight.

Then another pair of hands wrapped around her sister's forearms. Together they pulled, yanking her up over the lip of the hill just as the water crashed into where they'd been standing, splashing over the edge and upon them in a wave. The rush of water and a sickening thud cut off Starling's keening cry.

Mikira lay panting in the muddy grass, her muscles sore and screaming. Ailene sobbed beside her, her entire body shaking, Wolf nudging her face with his nose.

And on her other side, his face pale and splattered with mud, was Reid.

She gaped at him, struggling to form words. He was still dressed in his suit from the ball, his tie torn loose and his hair a wild nest. Before she could say anything, he was on his feet with Ailene in his arms. She looked so fragile against his chest, lying limp in his grasp as they hurried across the pasture.

They burst into the house. "In there!" Mikira gestured to the glow of the evening's dying fire in the drawing room, then shot into the mudroom. She retrieved her father's medical kit, a bottle of salve for cleaning the wound, and as many bandages as she could carry.

When she broke back into the foyer, she found Nelda peeking out from their father's study, the book she'd been reading clutched to her chest like a stuffed animal. For an instant, Mikira half expected to see her father's tired face over her shoulder, but there was only the darkness of the study she couldn't bring herself to enter since he'd left.

"Nelda." Mikira's voice broke. "Go upstairs, and don't come down, no matter what you hear. Can you do that for me, little frog?"

Face pale, Nelda nodded, bolting up the stairs.

In the drawing room, Reid had torn away the rest of Ailene's trousers up to her knee, revealing a bloodied mess. Mikira's stomach turned, but she forced the nausea down and dropped to the floor beside Reid, proffering the medical kit.

He took it and set to work. "I need light."

She retrieved an enchanted lamp from out in the hall and held it over Ailene's leg, moving it to the left or right each time Reid instructed. Wolf lay with his head in her lap, and she petted him mechanically with her free hand. She was vaguely aware of Reid cleaning the wound before he set the bone and began stitching. Time stretched so that it felt like he'd been operating forever when he finally slumped back with a heavy breath.

"It's done."

Mikira couldn't look. She lowered the lamp beside her and turned her back against the couch, staring at the dying embers in the hearth.

"She's going to be okay," Reid said softly. "It was a clean break. I don't know if she'll ever run on that leg again, but she'll be able to walk. We won't know until much later if it'll cause her any pain."

She nodded, and kept nodding, until her addled brain realized what she was doing, and she forced herself to stop.

"When you left the ball so suddenly, I got worried," he said awkwardly.

She wanted to tell him she was glad he'd come, but everything inside her felt numb.

An arm fell around her shoulders. It wasn't until she felt the heat of Reid's body against her own that she realized how cold she was. Bone deep, achingly cold. She leaned into him, and let him hold her until the fire turned to ash.

CHAPTER 25

MIKIRA

REID DEPARTED EARLY the next morning, leaving them with instructions to watch for infection and ensure Ailene stayed off of her leg, a task Mikira dreaded. Keeping Ailene cooped up on a couch for days on end was like sticking a wild stallion in a tiny stall. The last time her sister had been on bed rest, battling a fever, Mikira had come home to find her out racing the neighbor's boy in the freezing rain.

Now, though, Ailene lay with her arms folded, staring blankly at a spot on the wall. Wolf had wedged himself between her and the couch. She'd cried when Mikira told her about Starling, but since then, she hadn't said a word. Nelda had taken it upon herself to be at their sister's beck and call. She'd made her breakfast, kept an endless supply of tea coming, and read to her from the book she'd been carrying about. But Ailene kept staring.

She just needs time.

She wasn't the only one. The prince's stable master had arrived earlier that morning, and with the horse he'd wanted gone, Mikira had promised him his pick of another.

She waited for him now while he perused the selection she'd brought into the stables. He'd been looking for nearly an hour, popping out occasionally to question her about one or the other, and the wait was slowly wearing at her. They needed this sale. Only a purchase from the prince would break the embargo Rezek had effectively placed on their business, and if she didn't win the Illinir, they would need the money.

Mikira was sitting on the steps, picking a long blade of grass into tiny pieces, when the stable master's stocky form emerged. He walked with a limp, a wolf tattoo on his bronze forearm indicating he'd served in the Iziri military.

Dropping the grass, she clambered to her feet. Her hope rose and died like a wave as he frowned back at her.

"I'm afraid none of these are quite what the prince is looking for." His gruff voice was thickly accented. "You don't have others of the speed and danger line?"

Mikira's gaze strayed reflexively to Iri, who stood at the fence of his paddock, waiting for her. She'd ridden him only sparsely the last few weeks, too busy with Atara and the races, and his head hung just the slightest, as though he knew he'd been replaced.

You haven't, she promised him silently.

"He's of the same line as Starling, isn't he?" the stable master asked. "I saw it on his stall plaque."

Mikira flinched. "Iri's not for sale."

The stable master's frown deepened, and she nearly kicked herself. She needed to be on her knees groveling, begging him to buy another horse, not snapping at him like a testy mare.

"The prince will not be pleased if I return without his horse, Miss Rusel," he said, not unkindly.

She bit her lip, glancing between the horse and man. He had a thick beard that framed a hard-planed face. From what she'd learned about him, he was a respected enchant breeder from Izir who'd recently taken a position at the castle. Her father would have dug further, but she didn't have the time or the luxury to be so fastidious. He seemed kind enough.

But Iri . . .

He was all she had left of Lochlyn. She couldn't just . . . She wouldn't . . .

She dug her nails into her palms, focusing on the sharp pain rather than her welling emotion.

"Listen, lass." His voice softened. "I'm going to be honest with you. The prince wants this horse. If you think times are tough now, the last thing you want is Prince Darius as an enemy to boot."

Rezek had nearly destroyed her family. They could not survive the wrath of a prince.

"I can see you have an attachment to him," he said. "So I'll double the prince's offer."

No.

The word was a solid weight in her throat. She tried to force it out, to tell him to leave, but she knew she couldn't. Without that money, Ailene might never walk again.

And though it was like tearing out a piece of her heart, she said, "Okay."

MIKIRA WRAPPED HER arms around Iri's neck and held him as tightly as she could. The stable master had given her privacy to say goodbye, but alone with him now in his stall, she didn't know how she could. If only she'd been here when Ailene needed her, if only she hadn't been so wrapped up in the machinations that had consumed her life, maybe this wouldn't have happened.

"Miss Rusel?" called the stable master from outside the barn. "I have to be getting back."

"I'm sorry," she whispered, and squeezed Iri one last time. Then she led him out of the stall to the stable master's trailer. She couldn't bring herself to walk him up the ramp, so she handed over the lead and watched as the stable master secured him inside, closing the gate behind him. It barely even registered when he set a pouch of coin in her outstretched hand.

"You take care," he said solemnly, and climbed into the motortruck.

Mikira's hand closed around the pouch as the trailer trundled forward, thankful she couldn't see Iri inside. It was like losing the last piece of her brother, like watching him be taken away all over again. She wanted to chase down the truck and tell him she'd changed her mind. Wanted to fling the coin back into his hands and rip open the trailer.

But she didn't move.

A breeze tickled the back of her neck. The storm had blown over, leaving pure blue skies and clean, crisp air that betrayed nothing of what'd happened. It felt like a slap in the face. Starling was dead, her sister might never run again, and Iri—oh, Iri. Everything was coming crashing down around her, but the world didn't slow. It broke and broke and broke, but it never stopped to witness its destruction.

Mikira didn't move until the trailer was out of sight, then she pocketed the coin and gathered a bag of tools, setting out for the fence. If she stood still, she wouldn't be able to take it. If she stood still, she would fall apart.

She slowed as she approached the fence. The edges were blackened from the fire, but in the light of day, she saw something she hadn't before: hatchet marks. Dropping her bag, she knelt before the lowest rung, running her finger along the sharp break.

This fence hadn't been struck by lightning. It'd been hacked apart and set on fire to cover the evidence.

Someone had sabotaged her.

"Rezek." His name felt poisonous on her tongue. Who else would have done this? He must have been trying to prevent the prince's purchase.

This too was her fault.

If she'd never gotten involved with Damien, if she hadn't angered Rezek, none of this would have happened. Ailene wouldn't have gotten hurt, and Iri wouldn't have been sacrificed to the prince in Starling's place.

Staggering to her feet, she stepped over the fence's remains. Below, the rush of the river echoed. She released a small prayer that Starling's body had been washed away and glanced down.

It wasn't Starling's body she found.

A corpse lay on the nearest riverbank, tangled in the roots of a tree. The skin was pink and rubbery, the face bloated and distorted from days of decomposition. Its chest was a gaping red maw from where a bullet had torn through it. Bile rose in Mikira's throat, and she heaved her meager breakfast into the grass. It took her several moments before the nausea passed.

Using the exposed root of a nearby tree as a handhold, she climbed carefully down the muddy bank. The stench struck her as she neared the corpse, and she nearly retched again. Holding her breath, she grabbed the corpse beneath the arms and pulled, dragging it up the bank. The skin felt slimy and squelched beneath her touch.

Letting the body drop to the ground, she rushed to the river's edge and plunged her hands into the freezing water, leaving them there until the feeling of crawling flesh turned to icy numbness.

When she turned back to the corpse, something glinted. She lifted her shirt over her nose and crouched beside the body, a silver object clutched in its hand. It must have had it in its grasp when it died, long enough for rigor mortis to set in before the storm came, washing it downstream.

Before she could think too deeply about it, Mikira seized a stick and pried it between the metal and the corpse's flesh. It took some maneuvering, but she finally dug a thick silver ring free, and froze.

Set at the top was a hawk's wing formed of hematite and diamond. Black and silver.

Damien's missing ring.

She'd suspected Damien had made a fake ring rather than commission a new one to hide the fact that he'd lost it but hadn't known why. Now she wished she didn't. Damien must have lost it in the struggle.

"Rezek," she breathed, remembering his delight at learning of the missing ring. Was he involved with this somehow, or was this the exact kind of potential outcome that had made that information valuable to him?

She stared at the ring cupped in her palm. What was she supposed to do? She needed Damien. His sponsorship was the only thing keeping her in the Illinir. Without him, she couldn't help her family. And now with Ailene's leg, they'd need money for medicine and doctors, more than Iri's sale could cover. But with the winnings from the Illinir, they'd be fine.

If she gave the ring back to him, there would be no proof he'd ever been involved. Only her.

He killed someone.

Some part of her had always known who Damien was, but she'd buried that part beneath her desperate need for his help. Then she'd gotten to know him over the last couple months, seen the way he helped his community, the way people looked at him like a savior, and she'd thought maybe he was okay. Maybe she hadn't bound herself to a monster.

But now—now she wasn't so sure.

"You don't know the full story," she told herself, even as she stared down at the bloated face of the corpse. If Damien hadn't killed him, why hide the loss of his ring? She couldn't ignore Talyana's warning about the sergeant investigating him, nor how familiar the man looked. Had she seen him at Adair Manor before?

Mikira squeezed her eyes shut. If she won the Illinir, her prize money would be funneled through Damien. If he was arrested, would his funds be frozen? What if he discovered it was she who told? He could pull his sponsorship for a partial return of his money, but would he with so much riding on her winning?

Her eyes snapped open. Damien Adair did not take kindly to betrayal. She'd be lucky if all he did was withhold the money.

What would her father do?

He'd never stand in the way of the law, but he had always been unyielding, and her family had suffered for it more than once. It was her trust in the law, in what was right, that had lost them Lochlyn. But her father had also been a fierce and loyal man once. He would never have betrayed someone who'd done so much for him.

Mikira's fist closed over the ring. "I'm sorry," she said to the body at her feet. Then she placed her boot against its ribs and pushed, releasing it back into the roaring river.

CHAPTER 26

ARIELLE

ARI HAD NO idea where she was.

One moment, she'd been asleep in her room at Adair Manor, having retired early when the others went to the Ruthar ball. The next she'd woken to morning light and cold cobblestone beneath her bare feet.

A horn startled her, and she stepped onto the sidewalk as a motorcar revved its engine, flying past. Her heart kept skittering long after it'd gone, the small side street now empty and quiet.

There had to be a logical explanation for this. Was she dreaming? No, she could tell she was awake. Then how had she gotten here?

She looked down at herself and stilled. Her nightgown had specks of red on it.

Unease wedged beneath her ribs as she gently pulled the gown up to inspect the stain, though she already knew what she would find.

Blood.

She stared at the nightgown and at the fingers that held it. Her nails were crusted dark with blood.

"Ma'am?" asked a voice.

She whirled. The man behind her recoiled a step. He wore a dark blue uniform and clasped a bundle of posters in one hand. A military recruiter.

Just a recruiter. She forced herself to calm down, seizing control of her emotions and wrenching them into compliance.

"Are you . . ." He trailed off as he saw the blood.

"I was attacked." Her throat scratched like she'd been screaming. "I ran, but now I don't know where I am."

The man visibly relaxed. A woman in distress he could handle. She almost laughed, and it must have shown in her eyes, because a nervous twitch formed at the corner of his mouth. Perhaps he wasn't sure if he should smile or call for help.

She longed for a piece of verillion, for the singe of magic to calm her nerves, to make that decision for him so, so easily. He should scream, of course, though no one would hear him. It was too early, the street too remote. No one would come for him.

"Ma'am?"

Ari blinked, realizing she'd taken a step forward. Had those thoughts been hers, or the voice? It was getting more difficult to tell, the line between them wearing like a fraying rope.

She clasped her hands, setting her expression with fear and confusion. The latter was easy. She felt disoriented, like a leaf caught and thrown by the wind.

"Can you help me get back to a main road?" she asked. "I can call a coach from there."

The recruiter smiled. "Of course. Follow me."

THE WIND CARRIED the scent of lavender after her as she hurried back to her room at Adair Manor. She closed her door and leaned against it, as if she could lock the whole experience outside.

She wanted so badly to believe that there was a logical explanation. That she'd sleepwalked or gotten drunk and not remembered wandering out. But she knew those weren't true as surely as she knew the crimson on her gown was blood.

Something was happening to her.

Tearing off the gown, she tossed it into a corner and scrubbed the blood from her nails in the sink. Then she dressed in a loose black skirt and embroidered blouse. By the time she'd tied up her hair in one of her mother's headscarves and slid on her Saba's necklace, she felt more herself.

She slipped into Damien's room to the sound of hushed voices.

"I'm losing patience, Hyle," Damien said. He reclined at his desk, his chin resting on one fist. A thin, pale man with a lean face and long blond hair pulled back in a bun fiddled with various things on his desk. To anyone else, it might look as though Damien hadn't noticed it, but she detected the annoyance in the tilt of his lips. From the smile on Hyle's face, he did too, and seemed to be rather enjoying it.

Hyle set down the pen he'd been spinning in his fingers. "Maybe I can find that for you instead. Or perhaps a lock for your door?" His gaze slid to Ari, who hadn't moved from the top of the steps. There was something about this man that unnerved her.

"Speak freely." Damien waved his hand, and Ari descended into the room, seeking the teakettle.

"I always do." Hyle grinned. "Your ring remains as absent as my love life, though not yours, it would seem."

Ari's gaze flicked to Damien's right hand, where his signet ring adorned one finger. Was it a different one he was missing?

"Let me rephrase." Damien folded his hands atop the desk. "Speak freely about our business and then get out."

Hyle released an overdramatic sigh. "You're never any fun. Very well, you were right, as usual. Two other unlicensed enchanters disappeared before Keirian Rusel."

Ari paused mid-sip of her tea. Why was Damien looking into Mikira's father?

"Your source?" Damien asked.

"The Goddess herself whispered in my ear," Hyle replied with a cheeky grin. At Damien's flat glare, he added, "I tracked the paperwork on both of them through the Vault. Rezek has quite the network between himself and the Anthir jail cells. The paperwork shows the enchanters being executed, but there's no additional paperwork for the burial of their bodies."

"Which means they were never executed." Ari dropped into one of the armchairs. "Rezek took them, like he took Mikira's father."

Hyle's unnerving gaze found her once more. "Precisely. I found the berator responsible for the paperwork. It appears he owes a rather large betting debt to House Kelbra."

"Ensure that debt is erased," Damien instructed. "Whatever Rezek is doing with them, I don't want him obtaining any more."

Hyle dropped into a flourishing bow. "Done." He cast Ari one last, lingering look before leaving the way she'd entered. Ari watched him go, trying to discern what it was about him that left her so cold.

"Rezek appears to be collecting enchanters," Damien explained without prompting. "Since he could have traded Mikira her father's life for her ranch, he must want something in addition to it, and her father's powers were all I could think of."

She shivered. That could just as easily have been her. "For what?"

"I intend to find out."

"And your missing ring?" she asked.

Damien spun the signet ring around his finger. "This is a replica. I lost the real one, though I've begun to suspect it was actually stolen. Until I know why, I don't want to commission a new one."

"I see." She studied the dark outline of the Racari on his desk.

His gaze followed hers. "I've made some new discoveries you might be interested in."

Is one whether the effects of magic include losing time and a voice you can't tell from your own? Her hand tightened around her teacup. Maybe they'd been wrong about the impact of verillion on enchanters. Maybe it did poison them, just in another way. She hated the idea that the same power that had quieted her fear threatened to bring it back to life. She didn't want to lose control again.

"Arielle?"

"Yes, sorry. What did you find?"

Damien tapped his notebook. "The Racari talks of a fifth gemstone capable of conducting enchantments: bloodstones."

Her brow furrowed. "Meaning more types of enchantments?"

He nodded. "Though I haven't quite deciphered what kind. The application of magic was once much greater, and new discoveries are still being made. For example, did you know Iziri shadowglass is supposedly capable of holding enchantments to be used later?"

"I didn't." Yet another thing lost in the Burning. But if they could discover what the stone did—she met Damien's eyes and found them alight. That information could make House Adair far more powerful than it already was, could take her magic to an entirely new level.

Ari joined him at the desk, and Damien folded the Racari closed, tapping the red and green stone at its center. "This is a bloodstone. Do you sense anything from it?" He was in his shirtsleeves again, and the definition of his forearms pressed distractingly against the white fabric.

Ari ran one finger along the cool stone, sensing the faint buzz of magic. "Yes."

It pulled at her, drawing her in, and she snatched her hand away.

"Does the book say anything about the effects of enchanting yourself?" She leaned against the desk, his eyes tracking her movements. He was so very aware of her when she was near. She liked to pick out the tiny flex of the muscles in his jaw, the flick of his eyes across her face. His fingers curled into a fist on the desk, as if to keep from touching her. So controlled. A part of her longed to make him give that up.

"Not exactly." His voice betrayed none of what his face had. "It only warns against holding too much verillion without burning the magic as it may cause physical damage."

"Nothing else?"

The slightest furrow formed between his brows. "Why? Is something wrong?"

She lifted off the desk. Just the other day she was chastising him for keeping things from her, and now she was doing the very same. But she worried what telling him might do. Would he look at her differently if he knew the truth?

"Arielle?" She heard him approach, felt his hand settle in the curve at the base of her neck.

Ari had spent so very, very long keeping secrets. What she'd done to her Saba, what she was capable of, her magic—for once, she didn't want to handle this alone. She turned into his touch, his fingers sliding down her arm, and she captured his hand in her own.

"I've been hearing a voice," she told him, and he did not flinch. "At first, I thought it was just my own thoughts, the voice in the back of my mind. But it's been growing stronger each time I use my magic, and the things it says . . . They're not me."

Are you sure about that, little lion? whispered the voice.

She pushed it away, focusing on Damien's steel-steady gaze. "I think it's the book. I think it's . . . *talking* to me."

The strange feeling she got when she held it, the way she never wanted to put it down and couldn't be rid of it. There was no denying the voice grew stronger each time she used her magic, and it had only appeared after the incident with her Saba, but over the last few weeks, it'd been getting worse even without using magic.

She expected Damien to dismiss her, but instead, his eyes grew wide with realization. "That's it."

He released her hand, returning to the Racari. "There was a part I couldn't translate, but I think I know what it is now." She joined him as he flipped back several pages, scanning the words she couldn't read. His finger stopped on one. "Here. It's the same word twice, and I thought it a mistake. But it actually has two meanings: 'stone' and 'bond.' I think it means to *bind* the stone. I think the bloodstone creates bonds between things."

"That's why I can't get rid of it," she said. The Racari was *bound* to her. Had her parents known? Was that why they'd kept it hidden, why all her life their neighbors had been wary of their family? Had they known all along what she was?

Do you? asked the voice.

"Damien," she asked warily. "What happened to the Heretics?"

"No one knows for certain," he replied. "Most believe that they died in the explosion of the Cataclysm. Why?"

"A Heretic was the last one to be bound to this," she said. "What if ... What if part of them still *is*?"

In the back of her mind, something unfurled, its satisfaction spreading through her. Her hand went to her Saba's necklace, and the feeling subsided. A story rose to life in her mind, a piece of forgotten mythology from one of the Kinnish texts about a possessing spirit seeking revenge. A Dybbuk, it'd been called.

Damien's expression grew tight. "Do you always remove your Saba's necklace when you work magic?"

"When I create golems ..." She trailed off. Both of the incidents when she'd lost time, she'd taken her necklace off. The first time to create Atara, the second just last evening when she went to sleep. But she always took it off when she slept. Did that mean last night wasn't the first she'd spent wandering, or had something changed? What if she hurt someone else?

"Keep it on at all times from now on," Damien instructed. "Aslir's fang is said to guard against evil spirits."

Her hand tightened on the necklace. "Is that what you think this is? An evil spirit in the Racari speaking to me?"

"In truth, I don't know," he replied, and she could see how much it cost him to admit that, a man who prided himself on knowledge. "But for now, we play it safe."

Whatever this was, whatever was happening, Ari didn't think safe was an option any longer, and yet she could not bring herself to give it up.

She would never let this power go.

CHAPTER 27

ARIELLE

A PLATFORM HAD BEEN erected on a hill at the edge of the
Highbridge District on the east side of the city, where the third
race would follow the Traveler's Road around Veradell, across the Greystel
River, and into the Silverwood at the base of the Anfell Mountains.

As the ancestral hunting grounds of the royal family, the Silverwood
was usually off-limits to anyone outside their circle. The Adair coach had
taken them past the forest on their way in to give Mikira a glimpse of the
course, and Ari could see why they kept it to themselves. The trees had
smooth ivory trunks with graceful sloping branches laden with thick clus-
ters of silver-green leaves, as if the whole wood had a dusting of metallic
snow. It had the stillness of a land undisturbed, a tranquility that called to
her and was minutes away from being violently disturbed.

The air of the race was different than she'd expected, far livelier and
festive in a way that obscured the gravity of what was to come. Some of
the riders might not survive, their horses could be maimed, and yet the
only thing louder than the music were the chants of the crowd gathered in
the makeshift stands or reclining at the tables that dotted the hillside. She
saw more than one fan with homemade signs for Mikira, others wearing
professional racing jerseys with her family's name sewn across the back.

They make a sport of bloodshed, said the voice.

This coming from someone responsible for the deaths of thousands, Ari thought back. A beat of silence. Then: *That was never my intention.*

Ari didn't respond. She shouldn't have to begin with. They had yet to discover a way to sever her bond to the Racari, but in the meantime, she'd kept her Saba's necklace on and promised Damien not to entertain the spirit. But after spending so much time with it, it was difficult to ignore.

She joined the others by the trailer, where Damien was giving Mikira some last-minute stats on the riders left in the competition. The girl was only half listening. She'd been distant all morning, barely acknowledging Ari's explanation about the bloodstone discovery. The stones set in the hilts of her knives were the same as the one on the Racari, but while she couldn't be free of the book, Mikira's knives seemed to have no link of their own.

When the bell rang and she swung up into the saddle, Ari grabbed hold of her hand. "Be careful," she said. "And good luck."

Mikira gave her a small smile. "I'm glad you're here," she said, and then she was gone.

Damien watched with a look of dismay as she rode off to the starting line. "She's distracted."

"She's got a lot to think about," Ari countered. It was a feeling she understood, and she only wished she knew what was on Mikira's mind.

Reid picked up the mug of tea he'd set down in the trailer. "She'd better get focused or—shit."

"Is that all you ever have to say to me, Reid?"

The voice raked cold claws of dread down Ari's spine. Her hand went reflexively to the emerald in her skirt pocket, and she drew to life the burn of verillion in her gut as Loic Adair rounded off their circle.

His eyes were only for Damien. "I hear you've been looking for me, little brother."

A line of tension descended through Damien. "And I hear you've found a new partner."

Loic tilted his head, regarding his brother with amusement. "Are you jealous that your little friend prefers me now? You do have a bad habit of glaring at people until they run away. Ah, there it is."

Annoyance overtook Damien's face, though it quickly vanished. It seemed at least his siblings were capable of getting under his skin. "Whatever you're planning with him, he'll turn on you, L," he warned. "It's only a matter of when."

"You think I can't handle Rezek Kelbra?"

"That's not what I said."

Loic waved a dismissive hand. "Just because he outplayed you doesn't mean I'll make the same mistake."

"Outplayed?" Damien hissed. "Is that what you call him murdering—"

Loic seized him by the collar. "Do not finish that sentence. You don't have the right."

The burn of verillion tore through Ari, and she wrenched Loic back by the shoulder. He spun on her, but Reid leapt to his feet, and he and Damien closed ranks between them.

The grin that cut across Loic's face was half snarl. "Just a sculptor, hm?" His gaze settled on Ari like a clammy touch, and she fought the urge to recoil. "Did you find yourself a girlfriend, little brother?"

Damien ran a hand through his hair, then straightened his jacket. They were small movements, throwaways to someone who didn't know him, but Ari recognized them for what they were: distractions. Tasks Damien performed as a means of keeping himself under control. Straighten this, move that—and don't think about punching your brother in the face.

"She's not your concern," he said.

Loic's grin turned hungry, and for an instant, all Ari could see were Fen and Cardix. She felt their hands around her throat, smelled the stale stench of their breath. "Care for her, do you? Now, what could be so special about her that it would enrapture the great Damien Adair?" He laughed. "Perhaps I'll find out for myself."

Damien shed the last of his pretense. "If you go near her, I'll put a bullet between your eyes."

Loic lifted his hands in mock defense. "I won't touch her." A smile split his lips as his gaze locked on Ari in a way that made her stomach turn. "Until she asks me to, of course."

Reid seized Damien's hand as it went for the gun at his ribs. "You can't," he warned.

"Do it," Loic urged. "Shoot me and forfeit your right to the Ascension, little brother."

For an instant, it looked as though Damien would throw Reid off and draw the weapon. His fingers curled tight about the handle, his knuckles bleeding white. In the end, he only shoved it back into its holster.

"You and Rezek deserve each other," he said.

Loic snarled. "And you deserve no one, which is exactly what you'll have when I'm finished."

Damien straightened his jacket cuffs. "This isn't over."

"No," Loic agreed, drifting backward. "It's only begun."

Ari watched him go until the crowd swallowed him up. Only then did she relinquish the burn of magic.

You should have shown him what happens to people who threaten you, coaxed the voice. *You still can.*

She pushed its words aside and looked to Damien. "What is the Ascension?"

Damien's gaze strayed across the crowd, checking they were alone. Most of the spectators had moved to the starting line, where the announcer was running through her usual speech. He was delaying. Thinking.

She didn't give him the chance. "Does this have something to do with why Shira's been following us? And why Loic showed up at the manor that night?"

"Damien," Reid said quietly when his silence persisted. "She should know."

Damien ran a hand through his tousled hair, vexation breaking through his mask. "If I involve you in this, you become a piece on the game board. You become a target."

Ari thought of the way Loic had looked at her. "I already am."

He must have understood what she meant, because he visibly relented. "The Ascension is a tradition among the noble houses. Instead of the oldest child inheriting the household, a challenge is set. Whoever completes it first, or most successfully, becomes heir to their house."

She'd never heard of a competition to decide the next heir of a house, but she'd only been in Veradell a short time, and it sounded like a closely guarded process. Was this what Reid had meant by saying that he had a lot depending on the race? Not just House Adair's racing business and verillion, but its entire future. His future.

"And what challenge were you set?" she asked.

"Whoever deals the greatest blow to one of the other houses by the end of the Illinir will become my father's heir," Damien replied.

"That's why you made the deal with Rezek. That's why you hired me and Mikira. If she wins, Rezek loses the rights to the Illinir to you." It would be a crushing blow for the Kelbras, whose deep coffers were due largely to the Illinir's profits. "But then Loic, and Shira . . ."

"Shira's concern with you is her own," Damien said tightly. "She's not interested in heading the family, and I expect her to make an intentionally weak entry for the Ascension. But Loic . . . I've made the mistake of treating him like a fool. He's reckless and temperamental, but he's also charming and well-connected, and he has the distinct advantage of knowing me better than almost anyone."

And when people knew you, it gave them power over you.

"That's why he threatened me," she said.

Damien took her hand, looking almost pained when he said, "If he can hurt you to get to me, he will. And my brother is not known for his kindness."

Absently, Reid folded his arms across his sternum. He looked as uneasy as Ari felt. She'd thought herself done feeling like the prey of hungry men, but it was a feeling that crept inside you and set down roots, refusing to be ripped free. It was the sort of thing she had to deny again and again, lest it entangle her so deeply, it became her.

She wanted to exorcise it.

"Mikira should know too." She intertwined their fingers. "She's as much a target as I am."

Damien shook his head. "I shouldn't have even told you. My father would be furious, and the more people who know, the more complex the game becomes. We already have a rogue Anthir sergeant prying into our business. I can't afford for information to leak."

Ari read the words he wouldn't say. "Mikira would not betray you."

"In this sort of game, betrayal is not always a choice," he replied. "It's safer for me to keep everything close."

The idea of lying to Mikira sat terribly with her, but this was not her secret to tell, and she knew the worth of a secret.

"Very well," she said. "But she had better be kept safe."

CHAPTER 28

MIKIRA

THE THIRD RACE was as much about weapons as magic.

Beginning on the outskirts of the Greenwark District, the race's physical enchantments would be a test of strength, agility, and endurance. Most horses would be unable to run the distance out to Silverwood Forest and back. If any of the remaining twenty-five riders had horses without the necessary enchantments, it would mean their end—unless they managed to kill enough competitors that speed no longer mattered.

It was that which made it the most dangerous, and Mikira the most nervous. She didn't want to hurt anyone, but the violence sold her lie. Without it, Rezek would know her horse was a cheat, but this way, she could pretend her skills with a knife were what saw her through.

Talyana brought her bay mare up beside Atara, but Mikira couldn't look at her without thinking of the body in the river. The oily touch of its skin, its bloated face.

Damien Adair is a murderer.

"Kira?" Talyana asked uncertainly.

"It's nothing." She put thoughts of Damien out of her mind. She couldn't afford distractions now.

Talyana reached across to squeeze her hand, and Mikira focused on the warmth of her touch, on the reassurance in her best friend's eyes. Talyana had always had a way of steadying her that no one else did, a certainty that she clung to. But it was something more now. Something that made her curl her fingers back around Talyana's own and hold tight.

Then she felt the press of eyes.

Over Talyana's shoulder, Gren watched her like a shark that smelled blood in the water. He was hedged in by Dezaena's and Arabella's horses in a way that looked purposeful. Had they made an alliance?

The announcer gave the last call to reach the line, and the crowd's cheering redoubled. Despite the chill morning air, sweat dampened Mikira's back. Atara shifted beneath her, and she counted every shuddering breath.

Five. Six. Seven.

"For Enderlain!" came the announcer's voice.

Eight. Nine. Ten.

"For the Harbingers!"

Mikira sent up a prayer to whoever was listening that they survive the melee to come.

"For Sendia!"

The bell rang.

The first fumbling seconds of the race were the same mess of hooves and barked curses as the others. Horses tossed their heads and struggled to find space. Mikira tried desperately to put distance between her and Gren, whose eyes were still locked on her. She got Alren's horse between them, losing ground in return. Hooves clattered against wet earth. Overhead, thunder echoed, and the first sprinkles of rain misted her skin.

The herd of racers evened into a steady flow as each horse found room to run. She'd lost track of Gren, but Talyana was at her back, a second set of eyes.

The beginning of the course followed the dirt track of the Traveler's Road, a stretch that would become an all-out sprint on the return. Ahead, the Grey spanned the width of several streets, its current unusually quick for the summer months. Water crashed against jagged rocks and splashed over the banks, running swiftly even in the shallows, where the riverbed bore a thousand small stones to overturn unsteady hooves.

It'd been enchanted with speed.

"Kira!"

Talyana pointed upriver at a bridge. The herd of riders was splitting between those with speed, who could handle the detour, and those chancing the quick waters and uneven footing of the Grey, their horses likely charmed for surefootedness.

With their horses enchanted for speed, she and Talyana veered toward the bridge. Alren Zalaire raced ahead of them, thundering across the painted wood. Just as they reached it, some horses began leaping into the air, others jerking to a halt.

"There's a gap!" Mikira called back to Talyana as Alren's horse landed on the other side.

"We've got a strength charm!"

They drove their horses between two riders picking their way back across the bridge, choosing the river over the jump. Mikira freed a knife just as the nearest rider swung at her with a baton. She ducked flat to Atara's withers and heard a thud behind her.

Whirling, she spotted the rider on the ground and a grin on Talyana's face—that quickly vanished. Mikira spun frontward again—the gap in the bridge was nearly two and a half horse lengths.

This time, she didn't even think about stopping Atara, only lowered her head, lifted off the saddle, and balanced her weight—Atara did the rest. She arced over the gap and landed soundly on the other side.

Talyana's horse landed easily alongside them, and the melee began as the two paths reconverged outside the edge of the Silverwood.

Mikira caught the flash of a blade and heard the gurgling scream of a rider seconds before they fell from their horse, vanishing beneath the stampede of hooves. The high whinny of another horse cut above the noise as a spotted bay's forelegs gave out beneath a wicked slash.

Nausea turned Mikira's stomach, but she kept her focus on Atara. They had room to run now, drops of water flying from the hooves of horses ahead of her. Talyana rode close to her side, a throwing knife in hand. When a woman sent her mount careening toward them, dagger drawn, Talyana buried the blade in the woman's shoulder.

They barreled into the Silverwood, seeking out the checkpoint in the center, where they would secure a flag before flying back to the starting line. The ground began to slope the deeper into the wood they got, the terrain growing rockier and littered with bone-white branches to leap. Ahead, the ground jutted sharply upward in a steep hill, hitting the cliff face of the Anfell Mountains. Through the canopy of leaves, Mikira could just make out the plateau partway up where the flags waited.

"Take the straightaway!" Talyana called a moment before Mikira realized what she meant: the hill was sheer enough that switchbacks had been cut into the face, granting weaker horses an easier alternative, but a longer one. Cutting straight from base to plateau was another steeper trail, and Mikira sent Atara right for it.

Her pace faltered when they hit the slope, but she charged upward, her labored breathing audible over the strike of hooves in wet earth. Arabella's horse ran ahead of them, and two more galloped along the switchbacks.

A flash of metal, and Talyana cried out, clutching her arm where a knife had grazed her. Mikira sought the culprit, but the rider was already up the switchback on the other side, left behind as Atara and Talyana's horse crested over the top of the hill onto the plateau.

Flags had been positioned all over. Some were tied to pulleys in the trees that rose and fell, bringing the flags in and out of range of a rider traveling on horseback at lightning speed. Others were accessible only by horses capable of navigating the pile of boulders ahead, requiring a sure-footedness charm.

Mikira leapt off Atara's back, going for a set of blue flags on the ground, but no sooner had she snatched one up than it dragged her back down—it'd been enchanted for weight. Atara circled around her as she reconsidered her strategy. They could take the extra weight, but it would wear on them over time, and look suspicious to Rezek if he saw her with it. Atara couldn't navigate the boulders, which left the speed flags.

"Duck!"

Mikira dropped to the ground at Talyana's shout, a baton swinging over her head. Atara spun on the attacker, her teeth clamping down on the rider's arm. The woman screamed, and her horse reared, but Atara didn't let go. The rider tumbled to the ground with a crunch of bone, her eyes rolling up as she fainted.

"It's okay," Mikira pressed a hand against Atara's chest. "Let go."

It took a moment for the mare to obey, but she finally released the woman, and Mikira swung back into her saddle. Several other riders were locked in combat or attempting to retrieve flags, but Arabella and Dezaena already had theirs and were heading back down the hill, Alren not far behind. She sought some sign of Gren, but the chaos was too much.

"I'll watch your back!" Talyana positioned her horse between them and the others. "Get the flag."

Mikira directed Atara beneath one of the pulley flags, and the horse set her stance. Balancing atop the saddle, she reached overhead just as the flag came down and snatched it free. They switched roles, Mikira protecting Talyana as she secured her own flag, and then they were off back down the hill.

"We're near the middle of the pack," Talyana called as they hit flat ground. "You should go ahead."

Mikira hesitated, but Talyana was right. There was no guarantee they'd win where they were now, and Talyana knew what this race meant to her.

"Stay safe!" she called, and Talyana nodded. Then she let Atara go.

They easily caught up to the bulk of the other horses, led by Arabella. A space opened, and Mikira loosened her hold on the reins, preparing to give Atara her head—just as someone nearly collided with them.

Atara dodged the other horse, then snapped at it. Gren cursed, drawing his mount away.

Shit shit shit.

Mikira urged Atara on, but the horse refused to turn her back on Gren. She swung back in, biting for the stallion's shoulder.

Gren slashed at Mikira's throat.

She leaned back, the blade drawing a shallow line across the bridge of her nose, and almost lost her balance. But she clung hard with her knees and pushed a hand against Atara's hindquarters, thrusting herself back into her seat.

Gren struck out again but missed. She tugged on Atara's reins, digging her knees in, but the horse wouldn't respond. Her teeth had already bloodied the stallion's neck, and she kept throwing her weight against the other beast, knocking Mikira against Gren.

The road curved, the rush of the Grey swelling up around them. The trees thinned to Gren's right, revealing a deep river ravine. It thundered like the stampeding horses, ready to tear apart anything it touched.

Gren was going to keep hounding her until he killed her. Atara could cover any distance they were losing, but Mikira couldn't win if she was dead.

Gren swung his horse in again, but this time, he didn't go for Mikira.

He slashed into Atara's right shoulder.

The horse screamed as her leg gave out and they hit the ground *hard*.

The air rushed from Mikira's lungs as she rolled like a skittering stone, the rocky earth tearing at her skin. She slid to a stop in the wet mud of the ravine edge. Her entire body ached, pain flaring from a thousand tiny cuts.

Distantly, she was aware of hoofbeats pounding past, of her own ragged breathing, of leaves crunching beneath a softer, more human step— she sucked in a gasp and flung herself back a second before Gren's blade drove into the earth where she'd been lying. She scrambled to her feet, ignoring her body's protests, and drew a knife.

Gren snarled, his face splattered with someone else's blood. She whirled, searching for Atara. She couldn't lose another horse, she couldn't—Atara lay in the mud a few paces away, struggling to get her legs back under her. Her shoulder was a mess of dark blood, the red growing until it was all Mikira could see, until the fury of the second race's enchantments paled in comparison to the rage pounding through her now.

"I'm going to kill you!" Mikira shrieked, but Gren only laughed and hefted his blade.

"Come on, then, little girl."

She dodged his first strike and his second. Then the blade caught her along the arm. She stepped inside his outstretched guard, slashing his forearm. He dropped his knife with a hiss.

"You're not even racing," she panted. "You're just trying to stop me."

"Lord Kelbra has made it very clear that you are not to win."

Because Rezek's rider didn't need to win for Mikira and Damien to lose—she just had to fail.

Gren's lips twisted into a grin, and he slammed into her. She staggered back, dropping her knife. Mud turned to loose earth, the ground crumbling beneath her feet. Then it shifted as if releasing a sigh and gave out beneath her, sending her plummeting toward the river.

CHAPTER 29

MIKIRA

MIKIRA CLUNG TO an exposed tree root. The water pulled at her heels, trying to drag her under as she dug her boots into the riverbank, scraping and clawing for purchase she couldn't find. She tried to pull herself up, but the added force only tore the root looser, dropping her closer to the water.

She cursed, fear flaring wild inside her.

"Kira?"

Her head snapped up. "Here!"

Talyana's face appeared over the edge of the ravine. She lowered to her stomach and hooked her toes over another root, leaning over the edge to reach for Mikira.

Mikira flung up a hand, their fingertips brushing. The root loosened again, dropping her a few inches closer to the water. "I can't reach you!"

Talyana unhooked her toes from the root, leaning deeper over the edge, but they were still too far. Mikira didn't have any strength left; either she grabbed Talyana's hand now, or she wouldn't be able to hold on any longer.

"Try again," Talyana urged. "I've got you."

Mikira glanced at the crashing water, then downriver to where a group of sharp rocks jutted each way. She took a deep breath and lunged. Talyana caught her hand and pulled. Mikira tried to find purchase with her feet, but it was no use. They were both slipping.

Something seized Talyana's shirt from behind. A massive force pulled her backward, drawing Mikira with her over the ledge a moment before their hands slipped apart. They both lay panting and limp in the mud, Atara standing over them like a guardian, her nostrils flaring.

"Hells," Mikira breathed as Atara lowered her face to hers, huffing hot air against her skin. Gren was nowhere to be seen. Either he'd thought her incapacitated, or Talyana's arrival had chased him off.

Talyana was already on her feet. She seized Mikira's hand, pulling her up. "The race. You have to go."

But Mikira only shook her head, gesturing at Atara's injured shoulder. "There's no way I can win now. And you—You lost when you stopped to help me. I'm so sorry, Tal."

"You don't know that yet!" Talyana grabbed her bay's reins and shoved them into Mikira's hands. "Take my horse."

"I can't! I can't win on an enchanted horse." The words pulled something loose inside her. She seized the fraying threads, shoving her emotions down. She couldn't lose it now. There had to be another way.

Atara nudged her and tossed her head, the clearest indication she ever gave that she wanted to run.

"You're hurt." Mikira's throat closed. At full strength, Atara could easily make up the time, but her shoulder was matted with blood, her breathing heavy even at a standstill.

Atara whinnied and nosed her harder.

"I don't speak horse, but I'm pretty sure she wants to race," Talyana said, though she regarded the horse with a strange look.

Atara neighed again, pawing at the ground with her injured leg to show its strength. Indecision warred inside Mikira, but she couldn't just give up. If Atara wanted to run, they would run.

"Okay." She swung up gently into Atara's saddle, wary of her extra weight.

"Only a few more than ten racers are still in it," Talyana said. "You only have to beat out the last few."

She'd have to pass them before they were in view of the finish line. If Rezek saw her making that kind of comeback, it would only confirm his suspicions that they'd cheated somehow.

Talyana swung up into her own saddle. "I'll interfere with as many of them as I can."

Mikira reached across to squeeze her arm. "Thank you, Tal."

Talyana smiled. "Thank me when you win."

Mikira sent Atara straight into a gallop, Talyana close on their heels. If Atara's leg pained her, she forced her way through it. She wasn't as swift as usual—Mikira hadn't realized how accustomed she'd become to the golem's unnatural speed—but she was still incredibly fast, and Talyana's bay struggled to keep up.

They came upon a small group racing at an unenchanted speed, likely horses with only an endurance charm. Talyana rode into their way, heading off the horses and forcing them to swing wide.

"Come on, girl," Mikira whispered as she felt Atara wane. Even with an endurance enchantment, three miles was a lot to ask at a full gallop. It was an impossible ask on an injured leg, yet the hope that had turned to vapor inside her when Atara fell slowly came surging back.

Atara hadn't given up, and neither would she.

With the injury, they couldn't take the bridge back, and had to slow down to cross the Grey. Some of the horses they'd passed caught up to them, more than one charmed for surefootedness that saw them quickly across the river. They hit the far side at the same time as Mikira, but when she sent Atara back into a gallop, they surged past.

She heard someone curse as Talyana cut across them again, zigzagging her horse to keep the others from advancing.

By the time they reached the final stretch, there were no other horses on the path. Everyone else had finished or was behind them.

There was only Mikira and Atara.

"Come on," she said again. Atara's breathing came fast and heavy. Her stride wavered.

The finish line loomed. Were they already too late?

Atara's leg buckled. She caught herself before they fell, Mikira's stomach swooping. The horse tried to pick up a trot, but every step on her right leg pained her. She staggered between walk and trot, fighting, Mikira powerless to do anything but pray, to promise her apples and long walks in the forest and to bite whomever she damned well pleased.

"Come on," she whispered, leaning her weight back to keep it off Atara's front leg.

Atara tossed her head and threw herself forward, breaking into one final, limping trot across the finish line.

The announcer's voice cut through the thundering of hooves and blood.

"And in tenth place, Mikira Rusel!"

"WHERE IS SHE?" Ari barged into the makeshift stable, Damien and Reid at her back.

Mikira leapt up from where she'd been leaning against Atara's stall, her exhaustion nearly dragging her straight back down. Atara had her right foreleg bent to keep the weight off of it. She whickered softly when Ari entered, lowering her head to be petted, and Ari slowed to capture the mare's head in her hands.

"It's okay," she whispered, running her hand along Atara's side. She stopped above the wound.

It looked terrible, the flesh rent by Gren's knife down to the layers of muscle and fat beneath. Blood had matted in her dark coat and still leaked freely from the wound.

"Is there anything you can do?" Mikira held on to the stall door, helplessness overtaking her. If Atara couldn't race, they were finished, but more than that, the idea that the horse might be permanently lame made her want to be sick. She thought of Ailene lying on the couch, the spark gone from her eyes.

"I don't know," Ari replied. "I usually never see golems again after I create them, but there's a feeling . . ." She trailed off, her attention settling on something that the rest of them couldn't see.

"What is it?" Mikira leaned closer.

"My magic. I can sense it, like a connection." Ari pressed her fingers harder into Atara's shoulder, and the horse huffed in annoyance but bore the pain. "Everyone be quiet."

They obeyed as she closed her eyes and began to chant in Kinnish. Mikira watched in growing wonder as light wisped from her skin and gathered around Atara's wound, before slowly knitting the skin back together.

When the light faded, the wound was gone.

"Thank the Goddess," Mikira said in a rush of breath. "How did you do that?"

Ari stared down at her fingertips in distant wonder. It was Damien who replied, "I suspect since her magic formed Atara's flesh, she had only to do the same thing again."

Atara tossed her head, and Mikira grinned, collapsing into the nearest chair in utter exhaustion. She only realized she'd fallen asleep when she came to in an empty stall, Reid wrapping a bandage around her arm. She could feel the sting of disinfecting herbs across the bridge of her nose.

When Reid noticed she was awake, he seized a steaming mug of tea and thrust it in her face. "Drink this."

"What is tea going to do?" she asked groggily but accepted the mug.

He blinked at her in mild affront. "What is tea going to—" He bit off the words, muttering to himself as he finished binding the wound. She didn't miss how slowly he worked, his gentle touch, and the care he took.

"The others?" she asked.

"Are loading up Atara."

"Pity," said a saccharine voice. "I wanted to inspect the beast myself."

Mikira lurched to her feet, the sudden movement leaving her dizzy. Reid steadied her as Rezek peered at them through the stall door. His sharp eyes took in Reid's hand on her arm, and Reid quickly snatched it back.

Rezek traced one finger along the wooden groove of the door. "It seems you made an alliance. All anyone's talking about is the rider that kept the others from finishing, though no one seems to know their name."

Reid shot her a furrowed look of confusion, but Mikira ignored it. "That isn't against the rules," she said. "Not like targeting another racer and trying to kill them is."

A smile curved Rezek's lips. "Now, that would be a problem. I don't suppose you have proof?"

Mikira gritted her teeth, trying not to say something she'd regret. Rezek's fingers dropped to the door latch, and he flicked it loose. The door swung inward, and Mikira retreated a step, aware of every inch of space between them.

He took a single step inside. "Gren said your horse got injured. However did you manage to finish the race?"

Got injured, as if it hadn't been Gren's blade that did it.

"He was wrong," Reid cut in. "It was another horse's blood."

Rezek came another step closer, his eyes still on her. "If you're lying to me, Miss Rusel, the consequences will be far worse than any lost bargain."

Reid shifted between them. Mikira wanted at once to disappear behind him where Rezek's searing gaze couldn't follow, and to tell Rezek to go to all four hells.

In the stretch of silence between them, a distant humming rose. She and

Reid exchanged looks a second before the stable door flew open. A crowd had gathered outside, each craning their necks to get a glimpse inside. Their many voices coalesced into one: "Rusel! Rusel! Rusel!"

Every beat of her family's name tugged at the fear inside her chest, unspooling it and fitting something new in its place. She seized Reid's hand and pulled him past a scowling Rezek into the main stable. The crowd's cheers redoubled, surging through her like the adrenaline of the race, buoying her.

From the back of the crowd, Damien and Ari watched her with knowing smiles.

Mikira glanced back at Rezek, who was staring at them with barely concealed annoyance. "I'm going to win," she told him, and stepped into the crowd.

CHAPTER 30

ARIELLE

ARI CLOSED HER book of enchantments and rubbed her dry eyes, her head pulsing with a growing ache. She didn't know how Damien did this for hours on end. Even now he was lost in the Racari at his desk, scribbling translations as he had been for the last several days since the third race.

Healing Atara had set off his curiosity, but all it'd done was make her more uneasy. Though she'd continued to wear her Saba's necklace as he'd suggested, she couldn't shake the feeling that something was very, very off. Everywhere she went, she felt the press of eyes, the inescapable feeling that something was always just out of sight. Her mind felt foggy and distant, her thoughts elusive things.

More than once, she caught herself wondering what would happen if she simply tore the necklace away and gave herself to the thing in the dark.

The wind howled, beating against the windows and tearing branches off trees. She let the sound soothe her. She liked to think of the power of the storm, to listen to it remake the world as it pleased. It felt a lot like the look in Mikira's eye when the crowd had found her after the race—it'd changed everything about her, down to the way she'd held herself. She might not be able to enchant herself, but she had her own kind magic now.

Ari dropped the book onto a pile of others and went to pour herself and Damien a glass of whiskey, marveling all the while at how she could possibly feel comfortable enough to fix herself a drink in another person's home. It was a small act, but it was the act of someone who belonged, and that was something she wasn't sure she'd ever get used to.

"I think you might be obsessed." She set his glass beside him, sipping her own. The various flavors shifted over her tongue, a pleasant burn trailing down her throat.

He glanced up distractedly, then turned back to the book, before realizing what he'd done and looking up again. "My apologies. My sister says I tend to lose myself in things."

Mention of Shira sent a twinge of unease through Ari, though Damien claimed she had no designs on becoming heir. There were so many moving pieces circling around them: the Illinir, Damien's bargain with Rezek, the Ascension to determine the next Adair heir, her troubling magic. She worried that sooner or later, one of them would come crashing down.

Damien glanced at the clock on the wall. "Is it really that late already?" He ran a hand through his hair and stood. "I have something I meant to give you earlier."

He retrieved a flat white box from his room and held it out to her. She took it, curious, and set her glass on the desk. She ran her fingers along the black silk ribbon encircling the box. Foiled gold lettering repeated the same word over and over again: *Sinclair, Sinclair, Sinclair.*

It was a shop on Ettinger Street she'd only heard of in name, never thinking she'd have the chance to possess something from it.

"Open it," Damien said softly, so she did.

Inside rested a dress of the most magnificent design she had ever seen. With careful fingers, she lifted it from the box. Black silk unfurled, sleek and glossy as a panther's coat bathed in moonlight. Feathers of a deep crimson red gathered just below the waist and up along the sheer layers of black fabric that formed the bodice. Several trailed down the side, embers of color. They bobbed and shifted, like petals upon a pool of night.

"It's beautiful," Ari breathed.

"It's for the Kelbra ball. I thought you might want to come tomorrow night."

Once, that idea would have terrified her. Even attending the last race had been more public an outing than she'd had in a long time. But now the idea of stepping into that ballroom with Damien, Reid, and Mikira at her side only enthralled her.

"Thank you," she said.

"Do you want to try it on?" Damien nodded toward the open door of his bedroom. A little thrill went through her, and she nodded.

The enchanted lights inside his bedroom were dimmed, leaving the room caressed in shadow. The windows were draped in dark velvet curtains, the bed pushed against the far wall awash with black silk sheets, still rumpled from being slept in. A book lay open atop one pillow, and a small collection of empty glasses on the nightstand made being here feel suddenly personal.

She closed the door and changed. As she did a series of clasps beneath her arm, music drifted in from the other room. She felt her face flush. Thankful for the solitude and the dark, she pressed a hand to her chest, where the tip of her Saba's necklace pressed against the sweetheart neckline of the dress, and let out a slow breath.

Then she stepped into the foyer.

Damien surveyed the night beyond the windows, a glass in one hand, the other tucked casually into a pocket. He turned as she entered, his expression slowly slackening as his gaze ran along the length of the dress bit by bit. By the time his eyes returned to hers, Ari had forgotten to breathe.

"You look perfect," he told her, and she drew the words into herself. Over the last few weeks, the fear that lived inside her had given way to something else, something that burned. She had yet to fully unroot that fear, but she had learned to build atop it.

Setting down his glass, Damien offered her a small black box. "I had this made too."

She took it, removing the lid to reveal a thin gold band with an inset emerald. For a moment, all she could do was stare. The dress alone was worth more than she'd ever held in her hands, and *the ring.*

"The stone is flush with the band and without a back." Damien slipped it from the box. "It will be in contact with your skin at all times."

So she could use it to enchant herself at any time. He really did think of everything.

He gave her a questioning look, and she held out her right hand. Gently, he slid the band onto her ring finger. It fit perfectly.

"Do you like it?"

She ran her thumb over the band. "I love it."

He held out his hand, and she took it without thinking, the same warmth she remembered from before, the same callused fingers.

A steady melody encircled them as he placed one hand on her hip, the other clasped about her own. She set her free one on the solid muscle of his shoulder, her fingers pressing into his back. His body was warm against hers, his fingers lines of fire on her hip. She loved how aware she was of his touch, of him. Things that had once felt foreign to her felt right.

The dance was not quick. It was made of slow, sweeping motions and gentle, back-arching dips. It left little room between them.

As they turned and glided, the press of Damien's hips and hands guiding her, Ari's body came alight. Something burned inside of her. She clung to that feeling, to the power that coursed through her body with the understanding that the look on Damien's face, the intensity in his eyes, meant he felt it too.

The song slowed, then faded. They didn't break apart.

"If I didn't know any better, I might think you were trying to seduce me," she breathed, unable to bring herself to look at him.

"It seems only fair," he replied, voice low. "For what you do to me."

The words curled around her like verillion smoke, drawing her in. She closed her eyes, her hand tightening on his shoulder. This wasn't right. She didn't deserve this. Not after what she had done. This contentment, this happiness—a monster did not deserve those feelings.

"You don't understand," she said softly. "My power—" She drew back. "You don't know what I've done."

Damien held fast to her, closing the distance she'd created. One hand reached out, tilting her chin up so they were eye to eye. "I told you, I am not afraid of you."

Pressed this close, she could feel his voice reverberating in her chest. "You are magnificent, Arielle Kadar, and I will suffer no contradictions from anyone's lips, least of all your own."

Then he kissed her.

It was soft, and surprisingly gentle, like the brush of fingertips. She became utterly aware of the press of his hands against her body, one on her hip, the other sliding around to weave into her hair. Her fingers ran up his sides, curving into the lean muscles of his back. The pounding of the storm against the house drowned the skipping beat of her heart.

When he pulled away, her face felt flush with heat, her breath stilled in her throat. The slate-gray intensity of his stare held her pinioned, a bright desire alight inside them. She felt it too. Without a word, she pressed her lips to his once more, and lost herself to the storm.

SHE AWOKE TO find herself standing in the foyer.

It was dark, the lights extinguished for the night. Bit by bit, she became aware of the world around her. The dying embers in the hearth. The moonlight slanting in through the wall of windows.

She'd fallen asleep in Damien's bed—she didn't remember getting up, didn't remember walking out here. Taking a slow, controlled breath, she looked down at her nightdress.

No blood.

Relief swept through her. She checked the bottoms of her feet and found them clean. It seemed she hadn't wandered from the house.

Then her hand went to her neck—her Saba's necklace was gone. She spun, spotting it in a pool of moonlight on the floor by the bed. Had it come off in her sleep?

What do you want? she demanded of the voice, but only silence returned.

She went to the desk, where the Racari lay as if waiting for her. She ran her fingers along the leather cover, and the book pulled at her. *Come come come*, it seemed to whisper. She felt herself tipping forward, as if she might slip beneath the pages and curl up there, content with paper and ink and words that made magic.

No.

Ari seized the book and flung it across the room. It crashed into a lamp, sending it shattering against the floor.

"Arielle?" Damien's voice sounded far away. She clung to it, letting it draw her back up like water drawn from a well. He was in the doorway, wearing only a pair of trousers. Flashes of memory coursed through her: skin against skin, his gentle hands, words whispered on a breath. She'd never been with someone before him, and she did not regret her choice.

"The storm woke me," she said without thinking.

Damien looked from her to the lamp, then approached the hearth to stoke the fire back to life. The moonlight played silver across the smooth olive skin of his back, and the urge to run her fingers down it rolled through her.

She sat on the chaise, and Damien joined her once he had the fire going. His arm curled about her shoulders, and she let him pull her close, listening to the sound of his heartbeat in his chest.

"I'm sorry about the lamp."

"I don't care about the lamp," he replied. "I do care why you broke it, though."

Her jaw set. How could she explain when she barely understood it herself? She both loved her magic and feared it. Felt enthralled by it and furious at it. It made her strong even as it unraveled her. She might not know what was happening to her, but she knew it had to do with that book.

It felt like it was taking control of her.

"I was angry," she said softly. It felt like a lie. It felt like the truth. It encompassed none of what she felt and all of it at once, and it had taken her so very, very long to understand.

She was angry.

Angry at her family for how they'd kept her isolated for her entire life. Angry at the secrets they kept. She was angry at herself for what she'd done, angry that she'd fled. She was angry because she was scared, and because she was not. Angry that she didn't understand, and that even as she pulled more power from the book, it pulled from her. Because on some fundamental level, she knew that was what was happening, and yet she could not bring herself to stop.

"I'm angry," she said again. "And I don't want to be."

"Why not?"

She didn't know how to answer that. All her life, her parents had told her never to draw attention to herself. Never to let her emotions get the best of her, lest she catch someone's eye. She understood now that this was what they had been afraid of, that somehow, they'd known.

"Because it feels like losing control," she said at last, sitting up so that she could see his face.

Damien was quiet, one corner of his lips turning in a way she'd come to find endearing. It meant he was thinking about something that had his undivided attention.

"Rezek Kelbra was once my closest friend," he said at last.

That wasn't what she'd been expecting. Rezek hardly seemed the type to make friends, and Damien was no socialite.

"We met after my family became a noble house," he continued. "The other houses scorned us, the Kelbras included. We earned our position the same as any of them, but they still treated us as if we'd stolen it. But Rezek was kind to me. Neither of us quite fit in perfectly among our families, and we both had complicated relationships with our older brothers. And Rezek hasn't always been so . . . vicious."

It was difficult to imagine. From what Mikira had said, Rezek seemed to delight in his cruelty and control over other people's lives.

"Something changed when I was thirteen. His family's Ascension began, and Rezek knew he had no chance of winning. That he is not the son Eradas Kelbra wanted is the worst-kept secret in Veradell. His brother was the golden boy; Rezek was a problem." Damien tilted back his head, staring out at the waning storm. "Their challenge was to deal the greatest blow to another house."

The same challenge his father had set.

"We'd moved into all of House Kelbra's territories by then. Verillion, racing, enchanted horses. My father sought to take pieces of everything Eradas owned, and he succeeded. We possess nearly thirty percent of verillion-growing land in Enderlain now, and it's well known that our enchant lines are superior, our tracks more lucrative." Damien's voice grew tight, the only indication the story was becoming more difficult to tell. She slid her hand to his, their fingers intertwining.

"Rezek thought if he ruined us, the source of his father's greatest shame, he might win." A muscle flexed in his jaw. "And to do that, he killed my mother."

Her breath caught, and he continued, "I found her dying. Have you ever sat and watched someone's chest for every breath? Begging it to go up just one more time. Bargaining with any god that will listen. You'll do anything they want, if only they save them. Do you know what that's like?"

Even as he asked it, Ari could tell that he already knew the answer. He'd guessed, because things like that never slipped by him.

"Yes." It was all she could bring herself to say.

"It was only afterward that I discovered my brother hiding in the other room." His voice roughened, the only sign of his anger. "He watched Rezek stab her and did nothing. Once, I would have done anything to earn his approval. But after that night, I promised myself I would become the next head of the family."

His gaze found hers as he said, "My mother is dead because of the Kelbras. The Illinir is only the beginning of what I will take from them."

This was why he'd made that bargain with Rezek: not only to win his family's Ascension, but for revenge against the boy who'd killed his mother. And now his brother, a man whose respect he'd sought his entire life, was colluding with his enemy.

"The thing no one really talks about with grief is the anger," he continued. "At what happened, at whoever did it. At yourself for not stopping it. At the world or your gods, whether you believe or not. You've been hurt, and you want to tear the world apart in return."

Every word he spoke was stark with familiarity. She knew these feelings, these thoughts. She held them close to her fragile heart.

"But no matter what you do, it doesn't help. Because you're nothing in the face of tragedy. You have no control, and that realization, that understanding, it breaks you. And you don't ever come back from that. Not really." He ran the fingers of his free hand along one of her curls, the tips brushing along her jaw.

Silently, he slid from his seat to kneel before her, her hands caught inside his own. "I will never tell you not to be angry. When the world has taken so much from you, sometimes anger is all you have left. But if you do nothing with it, it will consume you."

His eyes were bright with firelight as he said, "So be angry, my lion, and let the world tremble in your wake."

It was as though he spoke a spell. A promise that wound its way through her and around them both, binding tight. She leaned toward him, her fingers sliding into his hair. This time when she kissed him, she wasn't gentle.

CHAPTER 31

MIKIRA

THE KELBRA BALLROOM was exactly as Mikira remembered it.
Hung with enchanted chandeliers laced with diamonds and
swathed in artwork wrapped in gilded frames, the room was draped in
wealth and bright as a sparkling gem. There were enchantments of every
kind, from the golden birds suspended on invisible wires that flew with the
grace of their living counterparts to the changing scenes on the countless
skylights, shifting from snowcapped mountains to sapphire seas.

She'd been here, once, a long time ago. Eradas Kelbra had wanted a
Rusel enchant to compete with the Adairs, but her father had refused him.
The Kelbras' horses had a history of meeting early graves. Mikira remembered that night with stark clarity. The way Eradas had tried first to bribe
her father, then to threaten him. He'd promised to destroy the Rusel business, to see her father imprisoned, to take everything. And her father had
merely smiled, asked High Lord Kelbra if that was all, then seen himself
out. Eradas had never followed through on his threats—but Rezek had.

What a poor legacy Mikira made. One threat, and she caved.

"Are you okay?" Ari asked as they entered. "You've been acting strange
all week."

"I'm fine." She flinched at the bite in her words. This was why she'd
avoided being around the others as much as possible the last few days. She

couldn't lie to their faces. Couldn't look at them without thinking about her meeting with Rezek and the truth of what burned inside her boot. The ring was warm against her skin, where she'd kept it safe, afraid of what might happen if one of her sisters found it.

It was only a matter of time before Damien saw through her, and she had no doubt what Damien Adair did to threats.

Ari hooked their arms together in response, which only made Mikira feel worse. "I'm sorry," she said as they navigated the swirling crowd in search of Reid and Damien. The boys had come ahead on their own when Ari insisted on weaving Mikira's hair into a braided updo that felt like a crown.

Armor, she'd called it, to face Rezek with.

She tightened her arm on Ari's. "It's just . . . I'm worried about Damien."

Ari slowed, pulling Mikira around to face her. "Worried how?"

Hells, how did she explain this right? She trusted Ari not to go to Damien with her suspicions, but she also knew the girl cared for him and had just as much riding on their success. She didn't want to drive a wedge between them with unfounded accusations.

"What if he's dangerous, Ari?" she asked quietly.

"He is," she replied instantly. "But so am I."

There was a fervency to Ari's words that unsettled Mikira. She'd always had an intensity about her, but it'd grown in the passing weeks as she leaned deeper into her magic.

Ari tilted her head. "Where is this coming from?"

"Nowhere," Mikira said quickly, already regretting her decision to bring it up. "I just want to make sure you're okay."

Ari hooked their arms back together. "He doesn't scare me, Kira. He makes me feel safe. You understand that, don't you?"

She did, down to her bones, but there was a part of her that was beginning to question what she had to give up for that safety. What Ari had to give up.

Two women swept up to them with proffered pens, putting an end to the conversation. Ari squeezed her arm and slipped into the crowd to find the boys. This time, Mikira accepted the pens with a smile, signing her name in their notebooks. It was easier than the first time, her amiability no longer forced.

A nearby group spotted the commotion and swarmed her, jokingly chanting, "Rusel! Rusel! Rusel!"

Like that moment at the end of the third race, she felt their adoration running through her like a current. She had a sort of influence here—just like her father once had. Their name had carried weight back then, and with it came lucrative offers, easily given favors, and a steady stream of customers seeking Rusel enchants. Now it did again.

"You're getting way too used to that," a voice griped beside her, and Reid pulled her free of the growing crowd.

Mikira didn't know how to explain the effect their adulation had on her. The way it made her feel ten times her size, like she could take on anything—even Rezek. So she only rolled her eyes and followed him to the small group Damien and Ari occupied, which parted to make room for them.

Too late, Mikira realized their company—Prince Darius Zuerlin and, beside him, Rezek. He wore a heavily embroidered ice-blue vest flecked with gemstones, his white jacket equally extravagant, and they leached what little warmth existed in his eyes.

Damien spoke before she could react. "Your Highness, may I present my jockey, Miss Mikira Rusel."

She curtsied stiffly.

Darius Zuerlin looked almost exactly like his cousin; pale hair, sharp features, and eyes like white ice that remained frozen even when he smiled. But where Rezek seized control of a room with clawed hands, Darius stood above it, secure in the knowledge that it would bow before him.

"I'm quite impressed with the animal you delivered, Miss Rusel," the prince said. "Almost as impressed as I was with your race the other night."

"Thank you, Your Highness." Her voice was steady, though thinking of Iri hurt. The prince might have lifted Rezek's unofficial embargo on Rusel enchants, but he was still a Zuerlin. Still responsible for the war that took her brother's life. If she told him about her father right now, he'd do nothing. In truth, he was just as bad as Rezek.

"I look forward to the final race." She held his gaze. "When I can show you exactly what I'm capable of."

The words came so easily. The confidence, the pride. She fueled them with the chants of her family's name and the adoration in the spectators' eyes. Weeks ago, she would have stumbled over herself, but tonight, donning this mask felt natural.

Damien and Ari gave her matching glances of approval.

"Indeed." The prince lifted his wineglass to Mikira. Something hungry smoldered in his pale eyes, and the realization that her words could be taken a very different way settled in her stomach with a twist. His gaze slid along the length of her dress with the carelessness of a man used to getting his way.

Her fingers curled into her palms reflexively, and she saw Ari's mouth turn down.

"I'd almost forgotten you purchased a Rusel enchant, cousin." Rezek tilted his head. "How do you find it?"

The prince waved a hand. "I haven't had the chance to ride it yet, what with Father's failing health and the Illinir to attend."

Mikira tensed, sensing a trap. Damien's gaze sharpened on Rezek.

"How unfortunate. You know, Gren's horse took ill just the other night, and the vet fears he can't be saved." Rezek's voice rang hollow with false pity. "If his horse doesn't survive the night, perhaps you'd consider allowing him to ride yours in the next race. To test him out for you?"

Mikira lurched forward. "You can't!"

The silence that followed her exclamation was thick enough to suffocate. She wished it would swallow her whole.

"Your Highness," Damien began carefully. "What Miss Rusel means is—"

Darius silenced him with a look. "Do you presume to tell me what I can and cannot do with my property, Miss Rusel?" he asked softly. Too softly. Here was the resemblance to Rezek; the predator lurking beneath.

She recoiled. "I—No, Your Highness. Of course not. I only meant to say that isn't it against the race rules to change horses?"

"Each rider is permitted to change horses once, but only if their previous mount is dead or physically incapacitated," Rezek recited with all the glee of a child given a new toy. "And seeing as Gren's horse isn't likely to survive the night, then it is well within the laws of the race for Darius to lend him a new one."

Panic clawed loose inside her, but it was Ari who spoke. "Your Highness, what if he's hurt? The race can be brutal."

Darius waved a dismissive hand. "A horse that can't survive the Illinir is not a fit mount for a prince."

"All the more reason to test his merit," Rezek said silkily.

The prince still hadn't looked away from her, his lips pressed into a frown. "And I intend to do just that, cousin. Your rider will have my horse. See what he can do."

Mikira gaped at him, another refusal rising. Iri couldn't race in the Illinir. He was too kindhearted, too soft. And with someone like Gren on his back? It made her sick to imagine. There had to be a way around this. She could not watch him die. She could not lose more of her family to people who did not care for the cost of their lives.

An arm looped through hers, pulling her flush against a warm body. "I think Miss Rusel could do with a moment of fresh air," Reid said lightly.

The prince pursed his lips. "Indeed. Good evening, Miss Rusel."

But Mikira couldn't move. Walking away felt like damning Iri, like leaving him to the wolves to be devoured. She had thought selling him had broken her, that the worst of it was over, but she should have known by now that when it came to people like the prince, like Rezek, there was always something worse to come.

This was what came of playing their games.

Somehow, Mikira performed a mechanical bow. Then Reid was pulling her away through too many people. More than one tried to stop them, to speak to her, but Reid elbowed them out of the way and drew her from the throng, just as her throat began to burn and the air grew too thick.

They emerged into a clear space near a wall of balconies. Mikira tore free of Reid's hand, rounding on him. "I didn't need to be rescued! I can handle myself."

"Punching the prince in the face is treason," he replied. "And you're welcome."

She shook her head. Suddenly her dress felt too tight, the air too thin. She struck out for one of the small balconies and pushed open the doors, stumbling out into the gathering dusk.

Clasping the railing, Mikira let her head hang as she caught her breath, her mind spinning with thoughts she didn't want. About her father somewhere in these halls, about the final race only days from now, about the ring in her boot burning against her leg.

There was no doubt in her mind that Gren's horse was fine, which meant Rezek was going to kill it. Kill it and replace it with Iri. It was a smart move. Gren's horse had been enchanted for strength and endurance, but the final race relied on ethereal enchantments. Iri's speed and ability to sense danger would be invaluable.

"Oh, Iri . . ." she whispered.

Reid shifted at her back. "I . . . I'll go get you some water." Then he was gone, leaving her blessedly alone.

Or so she thought.

"Did you know that surrounding a room in balconies like this is actually the Kinnish style?" She didn't look up as Talyana leaned against the railing beside her. "The Kelbras always have enjoyed taking things that don't belong to them."

Mikira leaned over the railing, hanging her head. "Not interested in a lesson right now, Tal."

"Really?" Talyana tilted her head. "You used to love them. Do you remember the nights we spent on the floor of your father's study, listening to him talk of far-off places?" She scanned the horizon as though she could see them, if only she looked hard enough.

There had been a time when all Talyana wanted was to explore the world. She'd tell Mikira about distant places she wanted to visit, things she wanted to discover—what had kept her here, tied to this job she'd never wanted?

"I remember," Mikira said softly. She faced Talyana. "What are you doing here, Tal?"

"Just because I'm out of the race doesn't mean I can't enjoy the free food."

Mikira shook her head. "Not here. *Here.*" She gestured at the city. "You never liked Veradell. Why come back?"

Talyana was unusually solemn as she replied, "I had some unfinished business." Her fingers traced the curve of Mikira's face, careful of the healing cut across the bridge of her nose.

A hush descended through Mikira. She thought only of the warmth of Talyana's skin against her own, felt herself leaning into it. The last few weeks had been a mess of danger, impossibility, and confusion, but in that moment, it all slid away, and she wondered what her life would be like if all she had to worry about in the world was if she was in love with her best friend or a boy made of shadows.

Then a rasping voice cut through the still air, jarring her back to the present. She recoiled, clenching the railing and looking for Rezek, but it was only a nobleman deep in conversation with someone on his arm.

"Have you thought any more about what I asked?" Talyana's expression was all too knowing.

Mikira's hand curled around the railing. "You act like I could put a knife in Rezek's heart and be done with him. It's not that easy."

"It could be," Talyana replied. "The house system is broken."

"They're not all bad," she said, thinking of Damien, then of the ring in her boot.

Talyana snorted. "Damien Adair is just the same, Kira. I hate that you're tied to him."

"He's helping me save my family."

"And tearing down another while he's at it." Talyana's voice dropped to a low hiss. "He's only helping you because you're useful to him. The moment you're not, he'll drop you. He's just like all the rest. A spoiled, rich noble who thinks the law doesn't apply to him."

She winced. That much she couldn't deny, not if the ring meant what she thought it did. If Damien had truly killed that man, if he'd done half the things the rumors said, was she any better than them if she stood by and did nothing?

Her hands tightened on the railing. How had she even ended up here, caught between feuding lords and wrapped in a web of conspiracy? Every choice she made held a thousand implications, and while she was busy trying to survive, Rezek and Damien went on with their game.

Even now, she wanted Damien to fix everything, to find a way to undo it all. How far had she strayed that her first instinct was to ask a nobleman for help? If he was truly responsible for that man's death, he had to be held accountable.

It all felt like too much. Too much responsibility, too many decisions. She was never any good at this. Every time she made a choice, she chose wrong. But Talyana—Talyana had always had an answer, even when they were kids. Maybe she could help now too.

Talyana's eyes narrowed. "What is it, Kira?"

She hesitated. "Promise me you won't tell anyone."

"I can't—" She cut off, then nodded. "I promise."

"Have you heard about the body that washed up on the bank of the Grey?" Mikira glanced over her shoulder, knowing Reid would return soon.

"Yes."

"Well, it washed up on my property first."

Surprise flashed across Talyana's face, but Mikira pressed on. "I found this in his hand." She fished the ring from her boot.

Talyana's eyes widened. "A House Adair ring."

"The one Damien's wearing is a fake." Mikira rushed on. "And the only reason I can think he would have hidden losing his ring—"

"Is if he couldn't have anyone knowing," Talyana finished for her. "Because he killed that man and that ring is the evidence."

Hearing it out loud, a fresh wave of guilt seized her. How could she have kept this to herself? If Damien had truly killed this man, she was enabling a murderer.

"Maybe it's a trick," she said weakly. "Maybe someone's trying to frame him."

"Kira," Talyana said, her tone off. "I need that ring."

Mikira stepped back. "What?"

"Please, I don't have time to explain." She held out a hand.

Mikira clasped her fist to her chest. "I don't understand."

Talyana cursed, and for a moment Mikira thought she was going to make a grab for the ring, but then she spotted something over Mikira's shoulder and indecision flickered through her expression.

Then she said very quietly and very quickly, "Remember that I'm your friend. What I'm going to do, I'm doing for you, and everyone like you."

"Tal!"

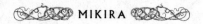

But she was already gone, disappearing into the crowd. Then Mikira saw who Talyana had seen.

Reid had returned, a glass in each hand, and he was staring at her like he'd never seen her before. "Why were you talking to her?" he demanded.

"Talyana?" Mikira asked, thinking him jealous. "She's my friend. Why?"

A scowl so vicious tore across Reid's face that she recoiled. "Because she's an Anthir sergeant."

CHAPTER 32

ARIELLE

ARI WOVE HER anger deep inside herself and held it close, no matter that all she wanted was to rip that satisfied smile off Rezek's face. Better yet, she wanted Mikira to do it, and she would when she won.

And if she fails? asked the voice. *Will you then?*

Ari ignored it, peering up at the enchanted birds and skylights dotting the ceiling. "Is there a room like this in your home too?" she asked Damien. Her arm was looped through his, and she wore the dress he'd gifted her. Her hair she'd left down in a dark wave of curls, her olive skin offset by the gold necklace he'd lent her and matched by the emerald ring. She couldn't resist spinning it about her finger.

"We never built a ballroom, no," he replied. They stood in a circle of guests, most of whom were wrapped up in the horrid story the crown prince was telling about the time he supposedly brought the Celairen ambassador to tears. The group had swelled so much with those eager for the prince's attention that they had relative privacy. "Mostly the greater houses have them. They were built for this exact occasion: hosting the Illinir balls."

Ari made a considering sound. "You'll need one."

As the new owner of the Illinir, Damien's house would automatically take the Kelbras' place in hosting the final ball. Only one race stood between them and that possibility, between her and the enchant license Damien had promised her. They were so close.

"That's an awfully bold assumption," said a cool voice.

Rezek had his back angled to the prince, effectively cutting them off from his cousin. She felt Damien stiffen, and she reached reflexively for the magic simmering in her gut, but Rezek only looked at her as if seeking something he couldn't see.

"Everything you are is built on a foundation of misfits and outcasts. Society's dregs." Rezek let out a low laugh. "Your family is less than the dirt on my shoes. Do you think a few verillion fields and distilleries make you equal to us? You'll never be anything but vermin."

He leaned close to Damien. "Just like your mother."

Damien's eyes widened a fraction. A breath, two, and Ari watched him seal away his rising anger. Rezek waited, a twisted glee in his eyes, but Damien held himself steady. It would take more than that to break him.

"Rezek!" An older man cut toward them, the crowd parting swiftly.

"High Lord Kelbra," Damien said as both he and Ari bowed. Eradas Kelbra shared his son's blue eyes and sharp features, but that was where their similarities ended. While Rezek was pale, Eradas was gilded, from the glow of his skin to the gold of his hair and the rings circling his fingers. And where Rezek smiled like a shark baring his teeth, Eradas's face was a mask of stone.

"I thought I made it clear you were to attend me this evening." Eradas didn't spare Damien and her a glance. "The Ranoen ambassador is waiting."

In those short seconds, Rezek transformed. The wild delight in his eyes vanished and his smile pressed into a firm line. "I apologize, Father. I got distracted by business."

"Your brother had no trouble understanding the importance of international negotiations," Eradas said. "Why is it that you struggle to grasp the concept?"

A muscle feathered in Rezek's jaw. Damien had told her that he was a child when Rezek's older brother, Warrick, vanished, but people still spoke of it: the day Eradas Kelbra lost his golden heir. He said they liked to whisper that Rezek had known no matter what he did, his father would never let him win their family Ascension, so he'd made his brother disappear, leaving his father no choice but to name him heir after killing Damien's mother.

"Well, boy?" A growl cut Eradas's words. When all Rezek did was bow his head, a look of disgust flickered through his father's stoic face. "Are you capable of finding your own way to the drawing room, or do you require help with that as well?"

"No, Father. I'm coming."

Rezek gave them a final, chilling look before following Eradas into the crowd.

"I don't know which of them I detest more." Damien straightened the sleeves of his cuffs.

Ari captured his hands in hers, stilling the fidgeting movement. "Something you and Mikira have in common, I imagine. At least he listens to his father."

"For now," Damien muttered.

"Speaking of detestation." Ari's gaze had latched on to Loic where he stood by the far wall, tall enough that he loomed over much of the party. Eradas had stopped long enough to acknowledge him, and several other nobles attended him, more than one of them brushing their fingers across his arms or laughing obnoxiously at things he said. "Your brother is here."

When Damien's eyes found him, Loic grinned and hefted his wineglass. Then he downed the ruby liquid in one gulp and wiped it from his lips like blood after a feast.

"I don't like him," Ari said.

"You aren't the only one," Reid muttered as he slid to Damien's side. His dark hair was a wild mess, and there were more shadows under his eyes than usual. Reid never slept well, but now he seemed not to have slept at all. He'd been fretting over Mikira's avoidance for days, though he wouldn't admit it outright.

"We have a problem," he said.

"I think we have more than one," Damien replied. Loic had left his entourage behind and was coming toward them.

Ari burned verillion on instinct but held off connecting it to the stone, the simple presence of the magic reassuring her.

They peeled away from the prince's group as Loic arrived. "Little brother." He had a flush to his cheeks from drink, but his words were clear and sharp. His eyes even more so as they surveyed Ari, who stared resolutely back at him.

"What do you want, Loic?" Damien shifted in front of Ari.

"I thought we might make a little bargain of our own." Loic snatched a champagne flute from a passing server.

"What need have I to bargain with you?" Damien's tone was steady, but Ari sensed his unease, and Reid moved restlessly at his back.

Loic dragged the moment out with a sip of champagne before he said simply, "You will forfeit your bid in the Ascension, and in return, I won't tell a soul." He leaned close, a smile on his lips. "I know your little enchanter's unlicensed."

The buzz of conversation faded as something cold and quiet spread through Damien. Ari went perfectly still, the burn of magic winking out inside her. That old, familiar unease came creeping back, and she fought to keep it under control.

Damien turned to her. "Go with Reid."

"But—" She stopped when she realized what was seeing in his eyes: fear. Reid took her arm, and she let him pull her into the crowd.

"She can't run," Loic said with a laugh. "Where will you keep her? Not the manor. Not the country estate." His smile grew with every word. "What a fun game this will be."

"You don't know the rules of this game half as well as you think you do, brother," Damien snarled. "I'll make you regret ever playing."

That was the last she heard before the crowd swallowed them up. Reid shoved their way through it with the persistence of an ox until they reached the entrance, where he released her. "Go down to the foyer. I need to find Mikira, and then we're leaving."

She followed the staircase down to the empty foyer, where she positioned herself by the exit to wait. Her eyes remained locked on the doorway, and she wrapped her arms about herself against the night's chill. The scent of roses hung heavy in the air, almost sickeningly sweet.

The crowd shifted, and then Damien appeared. She relaxed as he descended the stairs.

"Damien Adair."

A lean figure in the blue and white livery of the Anthir stood at the top of the stairs, her brown hair plaited down her back. Two constables flanked her.

Ari stepped into the shadows of the courtyard, sliding between the entrance wall and a low-hanging tree. Was this Loic's plan? Send the Anthir after her for being unlicensed?

"Sergeant Haraver." Damien greeted her stiffly. "To what do I owe the delight of your presence?"

The sergeant stepped into the foyer light, illuminating an angular face and affable smile that inexplicably irked Ari. It was the kind of smile that was meant to be disarming, but only put her on edge as she watched, mostly concealed by the roses.

"A delight, Damien, really? I'd have never guessed. You flatter me."

"Let me rephrase," Damien said shortly. "What do you want, Talyana?"

Ari inhaled sharply. Talyana was the name of the girl that Mikira had been meeting. Surely she would have mentioned if she was friends with an Anthir sergeant?

Talyana descended the staircase, the constables a step behind. Loic emerged onto the balcony in her place, champagne flute in hand. His laughter was practically palpable in the air.

When Talyana stopped a few feet away, she said in quiet simplicity, "I'm going to arrest you."

A line of tension ran through Damien like crackling ice. The clatter and noise of the party faded to a dull hum as Ari's magic flared to life. It took all her control to resist the urge to let her power flood her and go to Damien's aid. This was not a physical battle, and if she revealed herself, she'd only become a piece to be used against him.

Talyana's lips quirked into a smile. "Well, you did say get to the point."

"Do you warn all of your suspects before you arrest them?" Damien asked.

Talyana shrugged one shoulder. "What fun is a hunt if your prey doesn't run?"

Prey.

Damien betrayed nothing, though Ari knew the word bothered him. Like her, he'd worked too hard to make himself the hunter to suffer those who thought they could tear him down. Everything he had built, everything he had fought for, rested on his plans with the Illinir going smoothly.

If Talyana interfered with those, he'd make her regret it.

"Do you have a writ of arrest from your superior?" Damien asked Talyana.

Her jaw set, and Damien smiled. "I didn't think so." He advanced on her. The constables' hands fell on their batons. "I've heard stories about you, Sergeant. Apparently, you have a habit of disobeying orders and ignoring your superiors. I'd wager you asked for that writ and were denied, weren't you?"

Talyana's lips pressed into a firm line as he said, "And yet you came anyway. I wonder what Inspector Elrihan would have to say about that? He and I are rather good friends."

"So I've heard," Talyana ground out. "In fact, you seem to have a fair number of friends in high places. Been sharing your profits? Rigging races and selling illegal verillion has to pay well."

Damien clasped his hands and shrugged. "I wouldn't know."

Talyana looked ready to strike him down just for the sake of it. One of the other guards grasped her shoulder. "Let's go, Sergeant. It's not worth it."

"Listen to your friend," Damien warned.

The affable air that'd surrounded Talyana moments ago had grown into a thundercloud. For a moment, she stood poised on the edge of indecision. Then she said, "You're under arrest for the murder of Fen and Cardix Ridoux."

At the top of the stairs, Loic laughed.

Cold understanding swept through Ari, and she watched in horror as the sergeant withdrew a pair of handcuffs. She expected Damien to fight back, to *do something*, but he simply turned around and crossed his arms behind his back.

Well, if he wouldn't act, she would. She stepped forward, but Damien caught her eye and shook his head. She stopped.

The wind rose, making her curls dance around her face as the sergeant secured the handcuffs. An unfamiliar scent rode the air, something bitter amidst the rosy smell. Then a hand closed over her mouth. Strong arms dragged her back, her vision blurring. The last thing she saw was Damien's wide eyes, a shout forming on his lips.

Then everything went dark.

CHAPTER 33

ARIELLE

A RI WOKE GROGGILY on a cold stone floor. Her body felt numb and tingly all at once, but not in the pleasant way of the verillion. The buzz from the magic had faded, though she'd eaten enough verillion to last several hours. How long had she been out?

When she moved, metal clinked and something rough dug into her wrist. Blinking to clear her foggy vision, she looked down at the chains that bound her wrists, then up at the dark stone walls of the cell around her. An enchanted lamp burned just down the hall, casting a faint glow.

A sharp, wild panic reared inside her. Loic must have told the Anthir that she was an unlicensed enchanter. They'd arrested Damien for harboring her and locked her in a cell to await execution.

She pulled desperately on her empty store of verillion. If she could just enchant the ring, she could break these chains and escape, but the magic was gone. They'd hang her in a public execution, make her an example of what happened to enchanters who thought themselves above the law. They might even go after her family, if Loic accused her of Kinnish magic.

She'd been so close. The final race of the Illinir was only a day away. She'd have become a licensed enchanter, have had Damien at her side and the world at her feet. After everything she'd learned, everything she'd done, it was over. Her power meant nothing in the face of this.

Your power means everything, urged the voice.

A low moan echoed through the high arched corridor, answered by a bone-grinding growl. Ari stilled. Neither of those had sounded human. In tandem the sounds rose into a winding howl, cut through by the clank of chains and scrape of claws on stone.

What kind of jail was this?

A bolt shifted in the door, and it swung open to reveal two silhouettes. One she didn't recognize, short with a narrow face.

The other was Rezek Kelbra.

It wasn't an Anthir jail at all—it was the Kelbra dungeons.

The other man yanked a chain by the door. The manacles on her wrists pulled taut, drawing her arms above her head until her toes barely reached the floor. She bit back a cry as the metal dug into her wrists.

"I have some rather simple questions for you, little mouse," Rezek said in a honeyed voice. "All you have to do is answer them honestly, and I'll let you go unharmed."

Ari spat at his feet.

The other man backhanded her hard, and she bit down a cry.

"Mm, perhaps not a mouse," Rezek mused. "I suggest you don't give Kyvin here reason to hurt you any more than he needs to. He does have a tendency to get carried away."

Rezek leaned casually in the doorframe, arms crossed, as if watching a favored pet at play. "Tell me how Mikira is winning these races. No non-enchant can do what that horse has done."

She said nothing, even as something warned her to be careful, to not provoke them. It was a part of her that had shrunk over these last weeks. Hearing it now, feeling its pull, a fury lit inside her. She would not be that person again. She would not hide. Not before a man who wanted to watch her cower and beg, who took pleasure in her pain.

Not when another part knew that the moment Rezek had the information he wanted, he would kill her.

Kyvin's fist slammed into her stomach. Air rushed from her lungs in a pained gasp, the metal cuffs digging deeper into her wrists.

"Damien isn't coming for you," Rezek said softly. "It's just the three of us, little mouse." Her heart sank with every word. The sergeant had arrested him, but he'd seen her get taken. He had to know where she was, and if there was one thing she'd learned about Damien Adair, it was that he always had a plan.

He would come. He had to.

Rezek chuckled quietly. "Oh, you think he cares about you, don't you? How sweet." He drew closer, eyes searching hers. A faint, familiar buzzing leapt from his skin like static.

She recoiled. "What are you?"

Rezek smiled. "I think you know. You can feel it, can't you?"

"What are you talking about?"

He laughed, running one finger along the chains to her wrist before retreating to the doorway. "You mean only as much to Damien as you can do for him."

And she had done all she could already. The golem was made, the race nearly won. What use did he have for her now?

Stop it. She shoved the dark thoughts aside. If Damien didn't need her, he wouldn't have bought her that dress, wouldn't be helping her discover her new abilities, wouldn't have said the things he'd said.

She hated how little effort it took for her to believe that someone would discard her.

"You think I'm lying, don't you?" Rezek asked, a strange sort of twisted pity in his voice. "Didn't you ever wonder how those men found you?"

Her head jerked up before she could stop it, and Rezek grinned. "Damien told them where you were. He hired them to steal from you, to make you desperate so you'd work for him."

"That's impossible," she rasped.

Rezek made a disappointed tsking noise. "This is what happens when you put your fate in the hands of people like him. They use you."

Kyvin withdrew a small, sharp knife from a belt at his waist, and something old and familiar simmered to life inside her. Something she thought she'd destroyed.

Fear.

"Now, then," Rezek said in a low, dangerous voice. "I suggest you don't make me repeat myself."

As Kyvin grazed the point of the blade along her collarbone, Ari met Rezek's cold eyes and lifted her head. His words were poison, and she would not let them weaken her. Even if what he said was true, she would not bend. She would hear it from Damien's own mouth before she condemned him.

And she would tell Rezek nothing.

Kyvin pressed the point of the blade into the spot just below her bone with a grin. "Scream for me, little mouse."

CHAPTER 34

MIKIRA

MIKIRA DIDN'T KNOW what she was doing.

She and Reid had barely reached the landing outside the ball-room in time to see Talyana haul Damien off. Reid had gone after them to the Anthir headquarters, and she'd sought Ari, but unable to find her, assumed the girl had gone with Reid. She'd returned to the manor, and for several long minutes, simply stood outside Damien's door in a daze.

The world felt vast with possibilities. Her best friend had returned to her, only to manipulate and use her. Her sponsor was implicated in mur-der and had been arrested because of her foolishness. The final race for her family's fate began a day from now, and everything was falling apart around her.

That was why she'd come here. She wanted to see if she could find any more evidence, because she'd finally remembered where she'd seen the corpse's face: he was one of the men the Anthir had come looking for all those weeks ago. Still, she found it suspicious that this had happened after she told Rezek about Damien's fake ring. Had he orchestrated it somehow?

She rifled through Damien's desk, then his room, then stopped on the threshold of Reid's. It was not full of caskets like she'd thought all those weeks ago. Rather, it was the neat, orderly space of a soldier, or perhaps a mother hen, and it smelled of tea and paper. Directly across stood a four-poster bed, the dark navy comforter and sheets meticulously pressed. She'd drifted toward it before she realized what she was doing, her fingers brushing along the soft cotton, before she retracted her hand.

Scowling at herself, she quickly checked the nightstands and closet before moving on to the adjacent workroom. A narrow desk spread the length of the wall, stacked with neat piles of books and papers. Above hung an arrangement of drawings. The bones of the leg, the veins of the hand, the muscles of the lower back—they spread across the wall in charcoal and ink, precise, detailed, and methodically annotated.

She sifted through the stacks of papers but found only research and more anatomy diagrams. Careful to put everything back, she moved along the desk, but the only notable thing she found was a pile of thin glass packets whose purpose she couldn't discern. One was cracked and stained inside with ink, the others intact but with a tiny, needle-sized hole in the ends for loading the ink.

Her elbow brushed a stack of folders, sending one sliding across the table. Papers spilled out and she paused with her hand outstretched to gather them back. These weren't anatomical drawings.

She took in the curve of her own face, the hawklike bend to her nose, and the smattering of freckles across her face. Spreading the drawings out, she found one of her racing on Atara, another of her sitting by the fire with a cup of tea. The last showed a walk she and Reid had gone on after the second race—she recognized it because he'd drawn her clothes in exact detail, her hair still in Ari's complex braid.

A thought pulled at her, like a glimpse of something out the corner of her eye. It rocked through her in waves of guilt and gusts of understanding.

Unable to look at the drawings any longer, she stuffed them hurriedly back into the folder, and picked up a scrap of paper she'd missed. It read *I have a lead on the prince.*

"Mikira?"

She whirled about, crumpling the paper in her hand.

Reid stood in the doorway, his skin flush from exertion. "What are you doing in here?"

She opened her mouth and found no words. Lying had never been her strong suit, and the sheer open confusion with which Reid was staring at her drove back any attempt she might have made.

"I needed to know," she said at last. "About Damien. I needed to know who I was working with."

Understanding shuttered Reid's expression. "You're spying."

"I'm not! I'm looking for answers for myself." And she was—she just hadn't decided what to do if she found them. Once, she wouldn't have hesitated, but things had changed the last couple of months. *She* had changed, and she wasn't sure if she recognized herself any longer.

Reid stepped toward her. "Did Talyana put you up to this?"

The accusation sparked something inside her: a hot mess of indignation and guilt. She felt like a traitor. The look in Reid's eyes said she was one. "I don't work for Talyana. I didn't know what she was! Unlike you."

"What's that supposed to mean?"

"It means how can you be friends with someone like him, Reid?" She thrust a hand toward Damien's room.

Reid's jaw set. "I know the person underneath."

"The murderer?"

"My friend!" he snapped. "The person that gave me a home and a purpose when mine were taken from me." He ran his hand through his hair, the wild mess of it matching the look in his eyes. "The Kelbras pushed my parents out of their house and into the streets, all because their land could grow verillion. And because we resisted them, the Kelbras made sure my parents wouldn't find work anywhere. They starved, Kira. When Damien found me, I was alone and dying on the street, and he gave me—" Reid broke off, his jaw clenching.

"He gave me everything," he said tightly. "Because he understood what it was to have something you care about ripped away from you. And he's done the same thing for countless other people, you and Ari included, and this is how you repay him?"

The question prodded at her like a hot poker. Damien had told her that he wanted to make Enderlain a better place, and she'd believed him. She still did. He'd done more for her than almost anyone, and because of that, she'd ignored the rumors, ignored the possibility that Talyana might be right about him. Even now, she didn't want to condemn him without inescapable proof, but she drew the line at enabling murder.

She withdrew the ring from her pocket. "I didn't know who she was," she said. "I thought she was my friend."

Reid stared at the glittering ring in her palm. She watched the last of his reserve break. "You told her."

"No matter what he's done for you, it doesn't make what else he does right," she whispered, no longer sure who she was trying to convince. She couldn't ignore what she'd seen. She couldn't just close her eyes. But she wanted to, more than anything.

Reid reached for the ring. She nearly pulled back, but he plucked it from her palm. "You have no idea what he's done." He turned his back on her. "Just go home, Mikira."

The words felt like a slap in the face. The walls she'd built around herself, the ones that had slowly crumbled the last few weeks, rose once more. She let them cut her off, let them seal her away, and fled into the lavender-scented night, seeking the one place she could think of that felt safe.

Atara welcomed her with a hot huff of air as Mikira slid into her stall. She threw her arms about the horse's neck, holding fast and holding still as the world spiraled out of control around her.

Reid would tell Damien she couldn't be trusted. He wouldn't stop her from riding in the Illinir—too much rested on her winning—but what about after? Would he keep her share of the money? Ruin what remained of her family's business? Damien Adair was not known for his forgiveness.

And the look in Reid's eyes—the betrayal.

Mikira released Atara, falling back against the wall and sliding to the ground. She hugged her knees to her chest and buried her face in them, struggling to make sense of things she didn't understand.

A soft nose brushed the side of her face, and she looked up into Atara's knowing gaze. The horse dropped her head, and Mikira leaned her forehead against hers like she used to with Iri, and for the first time in a long time, she let herself break.

IT WAS LATE by the time she arrived home to find Ailene and Nelda laughing by the fire. The color had returned to her sister's face, and the aroma of Nelda's cooking wafted from the kitchen. The scene felt like a bubble, as though if she walked in, it would pop and send everything tumbling to the floor.

The thread between her and her family had frayed in recent years, creating a distance between them made of missing people and faded memories. It'd led her to resent herself the way you resented a wounded limb for hurting. It'd left her alone, and in that isolation, she'd turned to the only thing she had left: her anger. She'd wrapped herself in it like armor, told herself she needed no one.

But as much as she'd tried to fight it, her time with Ari, Reid, and even Damien had been like a candle against the dark. It'd eaten away at that loneliness, until she'd felt more a part of something than she'd been in ages.

Now she'd ruined that too.

Mikira stared at the closed door of her father's study, wishing desperately he were on the other side, until a heavy rapping on the front door startled her. She hadn't moved from the foyer, rainwater dripping into a growing puddle at her feet.

The knock came again. "Anthir! Open up!"

"Kira?" Nelda appeared in the drawing room arch.

"Stay there," Mikira ordered before opening the door.

"We have a warrant of search," said the foremost constable, and before Mikira could protest, they filed inside and dispersed like seeds in the wind.

Talyana was the last to enter, her crisp blue and silver jacket looking out of place in their dimly lit foyer. Her plaited hair fell over her shoulder in a long tail.

Fury rose inside Mikira like a rearing horse. "What is this?"

Talyana winced. "Can we speak in private?"

Mikira stomped toward her father's study, Talyana on her heel. She hesitated only briefly outside the closed door before throwing it open. For a moment, she simply stood there, the smell of a room long neglected making her heart twist.

The day Rezek took her father away, she'd closed the door and locked the place from her mind, unable to face any little reminder of him. Now moonlight bathed the study, illuminating the chair pushed away from the desk as though he'd left in a hurry, the surface still buried beneath a layer of papers and books. He'd spent many of his nights submerged in words, often reading to Mikira and her sisters about faraway lands and creatures they could scarcely imagine.

A note with her name sat on the desk. Mikira snatched it up and unfolded it, finding a short message in her father's looping hand:

Kira,

I knew you will have so many questions, most of which I cannot answer. I hope this can. Take care of it.

Love,
Your Father

She flipped it over, but there was nothing else. What was she supposed to take care of, the letter? Carefully, she folded it back up and tucked it in her pocket, alongside the note she'd taken from Reid's room.

"I missed this place." Talyana's gaze traveled the room, taking in the bookcases and art depicting foreign landscapes and beasts.

A smile curled her lips at the worn rug by the fire, where they'd once sat together while her father told them about the sea serpents supposedly descended from Lyzairin, or about the great instruments off the Yaroyan coast that made music with the sea winds.

"Your father knew so much," she said. "I remember—"

Mikira rounded on her. "Enough." She couldn't listen to her speak of the past. The past had teeth and claws, and it would tear her apart if she let it. "What lie did you come up with to get that warrant?"

Hurt flashed briefly across Talyana's face, but she recovered quickly. "Not a lie, per se." Her eyes drifted to a sketch of a pair of desert lizards, the pouches of their throats bright red with growing flame. "I suggested you might have evidence in the case I'm building against Damien Adair."

"Which is a lie."

Talyana looked back to her, her face half cast in shadow. "Is it?"

Mikira shook her head, unable to find words. Talyana was putting her family in danger by asking this.

"What does he have on you?" Talyana asked, and Mikira nearly laughed. All Damien had was what she'd willingly given him. The truth of that nearly broke her. To free herself from one noble's grip, she'd tied herself to another, and somehow during the last two months, she'd actually grown attached to the damned man. Was she that desperate for connection?

"Like you care." Her voice was a low rasp. "You lied to me. You used me."

"I didn't mean to, Kira." Talyana bit her lip. "You were a casualty I didn't intend."

"Is that what this is to you? A war?"

Talyana closed the space between them. "This city is a cesspool of corruption and greed. Did you know just last month, Lady Dramara evicted a family for refusing to work in her factories? And the Kelbras have begun targeting refugees with verillion? So yes, I am waging war on this city's elite, Kira."

She didn't know what to say to that. She wasn't against what Talyana was doing, but when it came to Damien, she couldn't just divest herself of the situation. They were bound.

Mikira peered at Talyana, the glow of the moon lighting her from behind, and saw a person who had changed. All this time, Mikira had been treating her like the girl she'd grown up with, but Talyana wasn't that person anymore, and neither was Mikira.

Talyana took her hand, her palm rough with calluses like Mikira's own. Her heat ate away at the ice settling in Mikira's veins, and she wanted so badly to lean into it, to let Talyana's arms encircle her, a barrier against the breach.

"Give me the ring, Kira," she said softly.

Mikira's lips curled in grim satisfaction. "I don't have it."

Talyana's eyes widened, and then Nelda's frightened voice called from the doorway, "Kira? Kira they're tearing everything apart."

Mikira ripped her hand free. "It's time for you to leave."

"Kira—"

"Now!" Her fingers found one of her knives, and Talyana recoiled, but Mikira didn't care. She'd torn a hole in Mikira's carefully constructed armor without caring that she'd made her bleed.

Talyana retreated into the foyer. "People like the Adairs are rotting this kingdom from the inside out. You could help me stop them." Something cold and hard settled in her gaze. "Or you can go down with him. Because I will bring him down, Mikira, and I'll take everyone on his side down with him."

Talyana slipped out the front door along with her constables, the rush of rain against the gravel drive swallowing up the sound of their departure.

CHAPTER 35

ARIELLE

*A*RI KEPT HER promise to herself—she didn't tell Rezek a thing. But she did scream.

Kyvin knew the most sensitive places to cut, the pain making her so dizzy that she couldn't tell if she was still screaming or if it was just the echoes of her shrieks inside her head. But she kept their secrets.

They'd left her alone in the dark. Kyvin had released the chains so that her toes brushed the ground. Pain radiated through her, blood sliding down her skin. Her throat felt ragged from yelling and her head pounded.

You will survive, promised the voice. *You will rage.*

I will die here, she thought back. *I will break.*

Be strong, little lion.

She didn't know how long she hung there. It could have been hours or days. Had the Illinir finished? Had Damien freed himself and left her here to die?

She flinched at every sound. Shied away at every hint of light. Only the voice kept her company, muttering a quiet litany of promises that soothed her. Without it, fear was her only companion. Fear, and the knowledge that when they came back, she would break, and she hated them for it. For taking away her carefully wrought power, for breaking her down to flesh and bone and terror.

We will make them regret every cut, soothed the voice, and Ari clung to it. *We will make them afraid.*

Noises scratched through the darkness. Bone-deep growls, high-pitched inhuman keens, and pained groans. She shut her eyes against them and told herself she was imagining them, but then she thought about a cold knife against her skin, of Kyvin's empty eyes, of the knowledge that even if she made it through this agony, there would be another waiting.

Be fearless, my love.

Ari choked on a sob, unable to stop the feeling of utter helplessness that descended over her.

You deserve this, she thought. *All of this.*

But another one rose above it. *You are magnificent, Arielle Kadar.*

A door opened down the hall. She recoiled, but there was nowhere to go. She turned away from a sudden glaring light, but not before she caught a glimpse of a face. Older, with thinning auburn hair and a neatly trimmed beard.

Not Kyvin.

Someone worse?

The door swung open, revealing an exhausted man with pale skin and a smattering of freckles across the bridge of his sharp nose.

There was something familiar about him.

He winced when he saw Ari and set his enchanted lantern on the ground. "I've come to help you."

Gently, he lowered her to the ground. First her toes, then the pads of her feet, then the weight of her body upon her knees—they buckled immediately, striking stone. She barely felt the resounding impact.

As her arms fell before her, the muscles screaming at the slightest movement, she swayed dangerously, but the man was already there, careful of her wounds as he held her upright. He pulled a bottle from his pocket and uncorked it, pressing it to her lips.

"Drink," he said. "This will help with the pain."

She turned her face away.

"Please." He sounded desperate. "I'm a friend. My name is Keirian Rusel. You know my daughter, Mikira."

He could be telling the truth, but Rezek would know that too. The thought sent a shiver through her. Surely, he wouldn't create this elaborate ploy just to get her to drink something he could easily force down her throat.

She allowed Keirian to tip the liquid into her mouth. It tasted of honey and began to work almost immediately, the sharp edges of her pain dulling into something manageable. When he helped her to her feet, she could stand, though she felt weak and disconnected.

"I can take you as far as the nearest exit," he said as they proceeded painstakingly from the cell and down the corridor. The enchanted lantern swung from one of his wrists. "But I mustn't be seen you with at any cost. I'm sorry I can't do more. My daughter—" His voice choked into silence.

She mourned the loss of it. Hearing it made her feel real again. It made her feel safe.

"I know you're working with her to win the Illinir," Keirian continued as they approached the end of the hall. "Thank you."

It was all Ari could do to remember to breathe, but she managed a small nod.

As they neared the door, something in the last cell moved. Ari flinched, then peered closer. The creature inside seemed neither man nor animal. With piercing blue eyes and shaggy yellow fur, it huddled over itself, its ribs pressing against thin, sallow skin. It lifted its head, revealing a mouth crowded with sharp teeth. Then they were through the threshold and into a small room, and Ari struggled to hold on to the image.

Keirian turned left, and Ari fell into the rhythm of her steps. Left, right. Left, right—then a sound. They both stopped. There was nowhere to hide as another light curved around ahead of them. A Kelbra guard filled the hallway holding an enchanted lantern. His other hand dropped to the revolver at his waist.

Inside, Ari screamed. She would not go back to that cell. She would not— the guard's eyes went wide, and he crumpled. A small dart stuck out from the back of his neck, and behind him stood Reid wearing a Kelbra uniform.

"Shit," the boy cursed as his eyes took her in. "Hells. Damien's going to kill Rezek. *I'm* going to kill him."

"A friend of yours?" Keirian asked warily.

She forced a breathy laugh and nodded. They'd come for her.

Reid slipped under her other side, and together they helped her to a propped-open door. Crickets sung a chirping song outside, carried in on a fresh night breeze. She breathed it deep. Then she stumbled, nearly taking both men down with her. Her body felt like stone. She could barely lift her head. Reid cursed again.

"Verillion," she rasped. She might not have the strength to enchant the stone, but just having the magic inside her would help.

"There's a field outside to the left," Keirian said. "This is where I leave you. Can you manage her alone?"

Reid took all her weight across his shoulders. She could feel him straining to hold her. "That guard won't remember anything," he said.

Keirian released a relieved breath. "Tell Mikira to read the journal," he said to Ari. "I left it on my desk. She'll know what I mean. And tell her I love her. Now, go!"

Reid pushed out the door, and the cool air washed over her in welcome relief. A moment later he was lowering her in the middle of a field. Gold light pressed against her heavy lids, and she heard the snapping of stalks and felt the press of a plant at her lips.

It took effort to open her mouth and chew the verillion. She swallowed it and a current of power rushed through her so warm and strong, she nearly wept. Gradually, her vision cleared, and she found Reid staring down at her like she'd just used his favorite shirt to clean up spilled tea.

"You better not die," he said.

Her lips twitched. "I never knew you cared."

"I don't. I'd just prefer not to die with you."

Her smile faded. "Damien?"

"He'll be fine. Right now what matters is getting you home."

A shadow moved over his shoulder. "Reid!" Her warning came too late. A guard wrapped a thick arm around Reid's neck, while another drove a fist into his stomach. Reid wheezed, prying uselessly at his throat.

Ari tried to stand, but her body struggled even with the verillion. "Just let him go," she rasped. "I won't fight you."

"I don't think so. Lord Kelbra will want to speak with him," said the second guard. She smirked down at Ari. "Right after Kyvin has another nice, long conversation with you."

The name alone sent a wave of nausea through her. Panic erupted like a flare, and she reached desperately for the verillion inside her as the guard approached. Her body resisted the draw of the magic, wanting to keep it inside, but she forced it through the emerald ring, muttering a binding.

The guard chuckled. "Praying won't save you, witch." She reached for Ari's arm.

Crush them, roared the voice.

Power snapped into place inside her. She seized the guard's hand and bent it back, breaking her wrist. The guard howled. Using her as an anchor, Ari pulled herself to her feet and drove her knee into the woman's stomach. Ribs cracked and she staggered, crumpling into a heap.

"What in the hells—" began the other guard. But she'd already ripped his arm away from Reid's neck. She drove her elbow into the guard's jaw, and he hit the ground hard, unmoving.

Reid stared up at her from his knees, one hand massaging his red throat. "I take back every insult I ever said."

She smiled. Then the verillion ran out, and she collapsed.

ARI WOKE SLOWLY. Everything hurt. Everything was dark.

She started upright. Rezek's men had found her. She was back in the cell—no. She was in a bed, not hanging from the ceiling. As her heart slowed, her eyes caught up to her surroundings. She took in the curtained windows of Damien's room, where soft rays of afternoon sunlight trickled in. The familiar scent of gunpowder and aged paper worked its way through her like a balm, and for a few moments, all she did was breathe.

Then the pain of her sudden movements came crashing down upon her. Her body ached as though she'd been battered like a shirt left on the clothesline in a storm. Yet it didn't hurt as badly as she'd expected.

She pulled away one of the many bandages Reid must have applied to her forearm, expecting stitches. Instead, she found scabbed skin and a little dried blood from where movement had pulled at the newly formed layer.

Carefully, she undid the rest of the bandages along her body. A couple of the wounds still leaked a little blood, but the majority of them were through the worst of it.

What is happening? she thought.

This is your power, Arielle Kadar, said the voice. *Embrace it.*

Climbing carefully to her feet, she walked slowly to the bedroom door and pulled it open. The sitting room was empty. A note sat on the nearest end table beside a bowl of glowing chopped verillion. She opened the letter, revealing Reid's mechanically neat script:

Went to tell Damien you're not dead. Though you're less dead than you should be. One of the perks of having magic no one else does, I suppose. Test it out for me? Try the verillion. A little to start, then more—I expect it'll correspond to the rate at which you heal. Don't actually die while I'm gone. The final race is tomorrow.

—Reid

P.S. I'll give Mikira her father's message.

She rolled her eyes. Only Reid would turn a near-death experience into an experiment. Setting the letter back on the table, she ate a few pieces of verillion. Magic flowed through her in a gentle rush. The scabbing on her forearm began to itch, the skin beneath it feeling tight. She scratched at the scab, scraping it away to reveal healthy skin beneath.

Ari grabbed the bowl of verillion and sat down on the chaise. She ate several more pieces before her weariness overtook her and she lay down. The magic might heal her physical wounds, but it took energy from her body when she burned it, and the fog of a lingering headache remained. She could only do so much at once. She fell asleep with the magic still humming inside her.

Dreams of darkness plagued her. Dreams of chains and pale faces, of silvery knives coated in blood, her screams echoing around her in an endless cacophony of agony. Twisted shapes writhed in the shadows. Inhuman groans coated the air. A beast with blue eyes whispered her name.

She woke gasping for air. It was several long moments before she remembered she was free of that cell, and several more before she was sure she wouldn't retch.

Ari knew these sorts of dreams. Knew the way they dragged you under and held you there until you drowned. The way they crept into your waking moments, tainting them with fear. Like the imprint of hands against her throat,

like the cold, quiet dread that pooled inside her when her Saba's screaming stopped.

Unless she did something, these dreams would consume her like all the rest.

Do not let them make you afraid, whispered the voice.

I won't, Ari thought.

This time, she was fighting back.

CHAPTER 36

ARIELLE

LOCATING KYVIN WAS easier than Ari expected. He'd made a name for himself as Rezek's right-hand man, so when she asked after him in pubs off Ettinger Street in the Crown District, people knew him. She learned he was a distant Kelbra cousin, the son of a butcher, who had taken a job working in the castle dungeons before Rezek had enlisted his services.

She also learned where he liked to drink.

Night had fallen by the time she spotted Kyvin inside the Whispering Rose on Rathsborne Street. She found a quiet alley with a view of the tavern and waited, occasionally eating verillion to keep up the store of magic inside her. She'd healed enough that moving was stiff, but not painful, though she'd stopped burning magic to reserve energy. The humming calmed her, but she couldn't quite shake the feeling of stalking a lion back to its den.

You are the lion, not him, said the voice, and Ari believed it.

Kyvin emerged from the Whispering Rose, his face flushed with drink. He turned down the street, whistling a low tune. It sent a spike of hot anger through her. He didn't care at all about what he'd done to her. Her screams didn't haunt him the way they haunted her.

Ari burned the verillion, pushing magic to the ring and muttering a binding. Strength flooded her body. She tracked Kyvin from a distance down the bustling street. People flocked from pub to pub, restaurant to shop, oblivious to her and her prey.

She dodged a pair of drunken women, and when she looked up, Kyvin had vanished. She hurried through the crowd, ducking to the edge to get around it better, but it was no use.

He was gone.

Hands seized her from the dark. She tried to scream, but one covered her mouth. In a blink, she'd been ripped from the street and thrust up against the wall of a dark alley. Kyvin's dead eyes stared down at her, a cruel smile on his lips.

"My, my, little mouse." He had a gravelly voice, so unlike Rezek's rancid honeyed tones. "You're supposed to be in your cage like a good pet." His thumb stroked her jaw. "Now that you're here, though, I suppose we can have a little fun. What Lord Kelbra doesn't know won't hurt him." He slid one hand down to her hip.

She drove her forehead into his. He stumbled back, and her fist cracked against the side of his head. He dropped.

For a moment she feared she'd killed him. Then she saw his chest move. She didn't know what to make of the relief that swept through her. Shouldn't she want him dead? Dead, he couldn't hurt her again. Dead, her nightmares might die with him.

She shook the thought away and withdrew a length of rope from her satchel, using it to bind his wrists behind his back. Then she picked him up, threw him over her shoulder, and turned deeper into the alley.

KYVIN CAME TO slowly.

When he opened his eyes, his pupils were blown wide, making him resemble a startled animal. Ari fixed the image in her mind. The way he looked about her workshop like the walls were coated in blood, the sharp intake of breath when he found her sitting on a crate in front of him. She would remember those things.

He leaned forward, but the ropes held strong, one arm tied to each side of the chair. She'd stripped him of his shirt, baring pale white skin like a fresh canvas.

"What in the hells do you think you're doing, girl?" He thrashed against his bonds in earnest now. "Release me!"

She gave herself a moment to enjoy his struggle, the lilt of fear in his voice. Then she lifted the gag she'd looped around his neck and tightened it between his teeth. He fought to get words out around the cloth as she faced her workbench.

Ari didn't have the arrangement of knives Kyvin did, but she had plenty of sharp objects and a working knowledge of living things from months of shaping golems. Perhaps after this she'd ask Reid to teach her about the most sensitive nerves, or the places where the skin was shallowest above the bone.

For now, her fettling knives would have to do.

She pressed the point of one to Kyvin's throat and said quietly, "Scream for me, little mouse."

Kyvin did scream, though the gag muffled the worst of it. What little sound escaped her small room would go ignored, just like her cries had the day those men robbed her. She exacted her fear from Kyvin's flesh. With each cut, she told herself he was just a man, and men could bleed. She could *make them* bleed.

A quiet piece inside her shuddered at the blood, but she shoved that part deep, deep down. This was about proving herself unafraid, about proving herself in control.

She was strong, said the knife as it cut.

She was safe, said the swelling rivulets of blood.

She was powerful, said the fear in his eyes.

You are magnificent, Arielle Kadar, said the voice.

By the time Kyvin fainted from the pain, Ari felt that constant, restless apprehension inside of her settle. She tossed the blade onto the workbench and stared down at her bloodstained hands. They were perfectly still. So still, they felt separate from her. These hands were not hers. They belonged to a monster.

The sound of scraping stone was all the warning she had before a chair struck her in the side, knocking her to the floor. Kyvin stood over her, one hand freed from the ropes, the other still bound to the chair.

"You think you can get away with this?" he snarled even as he swayed. Between blood loss and the pain, he could barely keep his feet. Yet he held the chair up like a bludgeon and swung it toward her. She rolled out of the way, and the chair snapped.

When Kyvin straightened, he had only a thin spike of wood still attached to his other arm. He grinned and pulled it free.

The shadow of her dreams reared back to life. She felt chains at her wrists again, a knife at her throat. Nausea choked her. Fear froze her.

He is just a man, said the voice.

And she—she was something more.

Burning verillion, she bound her magic as she clambered to her feet, strength coalescing inside her.

Kyvin struggled to keep his footing, using the workbench for support and wielding the wooden spike like a sword. He pushed off the bench, thrusting at her. She lurched away. The verillion might lend her strength, but it told her nothing of fighting. Kyvin on the other hand looked as comfortable with the spike as the scalpel he'd carved her with.

She backed up, seeking an opening. Kyvin followed like a rabid dog on the scent. His wide grin showed too many teeth, and blood flecked his lips.

Ari ripped one of the hanging baskets off the hook and threw it at him, forcing him to bat it away. In his moment of distraction, she leapt for him. They hit the ground hard, the tip of the stake slicing along her ribs.

Kyvin struck her in the face, then brought the spike around to gouge her in the side. She caught his wrist. He struggled against her unusual strength, but it wasn't enough. Bit by bit, breath by breath, she turned the tip of the spike toward his chest. His grip shifted, trying to push the stake away, but she leaned over him, flaring her verillion, and slammed it into his heart.

His eyes went wide, and he coughed blood. It splattered against her cheek. She didn't dare remove her hand to wipe it away.

She stayed that way, hovering over him, her hands tight around the splintered wood, until his eyes went dark.

ARI ALMOST DIDN'T notice the guards at the door to the Dark Horse pub, but they certainly noticed her. How could they not, stained with blood as she was? She'd followed the maze of back alleys that made up the Wrenith District to get here, some instinctual part of her remembering she shouldn't be seen like this. That part felt very far away.

One of the guards said something to her that she didn't hear.

"Shira," she said.

"What?" The guard's hand went to his revolver. She tracked the motion, burning verillion on instinct, but she'd used it all up in the fight with Kyvin, and all that replied was an empty echo.

"Shira."

The other guard said something and disappeared into the pub. A moment later, Shira Adair returned with him. Without a word, she took Ari's arm and led her inside.

Ari saw nothing of her surroundings. One moment she was standing in the dark of night, and the next she was sitting in a plush armchair by a crackling fire in a loft above the pub. She could still feel the squelching sensation of the stake sliding between Kyvin's ribs, the hot splash of blood against her cheek. It was still there. She could feel it dry and cracking against her skin.

Something soft and warm pressed against her hand, and she looked down to see Shira offering her a damp cloth. Ari took it, her movements mechanical as she wiped the blood first from her face, then her hands. It stained the cloth crimson.

For a moment, she simply stared at the stains.

Blood on her hands. Blood on the walls.

She sucked in a sharp, shuddering breath. Shira said nothing, only slid onto the wide arm of the chair and laid an arm about Ari's shoulders. Ari didn't even think, she just pressed her face into Shira's side and cried.

Sunlight was trickling in through the wide windows of the loft by the time she stopped. Some part of her knew that she had to pull herself together. That the final Illinir race was that afternoon, and Damien was still in prison, and Mikira didn't know what was happening, but her body felt hollow, nothing but a marionette with its strings cut.

She sat beside the fire now, a cup of tea going cold on the table. Shira had sent people to deal with the body, then brought fresh clothes that Ari had changed into like a ghost slipping out of its skin. The wound on her side had scabbed over thanks to the verillion, but it still smarted with every breath.

Shira didn't ask her what happened. If Damien was a vault, his sister was the iron that formed it. She could have sworn the woman lent Ari her sheer force of will, and Ari clung to it like driftwood in a storming sea. Everything inside her turned and turned, flashing images through her mind: Rivkah screaming, her Saba's cold, dead eyes.

Shira looked up from the book she'd been reading sprawled across the armchair. Ari felt the weight of her eyes, so much gentler than her brother's, but just as strong.

"Do you feel up for a short walk?" she asked.

Ari followed Shira out a back entrance and onto a quiet street. The shops were still closed, windows shuttered against the night. A newsboy rode by on a bike, tossing papers at doorsteps. Mikira's face stared up from them alongside images of the other Illinir finalists, the headline announcing the race's conclusion to come that day.

They turned down a narrow side street that emptied into a tranquil courtyard wrapped in trees. A fountain trickled quietly at the center, surrounded by wooden benches, and a set of low steps led up to a white-stone building on their right.

A Kinnish temple.

Ari stopped walking. "I can't go in there." She felt dirty and coated in blood, though she'd washed the last of it away hours ago.

Shira looped her arm through Ari's. "You have nothing to fear."

Words twisted and stuck in Ari's throat, but she didn't fight as Shira led her up the stairs and into the temple.

Lacquered cherrywood benches gleamed in the morning light trickling in through the stained-glass windows, illuminating the high arched ceilings and delicate gold decorations of the ornamental ark housing the holy texts. It was by no means garish, but it was rich with life and care, the sort of place that felt like coming home.

It was empty, the morning service not yet begun. It was strange to step inside and recognize the significance of the paintings of the Harbingers on the walls, to see the individual Arkala gathered in the shelves by the door, their covers worn away by countless fingers. She knew more about her people than she ever had, and yet she felt farther away than ever before.

"Sit." Shira slid onto one of the benches.

Ari followed, feeling lost and out of place. Sensing her discomfort, Shira laid a gentle hand on her shoulder. "You don't have to do anything, Ari. Just sit here."

She did.

She sat and listened to the silence of a holy place. She let it weave through and around her, let it fill her up like a deep breath after a lifetime without air.

And when she let it out, the whispered words came with it. "I killed him."

Shira let her talk.

"He told me to leave the book alone, but I didn't listen." Ari curled her knees up to her chest and wrapped her arms about them. "I just wanted to know what was inside. But once I opened it, I couldn't stop. I would sneak out every night to read from its pages, though I had no idea what the words said. They still felt familiar, like a word that's been misspelled, but you still know its meaning."

The first day she'd opened the spellbook had been like stepping from shadows into the sunlight. Its touch had made her feel alive, and she'd craved the feeling ever since.

She expected the voice to say something about that, but it was quiet inside the walls of the temple. Ari didn't know what to make of missing it.

"I found a page he'd translated." Her nails dug into her forearms. It didn't feel odd telling all this to someone she barely knew. If anything, it was easier, like talking to the gods, or the ocean, or a wind that would carry her words far, far away. But tell her she did. Of the golem, the attack, of Rivkah running to the sound.

"I couldn't take the fear and blame in my parents' eyes," she finished. "So I ran."

Shira's expression didn't change. She took in all of Ari's story without reaction, letting her empty the fear, the guilt, the pain. And when Ari finished, she didn't look at her any differently than before.

"People always want to blame someone when horrible things happen," Shira said. "But sometimes they're no one's doing. Sometimes they just happen."

Rivkah had tried to tell her that. She'd tried to say it wasn't Ari's fault.

But Ari had been terrified she might hurt one of them again. Terrified of herself, of the thing lurking inside her mind.

"What about the times when you make them happen?" she asked. "When you answer bad things with more bad things, but instead of canceling each other out, they just create more darkness?" They multiplied, like shattered glass crumbling underfoot, a single piece turning into thousands.

"It is easy to lose yourself to even a fleck of darkness," Shira replied solemnly. "Each new thing you do doesn't seem that bad because it's not much worse than the thing before. But eventually you look back to the beginning and you realize how far you've drifted."

She held Ari's gaze as she spoke. "And if you stop, if you stand still for even a second, it catches up to you. So you keep going and going, until it consumes you."

Ari was suddenly sure they weren't talking about her anymore. This wasn't the first time Shira had considered this, perhaps not even the first time she'd had this conversation.

"And what if it already has?" she asked quietly.

A surprisingly gentle smile pulled at Shira's lips. "Do you know the term *chet*?" Ari shook her head. "It is an archery term used to describe when an arrow has gone astray. It is the same word Kinnism uses to describe sin. Because that is all sin is, Arielle: a straying from the right path. You can always find your way again. But first you must find forgiveness."

Ari shuddered. "They'll never forgive me."

"There are many types of forgiveness," Shira replied patiently. "The forgiveness between yourself and the gods. That between you and another. And the kind that comes from inside yourself. The strength to forgive ourselves is often the hardest to find."

"What if I can't?" she whispered.

Shira placed a gentle hand on hers. "You can. To forgive is to make whole. Only once you forgive yourself can you make whole the rest."

She stood, running her fingers along the back of a bench. "All you can do now is keep moving forward. It is only when you stop that you lose the path."

She offered Ari her hand. "Now, if you're feeling up to it, my brother needs you."

Ari didn't hesitate. She let Shira pull her to her feet, and like a shadow snipped from her heel, she left the weight behind.

CHAPTER 37

ARIELLE

THE ANTHIR HEADQUARTERS were a squat, gray stone building in the Wrenith District. Ari was aware of every step she took inside, from the cold foyer to the monochrome waiting room. This was where she belonged. She should be in a cell right beside Damien after what she'd done.

You protected yourself, said the voice. *Nothing more.*

Where have you been? Ari thought back, but only silence answered.

Shira barely set foot in the place before someone was at her side, asking if they could help. Ari's attention strayed to the wall of faces to her left, depicting criminals the Anthir were hunting. Their crimes were printed beneath sketches or photographs. Most of them simply said REBEL.

"Arielle." Shira's voice pulled her back. "This way."

They entered a corner office with a plaque on the door that read INSPEC-TOR ELRIHAN.

The inspector was a broad-shouldered man with tawny skin, a thick black beard, and bright eyes. He sat behind a desk that took up most of the small, windowless room, the surface stacked with endless piles of paper.

Damien had told her about his friendship with the inspector, how he'd listened as the man, several drinks in, detailed how understaffed they were. How he felt trapped in his small office and longed to do something more meaningful, more recognized. In turn, Inspector Elrihan had accepted a generous donation for staffing and a renovation on the precinct due to start next month, and always had a minute to hear the Adairs out.

"Lady Adair." Inspector Elrihan leaned back in a too-small wooden chair. "I apologize for Lord Adair's treatment. If I'd known he was here earlier, I'd have seen to him immediately, but the paperwork has yet to be filed. I can assure you Sergeant Haraver will be suitably reprimanded."

Sergeant Haraver, she thought. *Talyana*. The same name as Mikira's friend. Had Reid told her what was happening when he delivered her father's message? She hoped that was where he was now.

Shira waved away his concern. "Not to worry, Inspector. The sergeant was only doing her duty. But I have someone here who can provide my brother an alibi."

Ari stepped up beside her. "I was with Damien at the time of those men's disappearance."

She expected the inspector to question her, to tear apart the lie that Shira fed her, but he only nodded. "Of course. I'll see him released immediately."

"Before you do," Ari cut in. "I'd like to talk to him."

A constable let her into the hall, where the pale light of dawn cast a blue sheen across the rusted bars of the cells on either side. Dark shapes shifted inside them, but Ari paid them no heed, even when they called to her.

We can silence them, said the voice. *We can silence them all.*

I know.

At the end of the hall, Damien paced the short length of his cell like a caged lion. His hands had been cuffed before him, his jacket unbuttoned from where they'd taken his guns. Even his curls were a mess. It was the most unkempt she'd ever seen him, and when his eyes locked on her, the look in them was nothing short of feral.

"What did he—" he began.

"I'm okay," she said, but the exhaustion in those words was a bottomless well. Reflexively, she burned a little verillion, seeking its warmth and strength. They'd given her the key to his cell, and she toyed with it in the pocket of her dress.

Damien's wrists strained against the handcuffs. "I will make him regret it," he promised, and she knew he would, if she let him. But she didn't want to let him.

She wanted to do it herself.

"I assume it was your brother who told Rezek I'm an enchanter," she said quietly.

"Yes." Damien leaned his forehead against the bars. They looked like the only thing holding him up. "I don't think he told him that you're unlicensed, just that you might know how Mikira was winning the race. But for this to have happened . . . Someone betrayed me, Ari." He bit the words out, as if they physically pained him. "I promised myself I'd never let this happen again."

Like it had with Rezek.

She realized then just how much that day all those years ago had broken him. How he'd spent every moment since putting himself back together piece by piece. There'd been no room for weakness, no place for vulnerability. Those things left you dependent on other people. They left you open to attack.

Yet he'd done it anyway.

He'd trusted Reid, and her, and Mikira. He'd trusted someone enough that this deception meant something to him.

But he was not the only one who had been deceived.

Ari traced her fingers along his jaw and said, so quietly the words were nearly lost, "Did you send those men to attack me?"

Damien flinched.

It was all the answer she needed. Her nails curled into his skin, but he did not pull away. Rather he caught her hand between his bound ones, holding it there. "They were never supposed to touch you." His voice was a low rumble. "They were to take your coin and leave."

"But they didn't."

His jaw tightened. "But they didn't. And I saw they were sufficiently punished for it."

He had. But was that enough? Once, she might have been uncertain where she stood with him. Might have doubted herself, unsteady and unsure. But he was looking at her now as if she was the only thing that mattered.

"Forgive me, Arielle," he said hoarsely. "That was before I met you, before I got to know you and your strength and your mind. Before I loved you."

He did not hesitate when he said it, though it left him breathless and vulnerable. Her eyes searched his, and he did not look away.

Those men would never trouble her again. He'd made sure of it—for her. She knew that, knew that Damien kept his truths clutched tight to his chest, knew the bars separating them were the very reason why. But if he wanted her, wanted her power and her mind and her soul the way she wanted his, then this would be the last time.

Her thumb brushed across his lips. "Never manipulate me like that again."

"Never," he promised, and she set him free.

✦ PART 4 ✦

But the Harbingers could not stop what they had set in motion,
and humanity's hunger grew insatiable.
Then came the Heretics.

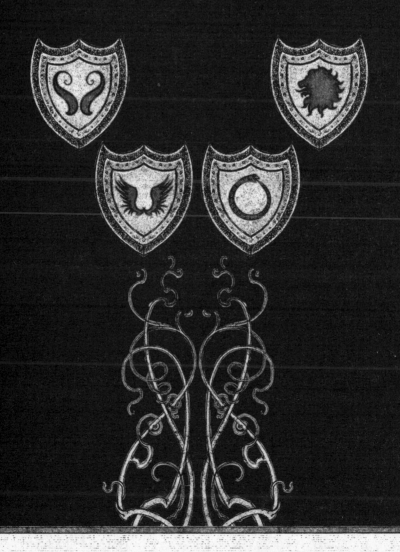

CHAPTER 38

MIKIRA

MIKIRA DRESSED FOR war.

At least, that was how it felt wearing the crisp black and silver linen shirt she'd been sent, her riding pants supple leather, her boots polished to shine. She removed the bandages on her arm, bearing angry scabbed skin, and slid her knife sheaths into place, studying the worn handles. Ari hadn't been able to tell her anything more about their enchantment since the discovery of the bloodstone's linking properties, but even without knowledge of their power, the blades made her feel invincible.

A note had come with the uniform yesterday morning, informing her that Damien had been released, and though she recognized Reid's handwriting, he hadn't signed it.

Had he told Damien what she'd done?

She hadn't been able to bring herself to visit the manor since the Kelbra ball. Reid didn't want to see her, and no last day of training would make a difference in the race.

This ended today, one way or another.

An enchanted coach arrived empty at her house that morning, and she felt the extra space inside it as it trundled up the King's Road toward the castle. First Reid, then Talyana—she'd managed to drive a wedge between herself and them both. Now she hurtled toward one of the most important days of her life, and she did it very much alone.

The castle's central courtyard was larger than half a city block and filled to the brim with horses and people. One area had been cordoned off for vendors, another occupied by canopied wooden viewing platforms for the nobility. The clouded sky threatened rain.

Thankfully, most of today's race would be underground.

The tunnels that snaked beneath Veradell began near the castle and emptied onto the Traveler's Road at the edge of the city. They would be dark, lending advantage to horses with ethereal enchantments, like the ability to never get lost or to sense danger. She had no idea what kind of charms they'd experience inside, only that once they escaped the tunnels, they would follow the Traveler's Road toward the finish line some three miles away at Kelbra Manor.

Mikira made her way to the saddling area, at once desperate for a glimpse of Iri and terrified of it. She desperately hoped the prince had changed his mind, deciding the horse was too valuable to risk, but she knew Rezek wouldn't let that happen. The stallion was here, somewhere. She could feel it.

So close to the start of the race, most everyone was already packing up and preparing to relocate to the finish line. Most of the spectators would watch the start, then take a coach to the Kelbras' estate to await the riders, who had already begun to gather by the starting gate.

"There you are."

She started at Damien's voice, whirling to find his arm linked with Ari's.

"Is something wrong?" he asked.

Her heart scrambled. "No—I just, you scared me." She searched his face for signs of anger and found none. That meant nothing. Damien could be plotting her death this very moment, and she wouldn't know it. He regarded her with a shrewd tilt of his head. Like the day they'd met all those weeks ago, she felt cut open by the steel of his eyes.

"Where's Reid?" she asked.

"Late." Damien said the word as if it'd personally offended him. Mikira knew exactly why Reid wasn't here yet—he couldn't look her in the eye.

Ari lifted her elbow, and a copper hawk alighted on her leather-gloved forearm. Its wide amber eyes showed no hints of the gold that indicated an enchant—a golem.

"Mazal is charmed to never lose a scent," Ari explained. "She'll keep an eye on you during the race, and Reid will follow from a distance."

Mikira nodded, gaze sliding over the other racers, many of them pulled in tight groups of friends or family. She felt every inch of space around her.

Ari stepped forward. "Come here. Your hair's a mess."

Mikira turned obediently as Ari guided the hawk onto her shoulder before undoing her sloppy braid and weaving it into something far more secure. By the time she finished, Mikira felt less like a pup nipping at the heels of a wolf and more like the girl that was going to help ruin House Kelbra.

Ari smiled as Mikira turned around. "You look perfect. You can do this, Mikira. And Reid will be with you the whole way. You're not alone." She squeezed Mikira's hand, and her heart gave an answering thump.

In that moment, those words were her lifeline.

"Oh, before I forget," Ari added with sudden urgency. "Did Reid give you your father's message?"

Mikira frowned. "My father?"

A strange look crossed Ari's face. "Do you know what happened after Damien was arrested?"

Mikira looked between them. "No," she answered slowly. "What?"

"I was taken by Rezek Kelbra." She said it so matter-of-factly. "Reid rescued me with the help of your father."

She thought of Reid rushing to his room. He'd known Ari was in trouble, and he hadn't told her. He hadn't trusted her to help.

She wrapped Ari in a hug before the other girl could protest. She looked okay, but Mikira knew from experience that not all pain was visible.

"Are you all right?" she asked.

Ari returned the hug. "Thanks to your father."

"Thank the Goddess." Mikira pulled back. "And my father? Is he . . ." She couldn't bring herself to fully ask, but Ari understood.

"He looked a little weary, but otherwise okay," she replied, and Mikira's shoulders slumped with relief.

She nodded. "Reid didn't give me any message, though." Most likely because he was avoiding her. He must have told Ari he'd deliver it to keep them from meeting alone. Did he think Mikira was going to tell Ari about the ring? She wanted to, but she also didn't want to put Ari in a position to have to lie to Damien.

"Odd." Ari's brow furrowed. "Your father said he loved you, and for you to read the journal in his study."

Mikira's mind strayed back to the note she'd found on the desk.

I know you will have so many questions, most of which I cannot answer. I hope this can. Take care of it.

He must have left a journal with the note. But then where had it gone?

Concern lined Ari's face. "Are you all right?"

"I'm fine." She could deal with the journal later. Right now she had a race to win. "Where's Atara?"

They led her to the mare, who tossed her head in greeting. Mikira wrapped her arms around her thick neck, burying her face in her hair.

Atara nibbled at her shirt.

A heavy-footed tread stopped beside them, and she pulled back to find a royal guard. "Weapons check," he said gruffly.

"What?" Mikira said at the same time Damien said, "Under whose authority?"

"By the rules of the Illinir, set forth upon its founding, no weapons shall be allowed in the course of the race," the guard intoned. "Every entrant is subject to search."

"Then search every entrant!" Mikira snapped.

The guard wasn't fazed. He wasn't much of anything; he just stood there like a door left ajar. "If you refuse to submit to the search, you forfeit your position in the race."

She looked to Damien, whose attention was on one of the wooden stands, where Rezek Kelbra smirked down at them.

In the end, he nodded stiffly to Mikira.

Her stomach sank, but she stripped the sheaths from beneath her sleeves and handed them reluctantly to the guard. "I get these back," she snarled. "Or I take them back."

"Threatening a royal guard is—"

"Leave." Damien's command was a thunderclap. The guard started, the first indication that he wasn't actually a machine. He continued down the line, but he didn't search a single other rider.

"We can give her other weapons?" Ari suggested.

"No. They're watching us now." Damien made a point of turning his back on Rezek. "We'll just have to hope you don't have to fight."

They had a better chance of Atara flying.

"Are you ready?" Damien asked as the announcer called the riders to the line.

A flutter turned Mikira's stomach like the upheaval of wings. "As I can be."

He nodded. "Good luck. We'll see you at the end."

If she made it there.

She guided Atara toward the other riders, where she mounted and allowed an assistant starter to lead them into the gate with the other horses. The positioning hardly mattered. It was merely tradition, meant to begin all the racers at the same point.

The space next to her was still empty, and there was only one rider missing, one horse. A sharp whinny cut through the air, and she craned her neck around. Iri reared, fighting the gate crew trying to bring him into the stall. As his front hooves came down, Gren jerked viciously on the reins.

Mikira choked down a cry as the crew finally forced Iri inside.

Gren laughed at the fury winding through her face and slapped Iri's neck hard. The horse fidgeted in the small space. He'd never been trained for this. He didn't know what was happening.

She snarled. "If you hurt him—"

"You'll do what?" Gren growled back. "He's my horse."

"To the line!" boomed the announcer's voice.

"I'll kill you!" she shouted.

The crowd's cry nearly drowned her out. "For Enderlain! For the Harbingers! For Sendia!"

As the bell rang, Mikira looked up into Gren's grinning face.

The horses took off.

CHAPTER 39

ARIELLE

ARI LAUNCHED MAZAL into the air. The hawk spiraled upward and set out across the sky, tracking Mikira.

"You're cutting it close," she told Reid as he approached the trailer. She'd expected him to be here in time to see Mikira off, but he'd appeared so soon after she trotted away that Ari suspected that he'd been waiting for her to leave. Did it have something to do with why he'd never delivered her father's message?

Reid untethered the reins of the speed-charmed stallion they'd brought with them. "I'm here, aren't I?" He swung up into the saddle, ignoring Damien's assessing gaze. "How will I know if she's in trouble?"

"Mazal will circle," Ari replied.

"Be sure the other riders don't see you," Damien warned. "Take the city streets to the Traveler's Road."

Reid clicked his tongue to the stallion, and the horse set off at a trot away from them. He'd volunteered to be the one to follow Mikira, but he looked more like they'd signed him up to watch a feral dog. Had something happened between them?

"Damien," she said, catching sight of a familiar face cutting through the crowd. A thin, blond man with a narrow face. "Isn't that one of your people?"

Damien's gaze followed hers. "Hyle. He isn't supposed to be here."

Hyle looked about before ducking into a nearby barn.

Damien and Ari followed. Dim light and the shuffle of stabled horses greeted them inside, where they moved quietly down the aisle, stopping when they caught the hiss of voices around the corner.

"Yes, yes, I know the place," Hyle said impatiently. "Would you like to tell me it all once more in case I can't repeat it backward and in Ranoen—" A resounding slap cut him off.

Another voice said. "Do not be late."

Loic.

Ari felt Damien's body go taut beside her. They both pressed into the shadows as heavy footfalls passed. After Hyle departed too, Damien took off after his brother with Ari on his heels. There was a part of her that had been looking forward to facing down Loic again, and she set her verillion burning just in case.

Loic was picking his way toward the royal viewing platform, where people were descending the stairs to make for the enchanted coaches that would take them to the Kelbra estate.

"If he's working for your brother . . ." Ari began.

"He betrayed me." Damien's voice sent a shiver through her. "A few weeks ago, I lost my house ring. Hyle was supposed to find it, just like he was supposed to dispose of Fen's and Cardix's bodies, something I'm beginning to suspect he failed at intentionally."

Loic reached the platform, bowing perfunctorily to the prince, before clasping hands with Rezek. Damien's jaw shifted. "I think Loic told Rezek about you to earn his trust."

"But why?"

"Hyle," Damien ground out. "He's a mercenary. An assassin. Loic has been cozying up to the race coordinator to learn the track for the final race. Then he befriended Rezek."

Ari's lips parted with understanding. This was Loic's Ascension move.

He was going to assassinate Rezek Kelbra.

CHAPTER 40

MIKIRA

IT TOOK TIME for Mikira's eyes to adjust to the darkness.

They were in a part of the tunnels she'd never seen before, narrow, with enchanted lights hung sparsely and the ghostly echo of hooves striking wet stone. Unlike the other races, there were no marked paths here. They had only to escape the tunnels, reach the Traveler's Road, and then finish at the Kelbra estate. Which meant the myriad of turns peeling off from the main tunnel could be paths to winning or to ending up lost beneath the city. The only indication they were even going in the right direction were the little miners' arrows nearly lost to the ash and grime.

They turned left, and something flashed. Mikira ducked the knife, twisting to find another rider who'd been waiting around the bend.

"Go, Atara!" The horse lengthened her stride. They tore down the tunnel, outpacing the other horse through several more branches.

Mikira had just started to relax when Atara suddenly leapt. Not prepared for the jump, Mikira nearly toppled over her head, but caught herself against Atara's withers. The horse's hooves struck stone—all but one. Her back hoof slid *into* the ground. Mikira's stomach dropped as Atara scrabbled for purchase.

She threw her weight forward, and Atara pushed off her front hooves, clambering to safety.

Mikira slowed her to a stop, giving them both a chance to catch their breath.

Hoofbeats clattered, and the rider that'd been chasing them burst into the corridor, galloping full speed.

"Stop!" Mikira screamed, but it was too late. The horse stepped on what looked like solid ground—and fell. The man yelped a second before they disappeared over an invisible edge. A sickening thud echoed below.

Mikira gaped at the undisturbed ground. "There's—there's a ditch," she breathed. With a concealment charm. She ran a reverent hand along Atara's neck. "Thank the Goddess you could sense it." The mare huffed, pawing at the stone.

The tunnel opened wide before them, a long straightaway she never thought she'd be so happy to see. On and on they went, past messages scratched into stone walls and posters with Aslir's disparaging gaze following them. The tunnels grew narrower, the hard-packed ground turning to squelching mud. The silence was almost as bad as the enchantments, the anticipation of what would come next gnawing at her, but Atara raced forward confidently, her ears twitching for signs of danger.

Even following the miners' arrows, there was no way of telling how close she was to an exit. The tunnels stretched the length of Veradell. The race could end while she was still fighting her way through the darkness.

The shadows coalesced at the end of the corridor, and she slowed Atara as they neared, expecting another concealment charm. Instead, she found a door. There was nothing remarkable about it, just simple dark wood and a brass handle. She'd never heard of doors in the tunnels, though she knew these corridors hid more than just Jenest's underground races.

Bringing Atara to a halt, Mikira swung from the saddle and approached the door. She had just grabbed the handle when Atara's head shoved her aside. The door flew open, revealing only empty corridor beyond.

"What was that fo—" She stopped. The corridor wasn't empty after all.

Standing on the other side was Lochlyn.

Mikira couldn't move. All she could do was stare at the easy grin on her brother's lips, the way his green eyes were warm even in the darkness. He was taller than she remembered, his auburn hair shorn in a military cut. But he was here. He was real.

"Hey, Kira," he said, and something inside her broke.

She flung herself toward him, but Atara stepped between them, shoving her back. "Move!" she screamed at the horse, unable to do anything but watch as Lochlyn started walking into the dark, beckoning her to follow. "Move, you stupid horse!"

Atara whinnied sharply, the sound rebounding painfully in her ears in the narrow confines of the tunnel. It struck like a shock of cold water, and she gasped as the magic released her.

Lochlyn was gone.

"It was an illusion," she breathed, staring down at her palm. The door handle had been enchanted to create illusions, and Atara's danger charm had sensed it.

She nosed Mikira's cheek, huffing indignantly, and Mikira dug her fingers into the horse's coat. "I'm sorry," she said, but Atara only shuffled aside, giving her room to remount. She took one last look at the door, at the magic that could bring back her brother, and sent Atara onward.

They barreled along corridor after corridor, no sign of another horse. On and on they raced, until a pinprick of white light illuminated the way ahead.

An exit.

Mikira leaned close to Atara's neck as the horse flew down the tunnel. But no sooner had the light appeared than Mikira realized something was blocking their way. She slowed Atara to a trot as they neared what looked like a series of standing boards.

"What in the hells are these?" Her voice bounced off the walls.

She led Atara at a walk to an opening in the line of boards. As they came around the corner, they entered a circle of mirrors.

They all reflected the same thing: her, sitting on Atara's back. Except something was wrong. Mikira's eyes were dark bruises full of anger, her jaw set in a hard line and her hands curled into white-knuckled fists. She'd never seen herself so angry.

As she watched, the reflection opened her fists to reveal hands stained with blood.

Mikira gasped, looking down, but her hands were the same pale white as always. But in the mirror, the crimson coating her palms was unmistakable. It was so thick it looked like she'd dipped them in a can of red paint.

What was this? An enchantment that reflected her emotions? Such a thing was incredibly rare and expensive, and by far one of the most difficult types of ethereal enchantments, as it relied on each individual viewer.

She couldn't look away from it.

The blood dripped from her hands, sliding down her leg and along the saddle, staining the horse beneath.

"Atara," she breathed.

In the reflection, there was only the shape of a horse, made entirely of clay. Slowly, she began to crumble apart, Mikira's chances at winning the race disintegrating along with her.

It wasn't simply her emotions the mirrors were enchanted to show.

She swallowed hard. "They're enchanted to reflect my fear."

A stone clattered and Mikira twisted in her seat. Standing in the entrance to the mirror circle, his black stallion's flank wet with blood, was Gren.

He stared at the clay horse in the mirror. For a moment, neither of them moved.

Then Gren kicked Iri with such vicious ferocity the horse squealed and reared. When his front hooves struck stone, he bolted.

"Stop!" Mikira screamed, but it was too late. He'd already torn through the opening on the far side and out toward the light.

She sent Atara after them, erupting out of the tunnels into the grassland and the storm above. Rain pelted them harsh and heavy, hounding

them past the checkpoint and onto the dirt road leading to the Kelbras' estate.

They tore after Iri and Gren, the realization of what this meant tightening like a noose around her neck.

Gren had seen Atara's true form. He knew she wasn't a normal horse.

And he was going to tell Rezek.

CHAPTER 41

MIKIRA

NO NO NO *no no no no.*

The word beat through her with every strike of Atara's hooves. If Gren told Rezek what he'd seen, their deal would be void. Ari's life would be forfeit, her Kinnish magic exposed.

She had to catch him. She could bribe him. Threaten him. Whatever it took.

Suddenly they were beside Iri and Atara snapped at his throat, gouging a chunk of flesh. The horse screamed, and Atara struck again, tearing deeper. He buckled, hitting the ground hard and sending Gren tumbling.

"No!" Mikira shrieked. Reining Atara in, she leapt off her back, rushing to Iri. The horse thrashed as blood leaked into the muddy ground. He kicked and writhed, his fearful heart pumping blood from his neck.

"Iri, please, you have to stop. Iri!" she screamed.

He kicked again, then lay still.

Mikira dropped to her knees beside him, clasping her hands against the wound. "Please no. No no no. Iri!" But no matter how hard she pressed, she could not feel the beat of the stallion's heart. He was gone.

Atara whinnied. Mikira staggered to her feet, spinning to find the mare dancing away from Gren. His lip was split and bloody, his face a patchwork of scratches and dirt. And in his hands, he held her knives.

Too stunned from Iri's death, Mikira could barely process what that meant. That this whole thing had been orchestrated against her again.

"What is this demon beast?" he yelled across the roaring wind.

"It's not what you think," she said. "The mirrors, they lie."

Gren laughed, advancing toward her. "Rezek told me about the mirrors, little Rusel. I've heard stories of Kinnish creatures made of clay. Did Damien's new pet make this beast for you?"

She shook her head, stepping back. Her boot fell in a puddle of Iri's blood, squelching as it melded with the mud beneath.

"I can pay you," she said. "I can give you whatever you want. You can work for House Adair when this is over. Damien will treat you better than Rezek ever—" She stopped when Gren smiled. He didn't care what she had to say. All he cared about was that she lost.

"Not that it matters," he said. "You won't be making it out of here anyway."

He lunged for her, and she leapt aside, stumbling over Iri's outstretched legs. A sharp cry was all the warning Gren had before Atara nearly ran him over.

"Not this time, you bloody beast." Gren yanked a long rope with weights on either end from his belt. As Atara came for him again, he swung the rope at her forelegs. It tangled around them, sending her crashing to the ground with a horrible thud.

"Atara!" Mikira scrambled for her, but the mud pulled at her boots. Gren's knife sliced across her forearm, and she hit the wet earth hard.

Gren struck down. She caught his arm, her wrist screaming with the effort. He grinned at her shaking strength. "I'm going to treasure these blades," he hissed. "I'll show them to your father and tell him how you died screaming."

Her hand slipped, sliding blood along the length of the blade as it drove through her shoulder. She cried out, and Gren ripped free the blade, aiming to stab her again. She seized his wrist, desperate to push him back, but there was no resistance.

Gren was staring at the blade in confused awe. The stone in the handle had begun to glow a pale, smoky red. He tried to push it down, but it wouldn't budge. It hung in midair as though it had struck a wall, pinned between their hands.

Then, slowly, it shifted direction.

Falling back, Gren released the knife to Mikira's hold, but she had no control. It pulled her forward, the point aimed for his heart. She grabbed it with both hands even as her arm shrieked at her, but she couldn't stop its slow crawl, no matter how hard she pulled.

Gren scrambled back, and as if sensing its prey escaping, the knife leapt from her grasp and buried itself in his chest.

Gren stilled, his head falling limply to the side.

Mikira stared at the hilt of the blade, at the blood staining her hands.

Then she screamed.

CHAPTER 42

ARIELLE

*A*RI AND DAMIEN commandeered horses from two late-arriving spectators and set off after Rezek's departing coach. They'd only just reached a gallop when Ari felt the tug of Mazal's magic. Prickles of emotion filtered through to her, enough for her to recognize that Mikira was in trouble, and they were riding in the other direction.

Take care of her, Reid, she thought.

The outcome of the race wouldn't matter if they didn't stop Loic. If he killed Rezek, removing House Adair's greatest rival's last heir, he would win the Ascension. Damien's deal with Rezek would be void; you couldn't barter with a corpse, and there was no telling what would happen to Mikira's father. Ari's chance at an enchant license would go up in smoke, and everything they'd all worked for would be tossed aside in favor of all-out war between the Adairs and Kelbras.

They broke out of a shortcut at the northwestern side of the city and into scattered farmland. The dirt road would empty into the Traveler's Road north of the Kelbra estate. But was Rezek ahead of or behind them?

Thunder boomed and the first sprinkles of rain fell. Their horses' hooves kicked up clods of earth as they raced past worn fences and long fields of grass. Ahead, the road disappeared into a copse of trees beyond a bend. They galloped around it and their horses shuddered to simultaneous stops, nearly throwing them both.

The Kelbra coach lay overturned in the road, a wheel blown off. Rezek, Loic, and a Kelbra guard stood beside it.

Loic's eyes narrowed. "Damien."

"What are you doing here, Adair?" Rezek sneered, a cut above his eye leaking blood.

Damien pulled a gun and leveled it at his brother's chest. "Call it off."

"I don't know what you mean." Loic's lips curled.

A gunshot rang, and Damien cried out. He dropped his gun and his horse startled, throwing him.

"Damien!" Ari leapt from her horse, using its body as a shield as she pulled him to his feet. Blood soaked through his jacket at the top of his shoulder. A nick, but enough that it must hurt terribly.

"I'm fine," he ground out.

Hyle emerged into the middle of the road, a revolver in hand and flanked by four others. "I'd really prefer not to kill you," he said simply.

"You can't." Damien's voice strained. "It violates the rules of the Ascension."

"I didn't hire him to kill you," Loic said with a shrug. "If he does that, it's of his own accord and in no way my responsibility."

"What exactly is going on here?" Rezek had backed away behind his guard, who had his own gun drawn.

Hyle cocked his gun. "Simple, Your Lordship. This is an assassination."

"Run, Rezek!" Damien whipped out his other revolver, firing at Hyle's people. They scattered, along with the horses. Damien swung the barrel back toward Loic, but he'd already bolted into the trees.

"To the coach!" Ari called, and they ducked behind it after Rezek and his guard, pressing their backs to the roof alongside them. Only Damien separated her from Rezek, and she longed to reach across him and wring the man's neck. She'd burned verillion on instinct at the first bullet, and it warmed her blood with a steady pulse.

"I'm going to string your brother up by his ankles and peel his skin off piece by piece," Rezek hissed. He snatched one of his guard's other revolvers, cocking it.

"More likely, Hyle puts a bullet between your eyes," Damien replied.

As if on cue, a bullet tore through the side of the carriage. Damien popped up, returning fire. She heard a woman scream and Hyle call, "Oh, nice shot! Can you do it again?"

"He's toying with us," Rezek growled.

"Do you have any useful ideas, or are you just going to complain until we're dead?" Damien snapped.

Ari pointed at Rezek's signet ring. "Give me that."

Rezek's eyes narrowed to slits. "Excuse me?"

"Give it to her," Damien ordered, realizing what she intended to do. He angled toward Rezek, leveling a gun at his temple. "Alternatively, I feed you to Hyle as a distraction so we can escape."

Another bullet broke through the coach, and Rezek flinched. "Fine," he snarled, tearing the ring free and handing it to Ari. She quickly threaded the verillion's magic into the diamond, muttering a binding and forming an intention.

"Come now, Damien," Hyle called jovially. "Move away from there so I can riddle it with bullets. I won't wait much longer."

Ari pictured the bullets flying past her harmlessly and shaped her charm into one of luck.

"Be ready to shoot." She clutched the ring. "I'm going for Hyle."

Damien turned onto his knees, ready to lay down fire, and Rezek and his guard did the same. "What exactly are you about to do?" Rezek demanded.

"Now!" Ari burned her magic and sprinted around the edge of the carriage. Bullets flew, missing her by a hairsbreadth. Behind her, the others fired into the open stretch of road while she distracted the attackers. People screamed as bullets tore into them. One man made a break for the edge of the road, and a bullet took him in the side of the neck. The Kelbra guard went down with a gurgling cry.

Hyle leveled his gun straight at her and pulled the trigger—it jammed, backfiring into his hand. He dropped it with a yelp, the two nearest turning to aid him. A bullet struck one in the head and the other in the leg, until there was only Hyle.

Ari threaded an enchantment through her emerald and punched Hyle in the face. He hit the ground hard and rolled onto his side, coughing blood. Someone moved beside her, and she nearly struck on reflex, but Rezek only stared at her as though he'd discovered something long lost.

Hyle groaned, and Rezek cocked his gun. His gaze lingered on her a second longer—then he put a bullet in Hyle's leg.

"Stop." Damien seized Rezek's wrist.

Rezek ripped his arm free. "I'll do with my would-be assassin as I please." He shot Hyle in the arm. The man wheezed and blood seeped from his chest; he wouldn't survive his wounds. Rezek was just ensuring he died painfully.

Without hesitation, Damien put a bullet between Hyle's eyes.

Snarling, Rezek rounded on him, gun raised to Damien's chest. A sharp smile cut across his face. "How convenient. I can leave you to die here in the mud, a victim of a highway robbery. Your brother was useful for something after all."

He cocked the gun. "Goodbye, Damien."

Ari flared her verillion. At the same time, something shadowed broke loose in her mind. It swirled through her like verillion smoke, wispy and light, but icy cold, curling about her magic like a beast about its nest.

Kill him, it whispered in a voice Ari knew well. *Now.*

Ari lunged, knocking Rezek's arm away just as the gun fired. A bullet ripped through her shoulder, but she didn't feel the pain. Just as quickly as the hole formed, it resealed, and Ari was upon Rezek. Her first strike knocked the air from his lungs, cracking ribs. The second sent him to the ground with a broken nose.

She'd killed before; what was another life snuffed out? Letting go felt right. Letting go felt easy. She had only to—

"Arielle!" Damien's voice cut through the haze descending on her mind. "Fight it!"

Fight? What was there to fight? There was nothing wrong. There—her verillion ran out, and the clash of ice and fire inside her vanished. She gasped, collapsing to her knees.

Damien was before her in an instant, holding her upright. "What happened? Your eyes—they went white."

Ari leaned into his embrace, seeking the steady *thud thud thud* of his racing heart. She'd nearly lost control. It'd felt like if she'd let herself slip, if she'd let herself go, she would have woken up after lost time like before, but never had she felt it happening like that.

Was it you? she asked the voice. *What are you?*

I am your power.

My power is my own, she told it. *You cannot have it.*

"Arielle?" The concern in Damien's voice was enough to snap her back to herself. She climbed steadily to her feet, and he rose with her.

"I'm okay." She took in the overturned coach, the carnage of bodies, and at last Damien, bleeding from a wound in his shoulder.

"What do we do with him?" She nodded at Rezek. Damien hesitated, clearly loath to let the topic of what'd just happened go. "We'll discuss it later," she promised, and he acquiesced.

It took some searching to find where Damien's horse had run off to. He led it back to where Rezek lay slumped, then hoisted the man across the horse's back like a sack of grain. He gritted his teeth, and Ari's eyes locked on the bullet wound. "Are you okay?"

"I'll be fine," he assured her, considering Hyle's body. It was Enderlish custom to bury the bodies of the departed, but what did Damien owe him now? The consideration on his face said something, but in the end, he turned away.

"Let's go." She offered him a hand up. He took it, swinging into the saddle behind her. Her clothes were wet from the rain, but her body was hot from the fight, and she was incredibly aware of every inch of him that pressed against her.

Damien leaned over to grab his horse's reins as Ari looked upon Rezek. She felt her magic rise, felt the presence that lurked in the back of her mind.

"He'll get what he's owed," Damien promised her. She turned to look at him, her back pressing into his chest.

"I know," she said simply. "I'll make sure of it."

His lips met hers, and she leaned into the kiss as the rain fell.

CHAPTER 43

MIKIRA

MIKIRA HUDDLED AGAINST the ground. Over the whirring of the rain, she heard the thud of boots in mud, and then someone was beside her, calling her name. She only stared at her red-coated hands as though they didn't belong to her.

"Mikira?" Reid tried again, reaching for her.

"I—I think I killed him." She stared at Gren's corpse, the knife hilt still sticking out of his chest.

"It's okay," Reid said softly, but she only shook her head.

"I killed him," she said again.

"By the looks of it, he tried to kill you first." Reid swung in front of her, taking her bloodstained hands. "Listen to me, Mikira. The race is almost over. You can't let this stop you. You're so close."

Mikira stared at him. Slowly, his words settled, and her heaving breaths slowed. It wasn't over. Not unless she fell to pieces right here.

Reid went to pull her to her feet, but she cried out at the pain from her shoulder. Cursing, he knelt beside her and pulled a small container from his pocket. "This will numb the pain, but this needs to be tended to as soon as you return."

She barely felt him smear the wound with salve, barely felt him guide her to her feet. "Where's Atara?"

The horse's name snapped Mikira back to herself. "In the grass. Gren—" She broke off, sprinting for an area of long grass that lay flattened. "Atara!"

The horse whinnied back, lifting her head. Mikira dropped to her knees beside her, prying at the ropes tangled in Atara's legs. Reid joined her, pulling his pocketknife free to shear through them. Atara scrambled upright, tossing her head indignantly.

"You're okay," Mikira breathed in relief, even as her heart clenched at the sight of the mare's bloodied snout.

Reid snapped his knife shut and marched over to Gren, reaching for the blade in his chest. "Don't touch that!" Mikira yelled.

Reid froze with his fingers over the hilt of the blade. Mikira sprinted over and yanked the knife free, staring at it for a protracted moment. It had been like the blade had a mind of its own. Ari had said bloodstones created links, and the moment her blood had touched it, something had snapped into place between her and the knives, a thrumming she could still feel but didn't understand. What kind of enchantment was this?

Later, she told herself, and snatched the second knife from Gren's hip. She sheathed the first and handed both to Reid. "I can't have these."

Reid's fingers closed around the sheaths. "Mikira—"

"Not now." She swung up into Atara's saddle and stopped at the sight of Iri's still form. The long grass bent over him in the wind, the rain darkening his coat until she could almost convince herself it was another horse, and not the remains of her heart shattered against the earth.

"I'll take care of him." Reid's voice reeled her into the present. She stared at him in silence, and he looked back at her with pleading eyes. In them she read a hundred questions she couldn't answer, trapped between want and reality, truth and lie. Enemy and friend.

"Thank you," she whispered, and then they were off.

Mikira had never ridden so hard in her life. Atara's long legs ate up ground. They left the Traveler's Road behind, cutting straight for Kelbra Manor across ground turned muddy and uneven by the storm. Rain pelted her face and wind tore at her hair as they raced faster, faster, faster.

There was no telling where the other racers had come out and when. Gren's interference had taken mere minutes, but that could be the difference between victory and the loss of everything dear to her.

One mile. Two. Ahead, a pair of horses raced. Atara shot past them to a whirl of curses and shouts, gaining on Alren Zalaire and Dezaena Fyas.

Beyond them, Kelbra Manor loomed, Arabella Wakelin's silver stallion bearing down on the finish line.

"Run, Atara," she breathed, giving the horse her head.

Somehow, Atara found more strength to push with. Her hooves skimmed the earth, her breath coming in heavy gasps. Even a horse enchanted for endurance couldn't fly forever.

Just a little farther.

Atara went to the right of the two, hugging the space between the nearest horse and a tangle of rosebushes. Alren did a double take. He shouted something, dropping his reins to lash out a hand to knock her from her seat, but she ducked flat to Atara's neck. It nearly cost her balance, but they pulled in front of Alren's horse.

Arabella looked over at her with wild eyes. A snarl tore across her bloodied face, and she slashed a knife at Mikira.

Mikira raised her hand on instinct to keep it from hitting her neck.

Metal clinked against metal.

Mikira stared at the weapon in her hand. Simple, well made, and entirely hers. Somehow, she held one of her knives again.

Arabella gaped, and Mikira seized the opportunity to strike. She drew a gash across her thigh. Arabella yelped, dropping her weight into her saddle. Her horse misstepped, adjusting for the change, and Atara struck out in front a second before her hooves hit stone.

They galloped into the courtyard and across the finish line to a wild roar. The noise filled her like thunder in her veins until she was screaming too, the past weeks' fear and frustration bubbling up her throat in a sound lost to the tumult around them. She felt Atara drop to a canter, then a slow trot, but her body moved on reflex, posting up and down with each beat of the golem's hooves.

She couldn't feel her hands, couldn't feel anything beyond that humming.

Pure adrenaline kept her upright as she took Atara around the wide circular drive, the other racers turning in after her. Arabella gave her a grim smile, Alren and Dezaena shouting something she couldn't hear. Gradually, she became aware of her fingers twisted in the reins, of Atara tossing her head and snorting heavily at the pressing crowd, a performer basking in praise.

All Mikira could do was stare at the radiant faces and clapping hands and try to understand what it meant.

They'd won.

The roar refined into a chant, her family's name echoing from a hundred pairs of lips. *Rusel, Rusel, Rusel.* With each cry, Mikira's heart swelled, and the pure, uncomprehending shock that had descended the moment she crossed the finish line disintegrated. A giddy relief bubbled through her, a grin breaking across her face that felt too small for the emotions coursing through her.

One of the gate crew stepped out to direct her around the house to the back. People craned their necks for a glimpse of her and Atara, waving when her wild gaze slid across them, and tossing roses at Atara's hooves. Mikira's jaw ached from smiling so wide, but she couldn't stop. The noise, the sights—they streamed past her faster than in any race. She couldn't hold on to any of it, couldn't settle the rising wave of jumbled emotion in her chest. It seemed impossible that they were here, and yet as they led her to a small alcove where cameras flashed and reporters pressed her for information, it all began to sink in.

It was over.

Rezek's threats to her family, the rigor of the Illinir, the lies and tricks—all over, it was over.

She wrapped her arms about Atara's neck, her familiar musky scent an anchor in the tide of cheers. "Thank you," she whispered, and held tight.

It was then that she remembered the blade. She had to hide it—except it was gone. She stared at her empty, bloody palm, unsettled.

"Mikira!" Ari's voice rose above the rest. The crowd parted for her, Damien, and Reid as Mikira swung down from the saddle; she flung her arms around Ari.

"It's over," Ari whispered, and Mikira sank into her embrace. After everything, they would both have what they'd wanted most. Safety. Security. A future unshadowed by a darker past.

When at last she pulled back, her face was wet with tears she hadn't felt herself cry, but she smiled through them, even as she caught Reid's eye. His arms were folded, his gaze half-averted as if he both wanted to look at her and refused to.

There was no room left in Mikira for the lie stretched between them. It was clear by now that he hadn't told Damien the truth of the ring, and that only made her regret the space between them now all the more. It was over, her family was safe—she would be happy, if only for this moment.

"Thank you," she mouthed silently, and smiled when Reid turned for Atara.

"I don't know what everyone's clamoring about," he said. "The horse did all the work."

Atara blew a hot breath of agreement into his face.

"I think everyone did plenty," Damien replied with a twist of his lips. Even his joy was a tightly constrained thing, though Mikira knew he had to be simmering with satisfaction. With her win, he'd torn something precious away from Rezek, and he would take his time enjoying it.

A woman wearing the gold and white livery of the royal family pushed her way through the crowd, bowing swiftly to Damien, then her. "They're ready for you at the podium, Miss Rusel."

It was only then that Mikira realized the crowd had peeled back at Damien's arrival. As they started along a path at the edge of the manor, reporters swarmed them, fans clapping her on the back and reaching for Atara's mane. She snapped at any fingers that got too close, and Ari laughed.

The path emptied into a spacious terraced backyard, several tiers leading down to the golden glow of the verillion fields. A platform had been built at the far end, where Prince Darius and Princess Eshlin stood, a bouquet of flowers in the princess's arms. They wore matching royal white, the bloom of flowers bright against Eshlin's dress.

The wealthiest of the event's attendees milled about, sipping champagne that they raised with a hearty cheer to her as she passed. A sharp call echoed in the air, and she glanced up to see Mazal circle once, then dive. The hawk landed on Ari's outstretched arm as she and Damien climbed the platform to join Rezek behind the royal siblings. His face was a bruised mess, and she realized now that Damien was holding one shoulder stiffly. A berator joined them, a leather briefcase in hand.

Prince Darius stepped forward, and the spectators' clamoring died to a murmur. He held out his hands as he announced, "Mikira Rusel is the winner of the Illinir!"

The crowd erupted.

Mikira soaked in the cheers even as she fought to comprehend what this meant. Her family would be safe and taken care of. Their debts to the Kelbras would be paid. Her father would be free.

It all felt like a dream.

Rezek whispered furiously in the prince's ear, but from the thunderous look that filled his cousin's face, she had a feeling Darius didn't appreciate whatever Rezek was saying. He gestured him back with a sharp word. Rezek retreated, his face crimson with fury.

The prince nodded to his sister, who descended the dais. She stopped

before Mikira, handing her the flowers. "You are all she promised," she said with a smile, and was gone before Mikira could respond.

The prince launched into a speech about the grandeur and importance of the Illinir's homage to Sendia that Mikira barely heard. The world fell away around her as bit by bit, an unfamiliar sense of peace stole over her.

It was over.

CHAPTER 44

ARIELLE

MIKIRA HAD WON.

Mikira had won, and so had Damien, and so had she. Soon Ari would be a licensed enchanter, safe from the reach of the law.

Not quite, the voice reminded her. *Your power will never be accepted.*

What do you want from me? she demanded.

Soon, little lion.

The berator who'd notarized Damien and Rezek's official deal laid his briefcase down on a table at the back of the platform, opening it to reveal the document they'd both signed, along with the deed of ownership of the Illinir, and those for the Adair verillion and racetracks.

Rezek stared Damien down over the case with a burning, furious hatred. Damien didn't smile, but she knew that he was reveling in every second of it. She certainly was. Damien had taken not only the Kelbras' greatest honor and one of their largest sources of income, but he'd stolen something Rezek loved from him.

She would remember that look of helpless fury.

"My lord." The berator presented the documents to Damien, who slipped them into his own case.

Rezek seized him by the injured shoulder as he was about to step off the platform. "This isn't over, Adair."

Damien held in a hiss of pain and looked pointedly at Rezek's hand. Ari's eyes flicked to the hawk on her shoulder, and Mazal snapped her beak, nearly catching Rezek's fingers before he wrenched away.

This time, Damien smiled. "My lord," he said sardonically. Then they were down the stairs, Ari linking her arm in his as they strode through the tumult.

"Where did Mikira go?" She scanned the crowd.

"Likely enjoying the celebration," Damien replied. "She has an invitation to the pub later tonight. I need to go now, though; I have a meeting to attend."

REID REMAINED INSIDE the coach when they arrived at the Dark Horse, having treated Damien's shoulder and having "no desire to be anywhere near Loic when he realized he'd lost."

The pub had been closed to the public in anticipation of the Adair family meeting, the air still thick with the scent of verillion and peat. Damien led Ari upstairs to the same loft that Shira had taken her to, where a gray-haired Celairen man sat in an armchair by the fire, a near-empty glass of wine in his hand.

Galan Adair had the same sharp-eyed observation and indelible calm as his son, and she felt Damien stiffen beneath his attention. "How are you feeling, Father?" he asked.

"Better, with another glass." Galan lifted his cup, and Damien approached to pour him more wine from the decanter by the fire. Another man stood beside it, a berator with light brown skin and thick spectacles framing earnest eyes that surveyed them both. He clasped a case in his broad hands, not touching his own glass of wine.

"I told you that you were asking the wrong child." Shira sat behind a great oak desk, her boots propped on one corner and a book splayed open in her lap. "I have a terrible habit of trying to prevent my ailing father from poisoning himself."

Galan's laugh bordered on a wheeze. "Only you would deny a dying man his last comforts, my dear daughter."

"Silly me," she riposted. "There I went trying to prolong your life again."

"A losing battle, I'm afraid."

She flashed him a grin. "My favorite kind."

A half smile pulled at Damien's lips as he filled the wineglass before rejoining her at the edge of the sitting area. Shira caught Ari's gaze and winked, as if they shared some great secret. Ari smiled back. Perhaps they did. She had expected to feel strange being here, like a flower growing out of season, but Damien had assured her that her family knew her attendance meant he trusted her irrevocably, a thought that warmed her to her core.

Sure enough, Galan and Shira had absorbed her presence without protest, and she might even have said that Galan looked pleased that she was there. Damien had warned her that his father often asked if there was anyone new in his life, and it had been a while since he'd been able to say yes.

They waited for some time, the clock on the fireplace mantel ticking away. At last, Damien addressed his father, "I don't think Loic is coming, Father. His plans didn't go as he expected."

Galan regarded him with somber gray eyes. "We shall begin, but your brother's absence does not forfeit him until the ceremony's end. Mr. Eross, if you please."

Mr. Eross joined Shira at the desk, where he laid out the Ascension document. "Whenever you are all ready, then."

Shira withdrew a paper from her pocket and tossed it still folded to the berator. "I present a trade deal with the Ranoen ambassador. They've decided not to resign with House Vanadahl and instead shift their shipments to Adair whiskey."

"Well done," Galan said as the berator marked down the entry. It was a solid move for the family, but also a very clear message from Shira: she had no interest in winning. It seemed Damien's assessment of her was correct. Which only made Ari all the more curious about why Shira had been so intent on keeping an eye on her and Mikira.

Galan looked to his son.

Damien set his case on the desk, withdrawing the deed to the Illinir and handing it to Mr. Eross. "I present the right of ownership to the Illinir, taken from House Kelbra."

Galan's face slackened with shock. Satisfaction curled deep in Ari's belly as Galan took the paper from the berator, his eyes racing along each line. When he looked back up, the pure, unbridled pride in his face made Damien straighten.

"I knew you would do something extraordinary, but this?" Galan shook his head. "Goddess help this city. Damien Adair, I name you—"

The door flew open, slamming into the wall. Loic's hulking form stood shadowed in the frame, something large and dripping dangling from his hand.

"Not until I've entered my offering," he snarled, and stepped into the light.

Hanging from his hand by the roots of its hair, was the head of High Lord Eradas Kelbra.

Damien drew his gun at the same time that Ari muttered a binding, magic flooding through her body.

"What have you done?" Damien demanded.

Loic flashed a wild grin. "I have dealt a deadly blow to our greatest rival. That is what I've done." All those weeks spent cozying up to Rezek—he wasn't the only one whose trust Loic must have earned. Eradas had let his guard down, had let Loic too close.

"You've started a war," Shira whispered.

"You've put Rezek at the head of the family!" Damien snarled.

Loic beat his empty fist against his chest. "I've taken my place as right-ful heir to the Adair family. Your pieces of paper mean nothing compared to this."

He bore down upon Galan. "Name me."

Galan looked from Loic to Damien. He couldn't possibly intend to name Loic? The man was unhinged, even Ari could see that. But Damien had said that he and Rezek had bonded over their tumultuous relation-ships with their older brothers, and Eradas Kelbra had always favored his eldest. Perhaps the same could be said of Galan, who likely felt some sat-isfaction at the death of his enemy.

"Name me!" Loic roared.

Footsteps echoed on the landing and Reid burst into the room, three constables on his tail.

"There he is." Reid pointed at Loic.

One of the Anthir stepped forward. "Loic Adair, you're under arrest for the murder of High Lord Eradas Kelbra."

Loic's nostrils flared. "No." He backed away as the guards advanced on him. "No! I am head of House Adair. You can't just arrest me. You can't—"

"Damien is my heir." Galan's voice cut smoothly across his son's.

A crazed look sparked in Loic's eyes. He dropped the head, going for a revolver at his hip, but Ari seized hold of him. He writhed in her verillion-enhanced grasp, but the constables rushed forward, cuffing his hands behind his back. If they had anything to say about the girl who restrained a man twice her size, they kept it to themselves.

Damien turned away as the constables dragged Loic outside. Unlike the smug satisfaction evident on Reid's face, Damien almost looked pained. Loic and he might have been at odds, but he was still his brother. Still family. It must have cut deep to see him fall like this.

A painful silence lingered in the constables' wake. In it, Damien's gaze

slid to Shira, who hadn't moved from her spot at the desk. They shared a brief look, then Mr. Eross held something out to Damien. A new house ring, nearly identical to the old one, save for one small difference: the loop of gold around the central stone, denoting the truth for all who saw it.

He was head of House Adair.

CHAPTER 45

MIKIRA

AFTER GETTING HER injuries tended to, Mikira spent nearly an hour looking for Rezek among the post-race celebration to no avail. Eventually, she tried the manor, but she'd barely reached the door when a Kelbra guard stepped in front of her.

"No one is allowed in at this time," he said.

"I have business with Lord Kelbra," she said. "My father—"

"I don't care about your father, little girl. Lord Kelbra will not be disturbed right now."

She stood there, seeking the words to make him understand and knowing that nothing she said would help. The race was done, the bargain set. Her father would be safe until tomorrow evening, when she could corner Rezek at the closing ball.

Mikira took Atara home.

Though she'd never really considered who the horse belonged to, Ari had made it clear that Atara belonged with Mikira, and Atara had made her choice on the matter even clearer. She gave the horse every apple she could find when they got there, before letting her out in what had once been Iri's paddock. The long grass swayed in her wake, and for a while Mikira just leaned on the fence and watched her run, thinking of another horse.

The images of Iri's death were imprinted in her mind, and there was a part of her that couldn't look at Atara without seeing them. The mare had only been protecting her, and she was unaware of how deeply she'd wounded Mikira in the process. She didn't blame the golem. Or at least, she didn't want to, but the knot in her stomach grew tighter each time she looked at her, until she couldn't bear it any longer.

If only she could undo the past.

Reid was true to his word, and someone arrived shortly after her return with Iri's body. She had only to direct them where to bury it and wait alongside them until they'd finished, leaving her alone at the edge of a grave. There she remained until she couldn't any longer, and then she turned for the house, some parts of her weighing heavily, others lighter than they'd been in years. The invitation to the party at the Adair pub sat folded in her pocket, but she had been away from her family long enough.

She found Nelda and Ailene curled up with Wolf on the couch. Ailene was asleep, Nelda buried in a book. She looked up when Mikira entered, then did a double take.

"Kira!" She flung the book aside, leaping to her feet.

Mikira caught her, holding tight even as her injured forearm complained.

"I'm so glad you're okay." Nelda's voice choked, and she squeezed Mikira tighter.

"Kira?"

They pulled apart, both facing a slowly waking Ailene. Her eyes found the bandages on Mikira's forearm and shoulder, and she sat up abruptly. "You're hurt—"

"I'm fine." She twisted her wrist to prove it. "How are you feeling?"

Ailene stared at her uncomprehendingly. "Kira. The race?"

A small smile tugged at her lips. "I hope you two are ready to be famous, because you're looking at the youngest person to ever win the Illinir."

Nelda gasped and Ailene yelped, waking Wolf, who, refusing to be left out, barked. Against Mikira's protests, Ailene met her halfway in a reckless hug. Nelda joined them, her thin arms wrapping around the back of their waists.

Mikira clung to the steadiness of her sisters, to their solid presences, and finally, the understanding of what she'd done began to sink in. Never again would they live in fear of the Kelbras. Never again would their family struggle to get by.

They were safe.

By the time Mikira finished recounting everything that had happened— leaving out only Gren's death—Ailene and Nelda had fallen asleep on the couch, their faces stained with tears at the news of Iri's loss. It was late, the fire burning low and the sky dark. She looked at Nelda, whose head still rested on her shoulder. Gently, she brushed her sister's hair back from her face.

Then her eyes fell on the black book by Nelda's feet. No, not a book—a journal.

Careful not to disturb her sisters, Mikira picked up the journal and laid it open in her lap. It was soft, supple leather, the first page inscribed with her father's name in careful script.

The first entry was dated nearly a year ago, marking the journal as one in a series. She flipped through the pages, scanning through aimless thoughts littered with information on enchantments and research into magical animals before finding the latest entry.

It was dated two months ago, the day before Rezek had taken him away.

I'm sure of it now: there's a fifth stone. How else to explain the enchantment on Mikira's knives? A charm to carry out their owner's intentions is surely ethereal, though well beyond anything I've witnessed, but the one that would bind the blades to her alone?

It's the bloodstones.

The journal slipped from Mikira's hands. She was right—her blood *had* triggered the bloodstone link. She'd been clinging to some thread of hope that Gren's death wasn't her fault, that she'd tried to stop it, but the knives said otherwise. If they were truly enchanted to carry out her intentions, then that meant some part of her, no matter how small, had wanted Gren dead.

And the knife had made it happen.

Was that how the knife had appeared in her hand in the final stretch, only to vanish when she realized she couldn't be found with it? Reid hadn't said anything to her about it, but he'd been occupied with getting back to the finish line and may not have noticed the blade's brief disappearance.

Mikira held out a hand. She'd left the blades in her saddle bag in the barn, but if she was right, then she had only to will them to her. Feeling slightly foolish, she called to them—and watched them materialize in her hand.

"Hells," she breathed. She let her head drop back, staring at the ceiling. This was all too much, and it wasn't over yet. There was still the closing ceremony ball, still the matter of freeing her father and seeing her funds transferred from Damien. Reid hadn't told him what she'd done yet, but who knew if that would change.

She had conned one of the most dangerous men in all of Enderlain. She'd won an unwinnable race. Against all odds, she'd saved her family.

She would weather this too, and come whatever may, she would take care of it herself.

CHAPTER 46

$\mathcal{A}$RIELLE

THEY CELEBRATED LATE into the night.

The pub was alive with music and dancing and drinks, and she recognized the faces of everyone from Adair jockeys to off-duty constables to the house's district tenants. Damien circulated through them all, shaking hands and accepting congratulations and requests to meet with the grace of a king. She'd been on his arm for nearly an hour, and never once did he forget to introduce her like a queen.

Mikira's absence was the only mark on the night. Damien had sent a messenger at Ari's behest, and Mikira had replied that she intended to stay home for the evening, but Ari wished she'd come. Everything they celebrated tonight was in large part due to her, and Ari missed having her there.

"He's going to have to pay for the fallout of Loic's move tonight," Ari said, now sequestered by the fire with Reid. They were both watching Damien in conversation with a retired general by the bar.

Reid snorted, half-slumped in his armchair. "As long as Loic pays for it more, it's worth it."

Ari studied his feigned nonchalance with a critical eye. "What did he do to you?"

He was silent at first, tracing the lines of one tattoo up his forearm, and coming to a stop at a particularly knotted mess of ink that resembled a crow. "When we were younger, he and his friends thought it funny to lock me in an old mausoleum. They left me there for nearly two days, refusing to tell Damien where I was. Eventually I was able to break the glass and climb out, but I cut my arms up doing it."

That was where the tattoos came from—they were covering the scars.

"A game," Ari whispered. That's what Loic had called it. Perhaps he'd gotten what he deserved. "But how did the Anthir know what Loic had done to Eradas?"

"Shira must have had the Anthir following him," he said. "But pulled them back when you and Damien engaged Rezek."

So that they wouldn't witness anything they shouldn't. But why see one brother arrested and prevent the other? Did Shira care for Damien that much more?

Ari peered over the heads of the crowd to the opposite corner, where a second fire burned. Shira was sprawled across one of the armchairs, her nose buried in a book. The crowd gave her a wide berth.

"Ari?" Reid asked.

Ari handed him her drink. "I'll be back."

The crowd parted for her with surprising ease, and she lowered herself into the chair opposite Shira's. The leather cover of her book had practically fallen away from the binding, but Ari could still make out the title. It was a romance novel.

"Exactly how many times have you read that?" she asked.

"One fewer than enough," Shira replied without looking up.

"At some point knowing what's going to happen has to ruin it."

Shira closed the book with a snap. "Ari. I'm reading."

Which translated loosely to *Tell me what you want before I bite your head off for interrupting me.* A trait that ran in the family it seemed.

Ari smiled. "Why did you call the Anthir on Loic?"

"A question I'd like an answer to as well." Damien appeared beside Ari's chair, laying a hand on her shoulder.

Shira didn't respond right away, and Ari could read nothing of her reaction in her face. How much of his emotional control had Damien learned from his older sister? He'd told her of his relationship with Loic, but not with her.

Eventually, she set her book aside. "They were supposed to stop him from doing anything foolish."

"You mean stop him from winning," Damien said. "You couldn't have possibly thought he'd make a better house head."

Ari agreed. Loic was as unpredictable as a wolf and twice as quick to bite. Surely Shira could see that?

Shira picked up a forgotten cup of tea from the table. "I think that winning the Ascension would have ruined him . . . and that losing it would have ruined you."

"Then we agree," Damien replied. "Loic is weak. He wasn't fit to lead this house."

Shira laughed softly. "How quickly we forget." He frowned, and she turned sideways in her chair to face him. "Do you remember when those boys cornered you outside the pub? Who came for you?"

Damien ground his teeth. "Loic."

"And what about when you took Father's prized racehorse out for a midnight ride, only to cause a sprain? Who took the blame?"

This time, more quietly, "Loic."

"We are all of us weak sometimes," she said. "You just like to forget when it is you."

Damien's hand tightened briefly on Ari's shoulder, the only indication that Shira's words had gotten to him. They always seemed to. His sister knew him well, and Ari suspected that was the very reason Damien avoided her. That, and what Ari now understood was Shira's deep desire to protect her brothers. This was why she'd followed her and Mikira, why she'd helped with the golem but wouldn't have agreed to the endeavor herself.

Damien downed the rest of his drink and set the glass aside. "The Loic you speak of is gone. He vanished when we became House Adair and Mother died, and he saw me as a threat to his position."

"That's the thing the two of you have forgotten." Shira picked up her book and settled back into her chair. "We've always been House Adair."

She cracked open the book to her marked page, and recognizing the dismissal, Ari and Damien returned to the party.

THE NEXT MORNING, Ari woke with a pounding head and a thirst for water so powerful, she nearly knocked over the pitcher on the drink cart scrambling for it. She'd downed three glasses before she thought to try verillion. It burned away the worst of the hangover in seconds, and she dropped onto the chaise, wishing it could do the same for her headaches when they pestered her. But she'd learned long ago the human body didn't always do what it was supposed to when it came to medicine.

Reid trudged out a short time later, looking far more disgruntled than she thought possible, even for him. He muttered something unintelligible and collapsed beside her. She reached behind them and poured him a cup of tea, which he accepted with another incoherent mutter.

Several minutes of silence and multiple cups of tea later, he finally looked at her. His eyes narrowed, taking in her obvious lack of discomfort, and said, "That is entirely unfair."

She smiled innocently.

The foyer door cracked open, and Mikira peeked through. She looked as exhausted as Reid. Her braid was a mess, her clothes wrinkled, and her sleeves unevenly rolled. Still, she smiled when she saw Ari. It faltered when Reid glared at her.

Mikira hovered in the doorway, returning Reid's stare with all the force of a burning fire. Then, without a word, Reid rose and poured her a cup of tea. He set it before one of the chairs. Mikira crossed the room and sat down, picking it up.

"Do I even want to know?" Ari asked.

"No," they said in unison.

"Right." Ari settled back into the chaise just as Damien emerged from his bedroom. Unlike the rest of them, he didn't have a single hair out of place.

He paused at the edge of the sitting room. "Is there a reason you're all glowering at me?"

"Ari," Reid said.

"On it." She woke the cord between her and the hawk perched by the desk. Mazal spread her wings and with a flurry of beats, sent a gust of wind straight into Damien's face.

A single curl of hair dropped across his forehead.

Ari groaned, thrusting a hand at him. "He looks even better like that!"

"We could try the talons instead?" Mikira suggested lightly.

Damien rolled his eyes. "If the three of you are done, we have some things to discuss." He sat down in the empty chair.

"Maybe we can start by someone telling me what happened to you two yesterday?" Mikira's gaze slid to Damien's shoulder, where the edge of a bandage peeked out from beneath his collar. Mikira's own injuries were still tightly wrapped.

Damien's expression grew grim. "My brother tried to kill Rezek with the help of a friend who betrayed me. We stopped them." The bitterness in his voice surprised Ari. How strong did that emotion run that he couldn't rein it in?

Next to her, Mikira had grown very still. The hand on her teacup trembled.

"I should receive the funds from the race winnings by the end of the week," Damien continued. "I'll have it transferred to your account, and I'll oversee your father's return from Rezek."

"I tried to get him back after the race." Mikira's voice warbled. "But the guard refused to even tell Rezek I was there."

Ari looked to Damien, who sighed. "That would be because his father was murdered."

Mikira gaped at him. "Eradas Kelbra is dead? But Rezek—" Her voice pitched, and she regathered herself, starting again. "He was the only thing that kept Rezek from spiraling out of control. He's been defeated on two fronts and humiliated. What will he do now without his father to control him?"

"We'll handle it," Damien said, unwavering. "Don't worry."

Mikira's jaw tightened, and she stared down at her half-empty cup, but she didn't argue.

Ari squeezed her arm. "I owe you my thanks, you know. For much more than just winning this race. You helped pull me out of a life I hadn't realized I'd stopped living. I'm grateful to have met you, and to call you my friend."

Mikira smiled weakly at her. "I'm glad we're friends too." She stood, her cheeks flush with color. "I just came to see everything was all right, but I promised Nelda I'd take her for a ride on Atara before the ball."

They hardly had a chance to say goodbye before she was out the door. Her departure itched at Ari, and a moment later, she followed her out.

"Mikira!" she called, stopping her at the edge of the corridor and joining her. "Is something wrong?"

Mikira's lips pressed together as if to trap the words inside, and she shook her head, but Ari didn't believe her. She'd been acting strange for days, avoiding them, sitting in icy silence with Reid, looking at Damien as if—

"Oh," Ari breathed.

Mikira's fingers curled into fists. "Did he kill those men?"

"He was protecting me," Ari said swiftly. "They nearly killed me, and they would have exposed me."

But Mikira was already shaking her head as if to block out the words. "He's a *murderer*, Ari!"

Ari gritted her teeth, driving her fingers through the knots of her hair. "We both are."

"What?" Mikira's voice was small now, unsure, and Ari watched the color pale from her face as she told her about her first golem, her Saba's death, her flight from the only home she'd ever known.

"That was an accident," Mikira said hoarsely. "It doesn't make you a monster, Ari. Not like him."

Ari bit out a sharp laugh. Would Mikira say the same if she knew about Kyvin? If Ari carved Rezek apart before her, would she still defend her? This was the difference between them. Mikira still wanted to be herself at the end of all this. Ari wanted to be something more.

Something untouchable.

"It's not what I've done that makes me a monster, Kira," she rasped. "It's that if given the choice to do it all over again, knowing what it meant—I'm not sure if I could give up this power."

A sense of satisfaction emanated from deep within her, that other presence preening with an unparalleled delight. It'd been waiting for this. Wanting it.

Mikira swallowed tightly, and aware of it or not, she retreated a half step. It was all it took for Ari to have her answer. Mikira couldn't know the truth of her darkness.

She couldn't accept it.

Ari didn't stop her as she left.

THAT NIGHT, WHILE Reid and Damien were in their respective rooms getting ready for the closing ball, Ari stood at the desk and stared at the Racari. This was the first moment of solitude she'd had to truly consider what had happened yesterday during the race.

She could no longer ignore it. Her magic was straining at her control, and it was connected to this book, to the bloodstone that bound them. It hummed beneath her touch, begging her to open it, to use it, its pearlescent ribbing almost pulsing.

Do it, said the voice.

"Arielle?"

Damien stood in the doorway to his bedroom, dressed in a crisp red shirt set beneath a slate-gray waistcoat. His black jacket hung over one shoulder hooked by two fingers, and dark strands of hair curled across his brow.

She pushed the book from her mind. "You look nice."

He stepped aside as she approached. "Not half so much as you."

The simple compliment brought a blush to her cheeks, and she ran her fingers across his stomach as she passed.

Inside, she washed and dressed, carefully finding her way into a new gown he'd bought her. Deep sapphire accented in gold, it hugged her curves in all the right places. Her hair she left down around her shoulders, her only ornament the emerald ring Damien had given her.

She stepped out to find him curved over his desk cleaning his revolvers. For a moment she simply watched him. He worked with a delicate precision, the look on his face familiar—it was the way she felt when she crafted a golem, both enamored with her power and utterly at its mercy.

It was how she felt about him, and how he felt about her.

He looked up as she approached, his gaze taking all of her in. She let herself bask in that look of wonder.

"There's something I want to tell you," she said.

He set down his tools, giving her his full attention. The words rose and hovered in her throat, and she thought of her golems, of how they could come undone, exposing their true natures.

She felt like that now. Like a fruit peeled to reveal the rot underneath.

Still, she forced the words out. "I killed my Saba a year ago, and the other night, I killed Kyvin."

She gave no excuse, no explanation. What mattered was the blood on her hands, not the reasons it had been shed.

Damien stood, and for a moment, she expected him to order her out of his home. To say she was dangerous. To say she was a monster.

Instead, he closed the distance between them. His eyes held hers with an affection bordering on reverence, and it was in that moment, her lips hovering before his, that she understood: she could destroy him if she wanted to.

If he didn't destroy her first.

Damien's lips met hers, and she melted into the kiss. Her hand traveled up along his neck to curl in his hair, and he let out a quiet moan as she tugged gently on it, then harder. His own hands were hot against her skin, finding the places where the dress was thin. Each brush of his fingers was like discovering sensation again for the first time.

A deep, long-suffering sigh sounded from the other side of the room. They broke apart, breathing hard, to find Reid standing in his customary all-black suit, his hair a ruffled mess.

"Oh good, you're done," he said. "Can we go now? The earlier we get there, the earlier I can leave."

Damien chuckled quietly, then slid his arm about her waist. She leaned into him, basking in that surety, that security.

Their strength.

Something jingled, the clatter of metal against stone. Widget darted after it, batting it once more with his paw.

Damien saw it at the same time Reid did. Reid snatched the glinting metal up, but Damien seized his wrist. They stood there, frozen, Reid's fingers curled into a tight fist, Damien's forearm taut. Neither one looked away.

"Reid," Damien said at last. "Show me."

Reid swallowed hard. Then he opened his hand.

CHAPTER 47

MIKIRA

THE CLOSING BALL was at the castle, and it put the showcase manors to shame. Nearly twice their size, it was built of pristine white stone and nestled in the hills of the northern city. Some of the stones were enchanted, changing color in unison from pale turquoise to brilliant orange to bright carmine. The ones in the center remained a vivid, shining white, forming the shape of the royal sigil.

Enchanted lights adorned the mazelike garden that framed the guest entrance, a gravel-lined path leading to the open ballroom doors. More festooned the shrubs and pastel green trees, and several small enchanted songbirds flitted from branch to branch, singing a harmonizing melody.

Some part of Mikira knew it was beautiful, but the larger part of her couldn't focus on the magic. She didn't care about the music or food or the magnificent dress that Damien had gifted her, made of black silk and embroidered in silver thread.

She had come for Rezek.

The problem was the bastard was nowhere to be found.

Had he not come? Between losing the rights to the Illinir and his father, she wouldn't be surprised.

"Hey, aren't you Mikira Rusel?" A tall, olive-skinned boy about her age with dark hair and deep brown eyes stood before her, a dark-skinned person with curly hair and an easy smile beside him. She tensed, waiting for their ridicule.

"My name's Wyer. This is my partner, Ilos." He took the other person's hand. "We just wanted to say how fantastic you were. We saw the whole end of the race. You came out of nowhere!"

"Thank you," she replied smoothly, grown used to this by now. Fortified by her response, they piled on, telling her how beautiful Atara was and how well she'd ridden and how much they'd loved watching her in the other races.

"I thought Lord Kelbra was going to lose it at the end!" Ilos exclaimed. Wyer chuckled, and Mikira did too. It felt surprisingly good to laugh with them.

They offered to get her a drink, and though the adoration in their faces pulled like a lure, she excused herself from their company. If she couldn't find Rezek, then she'd deal with another unresolved matter. Still, she left with a burning sense of satisfaction that she clung to as she dove back into the crowd, trying to avoid aggravating her injuries.

Working her way through the throng took a while as other guests stopped her to congratulate her or remark on her impressive race. By the time she pulled out of the mass of slapping hands and exclamations, she had several invites to tea, requests for private riding lessons, and more than one buyer interested in a Rusel enchant. She felt like a buoy rising above a raging sea and drank the fresh air in gasps.

But she hadn't seen Reid anywhere either.

"Well, aren't you the celebrity."

She spun, coming face-to-face with Talyana in her Anthir uniform.

"You've got to be kidding me," Mikira groaned. "I can't deal with this right now." She retreated, but Talyana grabbed her arm.

"Relax, I'm not here to pester you. I'm here to bring you to someone else who will pester you."

Mikira frowned, and Talyana looked to where Princess Eshlin sat at a table beneath a covered corridor. Sighing, Mikira followed Talyana through the crowd to the waiting princess.

Mikira bowed perfunctorily as they arrived, and the princess gestured for them to sit.

"Congratulations again on your win, Miss Rusel," she said. "That was quite the performance." As she spoke, her dress shifted around the shoulders. There was a pattern on it, a raised cylindrical outline. Was it enchanted?

"Thank you, Your Highness." Mikira glanced at Talyana, hoping for an indication of what this was about, but the other girl merely grinned at her. She never would have expected Talyana to look so pleasant in the service of a royal.

"Miss Haraver tells me that you've grown quite close with Lord Adair." Princess Eshlin laced her fingers together and rested her chin upon them. "I must admit I was surprised to hear that, considering your fraught relationship with the noble houses."

This time the glance Mikira shot Talyana was nothing short of hostile.

"Lord Adair's sponsorship helped my family out of a recent bind," Mikira replied tightly. "I'm grateful for his help, and that's all I have to say on the matter."

Besides, the princess and her family were no better. What right did she have to speak of the noble houses when her family's war was responsible for her brother's death among countless others?

Eshlin's brow rose, and for a moment, Mikira worried she'd been too blunt. But the princess didn't look put off, merely curious. "Tell me, are you happy with our current system, Miss Rusel?"

Mikira shifted uneasily. "I'm not sure it's my place to criticize—"

"Please." Eshlin cut her off. "Speak freely. Nothing you say will be used against you here."

Talyana's hand fell over hers. "We're not your enemies, Kira."

Mikira jerked her hand away. "And yet I still can't trust you. What are you even doing here with her?" She hadn't missed that Talyana had said "we," but neither could she process what that meant. This was the same girl who'd practically celebrated the attempt on Prince Darius's life.

Talyana recoiled, and Mikira looked to the princess, her frustration mounting. "I'll speak freely if you do, Your Highness. Tell me what you want."

A smile spread across Eshlin's full lips. "Ah, that's the fire Talyana spoke of." Something about the words drained Mikira's annoyance, making her cheeks flush. Here was a woman who was everything Mikira longed to be: poised and elegant as a winter flower, yet strong and formidable as Aslir, a princess who commanded the respect and loyalty of soldiers.

It was no secret that where her brother had the ear of the nobility, Princess Eshlin was backed by the military, a support she'd earned through her skill with a sword and years spent training in their ranks. She'd even served briefly in the Eternal War before her father forced her to return home when his mind began to fog.

The princess brushed a hand along her collarbone. As she did, the dress rose. Mikira blinked. No, something rose *from* the dress.

A snake lifted its head, forest green and thicker around than her arm. Its bright marble-like eyes watched her, its black tongue flicking out to taste the air. The dress wasn't enchanted; the snake was—except there wasn't a single gold fleck in its eyes.

A golem.

Eshlin ran a finger along the length of the snake. "Very well, Miss Rusel. I'll speak plainly. There is a certain organization in this city that could use someone of your mettle. An organization that intends to ensure equality among Enderlain's citizens."

Mikira almost laughed. Of course. Because her position wasn't already precarious enough, now the Princess of Goddess-damned Enderlain was requisitioning her, not in support of her family, but *against* them.

"You're rebels," she said in disbelief. This was why the rebels had only gone after Darius. This was why Talyana was here.

"Guilty as charged," Talyana replied with a smile. "What are you going to do about it?"

Mikira shook her head. "Nothing. I'm going to do nothing because I want nothing to do with this."

"Because you're loyal to Damien Adair," Talyana said with all the bite of acid.

"Because my family is finally safe," Mikira hissed back. "And I won't jeopardize them again. I don't care about your stupid war!"

Talyana leaned across the table. "The Mikira I know would never have turned her back on this."

"Like you had any idea who she was," Mikira snarled. "How could you? You left!"

Something pained flashed through Talyana's gaze, but she pressed on. "I entered the Illinir to use the winnings as funding. I gave that up to save you. But now you're exactly what we need."

"What's that?"

"A face," Princess Eshlin replied smoothly. "Every movement needs one. Ours cannot be a noble. But someone the people love? A legend among racers with funds no one is tracking?"

Mikira's hands curled. "You can't be serious."

Talyana's hand seized hers. "Think about it, Kira." Her eyes flitted over Mikira's shoulder, and she pulled back.

Mikira turned just as Reid broke free of the crowd. He looked from her to Talyana and back again, scowling, but forced himself to bow to the princess.

"Mikira, I need to talk to you," he said.

"What about?" Mikira snapped. "I'm a little busy."

"It's—"

"For me." Damien stepped from the crowd, his expression set in its usual implacable mask. "Your Highness, could I borrow Miss Rusel for a moment?"

"What for?" Talyana asked, but Damien didn't spare her a glance.

Princess Eshlin frowned just the slightest. It was her reaction that set Mikira on edge. "By all means, Lord Adair. But I'd like to see her again before the night is through."

"Of course." Damien bowed, then offered Mikira his hand. She sought Reid, whose panicked expression told her everything.

Damien knew.

"Mikira." Talyana sounded nervous, but Mikira didn't look at her. She forced herself to take Damien's hand. He led her out onto the dance floor, where the latest set had begun. His hand was cold against her waist as they took their positions, his movements stiff and sharp.

"Listen very carefully," he said in the cool, objective tone of a blade. The music struck up and the dance began. "We're going to make a new deal."

"Damien—" She cut off as his gaze snapped to her. There was nothing there of the boy who'd smiled at her earlier that day.

"I am going to keep your winnings." He guided her through the first turn. "I will distribute them to you in a monthly salary. In exchange, the information you know about me stays with you. You will not testify. You will not tell a soul. If you do, I will take more than your funds from you. Rezek is not the only one who knows your father's secret."

Her breathing came quick and shallow. Once, she'd wondered what it would take to get under his skin. Now she wished she didn't know.

"You can handle your father's release yourself." He spun her, bringing her back in a sharp motion. "Do we understand each other?"

She nodded.

"Good." He spun her once more, but this time he released her hand, allowing her to turn to the edge of the crowd. When she turned back, he was already gone.

Mikira stared at the spot he'd occupied, her heart thudding painfully in her chest. He hadn't even given her the chance to explain herself, to tell him how it had really happened.

He wouldn't care. For all she knew, Reid had already told him, and Damien had dismissed him.

This, too, is your fault, she thought to herself.

What had happened to Ailene and Iri—they were because of *her,* and her choices. She'd been so angry, so convinced the world owed her something, that she'd made decisions that once would have revolted her. She'd lied, and she'd cheated, and she'd thrown her lot in with the nobility whose power had crushed her family for years, all because she'd thought that for once, the rules should bend in her favor.

This was what came of playing a game of kings.

Yet Mikira could not bring herself to regret all of it. Bending the rules had seen her safely through the Illinir, won her father's freedom and enough money to save the ranch and pay for Ailene's medical bills, and brought her closer to people than she ever thought she'd be again. Her father's unyielding trust in what was right over what was necessary would never have allowed for that. But just as his rigid beliefs were impractical, neither was the answer to become like the very people she despised.

This was what happened when she let her uncertainty rule her. It was time she started trusting herself. If she didn't, the indecision would burrow beneath her skin and spread like rot. Her fear would rule her, as cruel and vicious as Rezek ever could be.

She was done allowing it to.

Lifting her head, Mikira cut through the crowd toward Princess Eshlin's

table. She wasn't the same girl Rezek Kelbra had forced to her knees. She was Mikira Rusel, the youngest winner of the Illinir in history and the best enchant breeder in Enderlain.

If Damien Adair wanted to make her his enemy, then his enemy she would be.

CHAPTER 48

ARIELLE

"DAMIEN," ARI SAID for the third time. They stood to the edge of the stage, where the orchestra was finishing their latest song. Reid hovered just behind him, withdrawn like a kicked dog. Damien refused to look at him—he was staring at the stage so intently, he didn't seem to hear her.

Ari placed a hand on his arm. "It was an accident. Mikira didn't mean—"

"Don't tell me she didn't mean it." The unbridled emotion in his voice surprised her. "She didn't accidentally hold on to the one piece of evidence tying me to them. She didn't accidentally forget to tell me." She watched him force his fisted hands to relax. "Mikira made her choice. I am only protecting myself."

She didn't agree, but before she could press him further, the song ended, and a feminine voice floated into the enchanted microphone.

"His Royal Majesty, King Theo Zuerlin of Enderlain."

The king emerged from a set of double doors at the back of the stage. His face was sallow and sunken, his broad-shouldered body now thin and emaciated. He walked under the support of his son and daughter, who guided him to the microphone amidst a heavy applause.

The king cleared his throat. "Thank you all for coming." His voice was thin and papery, but the enchantment carried it throughout the ballroom.

"Tonight, we celebrate the Goddess Sendia and her beautiful gift to humanity: enchantment. For the last four weeks, we have sung and danced, drunk and celebrated, and we have raced!"

A cheer went up, but none of the celebration reflected in Damien's dark expression. For once, Ari couldn't be sure what he was thinking.

"Tonight, we honor the winner of the Illinir, Mikira Rusel, and her sponsor, Lord Damien Adair."

The crowd's roar redoubled as Damien and Mikira entered on opposite sides of the stage. His expression was one of cool indifference, but Mikira's resentment was practically palpable. Ari wanted to tear them away from the stage, to force them into a room where they could figure this out without the pressing eyes of the crowd. Before it was too late to repair what'd been broken.

Pay them no heed, said the voice. *We have more important matters to attend to.*

What are you talking about? The voice had been uncharacteristically silent as of late, but she felt its presence more solidly now than ever before.

"Miss Rusel," the king continued. "You have shown incredible bravery and strength in the face of one of our kingdom's toughest trials. As the youngest person to ever win the Illinir, your name will never be forgotten. You've done your father proud. Please consider yourself the personal guest of the royal family."

Mikira bowed, the rigid lines of fury clear in her stiff posture. "Thank you, Your Majesty." Her tone was laced with acidity, the same way she sounded when she spoke of Rezek. But when she rose from her bow, her face betrayed nothing save a smile. It startled Ari. This was not the loose-tongued girl she'd met months ago.

"I understand that you've chosen to grant the royal boon to your sponsor, is that true?" the king asked.

Mikira met Damien's gaze. "Indeed, Your Majesty. Lord Adair was instrumental in my success, and in return, I'd like him to have the boon."

Clever. Portraying it like that made her look generous and deferent. She was not a commoner coming for the nobility's prestige and status, but also how endearing she looked, her red hair down in tumbling waves, her face flush from dance or drink or something sharper. The crowd whistled for her in earnest.

What game was Mikira playing?

Oh, Ari, sighed the voice. *You cannot save them.*

Save them from what? What is happening?

The king turned to Damien. "And what is it you would like to claim, Lord Adair?"

Damien lifted his chin. "Your Majesty." His voice rang clear and deep. "As my boon, I ask that House Adair replace House Kelbra as one of the four greater houses of Enderlain."

Utter silence reigned in the wake of his words. Ari sensed the wide-eyed stares of the crowd, felt the tension running through them in a taut string. But Damien did not look away from the king, whose dark eyes, so weary before, now held the shrewd awareness of a man who had once stolen a throne.

Seeing him now, Ari believed every rumor she'd heard. That he'd usurped his brother-in-law's line of succession, that out there somewhere was a child who could take everything from him. He had the eyes of a man who would do anything to have what he wanted.

"Is that . . . Can he do that?" Prince Darius asked. He looked baffled, his sister merely curious. She watched Damien with a knowing smile on her lips, the kind one player gave to another. A low murmur coursed through the gathering, and Mikira's astonished expression quickly shuttered.

"The greater houses have remained unchanged for decades," the king said, each word carefully measured. "But those positions are kept at my pleasure. There is nothing in the rules of the Illinir or in the law of the kingdom that prevents me from granting this request."

The murmuring rose into shocked gasps, people's words tumbling over each other in a rush of conversation. Some even laughed, their ridicule evident. They wanted the king to tear him down for his audaciousness.

"Father, please," Prince Darius murmured. "I admire Lord Adair as much as anyone, but Rezek will be furious."

"I do not take council from duplicitous snakes," the king replied in a low growl. Darius reared back like he'd been slapped.

The king stepped up before Damien. He was tall, the impression of the warrior's body his daughter had inherited still evident even in his old age.

"Damien Adair," he said, voice strong. "I hereby grant your boon."

This time, when Damien faced the crowd, no one jeered. They stared up at him in stunned silence. Then one by one, they bowed their heads, until only Ari was left standing tall.

"As the new greater house of the ethereal, so becomes your new crest," the king said. "Aslir, the white lion, the Bright Star, will watch over your house."

At that, Damien smiled—and that was the last she saw before something inside her shifted into place.

CHAPTER 49

ARIELLE

ARI DIDN'T KNOW where she was.

The ballroom lay far behind her, the empty corridor ahead arching high above like the rib cage of some stone beast. The music had picked up again, a phantom song at her back.

Had Damien seen her leave? Had he claimed his prize already?

Her body moved, but not of her volition. She was aware of each step, each breath, but could do nothing to stop them. It was like a dream you knew was a dream, your consciousness both in and outside yourself at once.

Her body carried her down the corridor and up a tight, spiraling stair. It emptied into a narrow hall with a dead end. The only thing other than slate-gray stone was a massive woven tapestry hanging on the wall, depicting an image of the four Harbingers and, above them all, the supplicating hands of the Goddess Sendia.

The tapestry pulled at her. Deep underwater, Ari's panic grew fiercer. She clawed and struggled for control of her body, but it was no use. Whatever had her would not let go.

Do not fight me, Arielle Kadar, said the voice in Kinnish. *I will not harm you.*

Her hand pulled the tapestry aside to reveal an open arch. They passed through it to an even narrower hall. A cold light illuminated the far end, and they stepped into a large, circular room.

On the far side stood a pedestal before a shining gold plaque. An aged leather-bound book ribbed in ruby gems sat upon it. She watched her fingers reach for it, watched them brush the hide, and felt nothing.

She shuddered and lifted her gaze to the gilded wall. Her eyes shone white as snow.

All at once she came slamming back to herself, her breath a sharp gasp in her throat. The cold of the tower grazed her skin, the soft touch of the leather beneath her fingertips too close to flesh.

She and Damien had been wrong.

The Heretic's soul was not inside the book—*it was inside of her.*

"Dybbuk," she breathed. Spirit.

A figure stepped from an alcove, his eyes white as hers. "I thought you'd come," said Rezek Kelbra, and she knew then that whatever had taken hold of her had hold of him too.

The book tugged at her, gentle, whispering, and something deep inside her stretched and cracked open an eye.

And the voice inside her mind, the voice that was not her own, laughed.

ACKNOWLEDGMENTS

IN MANY WAYS, this book has been my own personal Illinir. Sans the knives and enchanted horses of course, but just as much a saga from start to finish. It's more personal to me than almost anything else I've written, and it was so important to me to get it right, down to the last enchantment.

I couldn't have done that without my brilliant, steadfast editor, Kate Meltzer, whose thoroughness and vision helped take this beast of a book and turn it into something that's not only readable, but that I'm very proud of. I'm so grateful to have gotten to work with you on this story.

All my gratitude to my UK editor, Cate Augustin, for your valuable insight, to Emilia Sowersby for all your help and for writing the world's best synopsis, and to word cutter extraordinaire, Nicolás Ore-Giron. Thank you for all the time and attention you gave this story; this is definitely a team win!

To my agent, Carrie Pestritto—after five years and six books, I'm running out of ways to say thank you for always being in my corner and supporting my writing aspirations. This whole journey wouldn't have been possible without you, and I can't wait to see where things go next.

As always, I'd be a puddle on the floor without my Guillotine Queens: Jennifer Gruenke, Tracy Badua, Alyssa Colman, Ashley Northup, Rae Castor, Koren Enright (REID!!), Jessica Jones (for double-checking I didn't forget everything about horses), Brittney Arena (for reading everything before everyone else and then waiting years for me to do anything with it), and Sam Farkas (for reading my first draft and fixing it with a single idea, fielding all of my panics, and talking all things Jewish).

To my early readers and CPs: Rosiee Thor, Laura Southern, Rochelle Hassan, Linsey Miller, and Rowan Witebsky, your feedback and enthusiasm for this story kept me going throughout this journey. I'm such a fan of your all's work, and I feel remarkably lucky to know you.

To my SprintitySprintSprints, Shannon Price and Joss Diaz, who I owe several cups of coffee for listening to my rants, panics, and all-around publishing absurdity. I'm looking forward to reading more of your all's beautiful words. Shannon: in the pinecone we trust.

I also want to shout out to Arielle Vishny, whose insightful and thoughtful dive into the world of *This Dark Descent* helped flesh out so many of the Jewish elements and made the world all the richer.

Thank you to the seriously amazing Roaring Brook team: Kathy Wielgosz (Team Hiss!), Samira Iravani (you are a saint), Trisha Previte, Connie Hsu, Ana Deboo, Veronica Ambrose, Allison Verost, and Kristin Dulaney and Kaitlin Loss for making my foreign rights dreams come true. Thank you to my publicist extraordinaire, Morgan Rath, and marketing maven, Gabriella Salpeter.

There is also an incredibly talented contingent of artists behind the gorgeous artwork in the US and UK editions: to Katt Phatt for the most epic cover; Virginia Allyn for a map I could stare at for days; and Ashe Arends for bringing Ari, Mikira, Damien, Reid (and most importantly, Widget) to life.

To my parents, family, and all of my friends, who keep supporting me book after book, and to Brock, for letting me bribe you into helping me brainstorm the science-based magic system of my dreams.

I can't wait to continue these characters' stories. Until book 2!

THE SILVERWOOD FOREST

BARKHEATH DISTRICT

KELBRA MANOR

ZALAIRE MANOR

CANBURROW SQUARE

DRAMARA MANOR

PENDRON DISTRICT

ASHFIELD STREET

THE KING'S ROAD

TEA STREET

ROUGHSHAW BRIDGE

THE TRAVELER'S ROAD

RUSEL RANCH

KELBRA

DRADMRA